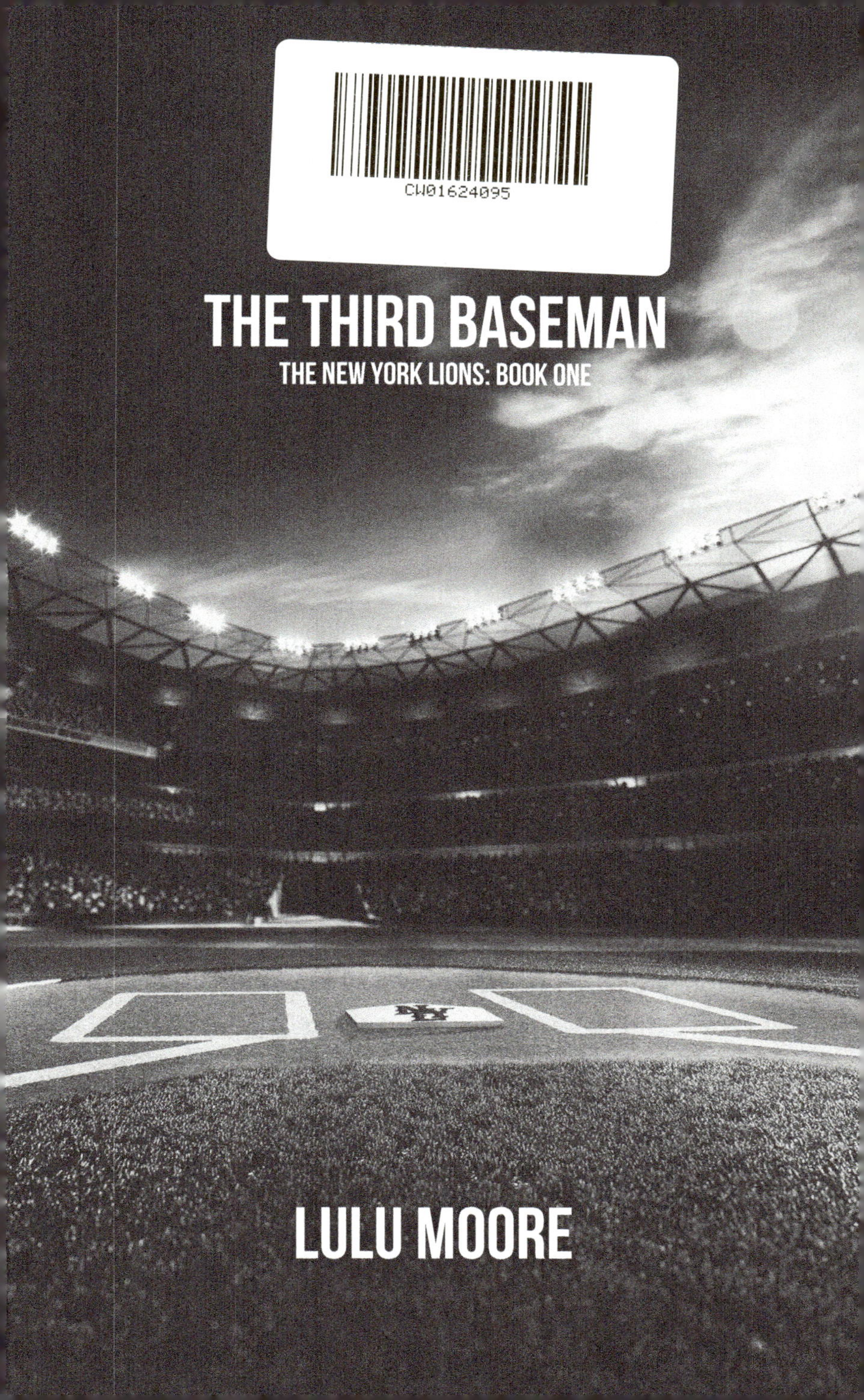

THE THIRD BASEMAN

THE NEW YORK LIONS: BOOK ONE

LULU MOORE

Cover Design by Emily Wittig

Interior illustration by Cleo Moran/Devoted Pages

Back cover shirt design by Lyla June

Editing by Katy Nielsen

The New York Lions Director of Baseball Operations Ryan Pegram

This book is for everyone who had a plan that didn't quite work out.
Don't give up. You might just have needed a different route.

Shoot for the stars, but if you happen to miss shoot for the moon instead.

Neil Armstrong

Prologue

Jupiter

I'm not prone to smiling, though you wouldn't know it from the way my reflection was grinning back at me like I'd just escaped from a 1950s asylum.

Even with my beard thicker than usual, I could still see the redness of my cheek through the whiskers; unsurprising given it was still stinging slightly. In fact, I could almost make out the form of her handprint.

Marnie Matthews had certainly put some force behind that slap.

So why am I beaming from ear to ear, you ask? Because she's *here.* In New York. And for the first time since I walked away, since I left her standing there with tears streaming down her face while my own heart was lying bleeding on the porch in front of her, I felt hope that I might *finally* be able to redeem myself.

That I might *actually* be able to win her back.

That she would be mine again.

Because if she didn't care about me, she wouldn't have moved two thousand miles – or however fucking far it is from Houston to New York – and come to work for my new club.

And if she didn't care about me, she wouldn't have packed a punch harder than Anthony Joshua. No, that blow had emotion behind it. Power behind it. And as long as there was a shred, a sliver, the tiniest fragment of feeling, then I still had a chance.

How had I gotten to this point? The one where I'd traded everything I'd known, at a place I'd spent my entire professional career, so I could come to New York and play for the worst club in the major leagues?

What did I do that set me on this trajectory of my life quicker than any curve ball?

I fell in love, that's what.

Fourteen years ago – June

The electronic pinging noise of the doorbell grated against every single one of my nerve endings, because every single one of them was already flooded with the adrenaline which had me shivering in the ninety-degree California heat.

I rarely used the front door; the tree outside her bedroom was my regular form of entry, and I counted twenty-two anxiety-inducing seconds before the door swung open.

"Jupiter." Noah Matthews' deep, booming voice always carried a degree of sternness whenever he addressed me. "I hear congratulations are in order. Dodgers, eh? Well done."

He stuck his hand out for a shake, which I reluctantly took. I wanted this over as quickly as possible. I did not want to be making small talk with my soon-to-be ex-girlfriend's father – who didn't like me anyway.

"Thank you, sir." I shoved my hands back in my pockets, trying to wipe away the clamminess while we stood in awkward silence.

I'd never been able to read Noah Matthews, never been able to tell whether he was happy or not. He was one of those men who always seemed slightly disapproving, though that was probably everything to do with the fact I was a jock dating his precious only daughter, the one he thought was ruining her life; her future.

I'd disapprove too.

He'd soon get his wish, because what I was about to do would have him sleeping soundly, filled with relief… and definitely hating me.

"Marnie!" he hollered into the house.

It wasn't the first time he hadn't invited me in, but this time I didn't care. There was no place for me in that house anymore.

She appeared like a tornado; a beautiful solar windstorm blowing away everything in its path, flinging herself into my arms with a squeal, her legs wrapping around my waist. The heat of her body that I usually relished set in motion a cold sweat which exacerbated my shaking.

I didn't notice Noah leave, but when I put her back down on the ground, he was no longer standing there, and the door was closed.

My lips found hers for one last time, tasting the cherry LifeSavers she always crunched on for me. My fingers lanced through her silky, dark chocolate strands until they cupped her cheeks… one last time.

One last time I held her to my chest and deeply inhaled the subtle coconut shampoo she always used.

I peeled her arms from around my neck and stepped back to look at her; soak in how beautiful she was, how her thick lashes always looked like she'd drawn around them with a fine tipped marker, how her cheeks were always the perfect shade of peach until I'd kissed her, when they'd darken to berry pink.

I needed to commit it all to memory.

One last time.

"Oh, Jupe! You did it. You did it! I'm so proud of you. A Dodger for life! You're a Dodger now!" she gasped, tears glistening in her bright, emerald eyes.

Aurora Borealis green I'd told her once, after she'd explained to me what the Aurora Borealis was. She was so fucking smart; my smartest Star.

The tension I was carrying in my jaw was giving me a throbbing headache.

"Babe, are you okay?" Marnie reached her soft little hand up and tried to stroke my cheek, the way she knew I loved.

But this time I stopped her hand from touching me. If she touched me, I'd never be able to do this; go through with it. I needed to let go of her hand, but I didn't want to. Couldn't.

I needed to look away from her face, but I didn't want to. Couldn't.

She watched me roll my lips, furrows deepening on her perfect, smooth forehead.

I coughed away the tension in my throat, or tried to. "Marnie, we need to talk."

That did it. I never called her Marnie. She was only ever Marn, only ever my Star. She stepped back; her eyes, which a minute ago had been glistening with love and excitement, were now filled with fear and confusion.

"Jupiter? What's going on?" she asked, her quiet voice far steadier than mine. The terror in it, however, shot right through my heart like a poisoned arrow through an apple.

I coughed again, but there was no loosening the pressure. "I'm a Dodger now, and I need to think about my future."

She began worrying at her lip, and it took all my strength not to pull it free from her front teeth.

"Okay."

"My future doesn't include you." I struck the first blow, harder than any heavyweight could handle. "I've got a job to do now. I need to concentrate on me, and I can't do it with you around. You're too needy, Marnie. You're clingy and you suffocate me until I can't breathe."

I studied her; it was possible she'd stopped breathing herself.

"It's becoming embarrassing. Everyone at school's been talking and I can't bring this with me." My heart ached from the lies I was spewing. "I don't have time for a relationship. I don't have time for you."

Tears spilled thick and fast, too much for her to be able to see properly, but she didn't wipe them away. She didn't attempt to speak which made it easier for me to spit out the words I'd been rehearsing since last night.

I'd prepared.

I rarely won an argument with her, and I knew she'd want to counter any point I made.

She'd want to talk about long distance, tell me what she'd been planning without my knowledge.

And I couldn't have that. I couldn't have her ruining her future for me.

"We're done for good. And when I pick a girlfriend, it won't be you."

The only way I knew she'd heard what I'd said was from the wince flickering across her horror-struck features.

"I don't love you."

It could have been a sharp intake of breath I heard, or it could have been the final crack of my heart, of my chest breaking open until its contents spilled out onto the ground.

Or maybe it was hers.

I stood there until I could bear it no longer and turned, walking away to the sound of her wail, followed by a thud as she slumped down onto her porch. But I didn't turn around.

I heard the door open and Noah calling to her, but I didn't turn around.

"Reeves! Reeves, get back here!" he yelled over her sobs.

I would say I'm sorry, but that would be another lie to add to my tally. I might not have been the smart one in our relationship, but I knew I was smart enough to make the only decision that was right for us – that we couldn't be together now.

Just like I was smart enough to know that Marnie Matthews was the only girl who would ever own my heart.

I knew… because I'd left it on her porch steps.

But what doesn't kill you makes you stronger. Right?

Let's see, shall we?

1

Marnie

Present Day

No one likes the first day of work.

They might say they do, but in reality, it's the nerves and excitement getting in the way of the truth.

First days of work blow.

Especially first days of work in a job you don't want and know nothing about; a job that required a relocation across the country, and came with new colleagues you've spent fifty percent of your life avoiding.

Yep, I'm the sucker who signed up for that in a moment of uncharacteristic idiocy.

"Want me to show you the way back down to your office, Doctor Matthews? Or do you remember?"

"No, I'm good. I remember, thank you. And I have the map." I tapped the folder I was carefully holding.

The guy asking was Mike, the head of facilities and security for the New York Lions. He'd handed me the folder like it contained nuclear launch codes, when really the only code I'd been given was the one to my office, along with a list of essential contact details, and a map of the eleven-acre New York Lions site.

He'd also peppered me with information, only twenty percent of which I'd retained – including, luckily, where my office was.

"Good. Make sure you always have your security pass on you. You won't be able to get through any door without it. Dial one from the phone on your desk and it comes straight to me or my office. You have a few days to settle in; most of the staff in your department tends to travel with the team so it won't be too busy down there this week. Not until the boys get back anyway."

I smiled and nodded. There was no way he could know quite how reassuring that news was.

It had only been two days since I'd arrived in New York; my home for the foreseeable future. And those two days had been spent ricocheting between varying degrees of annoyance, anger, anxiety, denial, dread, and excitement; although the excitement element was negligible compared to the rest of the emotions bouncing around my brain and my belly.

It wasn't until I remembered that the New York Lions team was on an away stretch this week, and therefore I wouldn't be running into anyone I didn't want to see, that I finally relaxed enough to take a full breath. Unfortunately for me that hadn't been until this morning, while on my way to The Lions Stadium.

I knew, however, that I only had this week to acclimate

myself, because I would be on the next away stretch.

And all the stretches until the end of the season.

The end couldn't come soon enough.

I waved goodbye and took off down the corridor toward the conditioning suites where my new office was located. Mike was right about it being quiet; I hadn't seen a single person beyond the security at the entrance and grounds keepers tidying up the outside, tending to the enormous lion shaped flower beds, and power-hosing the walkways.

It was still early, but I was used to the bustle of the Johnson Space Centre where there was always someone rushing off somewhere, no matter what the time was. In fact, in the seven years I'd worked there since graduating from M.I.T., I'd never been able to get a closer parking spot than the ones in Lot M, a quarter of a mile away from the main doors.

Spying the huge Lions logo on the curved wall at the end, I turned left and took the flight of stairs down two floors, where I was now on the same level as the field. The smell of dry wall and fresh paint was stronger down here.

On the brief tour I'd had this morning, Mike had told me that since Penn Shepherd took ownership of The New York Lions, the entire stadium had been renovated, and it was looking good; clean, polished, and shiny – 'slick as a space rocket', my old boss would have said.

Ugh.

Unease gripped my insides again, and I stopped walking until it passed so I didn't have a full-on meltdown my very first day.

Jesus, Marnie. Pull yourself together.

A small shiver zipped along my spine, but that was more due to the fact I'd left the seventy-eight degree Houston heat for New York's significantly lower temperature, and wrapped my sweater and jacket tighter around myself.

The weather – another reason I didn't want to be here.

Two minutes later and I reached the one space I was about to call mine, punched in the entry code, stepped inside and looked around for the second time this morning. When I'd briefly peered in earlier, I hadn't noticed much more than the size of the space – easily four times that of my last office – with an enormous desk at one end, and a blank white wall at the other, in front of which were two stainless steel tables. But on this second glance, I could see it also contained all the equipment I'd requested over the last six months, since Penn Shepherd had caught me at a weak moment and coerced me into joining his mission.

The mission being to turn his new baseball club into a winning team.

I remembered it as vividly as if it were yesterday.

That day had started with me filing for divorce. The day had ended with me accepting a job offer and a million-dollar salary to leave my role at N.A.S.A., and build a program that got the worst team in the MLB winning.

And how was I going to do that exactly? Astrodynamics and baseball are not the same thing.

Your guess is as good as mine.

So why did I agree?

The first reason we've already ascertained: I'm an idiot. The second… I didn't want to think about.

I closed my eyes and stood there in silence. I stood there so long concentrating on the stillness that I almost fell asleep to the muffled whirr of the lawnmowers on the baseball field the other side of the huge window at the end of the room. I startled myself back to the present when I nearly toppled over.

I walked further in, just a little further, but enough to drop my bag on the desk with a soft thud. Tentatively brushing my fingers over the cool edge of metal around the massive computer screen also placed there, I scanned slowly around and let out a quiet chuckle; my shoulders relaxed a fraction. Penn Shepherd must have emptied an office supply store for the amount of note pads, pens, highlighters, and sticky notes in every color, all neatly lined up like a rainbow.

Picking up the pink pad on the end, I mindlessly flicked the edges between my fingers while wondering – for the thousandth time – what had possessed me to come here, beyond the year-long air-tight contract I'd signed and couldn't get out of.

My therapist said for the closure, apparently, which I'd been repeating to myself like a mantra since I accepted the position.

But why do you still need closure after fourteen years? After you've already given yourself to another man in marriage? Is it really necessary?

Making the best of a situation that wasn't just bad, it was catastrophic – that's what this was, especially as this morning it seemed I was more interested in going out of my way to avoid seeing anyone.

Or one person in particular; the one I didn't want to think about – namely a very large baseball player; though in this building, that didn't narrow it down all that well.

But this one I'd last seen fourteen years ago, as I collapsed, sobbing on my front porch, and watched him walk away with my heart in his hands. Until two days ago, that is.

I looked back down at my palm. It didn't appear any different to how it usually was; small, fleshy, pink, but somehow I could still feel the bristle of his whiskers from when my hand made contact with his cheek.

It had been a long time since I'd imagined I could feel him next to me. Feel his strength; his smooth golden skin stretched across thickening muscles. Feel his hot breath as he smiled through his soft kisses.

And when I'd last seen him, he'd been a boy growing into adulthood.

Now Jupiter Reeves was all man.

I hadn't expected to be so shaken, so affected by his closeness; being in his presence.

I hadn't expected him to still be so beautiful, as if age had decided it would only harden the line of his jaw, and sharpen his cheekbones.

I groaned again and slumped down in the chair, spinning it around with the force of my movement.

What was I doing? Maybe I actually had lost my mind.

I'd lost something.

What a mess.

I pulled my bag over and dug around in it for the LifeSavers I habitually kept, then popped one in my mouth.

"Knock knock." I twisted back around to the door, stopping myself with my foot on the desk before I went a full three-sixty, to see two women walking through it; one with a sleek blonde bob, one with thick, glossy, dark brunette curls bouncing on her shoulders. "We wanted to come and see how you're settling in, and if we can steal you away for some coffee, if you're not busy."

The pair of them stood in the doorway, smiling like they'd won the lottery. The blonde one was Lowe Slater, the fiancée of Penn Shepherd. I knew this because when I arrived a couple of days ago, I'd been waiting in his office and he'd introduced me to her, at which point she pulled me into an embrace like I was her favorite stuffed toy from childhood and she'd found me in the back of a closet.

I hadn't had a chance to follow up as less than a minute later, Jupiter had walked into the room, and I'd lost the ability to speak, breathe, or stay calm. Every shred of self-control I possessed melted away as I stepped toward him, my eyes clouding with the reddest rage the closer I got.

He'd stood there, grinning down at me with his perfect smile that I wanted to knock straight off his perfect face.

I hadn't even cared that there were witnesses.

I soaked my hand in a bucket of ice that night; it was still a bit sore.

And now…

From the way they were both staring at me expectantly, I assumed Lowe had told this other woman exactly what had happened.

"Marnie, are you okay?" asked Lowe.

I blinked moisture back into my eyes and jumped up. "Um, yes, sorry. I'm… sorry, I'm in a bit of a daze. My first morning… this place…"

"Overwhelming?"

I smiled and my throat thickened out of nowhere. Now I had too much moisture in my eyes. "Yeah, you could say that," I croaked out.

Lowe stepped forward as if to hug me, but I waved her off because that's all it would take to get me going, and if I started I had no idea when I would stop. I'd already embarrassed myself in front of her once; I drew a hard line at a second time.

"No, no. Thank you, I'm okay. A lot has happened in the last week, and I think it's all about to hit like a sledgehammer." I let out a droll huff.

The brunette stepped forward on a pair of tan, gravity-defying heels with her hand held out, likely to stop me from embarrassing myself further. "I'm Beulah Holmes by the way, head of legal. We haven't formally met, but I signed your contract."

My contract. I wonder if she knew about the monumental headache I'd had the last three months because of my goddamn contract.

Deep breath, Marnie. Deep breath.

I took her hand and shook it, unable to stop a small grimace creeping up my lips. "Hello, sorry, this is really unprofessional. I'm not normally like this."

"Don't worry about it. First days of work are always hard. I was a wreck too, especially as Penn also strong-armed me into working here, and I knew nothing about baseball." She rolled her eyes. "He can be very persuasive when he wants to be. I do know more about baseball than I did a year ago though."

"I'm certain I've forgotten everything I knew about baseball." I gave a small groan of support. "Not that it was that much to begin with."

"You'll remember. I'm sure Penn will have a series of pop-quizzes lined up," she laughed.

I looked between the two of them, and it was clear from the expressions on their faces that they weren't joking.

"A baseball pop-quiz?"

Lowe nodded with a sigh. "Yeah, he loves them."

"Oh…" I replied, then wasn't sure what else to say.

"Anyway," Lowe started before the silence became awkward. "We're your welcoming committee."

A flash of my first day at N.A.S.A. when my new supervisor had handed me a stack of papers fifteen inches thick and told me to get reading because he expected a report by the end of the day – this was not that.

As much as I didn't want to be here, I could admit it was kind of nice.

"Thank you." I smiled genuinely at the happiness on her face. "I appreciate that."

"It's usually a bit busier, but…" she trailed off apologetically. "You're probably used to being busy."

"No, no. It's good that it's quiet." I chewed a little on my lip. "It'll give me time to figure out what I'm supposed to be doing."

"It was kind of why we wanted to take you out." Lowe's hand flicked between her and Beulah. "And we've been so excited to have you come here; to meet you properly."

"Really?" My eyes widened with surprise at her enthusiasm, along with Beulah's effusive nodding, and my cheeks flushed in a good way. I definitely wasn't at N.A.S.A. anymore.

"Yes, really. So what do you say? Coffee?"

Seeing as I was about to stifle a yawn, there was no way I was passing up the offer of caffeine. But something about these women made me want to go anyway. They were warm, welcoming, and instantly likeable. They also exuded an effortless type of glamour which wasn't present in my corner of Houston either. Even in their jeans and tees you could tell they were the type of women who stood out, whether they wanted to or not.

"Sounds great," I replied, mustering as much enthusiasm as I could. Plus, I still wasn't sure what I was going to do about my job, nor did I have any idea on how to do it, so perhaps they'd be able to shed some light on that particular problem.

"Awesome!" Lowe clapped her hands together, her blue eyes shining with glee. "There's a great place just outside the stadium, along the river."

"Sounds perfect." I hadn't yet gotten around to taking my coat off, so I grabbed my purse and slung it across my body before following them out.

"How do you like your apartment?" Beulah asked with a smile as I fell into stride next to her.

My mouth opened and closed. I was still a little speechless at the welcome surprise I'd had when I'd arrived on Saturday. The Lions had provided living accommodation as part of my job package; I was expecting an apartment somewhere close to the stadium, something slightly basic, comfortable, and clean. But I'd forgotten I was no longer funded by government dollars, so I wasn't prepared for the level of luxury and coziness I'd been given in an apartment so high I could probably touch the stars if the windows opened.

In short, it was incredible, and made soaking my hand that much easier. I'd spent my first night with a bottle of wine from my new wine wall – yes, *wall* – looking out on the twinkling lights of the city from my bathtub, while trying not to think about how the afternoon had played out.

My apartment was going to be hard to leave.

"It's beautiful, thank you. The views are stunning."

Lowe clasped her hands to her chest. "That makes me so happy. Beulah and I chose it. We wanted somewhere you had a great view of the city, but also the sky."

My throat thickened again slightly at their unexpected kindness and thoughtfulness. "That's really incredibly sweet of you. Thank you so much."

"You're welcome. We hope you feel at home. It's hard to move so far away, so we picked somewhere special to enjoy when you're not traveling with the team."

I thought back to the empty house I'd left in Houston.

Even when I'd been married it hadn't had much in it; the plus side of that was it hadn't taken long to pack up. No wonder we'd barely spent time there.

But my new place couldn't have been more perfect if I'd chosen it myself.

"It's the most gorgeous apartment I've ever had." I smiled widely for the first time since I'd arrived here. "I guess Penn told you I worked at N.A.S.A."

"Something like that," muttered Beulah, and I wasn't entirely sure it was a response she meant me to hear – especially when I swear Lowe nudged her slightly.

"Well..." I continued, "Perhaps you'd like to come over for dinner so I can thank you. I'm not the greatest cook, but I do make a mean fried chicken."

Lowe looped her arm through mine and squeezed it; something that I found oddly comforting considering I'd only just met her. "We'd love to."

I smiled then immediately forgot my train of thought when the sun blinded me as we stepped outside. Squinting until I found my sunglasses, we walked through the massive club grounds toward the stadium's entrance – the grand arch of climbing lions. Compared to when I'd been here on Saturday during the game, and the deafening levels of cheering, today it was more reminiscent of an eerie ghost town.

A well-kept one, but eerie nonetheless.

It would be the same this Saturday according to Mike on our tour this morning. We had a few home games coming up once the boys returned at the end of the week.

We were now walking past a grounds-man expertly trimming a lion shaped hedge. "Do either of you go to away games? Are you required to?"

Lowe's nose crinkled up. "Well, to tell the truth, this is

only the first week of the season. Penn took ownership at the end of last season, so there haven't been any away games to go to. Plus," she dropped her voice slightly, "Penn has been like a coiled spring leading up to this stretch, and there's only so much I can take."

Beulah let out a loud snicker. I wasn't in on the joke, though my only experience of Penn Shepherd was when he'd spent weeks trying to get in contact with me, then flown to Houston to find me in person when I didn't reply to his many messages and voicemails.

It wasn't hard to imagine what he was like when a game was on.

Intense.

"I run the press and marketing teams here, so we do have to have presence at every game – right now a couple of my guys are travelling with the boys to capture content. I'll attend in future, but I'm using this week to get organized. The club never had a proper communications team before so I'm trying to make it all run smoothly, and the social media is all new."

"I'm not required to go, but I'll join on occasion if I can get away," Beulah added.

We walked under the arch and turned left, heading along a blossom-tree lined walkway that led to the river. It was busier here, and I spotted several groups of tourists taking pictures along the outside wall of The New York Lions stadium which rose high above the Hudson, its shiny black and gold paint glinting in the sunshine.

Billboards ran along the side, plastered with a larger-than-life sized image of each player, one after the other. The more we passed, the bigger the shiver that whooshed across my skin.

"On game days, the river here is filled with boats of people all trying to catch a home run ball. When the season opened, we decided to have t-shirts made for anyone who caught a ball out there. They then have to collect it from The Lions merch store under the stadium. The shirt says 'I caught a Lion' and we ask them to post on social media. It was really popular on Saturday," grinned Lowe.

I forced myself to turn away from the billboards and ignore the gnawing slowly growing in my belly as we walked past the stadium, because I knew what would be coming, "Oh! That's what they were! When I arrived, I couldn't figure it out. I just saw them all stationed out there, like canoe-shaped battleships."

"Yeah, and you should have seen them fight it out. Two guys fell in," Beulah laughed loudly. "Lowe did a great job with it. She's been working her butt off in the offseason."

I didn't have a chance to respond or offer congratulations as I was knocked sideways into the two of them by a group of squealing young women not looking where they were going.

"Oh! Sorry!" one giggled. "We didn't see you."

"That's okay," I said, rubbing my ribs while Beulah glared at them.

"Actually, could one of you take our picture?" another asked, thrusting her phone at the three of us.

Beulah just stared disapprovingly, so Lowe took it from her. "Sure."

The sea of girls parted as they posed next to the board. Immediately my throat constricted, and my stomach plunged to the bottom of the Hudson.

Jupiter.

Though not Jupiter as I knew him.

Gone was the perfect smile, the mischievous glint, the fun.

Instead, those sensuous lips were schooled into a hard line.

I'd never seen him look so… menacing. Thick forearms crossed over his chest, almost covering The Lions logo embroidered on the left of his shirt. Huge biceps bulged and strained under the fabric; biceps covered in tattoos. So many tattoos you could barely see his bronzed skin.

My mouth dropped open, and I couldn't have stopped it with a gun to my head.

He'd been wearing a hoodie when I'd seen him on Saturday, so I never imagined underneath…

On Saturday he'd been beautiful, but this version… I couldn't look away.

I wanted to… but I couldn't.

He was staring down the lens of the camera, eyes bluer than I'd remembered. Pools of aquamarine, like Yellowstone hot springs, but not warm and lit with amusement like they used to be.

These were cold, and a little dangerous.

The shiver returned a hundred-fold, along with thousands of knots tying themselves in my belly.

The chatter going on around me cut through my thoughts like a hunting knife through fresh prey.

"He's so fucking hot..."

"God, I want his babies...."

"…I just want his dick."

Someone let out a groan so lascivious I could almost see the saliva dribbling out of her mouth.

"Could you imagine..."

Another groan was followed by a loud screech.

"Bet he's an animal in bed…"

"Yeah, and I'd let him…"

That comment elicited a cackle, and I couldn't help but stare in the direction it came from. My jaw popped and my teeth ground together until they squeaked.

"Those tattoos..."

"We need to find out where he lives now he's in the city."

Beulah pulled me away from the spot I'd become frozen to, my jaw wide open in shock while my eyes bulged in horror at what I was hearing.

"Are you okay?"

I blinked, and then refocused on Jupiter.

Stars.

Even from this distance, I could make out dozens of stars running up and down his heavily muscled arms, all different sizes, before disappearing under the fabric. Stars in between – I squinted – were they planets? Words? Squiggles?

Why wouldn't everyone shut up?! Why were those girls even here?

I wanted them all to leave so I could study him. I wanted to know where those tattoos went. How much of his body did they cover? What did they say?

And why?

Why had he covered himself?

A heavy throb punched me deep in my belly; too heavy for me to pretend it didn't happen, especially as tiny flutters followed in its wake, undulating deep in my core. My cheeks flushed as hot as the desert.

"Marnie?"

I turned to Beulah who was staring at me in apprehension, confusion, and maybe a little concern.

"His tattoos?" I managed to ask on a breath.

"What about them?"

"He's covered in them."

She paused a beat before answering. "Yeah, it's kind of his thing."

I tore my eyes away before I strained them, and found myself frowning at Beulah instead. "What does that mean?"

She was about to reply when Lowe returned. "Ugh, let's get our coffee or I'll be here all day! Those girls are demanding."

Those girls were still screeching next to the image of Jupiter as we walked off, and I wanted to yell at them to leave him alone. It was so reminiscent of being back in high school when Jupiter walked around campus followed by a gaggle of squawking girls, that it had given me a piercing headache. Bile churned in my belly.

Nothing had changed.

"Come on, Marnie. Let's go and talk about it before they combust under the glare you're giving them." She tugged on my arm like Beulah had, and I let her guide me away. "I'm sorry. I should have remembered the team images were along there before I suggested coffee."

"No, it's okay," I shrugged, way more casually and calmly than I felt, because I wasn't actually sure my insides hadn't melted away. "It was going to happen at some point, right? I just didn't realize…"

"Realize what?" Lowe asked when it was clear I wasn't about to finish my sentence.

And I'd have answered, except for the second time in as many days, seeing Jupiter Reeves had left me speechless.

2

Marnie

Present Day

I walked silently through the door to the coffee shop Lowe was holding open, and sat at the first empty table we found.

It was busy and loud; filled with a combination of moms and strollers, Columbia students with laptops, and tourists carrying New York Lions store bags. A table three down from ours was a family of four, and I watched as the two kids pulled new Lions jerseys out of their shopping bags.

REEVES was printed along the top of both, above the number five.

It's gonna be my number, Star. Five. I'm the fifth planet. And then he'd kissed me, and I forgot anything after that.

Lowe looked around as she sat down, noticed the family and incorrectly read the vacant expression on my face.

"Sorry, it's going to be hard to avoid him. I've got his face plastered over the city." She winced as my eyes bulged. "Not just his," she quickly added, "but he's around a lot more than most."

My head moved between the pair of them sitting opposite me, interrogation style, because that is the official seat placement if you're about to become the subject of an intense questioning.

Beulah leaned forward, her fingers interlacing into fists; the glossy red polish of her short nails matched her lips.

"Marnie, you didn't realize what?" she repeated Lowe's question.

"That he looked like that, I guess." My brows drew together slightly. "What did you mean about tattoos being his thing?"

"Jupiter's whole persona is tattoos, being moody and unapproachable, you know… doesn't give a shit about anything but the game."

I don't know why I was surprised. People change. He had – I had, too. But while the Jupiter I remembered was all about the game, he was also funny and sweet.

Popular.

He was not the guy I'd seen on the poster who looked like he could snap a bat with one hand.

I tugged at my top lip slightly in disbelief. "Really?"

The pair of them nodded in sync from across the table.

"And he's a pretty big deal."

It wasn't a question. Something about the arrogant stare down the camera lens for that picture plastered over the billboard… not to mention those girls. And I tried to forget the way he'd marched into Penn's office like he owned it.

That visual would be burned on my brain for an eternity.

He was a big deal, and he knew it.

Lowe leaned slightly forward across the table, her hands clasped in front of her. "Marnie, when was the last time you saw him? Did you really not know anything about him?"

I shook my head. "The last time I saw Jupiter was fourteen years ago – well, thirteen years, nine months, sixteen days."

Now it was Lowe's turn for her jaw to drop. Beulah also stayed silent, but I knew they wanted more. I could almost see the questions forming a line in their brains.

This wasn't how I envisaged my very first day of work going, but you had to rip the Band-Aid off sometime. But first…

"What do you know?"

"Not much, just that you guys dated when you were younger."

My huff was dark and low. "Jupiter was drafted to The Dodgers the day we broke up. After that, I did everything I could to avoid him. Avoid sports. At the end of the semester, I went to study in Boston for seven years, then I moved to Houston." I smiled weakly. "It wasn't that hard really. My old work colleagues weren't that interested in sports."

That was an understatement. In fact, if you ever want to avoid something, go work at N.A.S.A.

"Hi, ladies, what can I get you?"

Lowe and Beulah turned with obvious annoyance to the barista who'd interrupted us. He placed three glasses of water on the table, and stood back waiting for an answer.

"Drip coffee?" I glanced from Lowe to Beulah, my brows raised.

"Great," Lowe replied while Beulah nodded, more interested in my story than their coffee.

I turned back to the barista. "Make it three, please."

Besides my therapists, I'd never opened up to anyone about Jupiter. Never confided. Never talked about him. Never Googled him, even in my darkest, loneliest moments. Because if I could pretend he didn't exist on the outside, then maybe my heart and brain would get the message on the inside.

But they hadn't; they'd merely been put into a coma. And the signed divorce papers burning a hole in my purse was proof of that.

"Marnie, why did you come to New York? To this job?"

I chewed on my cheek while I figured out the answer, or the beginnings of the answer.

"I got divorced today."

Beulah choked on the water she'd taken a sip of. I grinned, passing her a napkin to wipe the dribble off her chin.

"Well, technically it was finalized last week, but I only got the signed papers back from my lawyer when I arrived here. They're in my bag. They were waiting for me when I got to New York."

"Does anyone know that you were married?" asked Lowe in a hushed tone while she scanned around to make sure we weren't overheard, as though I'd just told her I'd committed a federal crime.

I laughed loudly, which had a medicinal effect on the tension wrapping around my spine like a boa constrictor. "Yes, people know. It wasn't a secret."

"Does Jupiter know?"

"Well, considering we haven't spoken since the day we broke up, I'd say no." I shrugged.

"Penn never mentioned it."

"I didn't tell Penn."

The pair of them looked at each other sheepishly, like there was more to their statement, but it was at this point the barista came back with our coffees.

I took a sip of mine, savoring the warmth and its rich, potent flavors which almost immediately made my heart pound a little harder. At least I thought it was the coffee, but I was probably wrong.

I put the cup down and drew in a deep breath.

"Last year, I'd had to go to D.C. for a meeting at N.A.S.A. headquarters. I'd spent all day there, and it was late by the time I finally got to my hotel. I was in the elevator, and a group of guys got in and began talking. I wasn't really listening to them, but then one of them said 'Jupiter'." I picked up a sachet of Sweet'N'Low and began running the edges between my fingers. "Now, N.A.S.A isn't exactly the best place to go if you don't want to hear that word, but I'd normalized hearing it at work – especially as the agency is developing a new space mission to further study the planets. But I wasn't at work, and it took me thirty seconds before I realized they weren't talking about space. They were talking about baseball and Jupiter, my Jupiter. I guess The Dodgers were playing in the city or something, and he'd had a good game. As I was listening, it dawned on me that Jupiter was there, in the city where I was. For the first time since we'd broken up, or since I'd left for school, we were in the same place. By the time the elevator stopped on their floor and they got out, I was shaking like my body was going through G-Force training. I barely made it into my room before I threw up everything, which wasn't much. Then the crying started. I spent the next two days coming to terms with the fact that as much as I'd tried to get over him, our breakup had a profound effect on me. I was totally in love and totally heartbroken. All that time and nothing had changed. It's so dumb. I was sixteen years old! Everyone gets their heart broken, but here I am, thirty years old, and still crying about it."

I sipped at my coffee again, soothing my parched mouth from all my talking. I thought Lowe and Beulah might jump in with questions, but they didn't.

That would happen thick and fast, soon enough.

"I flew back to Houston and tried to gather my thoughts. David, my ex-husband, was on a mission, so I had time, but that was when Penn started calling me. He must have called twenty times." I chuckled as Lowe groaned loudly. "And I didn't know who he was, so I Googled him; he'd just taken ownership here, which made no sense to me. What would he want with me? I know nothing about baseball. I tried to ignore him, but he was so persistent. Then David returned and it became clear I had no interest in our marriage. We flitted from one mundane conversation to another, never touching, and I realized that while I loved David, I wasn't in love with him..." I began tracing my fingers around the rim of my coffee cup, "maybe never had been. We'd spend eight months of the year apart, and it always seemed acceptable to me. But in reality, it was avoidance. I filed for divorce. Penn kept calling, so I eventually went to meet him, determined to tell him I wasn't interested and to leave me alone. Working for a baseball team was too close to Jupiter's world. But instead, I came away with a new job."

I paused, waiting to see if Lowe and Beulah had something, anything to say, but they were both still staring with wide eyes, silently sipping their coffee. Or Beulah was; Lowe's coffee was untouched, and most likely cold.

"My life had imploded. I couldn't concentrate at work, I couldn't do my job, so I convinced myself that change would be good, that perhaps being in Jupiter's world would be good, help me move on. I promised Penn I would stay for a year, and signed the contract," I pointed to Beulah, "your contract."

Her mouth drew into a solemn line, the berry lips almost disappearing. She knew what was coming; I could see the remorse written all over her face. "You didn't know Jupiter had already signed at The Lions?"

I shook my head. "No. I tried everything I could to get out of it, but my lawyer said there was nothing I could do without it costing me a fortune."

"I'm so sorry."

"It's not your fault; you were doing your job." I looked between them. "We're required to go through therapy and psychometric testing at work, but I hadn't had my own therapist for over a decade. That morning I found one, went over, and downloaded everything onto her. I was there for three hours. Her diagnosis was that I had some kind of PTSD; I needed closure, and that's how I should approach the job. So here I am, in a city I don't know with a job I can't do. But... closure, right?"

I rolled my eyes at the last statement but sat back feeling lighter, as if the burden I'd been carrying had suddenly been diluted somehow.

"Sorry, that's a lot to take in. I didn't mean to dump. I promise I'm not a weirdo."

I gave them a second to absorb my life story. Lowe started first.

"Oh, Marnie, I'm so sorry." She reached over and covered my hand with hers, and surprisingly, I didn't want to cry in frustration, which was new. "That must have been so hard for you to deal with alone. Does your family know?"

"My brother, Will, is in the navy on deployment, so I haven't been able to talk to him. My parents think that David and I grew apart. It wasn't hard to believe, seeing as we barely saw each other. My therapist said I picked him because we spent so much time apart, so it was easy to keep my independence." I rolled my eyes again, and snorted because it was all so obvious now.

I was supposed to be smart, yet it had taken over a decade and someone else to figure it out.

Beulah put her coffee down slowly, and looked up at me. "I know we just met, but I'm proof you can completely change your life. It's never too late. And I understand what it's like to hold onto something for so long."

I smiled softly. I was positive she had more to add to that, but I didn't want to push it the very first time we'd met. I hadn't had a lot of girlfriends before, and was kind of liking it. "Thank you. I'll be okay, I'm just angry I've got myself into this situation. I should have never said yes to Penn. I could have dealt with my divorce and my feelings for Jupiter back in Houston. I didn't need to come to New York for that."

"If it makes you feel better, it's very hard to say no to Penn."

Surprisingly, that did make me feel a little better. Not much, though.

Out of the corner of my eye I noticed the waiter approach, then turn away. One look at Lowe and I realized her glare had stopped him from interrupting us a second time. I let out a small laugh, because I realized I was about to get to the one question I'm sure they'd been dying to ask all morning.

"So what are you going to do about Jupiter?"

I held my open palms out. "I dunno. I wasn't expecting to see him the other day. I'd been bracing myself to bump into him in the corridor at some point, but not on day one. I was totally unprepared." My head dropped into my hands. "I can't believe I slapped him! I shouldn't have done it, but it was like my body and mind had been hijacked by some other girl – a really angry one."

"Lowe said it was an impressive blow."

My head shot back up to find Beulah and Lowe grinning wide.

"Oh, God!" I groaned, letting out a deep sigh as my mind filled with the one other thing which had been bothering me more than I wanted to admit. I chewed a little on my thumb nail while I figured how to word it, but then decided I'd already told them enough, I may as well tell them everything. "I mean, it's just so typical isn't it? I feel like a poker thrust into the fire. Though I did think it was weird, Jupiter coming here. The boy I knew would never have left The Dodgers. All he ever used to talk about was being a Dodger for life – on and on and on about it."

Lowe and Beulah were both frowning at me. I knew I was going crazy.

I gave a heavy shrug. "Never mind, I'm just… frustrated I guess. I wanted to lick my wounds in private. I just hope I never have to meet his wife."

"Wife?"

"Or girlfriend, I guess. Jupiter was never short of females clamoring to get his attention. That hasn't changed based on that lot outside."

Lowe and Beulah exchanged that look again, just like they had earlier.

"What?"

"Marnie, Jupiter doesn't have a wife or a girlfriend." Beulah's eyes narrowed while she stared at me. "The only reason Jupiter came to play at The Lions was to get you back. That's why you're here."

I frowned, first at that statement, and second at my heart, which gave a hard thump. "Wait, what? How? That makes no sense… what does that mean?"

"He would only come to The Lions if Penn found you and offered you a job. I think he wants to try and win you back," she said simply, and not in any way like that news didn't hit me as hard as an asteroid.

No, not hit. Wiped me out was more accurate.

Lowe nudged her but looked at me. "He definitely wants to win you back."

My brain was on the brink of frying, my blood had passed simmer and was on its way to boil, and my stupid heart wouldn't stop thumping. "One more time please?"

Lowe sipped her coffee with purpose, then placed it slowly on the table and pinned me with a look I couldn't read. "When Penn took ownership last season, he was determined to build a winning team. He desperately wanted Jupiter to play for The Lions, and Jupiter would only do so on the condition Penn found you and offered you a job. He told Penn to give you anything you asked for. Basically, make you an offer you couldn't refuse."

My mouth closed, then opened, then closed again, all while I tried to make sense of any of this. "That's why he offered me a million-dollar salary?"

Beulah sucked in her cheek and nodded, while Lowe looked kind of apologetic. "Yep."

My mind whirred; that sledgehammer I mentioned earlier? It had just hit.

"So let me get this straight… fourteen years ago he breaks my heart and leaves me to put myself back together, then wakes up one day and decides he wants me back?! And I'm the dummy who fell for it!" I slapped myself on the head. "Oh, hell no!"

I could see Beulah on the verge of saying something, but it was then something else occurred to me.

"Oh my God! He's been dictating the course of my life since I was sixteen, and I haven't even realized!"

"I told Penn this would backfire," Lowe muttered with a head shake, and looked at her watch. "Okay, it's lunchtime, which means we can officially drink wine. And I think we need it for this conversation."

We sat in silence, each of us pondering the new information we'd been served, while actually being served three large glasses of wine and a bowl of fries. I don't think Lowe and Beulah were plotting Jupiter's downfall like I was, but they definitely looked deep in thought.

Well, not exactly downfall, but my thoughts weren't favorable.

"What are you thinking?" Lowe asked, breaking the silence.

I stopped running my thumb nail along my bottom lip and took a large gulp of wine.

"I don't know. I can't blame him for my marriage ending; I would have divorced David anyway. But I didn't need to be manipulated into coming to New York."

"You're being paid a lot though," countered Beulah.

"It's tainted money! It's blackmail. I was paid just fine in Houston," I grumbled.

"I say let's go shopping with it." Lowe raised her glass with a smirk, before laughing loudly at the expression on my face.

Beulah joined in and then I followed, because none of this made sense and it was sounding more ridiculous by the second. The three of us sat there laughing until tears poured down our cheeks.

And it wasn't even that funny.

But the more I thought about it the more I laughed…

until reality dawned on me, that my reality wasn't real. I was in a made up job I'd been conned into taking. But as first days go, this probably wasn't the worst. I had four more to figure out what to do about it before the team returned and things really got started.

I looked down at my cell as it beeped from an unknown number.

Private: *We're back in the same city, Star. Hope you've had a great first day. X*

I scowled at the screen, like that message was the cause of all my woes – technically it was. It didn't take a rocket scientist to figure out who'd sent it, especially since that rocket scientist was me.

If Jupiter Reeves thought he could click his fingers, or send a text, and I'd come running like every other girl, he was sorely mistaken.

I had until the end of the season to get the job done, and that was exactly what I was going to do.

3

Jupiter

Present Day

My bags landed on the floor with a thud, and I blindly searched the wall for the light switch. Six weeks I'd officially been living here, and still hadn't remembered where everything was.

At least the place was somewhat open plan, so I didn't have to go opening closet doors when I was looking for the bathroom.

I hated traveling, but this away leg I hated more than usual, and the mood I was in had me drooling for a beer, but scanning the shelves of the fridge, the options were non-alcoholic or non-alcoholic.

That'll be non-alcoholic then.

Twisting the cap, I flopped, exhausted, onto the couch

and flicked through the sports channels. The Cubs, Astros, and Giants were all playing tonight. ESPN was showing the Mariners game, but I passed through them all until I found the one I was looking for; The Dodgers game on FOX.

The boys were currently leading two-one against The Padres; I caught it just in time to see Freddie Freeman smash a home run that increased their lead to three.

Fuck, I missed it.

I missed being in Los Angeles.

Seeing the boys out there without me, on the field I'd played my whole career, was hurting more than I thought it would, and I was not looking forward to the day we played against them. I leaned back with a groan, once more wondering if I'd made a mistake.

That I'd taken on more than I could handle, with the potential to create an even bigger clusterfuck.

It was certainly a predicament.

We'd come off the high of our Opening Day win and gotten sloppy. We lost three games this week. Three games we should have won – or at least not lost by such huge margins.

All of a sudden, we'd gotten flat; each loss deflating the balloon a little more until we were nothing but shriveled rubber caught on the breeze.

I felt like crap, and I couldn't decide whether it was because we'd lost, or because Marnie hadn't replied to a single one of the messages I'd sent her... or because I should have been able to deal with the distraction.

I'd spent nearly half my life playing professional baseball, and I could legitimately say this was the first time I hadn't had my head in the game.

And because I always needed to prove myself right, I pulled my phone out and checked it. Nope. Not one. And it wasn't even like I'd sent many – just a daily check in; morning and night.

Ten in total.

I didn't expect her to come running back immediately, but I was beginning to think I should have known better.

That I couldn't atone for my behavior; that maybe I'd read it wrong and she didn't care. I'd spent fourteen years thinking about her daily, and now the reality was dawning on me that perhaps she hadn't thought about me at all.

But the slap…

I hadn't been a hundred percent sure she'd be in the boss's office when I'd headed straight up after the game, but since I'd woken up that morning, my body had buzzed with a latent energy I'd never felt before.

Some might have said it was simply Opening Day excitement, but that wasn't it.

I'd known.

I don't know how I'd known, but I had.

Marnie Matthews had finally arrived in the city.

I hadn't bothered to shower. I came straight off the field and ran up the five flights of stairs to Penn Shepherd's office, still covered in black and gold glitter from the canons going off after our win.

I stalked down the corridor and then stopped dead. The door to his office was ajar, and the second I heard her voice, I nearly fell to my knees. Still the same soft, lilting tones, but with a new sound; a delicate gruffness like she was getting over a cold. It coated my skin, covering me with the same protection it did back in high school, or before any game when she'd told me she loved me.

I'd stood outside for thirty seconds, absorbing the sound of her voice, quenching the nerves I'd never felt before in my life.

Or a handful of times before.

I chuckled quietly. Of everything I'd done in my life, Marnie was the only one who could get my nerves spinning like a fastball.

I pushed open the door and there she was.

Even though I'd known she was on the other side, I'd still been shocked into stillness when I'd seen her. Even if she wasn't burned into my soul or tattooed on my body, I'd recognize her anywhere.

She hadn't changed a bit.

She spun around at the sound of my voice, thick dark hair flicking into her face as she did. My fingers itched to run through it again, just like I used to.

It had once been my favorite thing in the world… it probably still was.

Yet one look at her face and I knew I had my work cut out for me if I ever wanted to do it again. Fourteen years, and the fire that burned in her eyes could have been lava if I didn't know better.

Then came the slap.

Another thirty seconds of being the recipient of her death stare, and she'd run off. I'd been left alone in the boss' office, standing there with a grin you could have seen from space.

That was six days ago, and I hadn't figured out what to do next.

My mind was still firmly on Marnie when I picked up the remote and turned off the TV. It was still on her as I took a hot shower and fisted my cock. And just like every other night, Marnie Matthews, owner of my heart, was the last thing I thought of as the tiredness I was drowning in engulfed me.

It dawned on me as my eyelids closed that I was nothing more than a lovelorn teenager.

I counted twenty-seven billboards with my face on them between my apartment and The Lions Stadium. No wonder the Yankees were pissed.

Penn Shepherd had taken over the entire city with the black and gold team colors.

I avoided Times Square at the best of times, but until the giant screens played something other than Lions interviews, and Lions social media on loop, not to mention the official team photos, I would be avoiding it forever.

It wasn't like all the images were of me. My twenty-five teammates were also included, but if I didn't know better, I'd say all mine had more airtime. If I could be bothered to prove it, I would. The New York Lions PR juggernaut was hurtling down the highway, and heaven help anyone who got in the way. This included said billboards, as well as social media presence, print interviews, and interviews across broadcast and network television. I'd had a request to go on The Tonight Show, but responded with a hard fucking pass.

Billboards were my limit, and that's only because I could hide among the rest of the team.

I was also plenty used to billboards and ad campaigns featuring yours truly. I could handle billboards. But since I'd moved to this city and my face was somewhere new, the interest in it had dialed up somewhat, to put it mildly.

For the first time I gave a slight fuck, because I now had a mission bigger than baseball:

Marnie.

There was a reason I lived in a very secure and gated community in Los Angeles. Thank fuck my apartment came with underground parking and security in New York, so I could avoid anyone waiting outside the main entrance for me; something that happened way more than it ever should. I wasn't sure if anyone had discovered where I lived yet, but it was only a matter of time before women started lining up outside and throwing their panties at me whenever I walked out, evidence of which was right here as I pulled up to the security entrance by the players gates.

I could hear my name being chanted over and over, and in fairness, New York had been incredibly welcoming to me. Less fair, I wish they'd stop hitting my car with each cry of my name. The atmosphere on game days was always heightened, but that didn't mean I wanted to send my SUV to get fixed every week.

"JUPITER! JUPITER! JUPITER!"

Bang. Bang. Bang.

I eased the car just beyond the barricades and out of reach. Flashing my pass at the security guard on the gates, I hit the gas to get through as quickly as I could, and into the quiet parking lot by the entrance the team players used.

I got out, removed the bra which had stuck under my wiper blade, and grabbed my bag from the trunk. Each step toward the building was spent squinting into the distance at the executive parking lot two hundred yards away, to see if Marnie was here.

Then I realized I didn't know what car she drove, or how

she traveled, period.

I knew where she lived – a little further north than my loft – but that was only because I'd overheard Lowe Slater and Beulah Holmes talking about it at the Opening Day celebration last week.

"Hey, Reeves!"

A cry from behind had me spinning round to find Stone Fields, the left fielder, jogging toward me.

"Hey, man," I tipped my chin when he caught up, "You good?"

He didn't answer my question; his wide eyes were focused on my left hand. "You had a good night or what?"

"Girls at the gate throwing stuff, it got stuck on my window," I groaned, tossing the piece of frilly pink lace in the trashcan as we passed. "Why are you here so early, anyway?"

"Hash browns," he replied while patting his stomach and making me laugh.

On game days we didn't officially have to be in until one p.m.

However, I was a terrible cook, and my chef had stayed in L.A. when I'd moved to New York, so every morning I was presented with the dilemma of how to feed myself. I hadn't been in the city long enough to be comfortable going out in public, given the issue of my face being everywhere. Even if I did, coupled with the renewed interest in The Lions, it would take me twice the time to do anything with all the interruptions and requests for selfies and autographs.

And since my youngest sister, Emerson, lived slightly upstate with her three kids, I couldn't bribe her to come and feed me.

All this meant, therefore, I needed to come to the club early. The plus side – I could squeeze a workout in.

"Me, too," though I'd be sticking with the staple spinach and egg white omelet with turkey bacon, because the season meant I watched what I ate. The off season, however, pass me the share bag of M&Ms… that I won't be sharing… "Hey, did you get into the grounds okay?"

"Yeah," he nodded. "But those gates, dude…"

I held the door open and followed after he walked through. "I know. I'm going to talk to security, or I'm sending them the bill for the repairs I'll need."

He chuckled. "Knew I could count on you getting shit done! I like that the fans are excited though."

"Yeah, just not at the expense of my car!" I huffed.

We both flashed our passes at the guards on the reception desk we'd stopped in front of, though it would have been just as easy to point to the enormous flags flying outside with our faces on.

"Good morning, Mr. Reeves, Mr. Fields. How can I help you?"

"Hey," I started, leaning slightly over the desk, "is there something we can do about the fans at the gates? Can we move them back a bit? They're banging hard on the cars when anyone drives in."

"Yeah, it's dangerous too, man," added Stone. "Someone will get hurt."

Yeah, that's the angle I should have gone for – safety, not damage to my car. And this is why I had a reputation for being a self-centered prick.

The security guard, Pablo, considered us for a moment, then answered in a deep baritone. "Sure thing. Let me check with Mike, and we'll get something figured out; maybe have some barricades moved back."

"Thanks, man, we appreciate it." I bobbed my head, trying

to look as genial as possible.

"No problem. Good luck today fellas; should be an easy win."

"Yeah," I replied as we walked away. "Thanks, man."

"God, I fucking hate it when people say shit like that. Like they actually know what it's like to stand up at the plate and hit a ball traveling toward you at a hundred miles an hour," Stone griped, his ever present cheery façade dropping.

A talented left fielder, we'd played against each other ever since he'd moved up from the minors seven years ago. He'd started at The Red Sox and then moved to The Astros before coming here. This was the first time we'd played together. Aside from seeing him at the usual sports award ceremonies and around the circuit, we hadn't spent much time together, but he always garnered massive respect from everyone in the leagues due to his affable, happy-go-lucky demeanor while smashing out a home run, like he was swatting a fly.

I'd always had massive respect for him as a player, especially as the press loved him – unlike me.

"Yeah, I know." I nodded in agreement. "You okay though?"

He took a large gulp of the water he was carrying, and dragged the back of his hand over his mouth. "Yeah, I'm good. Just had an argument with Carrie this morning is all."

"Is Carrie your girlfriend?"

"Yeah, but not sure for how much longer," he sighed, "Man, relationships are hard."

Finally, a conversation about relationships I could contribute to. Because up until I moved to New York, I had categorically stayed as far away from them as I possibly could.

I had no interest in them.

All I wanted to do was play ball how I wanted, and anyone

who got in the way of that could fuck right off.

Only one woman would ever change my mind, and it was the one who currently wanted nothing to do with me.

But… I couldn't deny that after last week, something was officially going on between us, even if it lived solely in the slap she'd delivered, and it meant I actually did know that relationships were hard.

"Tell me about it."

"You got a girl?" He stopped, his face filled with questions, like this was news he should have known.

"Working on it. But she doesn't want to know right now."

Stone's head fell back with a loud guffaw, and from the way he was looking at me I think he expected me to continue, but that was all I had. I also didn't want to divulge anything about Marnie until I had an actual plan. I'd seen plenty of players make moves on club staff and have it blow up in their faces. Granted this wasn't the same type of situation, but I still wasn't going to talk.

"That's all I got, sorry."

"Well, if you need help, you come to me," he thumbed his chest.

"You just said you were about to break up with your girl," I scoffed, pushing open the swing doors that led down to the training facility.

I'd played against The Lions plenty in my career, but never thought much of the stadium. Coming from The Dodgers', it always seemed a bit run down. All that changed, however, when Penn Shepherd took over. Even I didn't know how he'd managed to make it all happen in the five short months between seasons, but he'd transformed this place into a palace.

For starters, we had two locker rooms – one purely for game day, the one we began and finished each game in, then a second for every day. An everyday locker room – or Locker Room One, as it was known. That was where we were headed now.

The game day one was sleek, but Locker Room One was incredible; like a five-star hotel. Given we spent the majority of our time at the club when we weren't traveling, the boss made sure we had every comfort imaginable; and a locker room staff ready to serve us however we needed.

Locker Room, however, was slightly redundant, and a little misleading. It was more like a locker suite, spread across five thousand square feet. The entrance hallway we were walking down was lined with fridges, all filled with any approved drink we could want, plus shelves of snacks if we were ever hungry, which was all the time for some of the boys, including my current locker room pal.

Big screen televisions, huge couches for any downtime we were allowed, plus Xbox and PlayStation was neatly tucked away in one corner of the space, along with board games, playing cards, a fully stacked poker table, and bocce ball. On the other side of the playroom was a quiet space, with little bunkbeds if we had time for a nap.

And I hadn't yet asked, but I swear it had its own smell; calming like massage oil, but not the stinging, painful massage kind. More like the kind you got on vacation.

It was clever, too. We were a brand-new team, coming together almost like an expansion, and this place was designed for us to socialize, get to know each other on a personal level, become buddies.

Doors off the locker room lead to the team dining room, the gym, the pool, the rehab and conditioning suites, the executives' floor, and the only place in the entire complex I remotely cared about – Marnie's office.

I'd walked past it more times than I wanted to admit over

the last month as I waited for her to arrive.

Fuck. What was I going to do?

Sometimes it felt like my chest was about to cave in, I was so desperate to see her again. I'd even settle to just be in the same room in silence, but right now, it felt like she was behind a massive brick wall that I couldn't punch my way through.

I opened my locker, the one with my name on it, and threw my bag inside. Pulling my hoodie over my head, I fished around my pockets for my earbuds then stepped out of my track pants. "Fields, you working out first?"

He sat in front of his locker, pondering my question with a long stroke of his thick beard. "Yeah, I guess I can wait a bit longer for hash browns. I can even have an extra one if I burn it off first."

"Great, move your ass then." I waved over my shoulder as I headed out.

A little over an hour later, after a gentle six-mile run, some conditioning exercises, and a scalding shower, I sat down opposite Stone, and watched while he inhaled two of his beloved hash browns in less than thirty seconds.

I wasn't even sure he chewed them.

"You're going to give yourself a hernia if you eat any quicker – or at the very least, a nasty case of heartburn."

"I have to eat them like this." He took note of my raised eyebrow and continued, "If I eat them quickly, I can pretend I didn't eat them at all; that I did, in fact, stick to my nutritionist approved breakfast."

You had to admire the logic.

"Right, but all the food here is nutritionist approved." I pointed my fork toward his mouth. "It's not like they came from Mickey-D's. I think they're made with sweet potato."

His giant shoulder heaved upwards. "Same diff. I need to shed fifteen pounds this season, but I can't quit the browns."

"So you just eat them and forget about them?"

"Exactly!"

I swallowed my mouthful of omelet. "So what happened this morning with Carrie?"

He put down his fork and pinned me with a look of frustration, adding a deep sigh to boot. "She won't come to the game today; said she wanted to go shopping instead. Fucking shopping! We've been away all week when she could have gone shopping, but she does it when I'm back. It's bullshit."

Even in my very new and inexperienced position as a relationship participator, I could see that it was, indeed, bullshit.

"How long have you guys been together?"

"Couple of years, but if I'm honest it's been dying off the last six months. She wants kids, and I'm not ready. I'm still only twenty-eight. Plus," he dropped his gaze and began pushing the remainder of his food around, "she only seems to have an interest in spending my money, and I'm sure the kids part is to get a bigger chunk of change."

I stretched my hands out, linking them behind my neck. I'd never been in his situation, but I'd seen plenty of guys over the years get embroiled in a thousand court cases over kids and money. It was never pretty, and it never ended well.

I wasn't any better off though. My money was safe, but I'd been alone since I was eighteen.

Finding your forever person was goddamn hard – especially if you lost them once already.

"Man, I'm sorry. That really sucks balls. What are you going to do?"

"I dunno. Break up I guess. She didn't want to come to

New York anyway, so maybe it won't be too bad."

The door to the dining room swung open and Ace Watson, The Lions' pitcher, and Parker King, our catcher, sauntered in, with all the swagger a pair of twenty-two-year-olds in their second year of the major leagues could muster, thanks in no small part to the interview with Jimmy Fallon I'd pointedly refused to do, they'd taken my place, and New York had fallen in love with their bromance. It was rare to ever see them apart; they'd even started finishing each other's sentences like an old married couple.

I groaned to myself. They were at the more junior end of the ladder, and I hadn't decided yet whether I liked them. King was okay, but I could do with Ace talking less, because once he started, he never seemed to stop.

Stone looked over his shoulder to see who'd just come in, and dropped his voice. "Don't say anything about Carrie, will you?"

"Take it to the grave, man," I promised solemnly.

"Thanks," he looked up as the boys approached. "Hey, guys."

"Mind if we join you?" asked Parker.

I glanced up. "We're not in high school, King. You don't need to ask permission."

"You looked like you were having a deep and meaningful, that's all," he shot back with a boyish smirk, then sat down next to Stone, who looked longingly at the pile of hash browns on Parker's plate. "Didn't want to interrupt anything important."

"The only thing it looks like we're interrupting is the way Fields is eye-fucking your food. Here, man," Ace tipped half his plate onto Stone's. "Go nuts."

The expression on Stone's face had me chuckling behind

my cup of matcha as I sipped it. "Dude, just eat them."

He didn't need to be told twice, and two had disappeared before I'd even put my cup down.

"Hey, do you guys know what baseball science is?"

I pushed my empty plate away and started on my granola, which was far more interesting than anything Ace had to say. "Nope."

My mind went back to Marnie.

Maybe I should go and see her, just see if she'd talk to me.

How was I going to convince her to talk to me? Um…

Would it be weird if I waited outside her office? Yes, it would.

Maybe.

"Did you guys see the email about the new chick?" Ace asked through a mouthful of avocado toast.

"We're all new."

"No, she's super new, like from last weekend. We just ran into her in the hallway and man, she's hot. Her ass is…" he lifted his fingers to his lips and burst them open in a chef's kiss. "Fuck, I love older women. And this one is so… peachy. She looks smart too, wearing glasses like she meant business, instead of just… you know."

Stone and I both stared at him, making it clear we, in fact, didn't know. But that was not unusual with Ace, and we'd all learned quickly to filter the important stuff.

"He's right, she was," nodded Parker, with more enthusiasm than he needed.

Stone and I went back to our breakfast. Even if I wasn't thinking about Marnie, breakfast was also seen as a time of quiet contemplation, and a look ahead to the day's game,

something these two had yet to learn.

"I can't wait until Monday." The tone of Ace's sigh had all three of us looking at him.

"What's happening on Monday?" Stone asked, once he'd swallowed his current mouthful.

"We all have appointments to see her over the next few weeks. Coach scheduled them in our calendars." He picked up a piece of toast and crunched down on it. "She's the head of baseball science."

My ears pricked up, the important subject filter doing its job properly. "Who're you talking about?"

He looked at me like I hadn't been listening to him for the last five minutes, which of course I hadn't.

"The new chick." He scratched his head, obviously trying to remember. "Marnie, I think her name was."

I stood up so quickly I almost got head rush. Parker grabbed my chair before it hit the floor. "Marnie Matthews?"

He clapped his hands together. "Yes! Her, she's fucking hot. She's got…"

My hands slammed down on the table so hard Ace's orange juice toppled over and spilled all over the table. He jumped out of the way before he was covered in it too.

"What the fuck, Reeves?"

I stood tall, adjusting my ball cap, and slowed my breathing. I might not have known what my immediate plans were with Marnie, but they sure as shit didn't include having to fight off these two horny dipshits staring up at me like they'd never seen someone fly into a jealous rage before.

I leaned forward, palms placed calmly on the table this time, and stared down at them. I'm not gonna lie and say I didn't enjoy seeing Parker shrinking back slightly.

"Right, listen up," I began quietly. "No one, and I mean no

one, is to go near Marnie Matthews. I don't give a fuck if you are scheduled to see her. I'm canceling all the appointments now."

Stone looked at me like my mind had gone the way of the orange juice. "Er, Reeves, I don't think you can do that."

"Watch me," I snarled, knowing full well he was correct. I pointed to the open mouths of Ace and Parker. "And you two spread the word about it. No one is to go near her."

"Um, okay…" said Parker, his tone the level of calm I'd failed to achieve, and whom I then decided in that second I liked better. "But you want to explain yourself?"

"Not really."

I crossed my arms over my chest with a huff, realizing I may have just dropped myself into the deep shit-filled trench of club gossip, because there's no way my outburst wasn't going to get around. And while I didn't give a fuck, I didn't want Marnie dragged into anything.

"Jupiter, Shepherd will find out about this when no one is turning up to see this expert he's brought in. You saw the email."

I pulled my chair in and sat down. "I don't read emails."

"Well, it said that she's new to the staff and all our schedules have been updated with sessions to meet her."

"I'd definitely take a session with her," smirked Ace under his breath, but not quietly enough.

My head whipped round with an ill-concealed snarl. "I will knock your head off."

His palms shot up defensively. "Okay, okay. Chill."

I was not going to chill.

It became clear no one was going to say anything else. Only the *drip, drip,* of orange juice hitting the floor could be heard. I took a deep breath and rubbed my temples, willing my racing heart to calm. It had been years since I'd felt this level of rage over a woman. In fact, Marnie was the only woman I'd ever felt jealousy over.

In all my years since her, there hadn't been one woman who'd ever piqued my interest enough to raise an eyebrow over, let alone my pulse.

"Okay, dude, what the fuck is going on?"

I looked up at Stone, then the two rookies sitting and gawping. Stone turned to them because we both knew I wasn't going to speak in front of them.

"You two, breakfast time is over. Go find a mop or something."

They shot up and ran off without any argument. Stone simply looked at me, crunching down on a piece of toast he'd picked up off Ace's plate, then sat back and waited.

"Okay, but you keep my secret and I'll keep yours." I offered up the trade before I got stuck into the actual intel.

Stone gave a single nod, like he was fucking Mr. Miyagi.

"The girl I told you about earlier, the one I'm working on who doesn't want anything to do with me?" I looked at him dead-on. "It's Marnie Matthews, the new girl."

He threw the rest of Ace's toast down, picked up a napkin, and wiped his fingers clean. "Whoa, seriously? But she's only just started here! How did you fuck it up already?"

I shook my head slowly. "No, it's not like that. We were in high school together. She was my first girlfriend, the only girlfriend I've had. The only woman I've ever loved. I broke up with her the day I was drafted. It had to be done, but I've regretted it every single day since. I never thought I would ever have the chance to make it up to her, but then Penn Shepherd came to see me. I said I would only play for The

Lions if he found her and offered her a job."

"Holy fuck!" he yelled, then dropped his voice at my snarled *shhh*. "Sorry, but that was not what I was expecting you to say!"

"She moved here from Houston."

Stone's eyes opened wider. "What? Like me?"

I nodded. "Yeah, she was at N.A.S.A. It's why Shepherd brought her on for baseball science or whatever it is. It's all he could come up with. Marnie was a rocket scientist, is a rocket scientist. Well, an astrodynamicist."

"Holy fuck. What's she doing with you? You can't even pronounce it!"

I shot him a wry look, though he wasn't wrong. "She's not with me… yet."

"Have you spoken to her?"

"Not exactly," I cringed with a head shake and quickly explained the slap. Stone's jaw dropped further with each revelation, until I could see the whole length of his very pink tongue. "I've been texting her this week but she hasn't replied to any of them. I need to talk to her before that rookie gets in to see her."

"Dude, she's here. Ace said he ran into her, remember?"

My eyes widened. "Yes, he did fucking say that, didn't he?"

Stone lifted his hands in the air and trapped me with a hard stare. "What are you waiting for? Go."

He didn't need to tell me twice. I took off quickly, heading down the corridor and only slowing down to take the left at the stairs. It took a second before I realized someone was ahead of me.

It was another second before I realized that someone was my someone.

Fuck.

"Marnie."

She spun around, her green eyes locking onto mine. Her jaw tensed just before she shot right and slammed whatever door she'd gone through.

Turned out, it was her office.

This was already going much better than expected. And this time, I was going to learn to duck.

I calmly walked the rest of the way, and stood outside. Dr. Marnie Matthews, *PhD* was carved into a plaque on the door, above which I knocked hard.

After ten seconds, it was clear she wasn't going to open the door so I tried the knob, only to find it locked.

Not sure why, but it made me smile.

I knocked again.

Nothing.

"Marnie, I know you're in there. I saw you go in."

Silence.

"Star, please," I tried again. "I really want to talk to you."

"Well I don't want to talk to you. Go away."

I held in the chuckle that bubbled up because I didn't think she'd find my amusement amusing. I'd forgotten how stubborn she could be. "Can't do that I'm afraid, Star."

Still nothing.

My fist pounded out a slow beat on the door that matched my heartrate. She lasted less than a minute before it flew open.

Jeez-zus.

Like last week, I was unprepared for the onslaught of emotions, nor for the way my body reacted to having her stand in front of me.

My throat constricted. My chest seized. Blood raced to my dick.

All at the same time.

She was so fucking beautiful, even if she was shooting daggers of fire at me through the narrow slits hiding her eyes. I could just make out the black of her pupils, almost indiscernible from the brilliant green of her iris.

"What do you want?"

I wiped away the tiny bubble of spit which hit my face and buoyed my determination. It also helped me steady myself; my dick, however, was hardening by the second.

"Good morning to you, too. How was your first week? I texted you but didn't hear back, so I hope it was good."

Her knuckles turned white as her fist gripped the door, and her glare became decidedly more murderous. "Jupiter, what do you want?"

"Cutting to the chase I see. Are you going to invite me in?"

"No. And you've got thirty seconds before I shut this door again," she snapped hard, pushing her glasses back onto her head.

Shit. Maybe this was reckless... How the fuck was I going to put an argument across in thirty seconds?

Fuck again. I was wasting my seconds.

"Okay. Well, I came to tell you that I'm going to make it right between us. I want you back, Star."

"Stop calling me that!"

I shook my head. "No. I'm going to make it right."

Her eyes flicked up, but the way she was glaring wasn't solely with anger… there was interest, perhaps.

"I'm not interested, so don't hold your breath," she hissed, like she'd read my mind.

"You know I can hold my breath for a long time. Have you forgotten?" I leaned in slightly and winked. She blushed that shade of pink I used to get a boner for… and apparently still got a boner for.

Thankfully, my track pants were hiding most of it.

"I know you coerced Penn Shepherd into hiring me."

I rolled my lips and crossed my arms like she had, but casually, not rigid with anger. "Yeah, so?"

"You're so goddamn arrogant."

She wasn't the first person to call me that, and she wouldn't be the last. But she was the only one whose eyes sparkled when they said it. She was the most beautiful, and somehow the way she said it didn't make it sound all that bad.

Almost like a compliment.

Or that's how I was taking it.

"Still trying to control people's lives without a second thought, as long as you get what you want. Did it ever occur to you that had I known you'd be here, I'd have run fast in the opposite direction?"

Okay, perhaps not a compliment.

"Maybe, but I am going to win you back, even if it takes all season. I'm going to remind you of what we had."

"Fourteen years, Jupiter. You haven't seen me in fourteen years. Why am I here? Do you even remember the way you left me? You can't just click your fingers and expect me to come running. We aren't even the same people. You don't know me, and we don't know each other." The pulse in her throat was quickening with each point, and her voice had risen an octave. "It was a dumb teenage romance. You're delusional if you think it was any more than that."

My eyes hadn't left her face while she'd been yelling at me; the way her lip curved deeper into a Cupid's bow, the way her left eye flickered in the corner by her brow, and the way her jaw was now popping.

I leaned further into her. "Say that to me again without lying."

I didn't hear her breath catch, I saw it.

"Just as I thought." I stepped out of her space, no matter how much I wanted to stay there. I wanted to be right up in it. "I know I have a lot to make up for, and we have years to make up for. But I'm going to show you. I'm going to remind you exactly what we were to each other."

"What we were to each other?! You dumped me for being clingy the day you got drafted. Not girlfriend material. Embarrassing. That's what we were to each other, Jupiter." She laughed darkly, a tone which punched me hard in the gut. The glistening, unshed tears didn't help either.

"Are you coming to watch the game?"

"I have to as part of my contract. No doubt you had that added in too!"

I ignored her jibe, especially as I hadn't. She probably didn't realize it was a clause in everyone's contract, not that I was complaining. "Good. I can't wait to see you watching me again. Remember how you used to watch me?" I scanned her face again. "I'm going to hit a home run for you."

"Don't bother," she snarled.

I stared at her. She stared at me. The pulse on her neck was pounding now. I went to reach for her hand, but then thought better of it.

Instead, I told her, "I'm not sorry, Star. I'm not going to apologize for bringing you here and back into my life."

"Of course not. It would be foolish of me to expect otherwise, especially as the word isn't even in your vocabulary."

I ignored her snarl. In fact, the more I smiled, the snarlier she became. "It sure is. I'm sorry it took me so long to find you again."

Her fists clenching by her sides made my heart flip a beat.

"I'm going to remind you, Marn, then you'll see we're meant to be together."

With that she slammed the door in my face. My thirty seconds was up.

And I knew what I had to do.

4

Jupiter

Fourteen years ago - January

Man, my life is great.

January in southern California; the weather's a balmy sixty-eight degrees and today is my first full practice of the season. My final school season.

And by the end of it, I'll have been drafted to the greatest club in the world – the Los Angeles Dodgers. No question.

Because dreams really do come true.

Ever since I was old enough to hold a Little League bat, I knew all I ever wanted to do was play ball. Everything I've done since I was five years old has been with the singular goal of being the best at playing baseball.

Healthy? Probably not, but I'm happy because I get to do what I love, you know, in between the rest of the stuff that comes with being a teenager – school, a curfew, really annoying sisters, and semi-annoying parents.

But I have great friends, and there's always a girl around campus who'd be happy for a hook-up with me. Hell, there's usually a line.

And now, on this early Monday morning, there are exactly five months and twelve days between me and The Draft. My life will be a steady breeze of eating and sleeping baseball, and maintaining my C-average in order to graduate.

My professional career is inevitable, so why postpone it with another four years of pointless learning?

So yeah, life is great. Or it would be if my youngest sister would hurry the fuck up.

"EMERSON! GET YOUR ASS OUTSIDE!" I hollered, but kept the rest of my cursing to a low mutter in order to avoid my mom's hawk-like hearing, and any part of my allowance relegated to the swear jar said younger sister had created last summer.

I could also do without the lecture from my mom that *gentlemen do not swear, Jupiter,* before seven-thirty a.m. because if I'd heard it once, I'd heard it a thousand times.

Clearly it hadn't sunk in.

"Jupe, you're gonna burst your muscles if you keep hollering like that. You know, the ones you've been working so very hard on…"

I didn't need to spin round to know my sister's almost-more-annoying best friend was walking up my parents' driveway. "How about you stop perving on me, Mallory? I know it's hard for you, but you'll get eye strain one day."

"Yeah, you wish I was a member of that brainless harem that follows you about all day." In my periphery I could see her cupping her face in one hand, before she put on a high pitched squeaky voice. "Oh, Jupiter, oh look at your muscles, oh look at how hard you swing your bat, oh you're so handsome..."

She didn't manage her next dig before she dissolved into a fit of giggles. At least she was amusing someone.

"You're a dick, Mal, but whatever floats your boat." I finally turned to look at her, and my eyes popped wide instead of rolling deep like they were about to. "Um, what the fuck is that under your arm? I know you're not thinking of bringing that with you because I've already told you it's not coming anywhere near my truck."

"Keep your muscles on, Jupe." She righted the surfboard she was carrying and glared at me. "You understand the purpose of a truck is to put stuff in the trunk, right? Emerson and I are going surfing after school, and we don't have time to come back because we have a late math period."

"Not my fucking problem." I leaned on the horn again while I hung out of the truck window, "EMERSON!"

Mallory propped a fist on her hip. "You know, Jupe, based on my calculations, you owe at least fifty dollars in the swear jar from our delightful morning chit chat alone. I'll let it slide and keep it between us, if you can graciously give me and Stevie a ride this morning."

I looked at the clock on the dash; at this rate I was *actually* going to be late. I'd forgone my usual morning run in favor of one with my best friend, Jenson, at school, and if I was late for that, I'd be late for Coach, which he would not be happy about.

And this morning had started off so great.

"Who the fuck is Stevie? I never agreed to give any of your friends a ride! It's annoying enough as it is to have to wait on you and Emerson! And you better tell her she has thirty seconds to get here before I leave you both."

The horn blared out one more time.

"Stevie the surfboard," Mallory replied nonchalantly as she heaved it into the trunk of my Escalade, ignoring my glare, and then climbed in the back seat.

I don't know why I even bothered. Truth be told this is how most interactions with Mallory and Emerson went – me protesting, them doing whatever they wanted regardless. At least I didn't have to contend with Piper, my eldest sister, as well, who was thankfully away at college. Then when she left, it fell to me to provide the carpool, hence my beloved Escalade truck I'd received for my eighteenth birthday.

"Finally!" I cheered, once again omitting the curse words as my sister ambled – fucking ambled – out of the house like she had all the time in the world. My teeth gritted as I spied her surfboard, but didn't put up an argument like I would have done if she'd arrived fifteen minutes earlier when I was first outside and ready to leave.

I waited until it joined Mallory's surfboard in the trunk, then turned the key. The engine roared to life, ready to inch its way down the driveway the second Emerson opened the passenger door.

"Jeez, impatient much? Let me actually get in before you take off, please! I don't understand why we have to leave so early. Piper didn't make us leave for another half hour, and we were still early to class," Emerson mumbled through the slice of toast still wedged between her front teeth, while trying to pull her seat belt on.

Turning left out of the drive, we surged forward along the winding roads leading out of our neighborhood, and towards Santa Monica. Hopefully traffic would be light, and I'd be able to make up some time.

"Piper didn't have pre-school commitments; I do. I have squad training, followed by practice, and this morning I have a meeting with Coach, and I'm meeting Jenson for a run. So, yes, we need to leave early, and yes, I'd appreciate you moving your ass quicker."

She huffed a response I didn't catch and began fiddling with the buttons on the music system. I braced myself for another protest once I'd rejected whatever pop crap she'd chosen.

"Oh yes, Taylor Swift! I love this song," Mallory piped up, her head sticking through the space between us.

"Absolutely not, turn this shit off! It's bad enough you're making me late." I slapped my hand on another button and the music changed to a much more acceptable Jay-Z. I then pushed Emerson's feet away from where they were currently resting, and rubbed off the mark her sneakers had left. "No feet on the dash, you know the rules!"

I didn't miss the wide eyes Mallory gave to neither one of us in particular.

"I want to live in New York one day," Emerson sighed, pulling down the passenger visor to look in the mirror as she brushed her hair, no doubt getting her long auburn strands everywhere. She was worse than a shedding dog.

"Fuck no. New York is far too cold." I shivered at the thought. "And can you stop doing that in my car?"

She flicked the visor back up. "I wouldn't have to if you'd let us leave at a more reasonable time."

"Jupiter, what if you get drafted to the Yankees?" asked Mallory, far too innocently to fool anyone.

I narrowed my eyes at her through the rear-view mirror.

Emerson turned around in her seat. "Please don't set him off. I'm not listening to The Dodgers for Life statement this early in the morning."

Mallory snorted, and turned to look out of the window, making me flinch when she banged on it. "Hey, stop! Jupiter stop the truck! Em, look, it's that girl…"

"What? No chance."

"Yeah, it's that girl. She was in our math class last year, but then moved to the advanced group..."

"Jupe, slow down." Emerson pointed ahead to a figure on the sidewalk about fifty yards up and closing. "That's the girl that moved in next door. Her name's Marnie, I think. Slow down, we can give her a ride."

"No can do, I'm already late! Bad enough I have to drop you two off."

"It's not like you go out of your way to take us to our side of the campus, we still have to walk there!" Emerson hissed and ducked down in her seat. "You're such an ass."

My eyes flicked over to where she was now almost horizontal. "What are you doing?!"

"I don't want her to see me passing by and not offering a ride, then realizing I'm related to an ass. It's so embarrassing."

I glanced in the side mirror; I wasn't sure if the girl from next door had even noticed we'd passed given the way her head was down in a book. Though even from that angle, and the increasing distance, I could still tell she was cute, glasses perched on her head above a high ponytail swishing softly as she walked.

Maybe I should give her a ride…

I cleared my head quickly. Nope. No distractions going into the final season. The only thing I was committing to was playing ball and graduating.

"I'm sure you'll get over it by tomorrow morning, when

you need to get to school again," I snapped back.

"Ugh! I can't wait until my birthday and I get my car."

"Unfortunately for all of us, that's not for a while," Mallory piped up unhelpfully.

Emerson then decided she no longer wanted to acknowledge me, and instead unbuckled and climbed into the backseat like I was now their fucking chauffeur. But at least with them gossiping together it allowed me to zone out and concentrate on what I had to accomplish during the remainder of the school year, starting with my nine a.m. meeting with Coach Barr. I was pretty sure he was going to name me Captain of the Baseball Squad this year.

Captain of the Squad – it would only be a formality, seeing as I'd assumed the role last year when Chris Jackson, the old captain, had graduated, and no one had been named his successor. Technically, there hadn't been anyone suitable, and officially I was too junior to move into the role but I took it anyway, and as a result, we were going into the new season looking stronger, feeling fresher, and scoring higher than we'd ever done.

I'd taken my self-appointed role seriously; the early mornings weren't just for me, but to set an example for the rest of the guys – and they'd listened. We were lucky that California weather was mild through the winter, because I'd set us on a training program that started at sunrise. Even though they liked to grumble about it, not a single one of them had missed a session.

I wanted to leave school on a high, with our team name etched into the Southern California High School Baseball League trophy.

I was still mulling it over when I pulled into my regular parking space, at the end of which was Jenson Abrams, my best friend and teammate. He was perched on the top of a concrete bollard, his arms crossed over his chest.

"Hey, Mallory," he crowed as she climbed out of the backseat, followed by Emerson, both of them retrieving their surfboards.

"Hi," she frowned in response, then ignored him, which only made his grin wider.

Emerson shuffled her board under her arm, before looking over at me. "Jupe, don't forget we don't need a ride later."

"How could I forget something so awesome?" I grinned.

She rolled her eyes in response. "Thanks, loser. See you at home."

I retrieved my backpack from the passenger foot well and slung it over my shoulder with a loud laugh, though they were already too far away to hear me.

Jenson pushed off the bollard. "Mallory is so fucking salty, I love it."

"They both are. Honestly, sisters are so annoying. Or just girls are, period," I added as an afterthought before shutting the door. I hit the alarm on the car fob, listened for the beep, then we headed over to the baseball field and our state-of-the-art training facility which we shared with the other sports teams, which had been generously donated by ex-alumni athletes a few years ago.

"Ready for the top job?" Jenson punched me harder than he needed to as we took the steps up to the school courtyard two at a time.

I rubbed my bicep and shoved him with a smirk. "Careful, dude, that's my money-maker. And I've already been doing the job."

He sprinted up the last few steps to reach the top before me and turned round. "Five months!" he reached out and shook my shoulders. "Five months and you're drafted!"

"Fuck, yeah!" A grin split my face. "You could make that a we if you didn't insist on going to college first."

He groaned, his shoulders dropping. It wasn't the first time we'd had this conversation, but as adamant and sure as I was about getting drafted straight from school, he had never had the same plan. "Yeah, I know, but I promised my mom. Plus, it's sensible. What happens if I never make it out of the minors? I need a backup."

I stepped up to his level and twisted him around so we could continue making our way to the sports building, because I was still on the clock, no matter how much I wanted to reassure him.

"Dude, where's your believer's mindset? Of course you'll make it out. We both will, and we're going to dominate the next two decades of the game. Cities will name their streets after us, people will name their kids after us, we'll be written about alongside Jeter and A-Rod, minus the beef, obvs. Then we'll move into commentary." I waved my arm slowly in front of us, giving him a vision of our future.

"Damn fucking right." He slapped my hand in a high five, but then his face dropped. "Uh oh, incoming."

I looked to the left to see The Laurens – a persistent group of girls who all had the same first name, and therefore thought they should hang out together. It was one of the many rules their coven had, so unless you were called Lauren, you had no chance of getting in. They also all looked very similar; with their blonde hair in various degrees of bleached, tight Abercrombie jeans, and sweaters they'd all customized with a number. Because we were currently in hockey and football season, the numbers they wore belonged to any one of the guys on the aforementioned teams, and starting next month, the numbers would change to include the baseball team.

That wasn't to say they were fans of any of the sports –

they weren't. They were fans of status only; of the guys on the teams who played well, and won. And even then, only very few of the guys were interested in what The Laurens had to offer, because you could smell the trouble a mile away, and no one serious about their place was willing to trade a prime spot for the distraction of a pair of tits.

Not tits that came with their levels of chaos, anyway.

I was proud to say that I had never succumbed to exchanging body fluids with any of them, and under no circumstances did I ever have plans to, no matter how hard they tried.

And they really, really tried.

In fact, I'd gone so far as to warn the entire squad last year about hooking up with any of them after an incident at the football team's End of Season Party last year, and a fight involving the captain's girlfriend after she overheard two of The Laurens gossiping about her, and how they were going to break up her and the Cap, or so the story goes. I'm fuzzy on details though as I stopped listening, because girls…

But the moral is The Laurens cause drama, and my squad would be having no part in it.

"Hi, boys. Hi, Jenson. You looked so good at practice last week. Can't wait for the new season. You too, Jupe."

Jenson moved out of the way before Lauren M could stroke her hand down his arm. "Thanks, I appreciate that."

"Where are you off to? Have you been named Captain yet, Jupe?" asked the Lauren in the purple sweater.

I jolted slightly though I didn't know why, because the other thing about The Laurens is they knew everything. There was no unturned stone they weren't aware of. Usain Bolt is a snail compared to the speed they gossip.

"Not officially."

"You'll get it," she continued with a smile, "and then The

Dodgers will be waiting for you. You know loads of the major league players still have the same girlfriends from when they were at school. So romantic, don't you think?"

I didn't think it was romantic, but thankfully a swift yank to the left as Jenson grabbed my backpack meant I didn't have a chance to respond.

"End of the line, ladies. See you around never," he called behind us as he pulled me into the training facility.

The Laurens all stopped at the door – only school sports teams and serious athletes were admitted into the hallowed building. Everyone else had to use the older facility on the other side of the school. This was a place to concentrate, not fuck around, and mostly everyone respected that. Through the glass doors I could see Reggie, the guard on entry duty today, and they knew better than to push past him. He'd been an NFL hopeful in his day, but he'd suffered a serious knee ligament injury during the Combine that year, and struggled to play again.

"Jeez, they're getting worse. They're like sharks after fresh blood," Jenson snarled.

"Yeah, it'll get worse once the season starts and football finishes. Talk to the new junior squad again, will you? They won't know any better, and The Laurens will sense weakness on anyone playing well."

We stopped as we crossed the threshold, both of us soaking in the energy of the building for the briefest moment before heading in the direction of the locker room to dump our backpacks, and leave for our run.

An hour later we walked back into the building, our legs more Jell-O like than they had been this morning, given the pace we pushed ourselves. There wasn't a dry patch left on my shirt. I had enough time to towel-dry and change into a spare one before I had to go again.

Jenson plopped down on one of the benches and passed me a clean towel from the shelf. "I'll wait here for you."

I peeled my shirt off and took it, rubbing it over my torso just as a split second of nerves sliced through my belly. "Thanks, man. I'm hoping this won't take long. It's not going to be about anything else, right?"

He shook his head vigorously. "No, dude, you got this."

"Cool, okay. Cool. Yeah, 'course. It's in the bag." The confidence I usually carried with me filled my chest once more, and I dropped the towel in the laundry hamper. "Guess I'll see you soon."

I took off down the wide hallway, still pulling a fresh shirt over my head, and made my way to Coach's office, located on the second floor in the coaching wing.

"Hey, Reeves, wait up," a deep voice called as I reached the stairs.

I turned to find Mason Jones, the hockey captain, running toward me, and watched a couple of girls move quickly out of the way. Mason Jones was not someone you wanted knocking into you, even if it was an accident. At eighteen he was already a giant, like a wrecking ball, and one of the reasons the hockey team was having such a successful season.

"Hey, man, are you heading up to the second floor?"

I nodded. "Yeah."

"Cool, I'll walk with you. What you going for?"

The sports, fitness, and training department wasn't split up into separate teams like most people assumed, though we did all have priority schedules for when we could work out. Coach Barr's office and department was right across the hall from Coach Johnson and the football team; hockey was slightly further down next to basketball, along with swimming, wrestling, soccer, volleyball, and the individual division one sports.

"Coach called me in."

"Oh really, what for?"

I shrugged and ignored the slicing nerves again. "To officially make me captain, I hope."

"Oh, yeah? Cool! Although I thought you already were."

"Yeah, so does everyone," I laughed. "Hey, great game the other night. Nice goal!"

"Thanks, man. It's great to have another win. We have some good guys on the team this year and we're still holding the top spot, but Mission Pines is closing in," he replied, mentioning the high school every single team wanted to beat.

Located about thirty miles away from Santa Monica, we'd yet to meet a student there who wasn't a total dick. And more often than not, whenever we played against them, whatever the sports, someone came away with a black eye. Unfortunately, a lot of talented athletes attended Mission Pines, and they were always the school to beat every year.

"Another couple of goals like that and you'll take it." We reached the second floor where a handful of guys were hanging around, and began walking down to the coaching departments. "What are you doing up here anyway?"

Mason stepped to the side to let someone pass. "Got a meeting with the Athletic Director. Coach wants to assign me a tutor because my math is slipping."

At the bottom of the hallway was the unofficial NCAA office – set up by the A.D. to help student athletes get into NCAA colleges. He had a small staff who liaised with scouts, advised on tutoring, scholarships, and counselling. I never spent any time in there because I never had plans to go to college. In fact, I don't think I'd ever walked further down the hallway than Coach Barr's office.

"Oh, that's cool though, right? Least you'll keep your grades up."

His face told me he didn't quite agree with me. "Yeah, I guess, it's just what I have to do. But I'm busting my ass on the ice as well as off. I just need to keep my grades up so I can keep my scholarship for Michigan, and hopefully I'll get drafted next year then I can relax."

"You'll get there, dude." I stopped in front of Coach Barr's office and I thumbed to the door. "This is my stop."

Mason turned to face me, slapping me on the shoulder. "Good to run into you, man. See you at the next game."

"For sure," I replied, as he took off down the hall.

I stood where I was, watching until he disappeared through the doors, but mostly procrastinating my own meeting. I'd never been nervous before going into Coach's office, but this felt way more official than any other time I'd been.

I was pulled out of my musings by loud yelling from the direction that Mason had walked, but all I saw was a small, familiar looking girl leaving the NCAA office, carrying an alarming number of books. So many books that I was once again thankful I didn't have to go through college. A couple of jocks who were waiting on the benches which lined the hallway looked up and came to the same conclusion I did – that noise definitely hadn't come from her – so promptly went back to whatever they'd been doing seconds before.

Another loud eruption was followed by a flash of the orange jersey belonging to the football team, as Josh Ridley, one of the second team reserves, stormed out. Mason stepped out of the way, but the girl wasn't quite so quick, and Josh checked her shoulder so hard that she fell forward. She might have been able to hold her balance, but she was no match for the weight of the books too, and they all came crashing to the floor.

I frowned for a second then sprinted forward as Josh purposefully kicked the books out of her reach as she tried to collect them. I wasn't quick enough off the draw however, as Mason got there first and pinned Josh against the wall.

"What the fuck is your problem, man?" he growled at a struggling Josh, whose feet were almost dangling under Mason's strength.

"She reported me! Bitch got me benched," he snarled.

My jaw ground hard. My sisters might be annoying pains in my asses, and my mom might like to lecture me on not swearing, but it didn't take growing up in a house of women to understand what wasn't acceptable to say to one. And if someone spoke to my sisters like that, they'd be drinking through a straw for a month.

I stood next to Mason and stared at Josh. "What did you get benched for?"

Josh's eyes and lips narrowed, but the answer came from an angry higher-pitched voice behind me. "He refused to come to tutoring."

My nostrils flared and my eyes never strayed from his reddening face. "Then it's your own fucking fault. Apologize."

"Get fucked, Reeves," Josh choked, as Mason applied more pressure to his neck.

"Apologize, Ridley, and then you can go."

Josh was turning a deep shade of red, though I wasn't sure if it was from anger, or his windpipe being cut in half.

"Apologize," tried Mason again.

"Fine. Fucking sorry."

"Not good enough." Mason dropped Josh to his feet, but held onto him as he stared down at the girl still on the floor.

"I'm sorry I kicked your books," he snarled.

The girl on the floor rolled her eyes but said nothing. Mason let go of Josh, with a slight shove that had him storming fast toward the stairs.

"See! That wasn't so hard!" Mason called after him, then tutted. "He's such a dick."

"Yeah." I nodded, and peered down to see the girl still gathering up her books. I dropped to help her. "You okay? Sorry about that. The guy is a douche."

Her eyes shot up to mine as she swept back the thick brown hair which had come loose from her ponytail, and I nearly fell on my ass. Vivid green eyes, the color of the Malibu Ocean on an early summer morning, bored through me with all the annoyance she'd aimed at Josh. But with each blink of her thick black lashes it lessened, until she let out an enormous sigh.

"Yeah, I'm fine." She took the book I was mindlessly holding out for her. "Thanks for helping."

My tongue had caught somewhere because I'd been rendered speechless, but she didn't notice as she glanced up at Mason and smiled. "Thanks for that, I appreciate it."

"You're welcome," he nodded, and then looked at me. "Dude, I have to go."

"Yeah, no worries. I got this," I replied, picking up the last book. A Guide to the Solar System was heavier than it looked. As we both stood, a subtle scent of sherbet filled the air.

I glanced over her; she was wearing a striped t-shirt covered in shooting stars, with a little rocket logo over her perfectly handful-sized breast. I quickly looked away. She was easily a foot shorter than me, which meant she can't have been more than five four. No wonder she went flying. At least her jeans would have protected her knees from the hard floor.

What the…

I was still frowning at my internal monologue and the debate I was having on whether to give her one of the team backpacks to stop this from happening again, while also staring at her full and very soft looking pink lips. It was as she slipped the thick black glasses onto her head that I realized why she seemed familiar.

It was that girl, the one next door who Emerson and Mallory had been hounding me about, and I felt a pang of regret I hadn't stopped.

I didn't get a chance to speak before a door opened behind me, reminding me why I was on the second floor in the first place.

"What's all the commotion?!" boomed Coach Barr. "Reeves, what are you doing?"

I turned to look at him. "Nothing, Coach. There was an accident."

"Get in here," he ordered.

I spun back round to the girl, but she was already on her way out without another word, heavy books scooped under one arm, and I couldn't tell whether or not it bothered me as I stepped into Coach's office.

"Take a seat," Coach Barr ordered as he pointed to the chair in front of his desk, while he sat down on the other side of it and leaned back. "Now, tell me how it's going."

Coach Barr wasn't known for his small talk. It was almost like he had a competition with himself to use as few words as possible. He was tough, but he got results by making us work our asses off. He'd gone through the draft when he was at college but never made it out of the minors, and at the ripe old age of twenty-five decided to leave and build a career in coaching. While we didn't always like how hard he pushed us, we did like the wins, so we probably complained less than we would have done, or should have done.

I shuffled around, trying to get comfortable. "Um, it's good, Coach. It's good. We've been working hard over the holidays, and the beginning of the year. A couple of the guys have competed in tournaments as well. The team is ready for the season to start, and win it."

He linked his hands behind his head and nodded slowly, like this was news to him, which it wasn't. He had eyes and ears everywhere. "Good, good. Glad to hear it. You know why I called you in?"

I shook my head. "No, Coach."

He raised a thick eyebrow at me, because we both knew what I thought I'd been called in for, even if I wasn't one hundred percent sure.

"I was hoping you're gonna name me Captain of the Squad."

He pinned me with a piercing stare, and I was momentarily taken back to the girl outside and her incredible green eyes.

"Then you'd be right."

I stood up then sat back down. "Seriously?! Yes, Coach! Thank you, I won't let you down."

His lip curled ever so slightly in a smirk. "I know you won't. You've already been doing a decent job at it and you're going for the draft this summer, so I know you'll be working hard up to then."

My chest deflated slightly. I wasn't expecting him to say I was amazing, but they weren't the reasons I was hoping he'd be giving me the job – because I had too much to lose to fail. But then he took his feet off the desk and leaned forward.

"You're a fantastic third baseman, Jupiter; one of the best I've ever seen. You're going to go far. You lead the team well, and the junior guys look up to you, so keep your head screwed on and try to impart some wisdom before you go on to better things, will you?"

I grinned wide. "Yes, sir, I'll try to."

"Good." He flicked his fingers in the direction of the door, dismissing me, "You can go, and send Roser in if he's outside."

I stood up, and turned to the door. "Sure thing, Coach."

"You're up," I motioned to Dean Roser, a freshman pitcher leaning against the wall, who moved so quickly when he saw me he nearly slipped on the polished wood floor.

I smirked and took off back to the locker room to find Jenson and give him the good news.

I turned the key in the ignition and slowly backed out of my space.

What a fucking epic day.

Named Captain.

Decent run.

Great weights session.

Perfect practice.

English was cancelled.

Got a B in my biology exam.

It couldn't have been better if I'd written it.

The only thing that had been niggling in the back of my head was that girl, the one with the green eyes. The one who'd left without saying goodbye. The one that had me wishing I'd listened better to what Emerson had been saying when she was talking about her, because then I'd have remembered her name.

I turned on the radio as I pulled out of the parking lot and down the street that ringed the school campus. I was wracking my brain so hard I almost missed seeing her walking through the pedestrian entrance to the school gate, heading for the bus stop.

But there she was… three times in one day.

Oh man, whatever had I done to deserve this?

I slowed my car until it was inching alongside her, and rolled down the window. Though as her nose was back in a book and her earbuds were firmly plugged in, she didn't notice.

"Hey!" I called, but jeez, that book must be really interesting because her eyes never veered from it. I wonder if she walked into stuff a lot. She hadn't even noticed the car beside her. Any longer and this would get creepy.

"Hey! Stars and Stripes!" I called again. "Want a ride?"

I was about to honk the horn when she stopped in her tracks and turned slowly to face me. Removing one of her ear buds, she tilted her head with a slight frown which crinkled her nose, not dissimilar to when my dog was a puppy – except she was almost cuter.

She looked behind her then back at me. "Are you talking to me?"

"Don't see anyone else around."

"What did you call me?"

I propped my elbow on the open window frame and pointed to her with a grin. "Stars and Stripes, like your shirt."

I thought she might crack a smile, but she didn't. Instead,

she continued staring at me with a slightly confused expression. Maybe she hit her head when she fell, though I hadn't noticed.

"Do you remember me from earlier? The devastatingly handsome guy who helped you pick up your books? I notice you have a backpack now which could have helped you earlier," I winked.

The book she was holding closed with a soft thud. "Yes, I remember you. Thank you. But what are you doing?"

There was the million-dollar question. What *was* I doing?

"Apparently I live next door to you, so I guess it's your lucky day," I replied before I could think any more into this. I mean, it was just a ride.

"Oh yeah?" she popped her hip slightly and her head tilted. "How so?"

"Hop in. I'm giving you a ride."

"Why?"

"Told you, it's your lucky day," I grinned again, while also wondering why she wasn't already in the passenger seat next to me. "It's a service I offer to new girls. I'm Jupiter."

Her green eyes narrowed. "I know who you are, everyone knows who you are. And I'm not new."

Huh. My brow creased slightly, then a lot when she began walking again. I eased a little on the gas and moved forward next to her, unsure about what was happening.

"Okay, but you do live next door to me so I'm still saving you from a walk. And given how hard you fell this morning, your knees have got to be bruised."

She stopped again, and this time her face told me I was getting somewhere. She really was cute. Her thick, dark brown hair was now tied up in a messy bun, but there were enough loose strands falling around her face that made it clear she didn't really care what it looked like. I could imagine her sitting in the library, her head down as she studied, fingers mindlessly running through it.

And yes, I've been in the library… to make out.

"Why are you looking at me like that?" she asked.

I wasn't about to say I'd been wondering what it would feel like to run my own fingers through her hair… whether it was as soft as it looked; whether her lips were as soft as they looked.

Whether I was right about her tits being a perfect handful for me.

I cleared my throat. "I'm waiting for you to get in."

"And if I don't?"

"Then I guess we're going to cause traffic, because I'll be rolling alongside you as you walk." I smirked. "Do you really want to cause a traffic jam, Stars and Stripes?"

She pursed her lips at me. "My name is Marnie."

I snapped my fingers. Yes! Marnie! That was it! "Well, *Marnie,* you don't want to cause traffic to back up, do you?"

She sighed in defeat and crossed in front of the car. I leaned over to push the door open and waited for her to get in. The scent of sherbet I'd smelled earlier filled the air when she hopped up, dropped her backpack at her feet, then pulled the door shut.

I put the car into drive and turned to her as she clicked her seatbelt into place. "Ready?"

"Yes. Ready."

"So, what are you reading?" I asked after thirty seconds of silence, because it was clear that Marnie wasn't the chatty Cathy – as my mom liked to say – that my earlier passengers had been.

She smoothed her hands over the book resting in her lap. “The Fundamentals of Astrodynamics,” she replied.

I blinked. It was starting to become apparent that I was way out of my depth with this girl, and I couldn’t ever imagine her having a fight with someone about stealing a boyfriend or whatever – or trying to steal one.

I liked it.

“Okay then… what does that mean?”

“It’s the study of movement in space, like rockets or satellites, but also planets like Jupiter…” I caught her little smile out of the corner of my eye. “And moons, stars, asteroids… anything natural.”

“Did you know Jupiter’s the fifth planet in the galaxy?” I started and then groaned because the fact I loved to use to make myself sound smart only turned me into an idiot in front of this chick. “Never mind, of course you did. Anyway, what are you doing with all this space learning?”

“I’m going to M.I.T. in the fall.”

My eyes briefly flicked off the road to her. “Really? How old are you?”

“Sixteen, nearly seventeen.”

I forced myself to look back to where I was going before we veered off into the traffic cones. “And you’re already going to college?”

She nodded. “I applied for early admission.”

“No shit, seriously?”

“Yeah.” She began flicking the corner of the pages with her thumb, making a soft zipping noise.

“Did you apply anywhere else?”

“No, I only want to go to M.I.T. I’ve wanted to ever since

I was a kid."

I'm not sure I really understood what she was studying, but maybe we weren't that different. I could definitely understand the drive to want something that badly. "Yeah, I get that. I'm the same with baseball. What are you going to study at M.I.T.?"

"I'm studying a combination of aeronautical science, aerodynamics, and physics. I want to work on rockets going into space."

"Like the one on your shirt?"

She looked down and brushed her fingers over the little embroidered patch. "Yeah, something like that. This is the N.A.S.A. space shuttle logo. I want to work there one day."

"Really? I like that you know what you want, and you're going for it. Me, too. I've always wanted to play baseball, so that's what I'm going to do."

"Oh, yeah?" She turned slightly in her seat. "Good for you. I've never seen you in tutoring."

"Do I look like someone who needs tutoring?" I shot back, only to see her cheeks redden. I definitely wanted to do that again.

"No, nooo," she stuttered, "I just meant a lot of the student athletes get tutoring."

"They do if they're going to college."

"You're not going to college?" Her eyes widened like she'd never heard anything so preposterous.

"Nope. I've been busting my ass since I was a kid because I've always known that all I ever want to do is play ball, so what's the point of delaying it? I'm going to get drafted in July."

She looked like she was about to list off exactly what the

point of going to college was, but then decided against it. "What does that mean exactly? You get picked by a team?"

I chuckled; this was not a question I'd ever been asked. I wasn't sure I'd even met anyone who didn't know what the draft was. "Do you know anything about baseball? Or sports in general?"

She shrugged. "Not really, I mean I know some of the teams from the students I've been tutoring, although they just want to get to college, so we talk about colleges. My dad watches baseball, but I've never paid much attention."

"I guess you've been too busy studying to graduate early." I heard her scoff quietly. "Well, it means that one of the Major League teams is going to pick me to play for them. I'm hoping The Dodgers, because I've only ever wanted to play for The Dodgers. I guess like you and N.A.S.A. or M.I.T., I don't know what I'll do if someone else gets there first," I added.

"So then you'd be playing for The Dodgers?"

"No, then I'll have a couple of years in the double As; the junior teams," I explained when she frowned. "The Dodgers minors' teams are all over the country, but I'll probably be in Tennessee."

She nodded slowly as if she understood, then reached into her backpack and pulled out a roll of LifeSavers. After popping a pink one in her mouth, immediately the sweet candy scent hit me.

"Ohhh, that's where the smell comes from."

"What smell?"

"You smell like sherbet."

"I do not," she snapped, which I also liked.

I was liking a lot about this chick that I'd only just become aware of.

"You do. I smelled it earlier too. It's okay, it's not a bad smell."

She handed the roll to me. "You want one? I have different ones if you don't want any of these.

She fished out another couple of packets, and I took one from her. "Wow, you really like those, huh?"

"I eat them when I want to think, or when I'm a little nervous. It gives me something to do."

"I make you nervous?" I used my teeth to ease a LifeSaver out of the packet she'd given me. Cherry.

"I'm in a vehicle with a strange boy, so, yeah."

I frowned at that unwelcome piece of news, especially as with every passing minute I was enclosed in a tiny space with her, my fascination grew. "I'm not that strange. You already met me this morning, and you know where I live."

"No, it's okay. I just get nervous around new people sometimes."

For some reason, that didn't make me feel better. It made me feel worse, in fact. "And I made you get in my truck. If you open the compartment, my license is in there. You can see I'm telling the truth…"

"Thank you for helping me this morning," she replied, and I wondered if that was the only reason she had accepted the ride – that because I helped her, it was okay for me to take her home. The tension in my chest eased a little.

"You're welcome. Josh is always a dick. I don't know him very well, but what I do know I've never really liked."

We carried on in silence for a while. I turned left into a leafy tree-lined road which I always counted as the unofficial entrance to our neighborhood.

"So you're not new? And you tutor?"

She brushed her hands over the book again and rested them on her knees. I wondered if they were actually sore. Maybe I should give her some arnica. I usually had tubes of it scattered around the place for whenever I was injured.

"No, I've been here three years. I've only tutored since last September though."

I scratched my head. "I'm surprised I haven't seen you around more often."

"We've passed each other a couple of times," she murmured so quietly I almost strained my hearing trying to make out what she'd said.

"Really? You've noticed me?"

She snorted loudly, making me laugh. "It's hard not to. You're massive and loud, and usually surrounded by a gaggle of girls."

My chest puffed. The only part of that sentence I'd heard was that she'd noticed me, and I was massive; I was taking it as a compliment whether she meant it as one or not. The gaggle of girls was… well… not exactly false. Not that I encouraged it.

I almost told her I didn't encourage the attention, but then decided against it.

"And now you're my new neighbor, so I guess I'll be your driver for the remainder of the school year."

Her laughter filled the front seats, which had my chest puffing even further. It was a perfect sound and I wanted to hear it again. In the space of a twenty-five minute journey, I'd built a list of all the things I wanted from her again.

"No, I think this is a one-off. But thank you for the offer."

I wasn't about to argue and tell her she was wrong, but she was wrong.

"My place is just here on the right." She pointed to a Spanish style house with a tiled roof and a wide lawn in front, similar to all the houses around this neighborhood.

I pulled up, and she rested her hand on the door before opening it.

"Thanks for the ride, Jupiter."

"You're welcome." And because I wanted to see her blush again, I couldn't help adding, "I didn't know geeks looked like you."

"Like what?"

"Hot."

Her cheeks flared pink as quickly as her eyes widened, and I was still chuckling to myself as she got out and slammed the door closed. I didn't even complain she'd slammed it too hard.

"See you around, Stars and Stripes."

She looked back at me twice with a quizzical frown as she walked up her front path, and it had me grinning until bedtime.

5

Marnie

Present Day

Lowe hadn't been kidding about taking over New York with images of The Lions team.

In fact, if I stood on a chair and pressed my face against the corner glass of my apartment window facing due east, I could clearly see the highest billboard screen in Times Square…

the one where Jupiter's face appeared every seventy-five seconds.

The one I'd spent an hour watching yesterday, and the day before, while I sipped my morning coffee.

And that wasn't even the worst of it. If he wasn't content to haunt my days – his piercing blue eyes following me with every Lions poster I passed – he was haunting my nights too. I'd dream of his lips brushing along the surface of my feverish skin where a flurry of goosebumps followed the tickle of his hot breath. I'd dream of being trapped against the cage of his muscles, where I'd trace my fingertips around the delicate patterns inked into his skin. I'd dream and dream until I'd wake up dripping in sweat and shaking uncontrollably with longing, frustration, and anger.

I'd gone from nothing to all in.

From avoiding him, to him being unavoidable.

He was everywhere.

And since yesterday, our conversation had been playing on a loop in my mind. I hadn't lied when I said I didn't know him; the Jupiter I'd met this past week covered in tattoos compared to the high-school Jupiter I knew with his dimples and wicked smile were as different as night and day.

Except, *except,* when he pounded on my office door and told me he planned to win me back, I saw that eighteen-year-old, the one with dimples and a wicked smile; the one who used to pick me up for school and make me hot chocolate to watch the stars. The one who made sure the last thing he did every night was kiss me.

The one who was doing his hardest to get me to notice him again.

It was confusing as hell.

I took a deep breath as another bout of rage threatened to ambush me.

With one last look in the mirror, attempting to stretch out the new wrinkles which seemed to have arrived from all my recent frowning at Jupiter's face, I gave up and headed into the bustle of the city for my new commute.

I was so used to driving to work in Houston that I thought it might be fun to walk, but that lasted precisely one day when I realized it was nearly eighty blocks, and took an hour and a half. For the past week I'd used the subway, and managed to get my commute down to a slick thirty minutes. I wasn't counting the twelve it took to get through the two sets of security at Lions Stadium, across The Lions plaza and into my office, however.

But today things were a little different, as tonight we'd be leaving for a series of away games; my first ones.

Security waved my Uber through the gates and the driver pulled up at the executive entrance, where I tried to hop out but hadn't packed light, so ended up lugging my bag into the stadium. As with every morning so far, it was quieter around the club before eleven a.m., and I liked it. It wasn't exactly solitude, but there were few enough people around that I could absorb the space, the atmosphere, the love everyone had for baseball, and this club.

The club everyone longed to succeed.

The morning times over the past week had also given me an opportunity to think about how I was going to help make that happen. Or more specifically, what my job was and how I was going to do it. Because if I succeeded, then maybe I'd be able go back to Houston earlier than planned.

I was a little bit closer than I had been.

Grabbing some coffee from the team dining room, while also managing to balance a slice of toast on top of it, I made my way downstairs. After punching my code in, I used my free arm to push my office door open and finally dropped my bag.

I really need a wheelie case.

I scanned around the detritus. It was amazing to me how quickly I'd managed to make my new office resemble my old lab in Houston, but I guess piles of books and paper scattered about could make anywhere look familiar. I'd long come to the conclusion that while I probably should tidy up, it was never going to happen.

I was messy, and I'd made peace with it.

The books I'd been working through were spread across the metal desks at the end, and all were still open on the pages I'd been reading when I'd left every night over the past week; with subjects ranging from my usual aerodynamics or physics literature to – gasp – sports. I'd branched out because I figured if I could understand how teams and individuals got to the top of their game, I might be closer to figuring out how I could use my background to help them.

It would come as no surprise that it wasn't immediately obvious.

Turns out when something isn't rocket science, it's really hard.

I'd spent over half my life studying astrodynamics, engineering, astrophysics, and space. My most recent task had been working on a jet propulsion program at N.A.S.A, which in no way had anything to do with baseball – unless you counted objects moving through the air, something else Penn Shepherd seemed to think qualified me for this made up job I didn't ask for.

Still, I wasn't a person who liked to fail, so made up job or not, I was going to do my best to succeed.

I'd had a couple of ideas, but none of them had anything to do with my profession.

I sipped my coffee, then sat back and finished my toast as I stared at the wall – the white wall I hadn't realized was covered in writable paint, and now in my scrawl.

On one side I'd scribbled a formula for movement based on Newton's Second Law.

I'd mostly written it for something to do.

The other side was a list, and as much as I didn't want to

admit it, the list was probably the answer to success.

As I leaned further back, I spotted a large box on my desk. Very large; I'm not entirely sure how I hadn't seen it when I walked in, large.

A pink Post-it had been stuck on the top, and I reached to grab it. At this point my heart thumped hard and then flickered, before sending mini ripples to my belly as I picked it up and recognized the handwriting.

In case you need them. x

Grabbing a pair of scissors, I scored along the tape at the top, opened it up, and brushed away the packing peanuts.

Holy shit.

I had to bite down hard on my lip to stop the smile emerging.

It was there, I could feel it… but I definitely didn't want to acknowledge it.

He must have robbed Costco for this.

Staring back at me were boxes and boxes *and boxes* of Life-Savers. Mint ones, fruit flavored ones, variety bags of mixed flavors. I stood back and gawked at them, wondering what had possessed him to send these, then as I slowly removed a couple off the top layer, it became clear that the majority of them were cherry flavored.

There were easily a thousand bright red rolls.

Jupiter's favorite.

Before I could stop it, an onslaught of cherry flavored memories slapped me upside the head;

his demands to kiss me whenever I had them, because he loved the taste of them on my tongue.

And then what else his tongue would do.

In a nanosecond, millions of goosebumps spread over my

body, and I winced like I'd been scalded with hot honey.

My fist clenched around the bright pink paper, crumpling it into a ball as my teeth gritted and I shoved away all thoughts of his tongue and his face. Annoyingly it was becoming harder to do, especially now I'd been given fresh memories of this new, larger, more masculine Jupiter. Not that he'd never been masculine, but this one was…

Ugh.

The pink Post-it was dropped in the trashcan by my feet.

He wasn't getting to me that easily.

Selecting a roll from the box, I pushed it between my fingers, turning it over and over, and resumed my position in the chair. Jupiter used to insist I bring them to every game, because he claimed they helped him win, something I always made fun of him for.

But he maintained *I've never lost with them, Star.*

Not for one second did I believe LifeSavers helped him win. It was nothing more than superstition, and as a scientist, I didn't believe in superstitions.

As a scientist I liked data, facts, reasons, proof.

LifeSavers did not help you win.

But Jupiter's box of his favorite candy had reinforced an idea I'd been having. Searching through the books I'd spread over my desk, I found the one I was looking for and snatched it up, then took a quick snap of the wall. Security pass round my neck, I ran out the door and up to the owner's suite.

Penn Shepherd and I needed a little talk.

"Doctor Matthews, Marnie, how are you? Come in. Are you settling in okay?" He opened the door almost before I had a chance to knock, and something told me he already knew I was on the way… or maybe he could hear my huffing from all the stairs and the speed I'd run up them.

Penn stood there grinning, his wide, boyish smile and short blonde hair making him look far too young to be running a major league team.

This was not like walking into the N.A.S.A. Administrator's office, not that I ever had walked into the Administrator's office.

Or was even invited onto his floor.

"I'm good, thank you. It's my second week now." I nodded with a bashful smile, unsure of why I suddenly felt so intimidated.

Maybe it was because he was so tall.

Or maybe it was because I'd found out the real reason I was at his club.

Or maybe it was what I was about to say, and he'd think I was being dumb – though my PhD could prove him otherwise.

"Do you have a minute? Can I talk to you about a couple of things… ideas I've had?"

"Sure, come in. You want some coffee?"

"Yes, that would be good. Thanks." I took a seat in the chair opposite his desk, behind the plate glass window.

The view of the field I had in my office was at ground level, and I really couldn't see a whole lot beyond a stretch of green surrounded by arena seating. The view Penn had, however, was the owner's view. The entire field was below us; the rich terracotta fan of sand around three bright white bases, and the plate.

The New York Lions' diamond.

Even as someone who didn't really care that much about baseball, I could appreciate how lovely it was.

"Good, right?" Penn turned around from the window and sat down at his desk, hands clasped in front of him. "So what's up?"

When Penn Shepherd had first come to find me in Houston, he'd said he wanted me to use science to make his players better; to throw better and to hit better.

Science, he kept saying.

If you can put a rocket in space, you can get a ball to fly better – or a player to throw faster and hit harder, he said.

Like it was that simple.

If I'd been in the right mind I'd have interrogated his reasoning a little, or at all. If I hadn't been thinking about Jupiter, or trying very hard not to think about Jupiter, then I would have followed through with the sole reason I went to meet Penn Shepherd in the first place – to tell him no.

But I wasn't and I didn't, so some of that conversation was about to happen right now.

"Did Lowe tell you that she took me for lunch last week? Her and Beulah. It was fun, and eye opening." I raised a brow so he'd understand exactly what I was talking about, even though I knew he did.

Lowe had gone straight back to Penn and told him about our conversation.

I received his standard wry smile.

"Yeah, she did. I wondered what this meeting was about."

I laughed as the door opened. One of his assistants walked in with coffee and placed them down in front of us.

"That depends, I guess." I picked up one of the steaming cups and blew on it. "I've spent the last week trying to figure out how I can help you. You wanted me to use science, but it's not quite that simple."

Penn's brow furrowed deeply, tiny lines appearing on his boyish face, and I remembered Lowe telling me that it wasn't often he heard the word 'no'. That's if he heard it at all.

"I don't need to tell you that rockets and baseballs are not the same."

"I'm sure you can figure it out, Marnie. I'm paying you a million dollars."

Yeah. He was definitely the type of guy used to getting his own way, or finding a way around it. But I'd worked with many of those.

"Just take it off Jupiter's salary. That's the real reason I'm here, isn't it?" I snapped.

He had the good sense to look down at his coffee, but I could definitely see a smile curving along his lip. If Lowe was anything to go by, I'd wager he was also used to women not doing his bidding.

"Astrodynamics can't give you a winning team overnight. I can modify some formulas, and we can work on it, but it will also require the team to make physical adaptations to their game. That's harder."

I waited for him to argue again, but instead, he sipped his coffee and stared at me.

"Anyway, when we were in high school, Jupiter used to love LifeSavers. He had this thing about them helping him win. They didn't, but he thought they did..."

"But you let him think they did though, right? If they helped him, you encouraged that? Right?" he interrupted with a splutter.

I blinked at the expression on Penn's face, like he'd be horrified at any other outcome; that the idea of me not believing in Jupiter's LifeSaver fallacy was somehow unacceptable to him.

"Um… sure. Anyway... I've been reading a book on improvement data and the theory that if you can improve tiny things in your life by one percent, when added up, they can have a significant impact on overall improvement." Picking up the book I'd brought with me, I placed it in front of him, open at one of the pages I'd highlighted and pointed to it. "So this is what I think we should do. Improve tiny things at the club. It's what I think will get you – the team – to the top."

He didn't look at the book. Instead, he sat back with his arms linking over his head. "What kind of tiny things?"

I opened up my phone to the picture I'd taken, and passed it to him.

He was silent for a minute as he read it. His eyes moved slowly over the screen, while he stroked his stubble.

"Sweat rates? Energy expenditure? Sleep? Metabolism? Eating schedules? Hydration levels?" His eyebrows shot up as he worked his way down the extensive list I'd written on my office wall. "Pillows? What do pillows have to do with anything?"

I shifted slightly and uncrossed my legs to sit up straighter. "Sleep is vital to function properly. The team is traveling all the time, in different beds most nights. We know it's hard to sleep in unfamiliarity. If they bring their pillows from home, they have one piece of consistency to help them get a better night's sleep. Therefore, better performance the next day."

I couldn't tell if the grunt Penn let out was a good grunt or a bad grunt.

"Equipment storage?"

"Yes. Make sure all equipment is stored in the same way when traveling as it is during home games. It's just an example," I added quickly when Penn's frown deepened.

I sat there, waiting. There was still a ton on that list he

hadn't read out. Some were more easily explainable than the rest – like keeping to the same schedule – meal times, sleep times etc. no matter where they were. Which meant it would be easier to travel if everyone went to bed much later in the evening, and slept later in the morning.

He picked up the textbook I'd also shared, and flicked through a couple of pages in silence. "This is interesting, Marnie. Very interesting. I don't know why I haven't thought of it before. Why didn't I know about it?"

I shrugged. There was no way to answer that particular question.

He stroked his beard again then leaned forward, as if to confide a secret. "One of my plans here is to build an analytics team. There hasn't been one here before because this club hasn't had the budget, but the Yankees has one, and it's been working. Not to mention the A's."

"The A's?" My face scrunched slightly, which he correctly took to understand that I didn't understand, and needed him to explain further.

"The Oakland A's used analytics to win in the face of a low budget and players they couldn't afford. It shot them up the standings…"

I continued to stare blankly. The only word I really understood in that sentence was analytics.

"They made a movie about it."

Again, nothing.

"Brad Pitt was in it."

"Oh. I haven't seen it." I still wasn't sure what he was talking about, but I knew I hadn't seen a movie with Brad Pitt, because it had been years since I'd seen a movie, period.

It earned me an eye roll. "Anyway, the Yankees have an entire department studying the numbers, and I wanted something similar, but with edge." He pointed at me before continuing, "You just might be the edge."

I wasn't sure if I wanted to be the edge, but I also wasn't sure if I had a choice in the matter.

"I'm gonna set you up with Jesus Rodriguez, my deputy, and let's get the ball rolling. Work with Scott Fishman, director of the executive staff, and he'll send out the memos to the club for everything you need. Good work, Matthews."

I took it as a positive sign that he'd last-named me, instead of just Doctor Matthews or Marnie. I stood, as he had.

"No problem. I'll get working on a proposal and next steps."

"Great! Great. You'll be at the game later? And you're coming to Miami tonight, right?"

"Oh, yes, sir. I am, to both." I answered, even though he knew full well I was.

"Ugh, don't call me sir." He shuddered, and a decidedly evil looking grin appeared. "Perhaps I should send Reeves a gift basket of LifeSavers."

And with that, the meeting was over.

I headed back to my office with renewed buoyancy for my made-up job. I also figured that now it might actually become a legitimate role. I could work on changing the title I'd been given as Director of Baseball Science to something a little more authentic sounding. I was so deep in thought about how I could make the improvements that I failed to notice the corridors were starting to get busier; more crowded…

Or the very heavy and solid chest I walked straight into as I rounded the corner. A strong callused hand gripped my elbow to stop me falling over.

"Whoa, whoa, whoa. And where are you heading off to in such a rush, my little pocket rocket?"

I jumped back and peered up into the very blue, very dazzling eyes I had once been so familiar with, along with the smile currently beaming a million watts in my direction.

I turned to the guy next to him, who was equally as large and also grinning down at me, although his seemed less combative and more genuine than Jupiter's.

"Don't call me that. I don't even know what that means."

"Sure you do. You like rockets and you could fit in my pocket," he winked, which set off a flurry of waves in my belly that I did my best to ignore, and conjured up a scowl instead.

The guy next to him coughed out a snort, or whatever it was he was trying to cover up, so I scowled at him too, and he dropped his head. The smirk was still there though.

I focused back on Jupiter with my head cocked in curiosity. I didn't remember him being quite this annoying, or maybe I'd been blind to it. It wasn't hard to believe that I'd been dazzled by his beauty, especially as I was currently trying very hard not to stare at the fantail tattoo on his neck that disappeared underneath his collar… the one I wanted to run my fingers under.

He chuckled softly, snapping me out of my trance.

Goddammit.

Jupiter Reeves *was* annoying.

"Sure you don't want to admit we're meant to be together?"

My fist clenched at the familiar heat working its way across my skin.

"You're welcome for your gift, by the way!" he yelled at my back as I hurried off.

It was safer to shut the door to my office instead of replying.

Short, rasping breaths were all I could manage as I leaned

against it. Rubbing my nose hard, I attempted to dislodge the scent of him I'd inhaled when I'd smacked into his sculpted torso, which was working its way up my nostrils to lay claim to my memories. That scent… like summer nights, bonfires on the beach, and warm kisses. I pressed against my temples to halt the onslaught.

Where was a decontamination shower when you needed one?

The clock said eleven thirty; tonight's game began at seven. I had all afternoon to start work on the new plan, and more importantly, enough time to squeeze in a run because I now had a lot of latent energy to burn off.

More than I cared to admit.

"So talk me through it again. How's this going to work, exactly?" asked Beulah.

Beulah, Lowe, and I were sitting in the back of a car en route to LaGuardia, where The Lions team plane was kept.

After my meeting with Penn and my collision with Jupiter, I'd taken a longer run than intended, and spent the rest of the day figuring out this plan and whether I could make it work. My figuring was done in between all the time I wasn't thinking about Jupiter and the wall of sculpted muscle he now seemed to be built from. He may as well have been carved from granite.

I'd tried not to touch him, even pretend I hadn't, but I knew my fingertips had grazed along an impressive set of corded abs when I attempted to maintain my balance and my hand slipped down his chest.

"Marnie?"

I shook my head and turned in my seat to face her better. "Sorry… well, there's a theory that if you can make small, positive changes, then they all come together to make one big change. It's the one percent improvement rule."

"Huh." Her lips pursed, concentration settling on her face. "That sounds cool, kind of like when you want to lose weight, you only eat half the cookie, and not the whole thing; almost like you're deceptively dieting."

I nodded. "Something like that."

"Penn must be kicking himself that he didn't come up with it first."

I shrugged. "Maybe. He asked me how he didn't already know about it."

Lowe snorted. "Yeah, because he thinks he knows everything."

Beulah joined in, letting out a loud laugh. "You think it'll work?"

"I've been reading up on it, and there's no reason why it can't work. It seems to be kind of new in top tier sports, especially when there's already so much money pumped in to ensure they're at the top of their game already. But this could be the perfect opportunity to put theory into practice. The New York Lions aren't at the top of their game, and it's a brand new team. At the very least this could help them sync together, but that should then help them play together."

Lowe let out a little groan, and we all knew why. It was only ten days into the season, and the high they started on was swiftly deflating after more defeats than they'd expected.

"They need it. They barely scraped the win tonight. I know

I should be positive when they're already playing much better than last season, but no one else has to live with Penn! All I hear about is why they lost, and what they should have done better."

Beulah pulled her in for a consoling hug. "Surely that's what Coach Chase is getting paid the big bucks for? Send Penn to him when he starts giving you earache."

"Will it be bad tonight?"

Visions of the powernap I'd planned for the flight began floating straight into the night sky, and replaced with the visual of Penn Shepherd pounding down the aisle of the plane, pointing out every single thing we could have done better.

I'd had a tiny sample of it on Saturday when the boys had returned from their first away stretch, which they lost, but the massive win against the White Sox that day had stopped his train of thought.

There were four hours to go before we got to Miami, and I didn't want to spend it listening to a lecture – especially as it was nearly ten-thirty p.m. already.

"Nope, we'll get Lowe to shut him up with a little mile high action in the bathroom," Beulah laughed, then huffed loudly as Lowe elbowed her hard in the ribs.

I joined in, until I realized exactly what Beulah was talking about and couldn't halt the heat rising in my cheeks. I wasn't a prude. I liked sex just fine, but being in a relationship like that, where you couldn't keep your hands off each other no matter where you were... I'd only had that once – and it hadn't been with my ex-husband. Teenage hormones were not to be taken lightly.

"Marnie, what's that look?"

I blinked. "What?"

"You had a look, like you were thinking about..." she

grinned knowingly.

I blushed even harder. "Oh no, it was nothing. I was just… to be in a relationship where you… you know… sex all the time. I'd forgotten what it was like."

"What about David?" asked Lowe, ignoring Beulah's frown.

I dropped my head with a shake. "He was away a lot, and then when he got home it wasn't the first thought. He was always too excited to tell me about what he'd been doing, his new discoveries, that sort of thing. And then it was a lot of talking, and we'd fall asleep."

I didn't really understand the identical expressions Lowe and Beulah were wearing, but I knew I never wanted to see it again.

"What about Jupiter?"

If I thought I'd gone pink before, I'd now turned a deep shade of fuchsia.

"No, sorry!" Lowe waved me off before I could answer. "None of our business."

I swallowed thickly. "No, that's okay."

Because I'd never really had girlfriends before, not since school anyway, I'd never really had 'girl talk', where I could talk about my feelings or what I was experiencing. Yet I found right then in the back of the Range Rover taking us to the plane that I wanted to.

"We were teenagers; you know how it is…" I chewed on my lips as my brain flashed with more memories I was trying hard to forget about. "But, yeah, we were like that. It's not the same when you're an adult with jobs and responsibilities, though."

I look down at my lap. The dark of the car was doing a good job at hiding my face, both from the blush and the blatant lie. It was nothing to do with being an adult. I'd dated a few guys in college, and before David. Even though I'd had no one to compare Jupiter to when we'd met, it hadn't taken me long to figure out nothing would ever match up after so I stopped looking for it to happen, which made it easier to forget.

"I know what you mean," Beulah said, her hand resting over mine. "I was a pretty lonely teenager, so I didn't discover what is was like to be in a relationship until last year."

She smiled softly then her gaze drifted off, and I suddenly felt like I was intruding.

"Not sure I want to think about Jupiter Reeves as a teenager," Lowe snickered. "Was he as intense then as he is now?"

"Yes, but not in a moody way. As long as he was with me or playing baseball, he was happy. And when we were together, we were either having sex or studying. Sometimes both at the same time," I chuckled, then let out a long steady breath to calm the twisting in my loins before they heated to the danger levels of a nuclear reactor, "Phew, haven't thought about that in a long while."

Or at least since the other day, when the past had banged hard on my office door until I'd flung it open.

"Speak of the devil."

Because we'd been so deep in boy, sex, and relationship chat, I hadn't realized we'd pulled up at the airport and the car had stopped. I looked up as the driver opened the back door to see New York Lions painted along the side of a huge bus the team was disembarking from.

The three of us climbed out of the car and fell into line behind the enormous group. There were easily seventy people, made up of the players, coaches, and support staff.

As one of the tallest players on the roster, it wasn't hard to spot Jupiter, even with his short dark hair hidden by the same Lions ball cap everyone else was wearing.

It also wasn't hard to notice how broad his shoulders were, how narrow his waist was, how thick his thighs were, and how tight his ass was.

I'd always loved his ass.

In fact, for the first time since I'd arrived in New York, I had the luxury of looking at a real life version of him properly, without him noticing. Because it was perfectly fine to look if he didn't know I was looking.

Which is what I told myself right before he spun around in the crowd, his eyes finding mine almost immediately; like a tractor beam.

Like he'd always been able to.

He walked backward for ten paces, all without dropping his piercing gaze. His jaw popped, followed by a slight curve on the corner of his mouth. Then he winked.

That fucking wink.

And I wish I could say my panties were still dry, but winking was all he'd ever had to do to have me desperately needing to jump his bones.

Need. Not *want.*

"He'll get you pregnant with that wink." Lowe's quiet whisper tickled my ear, then she *ooofed* as I nudged her in the ribs. "Seriously, women's hearts all over the United States are breaking. I've never seen him wink, ever. He's become a completely different person since you arrived, like he's suddenly developed a personality beyond moody fucker."

I kept my smile to myself, and when I glanced back at him, he was once more facing forward, walking with the boys through the airport. The buzz of a message coming through on the phone in my pocket told me his head wasn't totally focused on where he was going.

It was only fifteen minutes later as we buckled into our seats for take-off that I dared look.

Jupiter: *I'm so fucking happy you're here, Star.*

The Jupiter I'd known with his dimples, winks, and toothy grins was impossible to deny.

The Jupiter with the tattoos and arrogance, all man and muscle, was becoming harder to ignore.

A combination of the two was deadly.

And it was anyone's guess how much longer I'd be able to hold out.

6

Marnie

Fourteen years ago – January

The concealer I'd rubbed in was doing nothing to hide the purplish circles under my eyes so I gave up trying, then pulled my hair back into my standard, boring ponytail. I didn't have time for anything else. I was already running late as it was.

The photography lab was always busy before the school bell went off, and I wanted to get these pictures printed out. Along with my tiredness, they were evidence of me staying up way too late, but the Milky Way was in full force last night, and I couldn't stop watching it.

I'd gotten some amazing shots.

"Mom, see you later!" I shouted to her while running down the stairs, gasping loudly as I jumped off the bottom step.

Whoa, jeez, Mom."

I turned back around and looked up the stairs. I could have sworn she'd been in her bathroom, but no, she was in front of me, appearing out of nowhere in a way that only moms could do.

"Marnie, there's no need to yell. I'm right here," she said quietly and pointedly.

"Yeah, you made me jump."

"Have you had any breakfast?" she continued with a raised eyebrow which meant she knew I hadn't.

"No, I don't have time for breakfast. I'm late," I inched toward the door.

"Here." She thrust out a packet of foil. "It's a good job I made you some waffles to take on the way then, isn't it?"

I paused my exit, "Are they banana ones?"

"Yes," she nodded.

I leaned in and kissed her cheek. "Thank you, Mom. Love you, I'll see you later."

"Have a good day. Try not to fall asleep at your desk." She pinned me with a look that told me I had definitely not gotten away with being on the roof most of the night. "Don't forget Daddy and I are out tonight, so you and Will need to fend for yourself."

"Money for pizza?" I fluttered my eyelashes at her, which won me an eye roll and an affirmative nod. "Oh, you're the best, Mom. Bye."

I looped my arms through my backpack and heaved it onto my shoulders while trying not to topple over. After I'd dropped all my books last week, I'd stolen my brother's old school backpack.

It was clunky and ugly, but I guess it solved a problem.

Slamming the front door shut, I headed down the path in the front yard, and took off on my usual route to school.

What a strange day that had been. Not to mention Jupiter Reeves. *THE* Jupiter Reeves spoke to me. Actually, he did more than speak to me. He gave me a ride home – in his truck.

Jupiter Reeves gave me a ride home in his truck.

When I'd walked in the front door, I'd sneaked a look out of the window and he'd still been sitting in it outside my house. I waited thirty seconds before he drove off, then ran upstairs and wrote it all down in my journal, just in case I forgot.

Not that it was likely that would ever happen.

And I don't know what he did after he got home, because later that evening I had a message from Josh Ridley with a very profuse apology for *behaving like a total dick,* as he put it, insisting he would never behave like that again, and would turn up to all his allotted tutoring sessions if I took him back.

I was going to reply, but when I got to school the next day, he'd already been assigned to someone else. And I had a funny feeling that was also to do with Jupiter Reeves.

So, yeah, weird day, and I've had a fair share of those.

I kept it to myself. If I had anyone to tell, no one would believe me anyway. I mean, I had people to tell, Lena and Byron – my Astro study buddies – but given they didn't know who Jupiter Reeves was it would fall on deaf ears anyway. And as I hadn't seen him since, I was beginning to wonder if maybe I did imagine it.

There were worse things to imagine.

I dug into my pocket for my iPod and earphones, stuck them in, and pounded my feet to the beat for the rest of the way to school while I was thinking about calculus and the challenge Professor Sureta had given us yesterday. He'd asked us to come up with an integral formula to solve the distance multiplied by the diminishing heat issues when delivering a pizza.

It was a hard one.

I'd planned to start it last night and then take a nap before the sky was at its best for viewing, but following the storm last weekend the sky had been much clearer than usual, and I'd been distracted... Hence no sleep and no homework completed – and the rush I was in.

I was so deep in thought about pizza, not to mention the music loud in my ears, that I didn't immediately notice the vehicle driving beside me – or the hollering from the driver.

My breath caught slightly as I turned, and not in the same way it had when my mom scared the shit out of me when she'd been standing at the bottom of the stairs.

If it was possible, Jupiter Reeves was even cuter today than he'd been last week, especially with his cap turned backward. It somehow sharpened his cheekbones and highlighted the freckles spread across his face.

In fact, I hadn't noticed before how similar his freckles were to the Milky Way. Probably because I'd never been close enough to him, but even in all the pictures of him posted around school they weren't that visible.

It took me a second to realize his mouth was moving, and I needed to remove my headphones to hear him.

"Sorry, what did you say?"

"I was saying you need to pull your earphones out," he grinned, which made a dimple pop in his cheek. "Honestly, Stars and Stripes, I've been following you for, like, three minutes. That must be good music."

The familiar heat which lanced through me whenever I

was put on the spot came back with full force, and I knew my cheeks were no longer my usual skin color.

I looked at my earphone, like it held all the answers. "Yeah, I guess."

"What is it?"

"Coldplay."

His lips rolled as he pondered it. "Coldplay, huh? Yeah, I could go for a bit of that this morning. Hop in."

His head jerked sideways to the front passenger seat.

"What?"

"Stars and Stripes, get in the truck. I'm giving you a ride to school. You've already been in here once so I'm no longer a stranger," he explained, like I was in remedial class. I hurried around before he asked again.

He pushed the door open just like he had last week, and I climbed in. Without making it too obvious, I took a deep breath and inhaled. It smelled just like it did before, not that it shouldn't have, but I wanted to remember it better this time. It smelled like sunshine, and boys; some kind of deodorant – sporty – and it made my belly flutter.

Way better than how my brother smelled, that's for sure.

"Thank you."

"You're welcome," he replied, looking at me expectantly.

I wiped my face in case there was still toothpaste round my mouth, or worse, banana waffle. "What?"

"Which Coldplay album are we listening to?"

I huffed a little smile of relief, and my heart immediately calmed. "Oh, I just had a mix on."

"Okay," he rolled his lips while fiddling with the buttons on his car stereo.

A second later, my hands shot up to cover my ears as Coldplay blasted out.

"Sorry," he smirked, adjusting the volume to a less ear-bleeding level. "This good?"

The violin intro for Viva La Vida played out. "Yes, this is one of my favorites."

"Really? Mine, too, though I don't listen to them too much. I prefer Eminem or Jay-Z, you know, something to psych me up in the gym, or before a game."

"You need to do that?"

Jupiter's wide grin warmed me to my toes. "Hell yeah. Gotta get in the zone to win."

I nodded, understanding. I never needed to psych myself up, but I also wouldn't ever listen to Coldplay if I was heading out for a run. Stifling a yawn, I watched as his big hands moved across the steering wheel and we eased back into driving to school.

"Want some coffee?" Without taking his eyes off the road, he pulled out a to-go cup from the center console I hadn't noticed before and handed it to me.

I tried not to freak out. In fact, it was quite easy not to freak out because I still wasn't fully convinced I'd woken up from a dream yet, so I sipped it.

"Why are you so tired?" he asked.

I placed the coffee back into his outstretched hand but couldn't stop my stare at his lips as they touched the exact spot mine had just touched.

"Um, I was up late."

"Obviously, but why?" he shot back. "Texting a boy?"

I scoffed so hard I nearly caused myself to have a coughing fit. "Uh, no."

I was now fully turned in my seat and facing him, which meant I saw a little smile curl his lip. "Tell me then."

Had he been this nosy last week? I didn't remember him being this nosy. I never really talked about my stargazing outside of my group, mostly because when I had, people responded with blank stares. But I also had nothing to lose; he knew I tutored in the NCAA office, and he knew I was a nerd.

"I was looking at the stars."

His bright blue eyes flicked over to me. "Stars? Like stars in the sky?"

"Um… where else would they be?" I replied with genuine confusion which made him laugh.

He waited for a car to pass before pulling out of the main entrance to our neighborhood, and onto the busy road which led to the freeway. I jerked back slightly as he stepped on the gas and we zoomed forward.

After we'd settled into our lane his gaze flicked to mine, before going back to the road.

"Okay, wiseass. You're going to have to explain a little better though. Can't you just stick your head out the window and see them? I don't understand why you were up so late."

I turned in my seat and faced forward, smoothing my hands down my jeans. It would be easier to explain this if I wasn't looking at him… then I wouldn't notice the expression of boredom which would no doubt hit once I got going.

Because I could talk about stars all day long.

"Do you know what the Milky Way is?

His right hand moved off the wheel and began snapping his fingers together. "Um, those little candy bars? Yeah, I love 'em."

"No," I replied with a head shake. "The one in the sky."

I caught his eye as he turned to me and winked, giving me the distinct feeling he was playing dumb on purpose, but I didn't know him well enough to tell. And that wink was making my belly feel like I was on a rollercoaster. I continued.

"The Milky Way is a galaxy. It's made up of billions and billions of stars and gas, and when you see it in the sky, it looks like a big hazy rainbow of light."

His thick brows knitted slightly, creating a line on his smooth tanned forehead. "And you were looking at it all night?"

"Yep," I nodded again. "I got a new telescope for Christmas and wanted to try it out properly. Last night was a new moon so the sky was dark, and Milky Way season is just starting."

"Milky Ways have a season?"

"Way. Just one. Milky Way, and yes, kind of. It's always there, but because of how the earth moves, we can't always see clearly it in the Northern Hemisphere."

"Huh."

When I've explained stargazing before, it's usually at this point most people zone out, which is what I assumed he'd done as he sat there in silence for a minute darting in and out of the traffic like a racecar driver.

But to my surprise he didn't, he just kept going with the questions.

"And this is all part of your space learning to get you to M.I.T. and N.A.S.A.?"

I tried not to show more surprise that he'd remembered what I wanted to do.

"Um, yes, part of it," I sighed wistfully. "But I find space so incredibly beautiful and interesting."

"So tell me about this Milky Way." He pointed a finger at

me with a smirk and added, "not the candy bar."

I giggled hard, and stopped short. Who was this Marnie Matthews giggling in Jupiter Reeves' car?

Like, what?

What was happening right now?

"The Milky Way is the galaxy which includes our solar system…"

"Including yours truly?" he interrupted, passing me his coffee again after he sipped it.

"Yep, including Jupiter," I smirked. "It's one of many galaxies in the universe, and it's reckoned some of the oldest stars in it are as old as the Universe itself. It's shaped like a spiral, so when you see it in the sky, it looks like a big arch of dusty light. But it's harder to see here because of light pollution. It needs to be really dark to see it properly."

"So all our planets and stars that we see are in the Milky Way? We're in it now?"

"Yep."

"That's pretty cool."

I grinned wide at him. "It is, yes."

"So it's gonna be there again tonight?"

"Yeah."

For the second time he turned and caught my eye with a smile, and the weird, unfamiliar flutters moved down from my belly and into my groin.

I crossed my legs.

"Are you going to look at it again?"

"Probably," I nodded, trying to ignore whatever was going on with my body. Maybe I was getting sick.

"Do you want company?"

"You want to come and look at the stars with me? You're asking to come over to my house and look at stars tonight?" My brow furrowed deeply because I swear that's what he was asking… which made no sense.

"Yeah, that okay? I can bring snacks."

"Um, sure."

"Great! It's a date." He pulled the car into a space and turned off the ignition.

I looked around to confirm we were indeed at school. I'd been so engrossed in him I hadn't even noticed we'd arrived. I opened the door and jumped down – actually had to jump – then heaved my backpack once more over my shoulders. At least with the ride I wasn't as sore as I probably would have been.

We met at the front of the truck.

"What time will you start with the stars?"

"Um, maybe eleven?" I raised a brow. "Is that okay?"

"Yeah, sure. I'll sneak out anyway; my folks won't know I'm gone." He pulled his cell out and thrust it at me. "Here, type your digits in so I can message you later."

I numbly did as I was told, and handed it back to him.

"I'm saving you as Star. Stars and Stripes has become too much of a mouthful, and I prefer my mouth to be full of other things." He smirked and laughed loudly at my gasp, his straight white teeth almost glistening in the sun.

My phone pinged with a message while I was trying to recover from the onslaught of heat and throbbing in every cell of my body. It was almost like I'd been dipped in lava.

"Now you have my number too. See you later for our date, Star. I'll message you."

He jogged up the campus steps toward the sports facility

building. It was the same direction I needed to go, but I wasn't sure I could cope with a walk together right after our car ride. I turned one eighty and headed toward the physics building.

I needed to cool down.

A bag came up first and landed with a thud on the flat roof outside my bedroom window. The next thing I saw was a navy beanie hat with the Los Angeles Dodgers logo embroidered into the rim, then the bluest of blue eyes I'd been seeing all day whenever I closed my own, which was a lot due to the lack of sleep from last night. I'd even power napped when I got home so I didn't fall asleep and miss a single second of this.

I turned my flashlight on so he could see where he was going and stood above him just as his foot hit the floor.

He glanced at his watch. "Under three minutes from my room to yours. Not bad, Star." His grin widened as he took in the space. "Holy crap, it looks amazing up here. Did you do all this?"

I looked round too, suddenly more proud of my little space than I'd ever been. When my parents decided to move house at the end of last year, my brother and I had been given veto rights on anywhere they viewed. While my brother hadn't cared either way, I hadn't initially liked this place until my dad pointed out the flat roof space directly outside my bedroom's side window, which hadn't been visible from the road. It wasn't really visible at all, given it was hidden by a cluster of large palm trees – one of which Jupiter had used to climb up.

It was my perfect little private space, and tonight I'd made it super cozy.

I'd been staring at the night sky for long enough to know exactly how to create the best experience, and seeing as this was Jupiter's first time, I wanted to make it a good one for him. I'd come out thirty minutes ago, bringing extra blankets and the soft-rollaway mats to lie on, plus a couple of the beanbags from my bedroom to lean on. Tiny electric lights were placed on a few plant pots I'd been keeping up here and on the surrounding floor, but not enough that it would disturb our view.

To the side was a hard cooler which I'd filled with snacks, because I assumed Jupiter would forget, along with my favorite fruit roll-ups and hot chocolate, though I'd already drunk most of it.

I'd need to go and make more. We might be in California, but it was still February.

"Yep. It's what we need." I grinned at his grin, because I'd discovered it was infectious.

"Consider me impressed." Then his eyebrows shot into his beanie. "Whoa, is that your telescope?"

I sighed softly and looked at the *Orion Celestial CGE 2T* telescope I'd been begging my parents for, for two years. I'd saved and saved all my pocket money to contribute toward it, because I'd wanted to show them how serious I was about owning a piece of technology more expensive than a computer.

And then this Christmas my dreams had come true. It wasn't the most powerful home telescope, but it was powerful enough that I could see the galaxy far beyond what the naked eye could see. I could see details on planets rarely visible. I could see the craters in the moon.

It looked impressive, too. All that power didn't come small, and I'd set it up in the middle of the roof on its heavy tripod; the shiny casing as black as the night, like a short, fat, long distance camera lens.

"Yeah."

"Can I take a look?" Awe soaked his rich voice, sending tingles down my spine.

"Of course," I smiled, and gestured toward it.

When I'd come up here to set up, I'd peeked through to make sure we'd have some good views tonight. Good in my opinion, not his, and I was fairly certain that tonight would be better than last night.

He stepped slowly toward it and turned round. "Okay, so what do I do?"

"See that lighter patch in the sky, almost like the sky is fuzzy? That's the Milky Way."

He stared up like he'd never properly looked at the sky before, and I loved it. I loved that I was the one to show it to him. "Wow, I can't believe I've never noticed this before… all these stars."

"It's a clear night tonight; it's not always like this. We're too close to the city for it to be really amazing. My parents are taking me to Joshua Tree for my birthday. Apparently the sky there looks like it's scattered with pin pricks of light."

"When's your birthday?"

"June seventeenth."

"And you'll be seventeen then?"

I nodded and looked back at the telescope. "I've set it up to give you the best view, so all you need to do is look through it. Sit down there," I pointed to the stool underneath the eye-piece, "and then get as close as you need to."

He glanced back at me one more time, and I nodded reassuringly that he was doing exactly what I'd told him to do.

He moved slowly and carefully, pulling back to glance at me again, before returning to his position. It made me smile because I realized he probably had the exact same look I'd had when I'd first peered through a telescope and had seen what he was now seeing.

"Careful," I muttered, "it's addictive."

I picked up his backpack which was much lighter than it had sounded, and carried it to sit on the beanbag next to him. He'd barely moved, except to stretch his long legs out in front of him. I cringed a little when he rubbed his knee. Given our height difference was nearly a foot, I'd made an educated guess at where I needed to set the tripod at so it was comfortable, but given how much he was crouching, I think I'd gotten it wrong.

But he hadn't complained, so I used the opportunity to properly look at him, because when they presented themselves, you had to take them, right?

Who knows when I'd get another?

Wisps of his dark hair curled under the bottom of his beanie, kind of blending into the shadow of thick stubble along his ruler-straight jaw. There weren't many boys at school who could grow beards quite so thick yet, but he was one of a handful, and it was probably one reason that made him so popular. That and the rest…

Lips.

Eyes.

Body.

He wasn't touching the telescope, but he'd positioned himself in such a way – with his elbow crooked on his knee – that I could see the outline of his bicep. I'd once heard one of the Athletics' Office staff say that Jupiter Reeves could splinter a coconut on the milkcan from a hundred yards with a ball off his swing. I had to Google what it meant and sitting here, staring at the defined curves under the sleeve of his hoodie, I could well believe it.

I was almost more content to stare at him, while he was glancing up at the sky, than stare at the sky myself.

"Holy crap! A shooting star." He pressed his eye closer on the pad. "Shit, there's another! You gotta see this!"

He turned away almost reluctantly, making me laugh.

"This is amazing, you were right. Come on, you're missing out on this. It's your turn."

I shook my head. "No, it's okay. I'm glad you're enjoying it."

I couldn't read the look he had in his eyes as he moved back.

"Okay then, tell me what I'm looking at. Teach me about space," he said earnestly, like we had all the time in the world.

His gaze bored into mine, eyes shining brighter than a supernova. Even though it was forty-eight degrees, a little bead of sweat developed and slid down my neck. Staring into his eyes was how I imagined a hypnotist worked, for the properties were the same, and I suddenly felt lightheaded, and more than happy to teach him about space for the rest of his life.

I blinked, releasing myself from my trance, and jumped up off the floor to work some air back into my lungs.

"Okay. Sure, I can do that." I repositioned the beanbag I'd been sitting on so it was next to the other one, his one. "Here, lie on this."

He got up and stepped back, then reached for his backpack and opened it. "If we're going to watch a show, we need sustenance."

He pulled out two massive bags of Garrett's popcorn –

one cheese and one caramel – the type my mom only gets at Christmas, and a bag of Dot's Pretzels. I took them from him while he continued digging in his bag, producing a thermos and a couple of rolls of LifeSavers; one cherry, one mint.

"After you gave me these the other day, I haven't been able to stop eating them," he grinned, then passed me the thermos. "I made hot chocolate."

I took it, mutely, my head spinning with confusion – and his closeness.

"Open the top; there are two little cups inside," he instructed, mistaking my shock for… I dunno.

For most of the day I'd expected Jupiter to cancel; to either not show up or message to say he couldn't make it. That was my headspace until the thirty minutes before I came up here, which was precisely after he'd messaged to say he'd be here in thirty minutes. So I was still getting used to the fact that Jupiter Reeves and I were sharing car rides, drinking the same coffee, taking up the same space. Never in a million years could I have told you this is how my evening would end – with Jupiter Reeves on my rooftop, drinking hot chocolate he'd made, and eating snacks he'd packed.

And while I was now certain I wasn't dreaming, I couldn't promise I hadn't fallen into a black hole to an alternate universe.

"Here I'll do it, you lie down." He took the thermos from me when I didn't move quickly enough, and poured out two little cups, steaming with sweetness. "Scooch over."

I shuffled from the spot I'd positioned myself on and took the hot chocolate. Our fingertips brushed together, and a single current of static shot through my body making me gasp, and him chuckle.

I sipped my drink to distract myself from the whorls of

energy spinning through me. I could feel it spiraling through my veins into my bones, and making its presence known as that single spark grew and grew, until I was convinced I might burst.

Did he feel it too?

A sudden gust of cold air slapped me round the face bringing me back into my body, and the bag of popcorn being ripped open had my head turning toward him. He thrust it at me, and I snatched up a handful.

"Thank you," I smiled. "Okay, lie back."

I switched off the flashlight and joined him as our eyes adjusted to the near total darkness. I could only see him out of my periphery looking up into the sky, but I could see his mouth open slightly, a smile cresting on his full lips. The solidity and warmth of his body had me wondering if we'd ever use the blankets.

I'd never had so much trouble focusing, though I'd never had a distraction quite like the one I had now, and mustered all my self-discipline to turn to the task in hand.

I pointed up at the sky slightly to the left of him. "Okay, you see those three stars in a row?"

His head shifted the tiniest fraction. "Yeah."

"Then the two above and the two below, so it's almost an hourglass shape?"

"Yes," he replied after a beat.

"That's Orion; he's the hunter of the skies. The stars on the top left and bottom right are some of the brightest. If you look for him on any given night, you can almost always figure out the rest of the constellations."

He said nothing, but his soft breathing next to me urged me to continue.

"Now if you look a little higher, can you see another bright star, kind of on its own?"

"Mmmhmm."

"That's Polaris, the North Star. It's directly above the North Pole and stays in pretty much the same place every night. Sailors used to use it for navigation."

"This is so cool." His head turned on the beanbag to face me. "Marnie, how do you know all this? Did someone teach you?"

I tipped my head to face him, immediately turning back when were practically nose to nose. I hadn't realized we were lying so close, close enough that I could feel his hot breath on my cheek.

"I mostly taught myself. I've always been fascinated with the night, since I was little. Everyone else was scared of the dark, but for me, that's when the stars came out. And as soon as I knew I could make stars part of a job, I wanted to do it, before I even knew what the job would be. I read books, and I've taken some advanced classes, but I still don't know a fraction of what there is to know."

He was silent for long enough that I could tune into the sound of my own heart, *thud, thud, thud.* It had finally slowed down for the first time since Jupiter had climbed up the tree onto the roof.

I sucked in a breath. I wasn't positive, but I swear one of his fingers brushed against my hand.

"You're really cool, Star."

"Thank you," I replied, because I wasn't sure what else to say, except, "Hey, you wanna see something else?"

"Hell, yeah."

I sat up and peered through the scope, twisting and turning the dial until I found what I was looking for – a beige striped mass surrounded by a bluish glow. "Here, look at this."

He leaned forward, kneeling instead of sitting, "Whoa, this is so awesome. What is it?"

"It's Jupiter," I grinned, more so when he spun around with his eyes wide.

"No shit!" he exclaimed before turning back the viewfinder. "Oh, this is so fucking cool."

I chuckled internally, watching him and how still he'd become. I wasn't sure how long we stayed like that – Jupiter looking at Jupiter, me looking at him – but I soon felt the night chill.

He finally stepped away. "Thank you. I can't believe I've never experienced this. Thank you for showing it to me."

I smiled as warmly as I felt. "You're welcome. I guess I never thought you'd be so interested."

"I'll tell you what, you teach me all about the stars, and I'll teach you about baseball."

"I want to learn about baseball?"

"Sure you do. You'll want to understand it for all the times you're watching me play."

Saliva pooled in my mouth, and I couldn't swallow it. "I'm watching you play?"

It felt like slow motion when his finger brushed away a strand of hair stuck to my forehead, "I'd say you probably will be, yes." His blue eyes held mine, still bright, even in the dark. "When I was little, my mom told me this poem. It was a nursery rhyme, so I never used to listen to the words, but now I think about it, maybe it came true."

He stepped back a fraction and cleared his throat.

"Starlight, star bright, you were the first star I saw tonight. Wish I may, wish I might, have this kiss with you tonight."

He smiled, nervously, "I changed the words a little."

I'd like to say I had experience in kissing, but beyond a couple of go-rounds with Seven Minutes in Heaven at a birthday party my brother was made to take me to last year, I had none. But I didn't have time to be self-conscious, because the next thing I knew, the lips of the most popular boy in school were grazing mine.

I didn't know what to do with my hands, but it didn't matter because he took them in his, lacing our fingers together. Then his lips pressed harder against mine, and I followed his lead as he teased my mouth open. I didn't know when he'd managed to do it without me noticing, but at some point he'd eaten a mint LifeSaver, because that's all I could taste on his breath.

Gentle was not a word I'd have associated with Jupiter before tonight, but that's exactly what he was being. Gentle. Like he could sense my inexperience, and didn't want to scare me away.

But I'd never felt safer, or more sure.

I let his tongue move softly around my mouth and stroke against mine, savoring the warmth and taste of him. I matched his pace, and soon I couldn't feel anything but my body melting into his like a marshmallow over the fire as he continued teasing me, until every cell in my body was buzzing.

And then a soft moan escaped his lips; a moan that hit deep in my core.

He slowly pulled away. My face must have been bright pink when he looked back down at me; there's no way it wasn't.

"This has been fucking magic," his lips brushed against mine again, "but I'd better go. It's getting late. Night, Star, see you tomorrow. I'll have coffee waiting for you when I pick you up."

He dropped my hands and scooped up his things, and then I watched him disappear back down the tree, in the same manner in which he'd arrived.

I waited three minutes, enough time for him to get back home, before I turned and cleared up the snacks we'd made our way through.

All with a massive smile on my face.

It was official. I had a crush on the boy next door.

And he'd just kissed me.

7

Jupiter

Present Day

The dugout was full.

A couple of the guys who'd already been up for bat in this inning were hanging over the railings at the end near where the coaches were sitting. Saint Velazquez, our Puerto Rican right fielder with a mean smash, was sitting in the middle of the benches, throwing sunflower seeds in his mouth like he was on the beach and about to order a piña colada.

As with every game when we were up to bat, there were twenty-five of us – plus the coaches – watching, monitoring, and observing our opposition. The twenty-sixth? Well, he was on home plate.

Right now that was Tanner Simpson, our shortstop.

"Shit, that was a fucking good catch," Stone grumbled as

he pulled on the peak of his cap then sat forward as the entire bench watched Tanner stop dead as he passed first base, and instead make his way off the field.

The Pittsburgh crowd was cheering so loudly I wished I'd brought earplugs. Even though we were still only two weeks into the season, the Pirates had been having a worse time than us, so a win for them here would be a big deal for them in the standings. A low chorus of 'bad lucks' sounded as Tanner stepped into the dugout, threw his helmet down on the floor then took a seat, head in his hands.

"Shake it off, Simpson," Coach Chase hollered over his shoulder without turning around.

Tanner Simpson – our resident rookie. This was his first season in the major leagues. He had talent, and he'd go far. It didn't make getting robbed of a hit any easier though.

He nodded to himself, caught a Gatorade one of the guys threw to him, and focused back on the game.

I was also trying to concentrate, but I was sitting next to Stone, and it was becoming next to impossible. He'd laced his fingers closed, then open, then closed, and was now rubbing his hands together. By the time Lux Weston, our center field, had reached home plate for his turn at bat, Stone had placed his palms on his jittery, tapping thighs… then sat back again; then forward.

"Will you stop fucking moving! You're twitching like you need a fix," I snapped.

"I do need a fix. I need to win this game."

"Just fucking chill, will you? It's tied at one in the fifth inning. There's a whole game to play for." We stopped talking as Lux smashed the ball on the first swing. It didn't get a home run, but it did get him enough to make third base, and let Parker King come home safely. I turned back to Stone. "See?"

I rolled my eyes as he let out the long breath he'd been holding.

Tensions were all running slightly elevated today, even more so than they had been over the weekend. We'd won the game against the Marlins, we'd lost the next one against the Reds, and now we were in Pittsburgh before we went back to Miami this evening for our final game tomorrow… then home. We were a team made up of elite players, none of whom were used to playing for a team at the bottom of the overall MLB standings, and all of us were antsy.

We were currently second from bottom.

If we won this game and the Tigers lost against the Royals, we'd move up to third from bottom. And we all wanted to keep moving up, including me, but it didn't help when Twitchy McTwitcherson next to me started panicking.

I had my own process, which right now was trying to stay as still as possible and concentrate on the game, specifically on the Pirates' current left fielder, who seemed to be limping. I'd been watching him for the last two innings, and now as I squinted, I noticed he was definitely doing something.

The way he kept popping his hip didn't look right.

I leaned into Stone. "Look at left field, I think something's up with his leg."

Stone pulled off his sunglasses and scrunched his eyes up like I had; leaning forward like being a foot nearer would get him a better view.

"Yeah, what is that?"

"I dunno." I shook my head. "He seemed to get round the bases okay, but I'm sure whatever it is has gotten worse. My guess it'll get you an inside-the-park home run if you aim for him. I can't see him catching anything right now if he has to jump."

Hitting a weak spot… was that dirty? No, that was baseball. Looking for an opponents' disadvantage – it could be nothing, or it could be everything. Their manager saw fit to put him in the field, so it was all fair game.

"Okay, you're up." I passed Stone his helmet as Lux made it off the field and back into the dugout following a perfect line drive courtesy of Boomer Jones, The Lions' first baseman. "Go for left field."

He made his way out, grabbing his bat from the first base coach on the way. The coach leaned in and whispered something which earned him a solemn nod in return, before Stone took to the field looking way more relaxed than he had a minute ago.

I cupped my hands around my mouth and hollered, "LEFT FIELD!"

A subtle raise of the bat over his head told me he'd heard.

As he stepped into the batters' box, The Lions' fans who'd travelled the distance to support us cheered even louder than the Pittsburgh fans had. For so early in the season, it was amazing to see just how many had made the journey. I was still used to Dodgers fans who weren't known for traveling far, but there were usually so many spread across the United States that it didn't really matter. Tonight, in fact, this entire stretch, our Lions' fans had been out in full force, easily filling about twenty percent of the stadium.

This could have had something to do with Penn Shepherd, because since he'd taken ownership, along with the inordinate sums of money he'd spent, he'd made a promise to the fans to bring the glory back to the club. As part of this, he'd provided discount travel and accommodation costs to all away games, hoping to get as many fans attending as possible.

It was working, though it likely also had something to do with the fact The Lions were no longer bottom of the standings for the first time in over a decade, and there had been a renewed enthusiasm about the club.

Stone hit the first pitch foul and got into position again.

It was at that point my concentration was once more interrupted.

"So I heard something interesting," started Ace, who'd slid a couple of spaces along the bench from his seat as starting pitcher.

The thing about the dugout – you sat where you wanted – but the one rule was to always save a space next to the water cooler for the starting pitcher.

"Oh, yeah?"

"Yeah."

Stone jumped out of the way of the second pitch.

"Are you gonna share it or keep it to yourself? Because honestly, man, I don't care. I'm trying to watch Fields and see if I'm right about left field. Just let me know whether I need to listen or not."

Ace leaned forward. "Yeah, there's something up with his hip."

"Right, 'cept it's his leg." The left field guy, whose name I didn't actually know, was now stretching his quad. Definitely something up with his leg.

"Hip, I'm telling you."

I pinned Ace with stare. "Why are you here?"

"Told you, I heard something interesting."

"Then spit it the fuck out!"

Stone was now swinging his bat around, working his shoulder and getting ready to resume his position.

"Alright! So anyway, you know how we're flying to Miami

tonight?"

"Yes."

"And you know how we're staying at the same hotel?"

"Fuck, I hope this story gets better," I muttered.

Smash. Stone drove the ball straight through the left fielder, who missed it. The center fielder sprinted after it, scooped it up from the ground and hurled it over to the Pirates' third baseman, who caught it a second too late. Stone was grounded on third.

"It does! So King was hitting on the chick who's in charge of room allocation, because he wanted to get his room with a balcony overlooking the beach, because he's got this thing about fucking on a balcony to the sound of the waves."

I groaned at that announcement. I could give a fuck what the rookies got up to, but as the most senior member of the team, I also had a responsibility to make sure that they were a) safe and b) didn't do anything stupid enough to get us reported to the media and/or the league.

"Watson, please tell me you're not doing anything stupid?"

He ignored me and continued. "She said no, the allocations have already been made to the players and it's against policy to change. So he thought he'd do it himself, and stole a copy of the room numbers when she wasn't looking to see if he could find someone to switch with his garden view."

I turned to him. "Watson, I really don't know where you're going with this, but I can tell you now it's neither interesting, nor a good story. Or one I care about."

"Just wait, I haven't got to the best part yet."

"Oh, goodie." I clasped my hands together in the way my two-year-old niece did when she spied a brownie, and then focused back on the field.

"And you have an ocean view."

I side-eyed him. "I know you know better than to come over here and ask me to switch my room."

"I'm not," he paused, and I thought maybe that was the end of the shittest story ever, but no… "You know who else has an ocean view?"

I stared at him. Maybe if I didn't respond he'd get to the point quicker.

"That science chick you have the hots for."

"She's Doctor Matthews to you, and she should have one; she's on the exec board."

"It's right next door to yours."

Huh. He'd been right. He hadn't yet got to the best part.

My eyes shot to his. "What?"

"You guys are sharing a wall, and a connecting door." He waggled his eyebrows.

"First off, don't ever do that again. Second…"

What was my second point? Did I have one?

I'd seen Marnie a total of nine times over the past three days, six of which had been on the plane. I wanted to think it was down to the grueling schedule we had and not because she'd been avoiding me, but it was most likely fifty/fifty.

The upside, I wasn't totally sure, but I'd almost convinced myself she was frowning less at me each time. In fact, last night, Stone had nudged me on the flight to Pittsburgh and said he'd seen her looking at me, but whenever I looked up, she was deep in conversation with Beulah Holmes. And I'd kept looking. I'd even made Stone switch seats so my eye line was more direct, but not once did I catch her.

The other three had been during our games. I'd figured out where she was sitting before each had started, and I made sure I found her whenever I went out to the field. Even from the distance we were separated, I was certain she'd been looking directly at me every time. And knowing she was watching had added a buzz to my game I hadn't felt in a long time.

I'd made three direct catches and hit two home runs – because of her.

A tap on my shoulder from Sawyer James heading out to bat reminded me I was up next. And in case I needed another reminder, Coach Chase was making his way over with Tanner Simpson.

"Reeves, try aiming for left field, because there's something up with his leg. No idea why he hasn't been switched out yet."

I ignored Ace murmuring "hip" under his breath.

"Yes, sir."

Then he turned to Ace. "Watson, just a reminder – when I put something in your calendar, I expect you to make it."

Ace's eyes shot up in surprise. "Coach?"

Coach crossed his arms over his chest. "You were scheduled for your first meet with Doctor Matthews."

I could almost see the entire situation taking place in slow motion, especially as that was the moment Tanner Simpson decided to input into the conversation.

"Is this the doc that Reeves said we couldn't visit yet?"

Shit. I groaned internally and concentrated harder on the game than I'd ever concentrated on anything in my life. I could just make out the deep frown on Coach's face from the corner of my eye.

"What? What does that mean?"

"Nothing, Coach. Sorry. I'll make sure I go to the next one, and I'll apologize."

But Coach wasn't listening to Ace's slight panic; his attention was now fully focused on me.

"Reeves, what is he talking about?"

I rolled my lips and stayed silent. If I could hang on another ten seconds, I'd be on the field.

"Okay, Reeves, you're up." Coach returned to the other end of the dugout.

I stood up and reached into the cubby to grab my helmet.

"You're going to get it after this game is done," announced Ace, both unnecessarily and unhelpfully. "Better think up a good excuse."

I ignored him and pulled my bat from the bin; the one with my name on it.

I walked slowly out to home plate, soaking in the roar of the crowds. And it wasn't just Lions fans – it was the whole stadium.

There'd been a lot of confusion when I'd left The Dodgers; confusion and anger. As far as anyone – the media, the fans, the club – knew, I was a Dodger for life, so the rumors erupted. For months, speculation on my departure fluctuated between strife in The Dodgers' camp and Penn Shepherd's deep pockets with offers I couldn't refuse, to me being too arrogant and that I wasn't as good a player as I thought (though that was mostly put out by Dodgers' fans).

But the single reason for me leaving the Los Angeles Dodgers was sitting to the left in the stands as I walked out. I glanced over; and even though her gaze was mostly hidden by the peak of her Lions ball cap, I could see enough to lock eyes with her for a split second.

It was all I needed.

I stepped into place.

Much had been written about my rituals every time I was

at bat; what I did, why I did it, what it meant, and every time I merely offered the reporter a shrug and a "just one of those things, man," then continued with the interview.

Using the tip of my bat I drew out the letter M.

M for Marnie.

I might not have known where she was for the past fourteen years, but writing her into the sand by the plate meant I had her with me. I blew the dirt off my bat and stood tall, cracked my neck left then right, and took position.

The Pirates' pitcher rocked on his back foot, his knee raised, his arm shot back then…

I had four attempts to hit a home run. I only needed one.

The crack reverberated through the length of my arm, and the ball soared higher, higher, higher – straight into the crowds.

Yeah, no one was catching that one.

I turned and found Marnie, my eyes locking with hers again, and winked; because I knew she'd never been able to resist it, then flipped my bat high in the air as the crowd roared. I took off for a slow jog around the bases and didn't see her again until I passed second.

She wasn't screaming or cheering like the rest of the crowd, but she was smiling as she stood next to a hollering Penn Shepherd. It was a smile I knew well, and one I hadn't seen for a long, long time.

This might not be a game where she'd be throwing herself into my arms the second it finished, like she'd done when we were still at school; her hot, excited body wouldn't be wrapping around me until I'd needed to find us a quiet space where I could continue what she'd started, not able to wait to get home so I could sink into her properly.

But the smile she shot my way the second before I ducked

into the dugout was just as good.

We won, five to two.

The best score we'd had since Opening Day against the Yankees.

And in less than twenty minutes, we'd run off the field, showered and changed, then boarded our bus to take us to the plane. And there, we celebrated, with Gatorade, hot tea, water, and a bucket-load of popcorn.

I'd been separated from Marnie by the length of the plane. I'd tried to catch her eye again but it was hopeless when so many of the guys were up and down in their seats, each dissecting a different play.

Unfortunately, I hadn't been separated from Coach who chose that moment to bring up why I'd been threatening the team with not seeing Marnie. It was a conversation that went surprisingly well, though not in the way I'd expected.

But suffice it to say that all team appointments with Doctor Matthews would be cancelled until further notice.

I ran a towel over my wet hair, then wrapped it round my waist and wiped my hand across the steamed-up bathroom mirror. I really should get my hair cut. I'd always worn it short, but it had been so long since I'd taken the clippers to it that it was starting to blend into my beard again.

Grabbing my toothbrush, I wandered back into my room and stopped by the connecting door. I'd opened up my side, so the wall was that much thinner, but I still hadn't been able to hear whether she'd gone to bed or not.

Sliding the balcony door open, I stepped out into the balmy Miami air, and tried to peer around, but couldn't make out anything. Our rooms were too high up, with too much privacy.

I went back to the bathroom and spat the toothpaste into the sink.

I probably shouldn't knock to check.

It was as I was slipping into bed that I heard a noise – a thud, followed by some soft banging. I launched myself across the room and pressed my ear as hard as I could against the door.

Voices. A man's voice… and Marnie's.

I pressed harder, seeing if I recognized it. I didn't.

My stomach plummeted. I never imagined she'd bring a guy to her room.

Then I remembered who *she* was. No, there was no fucking way she was having a hookup. Not the Marnie Matthews I knew.

Though… did she know I was next to her?

Maybe she was trying to make me jealous. Mission accomplished, if that was the case.

After a minute, where I'd barely let out a breath, I heard the door shut. Sprinting to mine, I yanked it open and peered into the corridor, but there was no one to be seen.

I returned my ear to the connecting door.

I *think* I could make out the shower.

My heart was pounding harder than it had during the game tonight.

Then I heard a thud… some furniture moving, possibly. And was that a scream?

Yes, it was definitely a scream.

I pressed harder against the door. A cry?

"Marnie!" I banged on the door. "Marnie!" I rattled the handle. "Marnie!"

No answer, or maybe there was some mumbling.

Shit.

The door looked pretty flimsy, plus it opened from the inside. I lowered my shoulder and slammed into it. It gave an inch and the newly formed crack by the handle meant it wouldn't take much more to knock through.

Two more times in fact. I fell into the room to find Marnie looking up at me from the floor, her face filled with horror, and maybe a little fear. I ran to her as quickly as I could.

"Where is he, Marn? Did he hurt you? Are you okay?" I scanned round the room. Unless the guy was hiding in the bathroom, there wasn't anywhere he'd be able to go. "Star?"

I glanced back down at her, wondering if perhaps she'd been scared mute… which is when I realized she wasn't scared; she was angry. In fact, seething to the point her body was vibrating.

"Jupiter! What on earth do you think you're doing? The door!" she screeched.

I turned around to see it was hanging off its hinges.

Shit. I'd need to pay for that in the morning.

I stood up and held my hand out to pull her up, but she batted it away.

"Answer me!" she ground out.

"I heard you scream, I… thought you were in trouble… I…" I looked around once more, and it quickly became apparent I'd been very, very wrong. "You screamed."

"I stubbed my toe!"

"Why are you on the floor then?" I shot back accusingly, though we both knew I was on the losing end of this argument.

"It fucking hurt!"

I took a deep breath, and then remembered… "The guy, who was the guy I heard? I heard a man's voice."

"The bell hop brought my bags up." She pointed to the offending bags like they were evidence in a court case.

Double shit.

As I took another step back, more came into clarity; her hair, slicked back and wet from the shower; the tiny towel she had barely wrapped around herself which was grazing her thigh in a way that could definitely be described as indecent. In fact, half an inch higher and I'd be getting a very direct look at the home I used to bury my face in every chance I got.

It took less than a second for the images I was conjuring to reach my dick.

The rest of the second reminded me I was only in a flimsy pair of cotton pajamas pants that were becoming tighter.

"Turn around!" Marnie's terse command pulled me back to the present. "I need to stand up."

I did so without argument. Though she'd forgotten there was a mirror behind me, I tried to do the gentlemanly thing and look away, but only after I caught the tiniest swell of her boob as she tucked her towel back into place.

I waited, silently. When I finally built up the courage to peek again, I could see her staring at my back, eyes wide.

No, not staring. Studying.

My tattoos.

I turned slowly, her gaze following me. My chest hit her eye line, and her eyes had widened so much I could see the full, round shape of her iris, the brilliant green I knew so well; exactly like the pair on either of my triceps.

But that wasn't what had her hand shooting up to cover her mouth, or the sharp gasp she let out. Her hand dropped, but her mouth was still wide open.

I'm not sure she'd blinked.

"You've always been with me, Marn," I whispered.

She reached out to brush across my chest, then clenched her fist and brought it back down to her side like she thought better of it.

"I got it the day after I was drafted." Her eyes shot up, now shining with tears which made the green even brighter, because the alternate way to say that was the day after I broke both our hearts. The day after I left my heart with her.

And that's exactly what it was. On my left pectoral, above the heart beating for her right now…

Thud. Thud. Thud.

An intricate drawing of a brilliant star sliced in two, one half lying on the ground, and inside the other half was a beating heart. Hers. Mine. Our tiny initials intertwined in the middle.

The exact replica of initials we'd carved into the palm tree I used to climb up to her room.

My eyes followed the path she was taking; absorbing the artwork in front of her until her head dropped down to my waist, to the start of the longest tattoo I had – both figuratively and literally. It had taken nearly three years to complete.

To the casual observer; namely every girl I'd slept with, most of my teammates, and anyone else who'd cared to ask, it was a shadow, a cloud, a swirling smudge of light and dark tinged in blue. To Marnie, however…

"The Milky Way," she rasped. "Jupiter..."

Her fingertips were cool against my skin as she traced the constellations stretching the length of my torso. I stood as still as possible, trying hard to enjoy the moment but also not scare her away with my rapidly thickening cock. But she continued as though she hadn't noticed, and I wasn't sure whether or not to take offense.

The main concentration of tiny stars worked their way along the deep V-line girls loved to comment on, disappearing below my waistband, but reaching up toward my chest and bursting across my abs. It was here her fingers stopped and she took hold of my arms.

I straightened them out for her.

"I wondered what this said," she began, her voice barely audible, and my heart thumped hard with a little internal jump for joy that she'd been wondering about me. "On my first day I saw a poster of you... I didn't know... I didn't realize you had tattoos."

That news hurt more than a misthrow to the side of the face.

I was almost associated with my tattoos as much as I was with baseball. If she hadn't known about them then she really had been hiding from me, or avoiding me. She hadn't once Googled me, or seen a picture, or been curious about me.

Even in my fantasies, I'd had her following my career in some way.

When in reality, she'd made sure I'd no longer existed for her.

"I wanted to know what they said." Her voice was so low she was almost talking to herself. "This date..."

"The day we met." I raised my other arm slightly higher, pointing to an identical entry. "And this is the date of our first kiss."

At some point the air had become static, silently crackling with electricity. It was so thick and heavy it was getting harder to breathe. She was standing so close to me that she needed to tip her head back to look up at me; so close I could see straight down her towel.

Her breath shallowed.

I took a chance, reaching out to brush a strand of hair away from her face. She didn't flinch, she didn't move away. She simply stood there staring up at me, her lips parted with the narrowest gap.

I didn't notice myself getting nearer. My attention was only on her, and the blush spreading across her cheeks, down her neck, and onto her chest.

Just like it used to every time we had sex.

It was my favorite color.

She still hadn't moved. I could feel her breath on my face. My lips were *this* close to hers. I could almost taste her.

Almost.

"Starlight, star bright," I whispered.

I should have kept my mouth shut.

"No!" She shoved me so hard I actually had to step back. "What the hell?! You don't get to break into my room, naked with your body all... that," she angrily circled her palm at me, "and your tattoos all... and pretend like it hasn't been half a lifetime since we saw each other and you didn't rip my heart from my chest! I'm not that meek girl whose stars and moons once revolved around you. I've grown up. You can't just snap your fingers and expect me to come running. No, Jupiter," she repeated, though it sounded more like she was trying to convince herself.

"Star... please..." I reached out to her, but she was already standing by the door still hanging off its hinges. "Give me a chance to explain."

"Go to bed, Jupiter," she exhaled wearily, refusing to meet my eye. I didn't push it.

I passed her, stopping briefly to make sure the door was safe and drop a kiss on her head. "Sleep tight, Marn."

I didn't turn around, just made my way to the bed and slipped between the sheets. I waited for the other door to click shut, and only when it didn't come did I lift my head from my pillow to see a shard of dim light shining through from her room.

She'd left it ajar.

I smiled into the darkness. I was taking that as a win.

Hopefully she'd be less hostile to me tomorrow, especially as I'd saved the news about the fact we now had to work together.

Because the reason the guys no longer need to see her? Coach had appointed me club liaison. And for the foreseeable future, I would be the only team player working with Doctor Marnie Matthews.

8

Marnie

Present Day

A vaguely familiar, burly looking man was waiting outside my office. I pulled my glasses back down to my nose.

Burly, and fit.

I'd always thought the astronauts program at N.A.S.A. demonstrated the pinnacle of physical fitness, with bodies that could withstand G-Force six, zero gravity, and months at a time in space. But astronauts and baseball players are not the same. For the past two weeks I'd been surrounded by guys who kept their bodies in check for a living, and if the guy standing here with the lethal set of biceps crossed over his chest like they'd be comfortable down at the shooting range was anything to go by, fitness wasn't mutually exclusive to The Lions' forty-man roster.

Fit seemed to be the requirement for working here.

"Hello?" I punched in the code to my office, and the door swung open.

"Doctor Matthews, I'm Jesus Rodriguez, Assistant General Manager."

Oh yes… now I remembered. I'd seen him a couple of times over the past week, usually deep in conversation with Penn Shepherd. It took me a second to realize he wasn't wearing a ball cap, which, coupled with some other kind of Lions attire, was the uniform around here. And he looked surprisingly different without it.

"Hello. It's good to meet you finally. Please come in, and call me Marnie." I threw the remainder of my bran muffin – my own attempt to join the fitness fanatics – in the trash and rinsed away the cardboardy taste coating my tongue with a large swig of coffee. I'd also run five miles this morning, but that hadn't had anything to do with wanting to keep fit. "Mr. Shepherd said you'd be able to help me with an idea I had."

I gestured to the stools underneath the steel tables, but he didn't sit opposite where I had.

"Yes, the one percent."

I took a beat, ignoring the bite of skepticism in his tone, and crossed my legs ready to get comfortable for the long haul. "You don't sound convinced."

Jesus walked slowly around my office, picked up a pen and put it back down before stopping in front of the white wall. "How's it going to work?"

I pulled over a couple of the books I'd been reading up on data theory, passing them over the desk to him just as I had with Penn Shepherd. He flipped through the pages with disinterest, and closed the books. His hands wrapped around the back of the stool and he leaned forward.

"We've got a busy season ahead, Doctor Matthews. The schedule is hard, and the team is new. It's not the same as one or two guys coming in to join the ranks; we have an entirely new starting nine made up of players who've never competed together before. That means we've got our work cut out for us. Me and my team of coaches..." he paused, making a clicking noise as he sucked his cheek in between his teeth, and I waited because I knew there was more to come. Then he said, "we don't have time to work on this project with you, and we can't have the team's scheduled disrupted. However, as a compromise, Coach Chase appointed one of the guys to be the liaison between you and the team. He'll work with you on how the team functions day to day. It's better than you meeting with forty individual guys. It'll be a better use of time, and less distraction all around."

His gaze was a challenge, like he was daring me to disagree. Even if I had, I'd never have given him the satisfaction.

"Yes, good idea. I did wonder why no one had turned up last week. I was scheduled to meet a couple of the guys."

"Yeah, sorry about that," he replied, not sounding in the least bit sorry.

"So I'll be working with..."

"Me."

I whipped around to the door to find my new tormentor standing there, the ever-present smirk plastered on his face like he'd had it tattooed on with the rest of them. The equally tormenting butterflies woke up and began battering their wings against the lining of my belly, making my heart beat erratically.

Again.

Since he'd broken into my hotel room two nights ago, I hadn't seen him, except on the field. As sleep had eluded me for the rest of that night, I thought that he might have been as tired as I'd been, but instead he'd played his best game of the season so far; four home runs in one game, something that less than two dozen players had ever done before apparently. Reporters had jumped on him, and I didn't see him again until he boarded the plane and sat at the other end.

Not that I'd been looking for him.

And now here he was, holding two cups of coffee.

"Doctor Matthews, this is Jupiter Reeves, The Lions' starting third baseman. He'll be your club liaison and will work with you to see how we can get this project off the ground. He'll be the one to let you know whether something is feasible or not."

Of course I'd be working with Jupiter; because there's no way it could have been any of the other thirty-nine players.

He walked toward us with a swagger he usually reserved for after he'd hit a home run – like he had in Miami. "Oh, Doctor Matthews and I go way back. In fact," that devious glint appeared in his eye, "we're old study buddies. Isn't that right, Marn?"

I was getting better at holding back on the volcanic heat which coursed through my body and lit my cheeks brighter than a supernova whenever Jupiter summoned it, but not enough, it seemed, that Jesus Rodriguez couldn't tell exactly what Jupiter was referring to – even though we had *actually* been studying. Most of the time.

Some of the time.

He handed me one of the cups of coffee, and I took it silently. I didn't need to remove the lid to know this coffee was exactly how I take it. Not too heavy, with a drop of half and half, and a packet of sweetener.

"No snarl today," he whispered from the corner of his

mouth, "baby steps, eh?"

Jesus stood up, smoothing down the whiskers of his moustache. "Great, that saves me the introduction. Both of your calendars have been updated; Jupiter is at your disposal, and we've set aside an hour of his time every morning."

An hour?!

Every morning?!

The butterflies in my belly transformed into anxious excitement. Fifty/fifty. My head knew this was a bad idea, but my heart was jumping for joy, and my vagina was throbbing hard, because I couldn't seem to stop her whenever Jupiter was within a hundred yards.

She remembered everything.

Maybe the excitement and anxiety was seventy/thirty.

"Um, Mr. Rodriguez, perhaps it would be better if I saw the starting nine at least. Jupiter doesn't have time for all of this, I'm certain."

"The coaches and I make the schedules around here, Ms. Matthews, not you. This is what's happening now." His annoyance flicked to Jupiter, giving me the distinct impression he wasn't an innocent party in whatever was happening. "This is the change of plans."

"It's Doctor Matthews," Jupiter corrected him, and received a glare in response.

"Let's hope Penn Shepherd is right about you, but I won't be expecting miracles," was the last thing Jesus Rodriguez said before leaving my office.

For a second I forgot about the guy to the left of me, as I stared at the empty doorway where he'd failed to close the door behind him. Before I could follow him and do it myself, Jupiter ran across and kicked it shut.

"Don't mind him, he's a grumpy fuck. He's been with the club a while and he's stuck in his ways. Between you and me, I'd heard that he presented Shepherd with a couple of ideas for how we can improve as a team, but Shepherd wanted to go with yours. Congratulations." He raised his coffee to me with a grin and sat down in the stool next to mine, not opposite.

My nose tingled as the scent of him enveloped me, making me lightheaded. It was the scent of California; of summer on the beach, of nights under the stars; of home.

"Also, nice office, and that's a great view."

I glanced out of the window where a team of grounds keepers were readying the field for the game tonight.

"What did he mean just now about a change of plans? Why is it just you here?"

To give him credit, Jupiter didn't even look guilty. "I thought it was best if I helped you, not the rest of my teammates. I suggested it to Coach, and he mentioned it to Rodriguez."

I pushed my glasses back onto my head, which was more habit that anything. "What? What does that mean?"

"It means if you're going to spend time with anyone around here, it'll be me." He shrugged and leaned back, then stretched his long arm to snatch up a packet of LifeSavers out of the box still on the floor. To be fair, it was so big I could put it in the dining room for the entire roster, and there'd still be some left. "I'll take these…"

I blinked, trying to figure out if I'd heard correctly, and given the look on his face, I had. "Are you serious? Do you know how childish that is? It's bad enough that I'm here because of you, and now you're the only one I'm allowed to work with. This isn't fair, Jupiter!"

His blue eyes flared like the word neon had been invented to describe them.

"I don't give a fuck! The field is the only place I play fair. When it comes to you, all bets are off."

I shot him a look which conveyed exactly what I thought of that. "I'm not a game, Jupiter. You can't play me."

"Okay." He schooled his mouth into a line, though I knew he was holding something back. "I'll make a deal with you. I'll let the guys come and see you... if you tell me what you meant the other night when you said my body was 'all that'." He perfectly mimicked the hand movements I'd made, and his head fell back in a loud guffaw until he nearly fell off the stool. I kind of wished he had. He righted himself and took one look at my face, though his wide smirk hadn't dropped. "Thought not. You and me it is then, especially when your hair is down like that. You know I can't resist it."

My teeth gritted and I snapped the band off my wrist, scooping my thick strands into a top knot, but it only made him laugh, which set off those waves in my belly again. I picked up a pile of papers to distract myself from his presence. He might be wearing more clothes today, but it was still only a t-shirt and track pants, and I could still see his muscles rippling underneath them.

It was borderline obscene.

"Come on, Marn." His voice dropped, almost pleadingly; a tone which laved every inch of my body until it tingled. "Run your ideas past me. You always used to... tell me what that list is." He nodded at the white wall.

I huffed, trying not to look at him. He was too close, he was too big, and he'd clearly come straight from the gym. The strands of damp hair curling along his collar had lightened a little, and were now long enough to see the dark mahogany color transforming into a shade resonant of a fox's pelt.

In the billboards around New York, Jupiter's hair was cut short like he was about to join the army; but now… now he was transforming into the boy I'd known.

The second I'd got home last night I'd collapsed in bed. I'd been too scared to sleep on the plane, for good reason. My dreams were becoming more pronounced. In the brief few hours I'd managed in Miami, all I'd seen when I closed my eyes was Jupiter's naked body covered in tattoos… like he himself had been tattooed on the back of my eyelids.

It must have been years' worth of work.

I could still feel the throb between my legs as I glanced over at him, or maybe it was still throbbing; every cell buzzing like a pylon, just like I was sixteen again.

I wanted to drag my tongue over the outline of stars and through the constellations, along the Milky Way imprinted into the thick divot of muscle over his left hip and splayed across his body; it had been so perfectly captured that for a second I thought I'd been looking at the night sky. And I wanted to look. I'd wanted to follow it under the pajama pants, especially as I very clearly remembered what would be there waiting for me.

My heart and my head might not be convinced that being in New York was a good idea, but my body was a salivating, wanton harlot.

I moved to the stool on the other side of the table, because if I had to be in a room with him – which I seem to do – then I needed space between us if I was required to think.

I cleared my throat. "Okay, you know about Sabermetrics, right?"

He scoffed. "Of course; the analysis of baseball stats taken during each game, everyone knows that."

"Yes, well... this is kind of… the exact opposite of Sabermetrics."

He looked between me and the list on the board, and back again. "Dumb it down for me, Stars and Stripes."

"I'm not dumbing down anything for you," I gritted out and rolled my eyes. "Simply put, winning isn't going to happen overnight. Sabermetrics is clunky. This – the one percent – is about working with surgical precision; changes so small and delicate that you barely notice them, but when they add up, the difference is massive."

"Like the atomic bomb?"

My brow furrowed, "Um, no. Nothing like it, and that's a terrible analogy. It's like… fixing the annoying things that you think don't matter, but in actuality they really do."

He thought for a second before he started speaking. "Like taping Ace's mouth shut so I can concentrate on the game, and what the opposition is doing?" he grumbled, and I couldn't stop the little giggle that erupted.

"Hooo!" His eyes widened, as did mine, and he pointed right at me. "What was that?"

I set my mouth in a hard line, hiding the evidence. "What?"

"That. That what was on your face just then? You smiled, I made you smile!" He cupped his hands round his mouth, and hollered "Hallelujah! She smiles!"

"Shut up," I huffed. "We're working."

"Nah, I'm not working, I'm celebrating." He leaned over the desk to where his LifeSavers had rolled, and broke it open, "Mmm, cherry. My favorite."

Goosebumps rippled across my skin the second he stuck his tongue out to show me. The shiny pink candy glistened with his saliva, and my throat thickened as he slowly pulled it back into his mouth with a loud crunch.

Distracting. Wholly distracting. In fact, I'd never met a bigger distraction than Jupiter Reeves.

"Please, continue," he grinned, but I'd lost my train of thought, and any memory of what we'd be talking about – and he knew it. His eyebrow rose. "Is it, or is it not like taping Ace's mouth shut? Please say yes."

Jupiter stared at me, eyes wide, waiting to see if I'd crack a grin. I relented with a tiny smile. He sat back like he'd already won the Commissioner's Trophy.

"Kind of. But speaking of tape, that could be a thing. Something as small as making sure the tape's right." I sipped my coffee before continuing; it was perfect. "Okay, say the tape you've been using hasn't had the right grip, or it's rubbed your hands slightly, or slipped, maybe all three. And when you went to bat, it caused your hand to drop the tiniest fraction, which caused you to be slightly off center when you made contact with the ball. It could be the difference between a line drive getting you to third base, and a home run."

Jupiter sat back on the stool and pulled a face. His thinking face. His impressed face, though I wasn't sure if it was due to the idea, or the baseball reference.

"Marn, seriously, where've you seen this?"

"I've been reading up." I waved around the piles of books and magazines. "There's a lot of data to back this up. Sports teams have won with it."

"Which teams?"

"Foreign ones… an Olympic cycling team."

"Hmmm," was all he said before he glanced over to the board. "Okay, so what else? Pillows?"

"Yes, well, the sleep routine as a whole. Going to bed and waking up at the same time every day. If we can get the team on a schedule which works for away games and the time differences, that would be really helpful, and sleeping with the same sheets and pillows as they do at home so there's an element of familiarity in a hotel room. The scent of home is a powerful relaxant."

"Okay. What else?"

I pursed my lips. "Why are you here, again?"

"To help… and to look cute," he added, with a wink.

My body did that thing again where it felt like it was about to malfunction. I looked away.

"Then give me some ideas, small things that annoy you."

"More than Ace?"

"Yes, more than Ace." I snorted quietly, making Jupiter smile.

He ran his fingers through his hair, stretching his arms over his head when he was done. "I don't like how our bats are all jumbled together. I know they have name tapes on them, but they come off sometimes, and that makes them harder to find when we're traveling."

"What? You want everyone's bats separated in their own little baggies?"

"No! But now I do." His eyes widened, followed by a smile. "I kind of like the idea of our bats all being placed carefully in their own velvet pouches, like they're precious jewels. Maybe even sealed in walnut cases, and presented to us officially before each game."

"That's not what I said."

"It's what I heard." He shrugged, nodding to the board. "What's that about sweat rates? And hydration levels?"

"Playing ball in Texas is going to be different than playing in Seattle. There's a vast difference in temperature, as well as the type of air. It's drier in Texas. If we can monitor each player for their optimum hydration levels, as well as how much they sweat per game, we can ensure that everyone works at the exact requirements for their body."

He studied me for a second. "I've read something similar to that… they were talking about it at The Dodgers."

"Yeah, but this would be monitored through your shirts with micro-sensors, in real time. Therefore, it can be adjusted during each inning. There's a material being tested right now in Germany…"

He chuckled. "Of course there is, and of course you know about it already."

I shot him a smug grin, which he returned with a knowing cock of his head.

"It's similar to the material astronauts wear in their base layers," I conceded.

He put his coffee cup down and leaned forward, his smile vanished. "Did you ever get to space, Marn?"

I dropped my head with a shake. It was on the tip of my tongue to tell him I'd been approved to start the training program, but that was the day I'd taken the elevator ride in D.C. Then I'd have to explain why I didn't continue with it, because there was no way he'd let it go. And that was a black hole of conversation I did not want to fall into.

Instead, I just went with a simple, "No, they needed me on the ground. Training is eighteen months minimum after you've been cleared, and I wasn't ready yet."

"Oh." He picked his coffee back up, thankfully dropping that subject, but started on another. "How did you sleep the other night, Marn? Did you sleep well?"

I ignored him, and turned to the white wall.

"What about stargazing? Done any lately?"

"Can we stick to work, please?"

"I am working; humor me."

I placed the lid back onto the marker pen he'd removed then shook my head. "No, I haven't. I left my telescope in storage in Houston and haven't had a chance to buy a new one. The city lights are too bright anyway, but I do have incredible views from my apartment, so that's something."

I hadn't had much chance to view them considering I now seemed to live at Lions Stadium, but I had enjoyed watching the sun rise over the Hudson on the mornings we hadn't been traveling.

"Oh, yeah? Gonna invite me over?"

"I don't have any current plans to, no." I held his gaze with determination, though I didn't think the lack of invitation would stop him from coming over. There was a broken door in Miami which was proof of that.

"Maybe you could come over to my place then? I can show you my telescope..." His eyes flashed with mischief.

I bit down hard on my cheek, trying to quench the fire raging through me. "Jupiter..."

"Yes, Star?"

"If we're going to work together..." I began, but stopped. My head was a minefield of confusion and I was doing my best to step carefully through it, yet every time I was near him, hell, every time I caught his eye I lost focus, and had to start all over again. At this rate I was going to tread somewhere I shouldn't, and I didn't relish an explosion. Another one. "I've been given a job I'm trying to do well, and it doesn't help when you say stuff like that. I can't concentrate. You need to let me breathe... please."

Even the freckles on his face seemed to stand still as he held my gaze, and for the first time, I couldn't tell what Jupiter was thinking.

He broke away from where our eyes were locked, to check his watch.

I desperately wanted to ignore the tiny plummet which gave out in my belly when he stood.

"Okay, as much as I don't want to, I have to shoot. I have stretches with my PT."

He bent down to kiss me and I let him, this time taking the opportunity to inhale every drop of him I could; commit to memory the sensation of his lips pressing softly against my cheek, and savor the tickle of his beard.

"Thank you for my coffee."

"You're welcome. Same time, same place tomorrow, Star." Then he was gone, only to reappear with his head round the door a second later. "Actually, I'll see you at the game later. Make sure you cheer for me." He winked and left for good, and me feeling like a freshly rung bell; the vibrations still echoing in its drum.

I went back to work. I stared at the white wall for a good hour before I decided it would be more productive to write up what Jupiter and I had discussed – or what I'd told him while he nodded and asked 'what else', but I did add in his tape suggestion and his bat pouch request, omitting the velvet and walnut box.

I allowed myself to have a little chuckle and it felt good, like maybe I could do this, maybe it would be okay.

I sent a memo to Penn Shepherd and Scott Fishman.

But as the day progressed, I became more and more jittery. Every atom in my body was bing-bonging in confusion.

My mind couldn't concentrate, and my body didn't want to.

Both knew Jupiter was somewhere close; somewhere in the building.

By the time I got home that night, I'd realized some surprisingly hard truths.

The wall built around my heart was slowly being knocked down, brick by brick, by the boy who'd put it there in the first place.

And that was not something I'd planned for.

9

Jupiter

Fourteen years ago – February

"Hey, did you guys know Jupiter's gotten himself a girlfriend?"

I nearly spat my Dr. Pepper across the table, but managed to hold it together when the heads of my mom and dad both whipped around in surprise to where I was sitting. From the confusion on their faces, it was quite possible they hadn't even realized I was there, though that was just wishful thinking when my mom's expression turned to one of undiluted glee.

"Oh, Jupey, is this true? You haven't said a word."

I shot Emerson a homicidal glare before she contributed anything else to this unsolicited conversation, because now I was in a bind.

A dilemma.

I'd never had a girlfriend before, just girls who came and went.

I'd never planned to have a girlfriend; they were too much distraction.

But in the month since Marnie and I had kissed on her rooftop, I'd seen her almost every day... and kissed her almost every day.

The days I hadn't seen her or kissed her were down to me traveling for games, or because she was studying late in the science department, or I had to be in school for sunrise training. Plus the one time she went on a field trip to northern California to look at some shooting stars or something.

The days I had seen her were usually down to the rides to and from school. The ones which didn't include Emerson and Mallory were my favorite, because on those journeys, I got to hold her hand in my lap, while she asked me questions about baseball in between explaining to me how the stars changed like the seasons, switching from the northern to the southern hemisphere as the earth spun on its axis. And I'd quickly take my eyes off the road to glance over at her, and wonder if perhaps I was currently spinning off *my* axis.

I'd never met anyone like her before. She was so open and genuine, and interested; genuinely interested in *me* instead of the social standing I came with. She was interested in learning about baseball; about why I'd fallen in love with baseball. I'd never talked so much to a girl in my life outside of my family, and she was asking questions no one had ever asked. She wanted to learn about the draft, about what I would do if I got picked by a team before The Dodgers. And she tried to explain to me about astrodynamics, but mostly I watched her mouth move and the way her top lip deepened to create a perfect line of symmetry down her face. Then she told me everything she knew about Jupiter, and I vowed to pay attention to every single word she uttered.

One time we went to the library; I had English homework, and she'd had trigonometry. I hated math, yet found myself captivated by the way she explained it to me like it was the easiest subject in the world.

She was two years younger than me, and I'd wonder, again, how I'd managed to convince this incredible girl that I was a guy worth spending time with.

We hadn't discussed what was happening.

I hadn't asked her to be my girlfriend.

Between baseball practice, games, and studying, save a few rare moments in the Sports Building where she'd shoot me in the chest with one of her perfect smiles and renew my energy for the day, our paths never crossed, so I'd never been asked by anyone if I was dating Marnie Matthews. Even Jenson had assumed she was a friend of Emerson's the first few times I gave her a ride to school

Until he saw me kiss her goodbye.

Then he just smirked, patted me on the back with a 'nice', and we'd taken off for practice where he'd eventually forgotten about whatever it was he'd planned to ask me.

A month in, and still no one had asked, so this time right now at family pizza night was the first time I'd really contemplated the answer to that question.

Was Marnie Matthews my girlfriend?

I tried to imagine what she'd say if I asked her. The thought of her saying no made it feel like the Meat Feast I'd been eating was about to come right up.

Maybe *that* was my answer.

Yes. As far as I was concerned, yes, Marnie Matthews was

my girlfriend. I just needed confirmation from her before I announced it more widely. I'd never been shot down before and I didn't intend to start now, but there was no harm in being cautious.

"Well, sweetheart?"

My eyes flicked from Emerson to my dad, then finally to my mom. I sighed, "Yeah, maybe. I dunno. I haven't talked to her about it."

"She gets a ride with us nearly every day to school," Emerson smirked before stuffing more pizza in her mouth.

"Fuck's sake, Emerson. Can you keep your big mouth shut for once? And might I remind you it was your idea in the first place to give her a ride?"

She grinned as my mom tutted, then pointed to the swear jar.

"I'm not putting anything in there for being baited."

"Emerson, knock it off." My dad frowned at her, which was unusual in itself. He was wrapped around her pinkie, and she knew she'd never get any kind of actual punishment. "Jupiter, you could have told us."

"There wasn't anything to tell. We've just been hanging out, I didn't think it would be front page news or anything," I grumbled.

"Could we get a name, at least?" Mom begged.

I still hadn't gotten used to the kneejerk reaction I had to smile whenever I thought of Marnie, or the way my heart pumped harder. It was pointless trying to hide it now. "Her name's Marnie. Marnie Matthews."

My mom and dad gave each other one of those looks, then my mom turned back to me. "As in Noah and Bryony's daughter? The Matthews' next door?"

I nodded. I hadn't met her parents yet, but I knew their names. "Yes."

The smile on my mom's face dropped a little and her whole body turned toward me. "How old is she?"

I took another bite of my pizza and swallowed it down, ignoring the slight clenching in my chest. "She's nearly seventeen."

"Jupiter, you're eighteen. That's a big gap at your ages. Please tell me you're being careful."

I scowled at Emerson making puking gestures at the other end of the table and focused back on my mom, who now had that look all moms get. "Jeez, mom, yes! God! It's not like that, anyway."

Emerson slurped her soda loudly. "Ainsley is going to be crushed."

Heads all turned back to Emerson. "Who?"

"You know, Ainsley McAvoy, one of the McAvoy twins. You made out with her."

I scoffed. I had no recollection of this claim, though that didn't necessarily mean it wasn't true. However, as Emerson was always trying to convince me I'd made out with her friends, I was dubious because I mostly avoided them like the plague. "When?"

"OMG, Jupiter, you're so gross! How can you not remember making out with someone?"

"Alright, Emmy, enough now," my dad tutted. "Jupiter, ignore her."

But once Emerson was under my skin, she was almost impossible to ignore. I tried to wrack my brain through the yearbook of my sister's friends, most of whom looked the same. I was still coming up blank.

"Can we get back to the subject of Marnie?" my mom interrupted. "When are we going to meet her?"

I groaned; this is why I didn't have girlfriends. Parents, ugh. "I dunno, Mom. Can you just let me figure it out first? Don't make this a big deal, please!"

"Okay, Jupe, but don't leave it too long or I'll be marching over to invite her parents for dinner." My mom picked up her wine glass. "In fact, we've been saying for ages we'd have them over, this could be the perfect moment."

I was a second away from banging my head on the table. Emerson was going to pay for this.

"Dad…" I pleaded down to where he was eating his pizza in silence, because I needed someone to be my ally in this situation, but he just shook his head with a smirk, leaving me to be eaten by the wolves. "Mom, just chill out, will you? It's nothing."

She got up and wrapped her arms around me, her chin resting on my head, "No, Jupiter, I won't chill out. I'm happy about this. Your grades are good, and you need something to show you there's life outside of baseball. It's what you need. You've got a few months left until we all hope you're drafted; just enjoy the time while you can. The hard work will really start then, and I don't want you to have any regrets."

I stayed quiet while I let my mom's words sink in, ignoring the 'hope' part about being drafted. I thought I'd always had a life outside of baseball; I had great friends, I was popular with a decent social life, but everyone knew baseball was my love, and I couldn't be persuaded otherwise.

But maybe my mom was right, and I definitely didn't want to have regrets.

"Okay, thanks. May I be excused? I have homework."

"Yes, but plates go in the dishwasher. The dishwasher, Jupiter, not by the sink next to it, or in the sink, or on the counter. In the dishwasher."

I rolled my eyes but did as I was asked. Firing off another glare at Emerson, I walked out of the kitchen, muttering "you can make your own way to school tomorrow."

"I already have plans with Mallory," she called after me, and I could hear her laughing with my parents as I ran up the stairs two at a time.

I wasn't lying when I said I had homework. It wasn't a lot, but I'd been procrastinating for the last week, and it was due tomorrow. I also wanted to see Marnie. Beyond a few texts we'd barely spoken today; she hadn't ridden in with me as I'd needed to get into school early for a workout with Jenson and she'd wanted to sleep longer, so it had been almost twenty-four hours since I'd last laid eyes on her. I was desperate for a hit.

Plus, after all the girlfriend conversation, I had a question for her which couldn't wait.

Jupiter: *Are you home? I'm coming over quick, 'kay?*

Star: *Yes, see you soon.*

I closed my bedroom door. I could still hear my parents and Emerson laughing in the kitchen – no doubt about me – but which should at least last for enough time for me to get out and back. Easing open the bottom half of the big sash window in my bedroom, I climbed out.

Luckily my room was at the back of the house and above the living room with its huge arched doorway. I'd learned a few years ago that I could balance on the arch, and walk my feet down while clinging to the edges. I jumped off just before I reached the ground, then jogged around past the pool and out through the gap in the hedge at the side, which led through to the cluster of palm trees outside Marnie's bedroom.

She was waiting for me on the balcony, her smile warming me better than the dying heat of the day's sun. She was wearing a pair of running shorts, *short* running shorts… elongating her toned legs; and a tank top which shaped her tits and accentuated her taut nipples in a way that made my cock pay attention… though it didn't take much to get hard around her. Sometimes I'd catch the scent of her shampoo when she climbed into the passenger seat, and my dick would twitch.

As ever, her hair was piled on top of her head, her glasses pushed into it, and I knew I'd interrupted her studying. But from the way her eyes sparkled as I pulled myself up over the railings, she didn't care.

It had been a month and I was still marveling at how I'd never really noticed her around school, because now I'd seen her, it was beyond me how I'd ever missed her.

She was so beautiful. More than beautiful. She was a star-filled night beautiful.

Yes, I wanted her to be my fucking girlfriend. My first girlfriend. And in return, I wanted to be all her firsts.

"Hey there," she started.

"Hey, yourself." I wrapped my arms around her waist and pulled her into me, taking a deep inhale against the warmth of her skin, before dipping down to quickly capture her lips with mine. "I won't be long; I just wanted to talk to you about something."

She tipped her head up to look at me, a tiny crease formed on her brow as her green eyes flared. "What's up?"

"Nothing much, I just wanted one of these." I pressed my lips to hers again, feeling her smile underneath. "And also to tell you Emerson outed us to my parents, and then the question came up about whether you were my girlfriend or not."

Her body moved in my arms like she was trying to pull away, but I held firm. "Okay..."

"So I guess I wanted to come here to see if it was something you'd thought about…"

"Being… your g…g… girlfriend?" she spluttered.

I nodded slowly. "Yeah, because I hadn't really thought about it… but we've been spending all this time together, and now that we have, I kind of like the idea. So I guess what I'm trying to say is… Marnie Matthews, will you be my girlfriend?"

I didn't expect her reaction to be hysterical giggles; therefore wasn't sure what to make of it. I'm not sure a girl had ever burst into hysterics over me before, unless you counted The Laurens, which I didn't, so I wasn't clear on whether it was a good sign or not.

"Um, Star?"

"Sorry." She wiped her eyes, and straightened herself up. "I feel like I'm having an out of body experience. Jupiter Reeves, captain of the baseball team, is asking me to be his girlfriend."

"I am," I grinned. "So what do you say?"

Her face dropped and she suddenly became serious. "Jupiter, I've never had a boyfriend before."

I didn't want to admit that it was one of the things I liked about her, that she wasn't the girl who chased after guys, or been through an entire team. I liked her innocence. I liked that when we kissed for the first time, she was following my lead. I liked that she didn't try to impress me with all the sexual knowledge she'd obtained from whatever magazines my sisters read, like I was a practice dummy.

And I really liked that when she looked up at me, she expected me to provide her with the answers. Me, giving answers to her. The smartest girl I'd ever met.

So hearing her confirm I would be her first boyfriend made my dick twitch and belly fizzle simultaneously.

I dropped a kiss on her cute button nose. "That's what makes us so perfect for each other, because I've never had a girlfriend before. Come on, Stars and Stripes; put me out of my misery, I beg you."

Her soft smile shot bolts of lightning through my core. "Yes, yes of course I will."

My mouth captured hers once more, and now I got to take my time. I wasn't sure there would ever be enough time for all the kisses I wanted to give her, especially when I could feel her smile pressed into mine; almost taste her smile laced with the sweetness of the candies she'd been eating as my tongue slid slowly against hers. I would never get tired of making her smile.

In the last month I'd learned that she loved it when I cupped her cheeks with my hands; a soft moan escaped every time I did. A louder moan sounded whenever I pushed my fingers through her hair and tugged on her pony tail. I got bonus points if I pulled it free from the tie and wrapped her hair around my fist.

I also knew she loved when I cupped her ass and lifted her up to me, her nails digging into my shoulders for leverage while her legs instinctively wrapped around my waist so she could kiss me deeper. So deep.

Because if I'd learned anything in the past month, it was that she had a fire inside her I seemed to unleash. Me, all me, and only me.

And that was something that *I* loved.

I pulled my head back but kept her hoisted on my waist with one arm, using a free hand to brush away the dark strands of loose hair which had fallen across her eyes.

"My girlfriend is so beautiful." My heart squeezed at the laugh she let out.

"Well, my boyfriend is the most handsome boy in school." She smiled back softly, her thick black lashes dusting across the tops of her pink cheeks as she dropped her gaze.

"You know it." Brushing my nose against hers, I said, "I have to go and finish my English homework, but I'll see you tomorrow morning. 'Kay?"

She nodded. "Sounds good to me."

I dropped one last kiss on her peachy lips, and shimmied back down the tree. As predicted, I could still hear Emerson and my parents in the kitchen by the time I was in my room and at my desk… then I realized my mistake.

I should have finished my homework before seeing Marnie.

There was no way I could concentrate on anything except the memory of her lips against mine.

It was going to be a long night.

I slipped into my usual space and cut the engine, letting go of Marnie's hand for the first time since she'd jumped into my truck.

But then I picked it up and kissed her fingers. "How busy is your day today?"

She twisted in her seat to face me better. "Pretty busy. I have a study period after lunch, but then I'm in the physics lab all afternoon."

I pulled a face at the thought of half a day of physics, making her laugh. "So you have lunch free? Meet me for lunch today?"

She nodded, "Yes, I can do that. Sounds good."

I kissed her again because I needed to take advantage of every opportunity when we'd be separated for most of the day. It was a strange, foreign sensation, this needing to be close to her all the time; my body was starting to feel like it did whenever I went long stretches without playing ball.

"Perfect."

She opened her door and hopped out, meeting me on the steps right where Jenson also happened to be.

"Morning, homies."

I passed Marnie her bag that I'd collected from the back seat and slung my arm around her. It was time to make a small announcement.

"Hey, dude, I want to introduce you to Marnie Matthews, my girlfriend." I grinned at him, and to give him credit, he only smiled back, "Star, this is Jenson, my best friend."

"But we met already, the other week."

"Not officially as my girlfriend though," I winked, and the tiny pink tint rose on her cheeks.

"Okay, well, good to meet you, Jenson."

"Bring it in," was all the warning he gave before pulling her into a bear-like hug. A rumble ran through my chest, and a beast began clawing at my insides.

Huh.

"Okay, that's enough of that." I yanked her away from him, only to receive raised brows from both of them. "What? She's my girlfriend; only I get to touch her."

Marnie's neck craned back, and she frowned. "That's a bit

caveman of you, isn't it?"

I shrugged. "Hey, it's a surprise to me too, babe. But what you gonna do?"

Turns out, roll her eyes.

"Okay, I need to head off. See you at lunch. Bye, Jenson."

"Bye, Marnie." He smiled at me as he called after her, waiting until she was out of earshot before starting on me. "Wow. Dude. Whaaaaaaat?"

I didn't look at him, just started up the steps to the Sports building. "What, what?"

"You know what."

I spun round and grinned. "I like her, Jens. I like her a lot. She's cool, and different."

"At least now I know why you've been running off at the end of every practice." He punched me hard in the arm, but I could see the grumble was just for show. "Nah, it's good. She seems like a nice girl. But promise me something…"

I narrowed my eyes. "Depends what it is."

"Promise that I'm there when The Laurens find out." He laughed so hard he nearly walked into the lamppost. "In fact, when all the girls find out."

"Shut up," I shoved him back. "It's not that bad."

He stopped dead. "Oh, dude. It really, *really* is. There's going to be mutiny."

I shook my head and laughed, trying to ignore the unease making itself known. It never occurred to me anyone would care; I just assumed it would be accepted as fact. I now came with a girlfriend, and given I rarely thought about The Laurens or any of the girls, I also hadn't thought that they might have an issue with it.

"All I'm saying," he went on and I wished he wouldn't, "is

the past few years it's been widely acknowledged that you don't date, therefore coming out of the blue with an unknown girlfriend is going to cause a stir."

I groaned which was all I could muster, before pushing it as far as I could to the back of my mind so I didn't have to think about it.

We nodded to Reggie as we walked through the doors and headed down to the locker room. I tipped my chin to a couple of the guys from the football team who looked like they were about to head out, and save for them, the place was empty.

And I suddenly couldn't be fucked for the eight miles we'd planned.

"Hey, let's skip the run today and hit the batting cages instead. I feel like smashing something."

Jenson threw his backpack into his locker. "Fuck, yeah!"

I threw on my shorts, grabbed my gloves, and followed him out to the bullpen where we spent the next two hours.

Maybe it was the change of plans for the morning, or the three buckets of balls I'd knocked out, but my body was coursing with electricity; like unstruck lightning. My muscles should have been tired, but I felt like I could go another twelve rounds. Not only that, Mrs. Philips, my English teacher, had graded my paper on the spot and given me a B.

Not sure who was in charge of making today, but I wanted to shake their hand because I was winning – especially when I rounded the corner to find the most beautiful girl in school sitting at the picnic bench outside the cafeteria where we'd arranged to meet. I'd picked up two pastrami sandwiches, water bottles, and a share bag of chips ready for our lunch together, but first…

My lips found hers; my free hand wrapped around the back of her neck and held her to me until I was ready to let her go… though it suddenly occurred to me I wasn't sure I'd ever be ready.

"Hi, how was your morning?" I peered down at her flushed face.

"It was good!" she replied and her eyes lit up. "Professor Foster has a new particle accelerator, and we got to use it this morning to make our own lightning. It was so cool."

I laughed, warmed by her enthusiasm, even though I had no clue what she was talking about. "You made your own lightning? I gotta see that."

"I'll show you, it was seriously amazing," she beamed up at me.

I held up the paper bags with our lunch. "I also have something amazing; I hope you're hungry."

"I sure am."

"Good." I held my hand out to her. "Come on."

"Where are we going?"

I laced my fingers through hers. "You'll see. It's one of my favorite places."

I led her across the picnic area, ignoring the turning heads, the whispering, and the looks I hoped Marnie hadn't noticed. Maybe Jenson was right.

Good job I didn't give a single fuck.

Passing the hockey building, the silver cylinders which pumped cool air into the rink caught the sunshine and spotlighted the path we were heading down, in the direction of the playing fields. All the teams – football, lacrosse, baseball, soccer – played in the same area of school. It had been purposely built like this so the school's supporters could cheer for any team if there happened to be games played on the same day. And when we turned the corner, all the fields were laid out like a patchwork quilt below us; the bigger ones with bleacher seating situated in the middle – the smaller fields all spread around the outside of them.

"Wow, this looks amazing. I've never been down here before."

My eyes shot wide. "Seriously? You've never watched a game? How's that possible? I thought all students had to support the teams."

"Not if you have an early acceptance pass which means you have to study." She shrugged.

"Well, shit." I stopped us walking and pointed out to the far left. "Over there are the football fields. There's one for the senior team and one for the junior team." My arm moved a little further to the left, "And there are the baseball fields… you can see the diamond. Best place on earth."

She squeezed her hand in mine, and she may as well have stroked my balls for the effect it had on me.

"What are the other ones?"

"They're the soccer pitches, and that one is lacrosse."

We carried on past the fields.

"Nearly there." I practically dragged her through the final stretch, so desperate was I to be alone with her, because as big as this campus was, it was virtually impossible to find a quiet space. Then there it was. "Here we go."

She spun, then spun again. "How did I not see this from the path?"

This was a raised platform, about eight feet by eight feet, that I'd stumbled on one day when retrieving a ball that had gone wide at practice. It was completely hidden by a large oak tree, but when you stood on it, you had a perfect, uninterrupted view of the baseball field – the big one.

That had been two years ago.

"I dunno, but you can't. I've tested it," I replied, and then wish I hadn't.

Her shoulders dropped, not a lot, but enough for me to notice, especially when her smile dropped too.

Because as much as I liked that I was her first everything, she wasn't mine. I couldn't erase that fact, but I could try and make it a little better.

"Star, come here." I crooked a finger and she made her way slowly to me, until the tips of our sneakers were almost touching. "I want to kiss you properly."

Like I'd flicked a switch, her smile returned and I took it prisoner with my own. I could kiss this girl forever.

"Jupiter?"

"Yes?"

She didn't say anything immediately, just looked down at her feet. But then I heard, "Are you ever going to do any more than kiss me? You know, now you're officially my boyfriend?"

I swallowed thickly as I absorbed her words and tried to calm the adrenaline that had shot up and was racing through my veins. "Do you want to do more?"

Her gaze hit me square; the ruby glow had reappeared on her cheeks, making her eyes even greener. She didn't say anything, but nodded slowly.

I had a sudden panic that perhaps being here was making her feel like I wanted more from her than she was ready to give, which simply wasn't true. For the first time in my life I felt like I was moving at a pace I was happy with, because whatever waited for me at the end would be totally worth it once I got there.

And I wanted to savor it.

"Marn, I don't want to rush you. You don't have to do anything because of me. Whatever we do is because you're ready, and for no other reason."

"I'm ready, Jupiter." She smiled a smile that jump started my heart. "I promise."

"Okay… okay." I rubbed my hands together. Fuck. She might have been ready, but I was not prepared for this. "Okay."

I reached behind me and pulled my sweater off, laying it down on the ground as a makeshift blanket. Then I stood tall, and kissed her once more.

"Okay," I said for the thousandth time, suddenly overcome with nerves, while she looked as cool as Kobe stealing the win in the final seconds of the Lakers game last night. "Sit here with me."

I dropped to the ground, and held my hand out to guide her into my lap.

"Shouldn't I lie down?"

It took me a second to realize her meaning. "Marn, we're not going to have sex."

Her eyes shot open. "We're not?"

"Not up here we aren't. Not for the first time anyway. When we have sex, it'll be in a bed."

The fact that I felt every muscle in her body relax was enough for me to know I'd made the right decision, not to mention I wasn't ready either. I'd never had sex with a virgin before, and I needed to have my head in the game to make it as perfect for her as I could.

And that wasn't this platform.

I wrapped my arms around her and pulled her closer. My lips found hers again, soft and pliant, and so fucking kissable.

"If you ever want to stop, you just say the word. Deal?"

She nodded, and my mouth returned to hers.

I might have been with girls before, but I'd never appreciated the luxury of time; of how sexy it was to feel a warm tongue slide softly against yours, and within seconds, my pants were too tight. She giggled quietly as I shifted her slightly without breaking contact, then her moans spurred me on a little further.

My hands slipped down, across the soft curves of her waist and down to the edges of her sweater. I slowed, making sure they were warm, before pushing up under the cotton, until I made contact with heated skin. Her body jolted and a flurry of goosebumps shot across her skin as my palms continued on their journey until they reached the edges of her bra.

I'd been dreaming about her boobs since the day I'd first met her. It was hard to even believe I'd lasted an entire month without touching them, but I'd been so fucking right when I'd said they were the perfect handful. They fitted in my palm just right.

Her nipples were as hard as the studs on my cleats.

I swallowed her loud gasp as my thumb brushed over one. She pulled back, her glassy eyes making my dick impossibly hard.

"You like that?" I did it again, and her jaw dropped. "I'll take that as a yes."

My lips found their way onto the slender column of her neck, and she shivered against me.

Fuck, this girl...

Every single place I touched her set off an avalanche of shudders.

And I felt *every single one* in the depths of my balls. It was going to take all my discipline not to bust one in my pants.

Her breathing had become more labored; I could feel

each rise and fall under my hand splayed across her back. My breathing was also alarmingly unsteady considering I was planning to become a professional athlete within the next few months.

My palms slid slowly across her body as if trying to memorize every curve, every dip and bend… every reaction so that when I finally did get her naked, I'd be able to match the touch to the sound. Like now, when she groaned the loudest yet as my fingers grazed over her pelvis.

She was wearing a short skirt today, one of those ones that puffed out, so it looked longer than it actually was; I let go of her for as short a time as possible, moving one hand to the top of her thigh, right underneath the hem. Without dropping her gaze, I pushed it up until the bright white cotton of her panties came into view. I waited, expecting her to stop me, but instead, she tilted her hips a fraction, pushing herself into me as her hand gripped my neck.

Her eyes were fully glazed, almost hooded, and I was suddenly desperate to slow down this moment. I wanted to savor it; capture it in a little vial I could wear round my neck or keep in my pocket.

"Kiss me, Marn."

It was so gentle it nearly broke me. Her tongue slipped past my lips and tangled with mine, tasting me as I'd tasted her.

My fingertips took on a life of their own, running up and down the warm path of her panties, right through her center; the one getting wetter by the second.

"Oh… ohhhh, Jupiter," she groaned into my mouth as I grazed my thumb over her clit.

"I know," I whispered against her lips. "I'm gonna make it feel so good."

Though in actual fact, I didn't know whether that's what I was doing; I only hoped and prayed I was, because I realized that these little moans she was making, the bursts of air she was gasping for… the way her chest rose and fell like it might explode, I'd never seen a girl do before.

Not in this way. Not so uninhibited.

The only thing I knew was that it was making my chest puff wider with every sound she made.

I slid the scalloped edges of her panties to one side, my fingers instantly drenched in slick warmth. She gasped hard as I eased one finger inside her. Eased was the wrong word, there was no easing. She was so wet she pretty much suctioned on and pulled me inside.

"Oh God… this feels…"

Her hips did the rest of the talking, thrusting forward and urging me on. My tongue plunged into her mouth as I plunged a second finger into her pussy, my steady rhythm of matching one for one. Her panting increased, her lips left mine. She peered down, mesmerized, to where my fingers were still moving in and out; like her own, private sex show.

I couldn't take my eyes off her.

"You like that?"

Another twenty seconds and she was convulsing in my lap; intense, almost violent quaking as she arched away from me, her mouth forming a perfect O shape while her eyelids fluttered like a hummingbird's wing. I swear her eyes rolled back.

Then I felt it; gripping my fingers like they were giving her life, she came in my lap.

I'd had some experience during my teenage years so far; fooled around with a handful of girls, had sex with another handful.

But none, not a single one, had looked at me the way Marnie was looking at me now – like I was the answer to every question she'd ever asked.

It engulfed me until I couldn't breathe. Until my heart was pumping so hard I was convinced I was having a seizure. And if I'd had a mirror, I'd have found the exact same expression on my face, too.

Because if I was the question, Marnie Matthews was my answer.

10

Marnie

Present Day

I pulled the pillow over my head, wishing whatever the obnoxious noise was that had wrenched me from sleep would go away.

But it didn't.

I reached for the intercom by my bed. "Hello?"

"Doctor Matthews, we have a delivery for you. Can we bring it up? It's large, heavy, and we can't keep it in the lobby."

I glanced at the clock; I'd only been in bed for five hours. We'd had a flight home after three away games, and it was Saturday.

I'd really wanted to sleep in today.

"Okay, come up," I croaked and hung up, or more accurately, dropped the headset down the side of the bed.

I picked up The Lions' hoodie I'd flung onto the chair in the corner and tugged it over my head, then made my way to the front door, all while trying to rub some sight into my eyes. My eyesight wasn't bad enough that I couldn't see without my glasses; they just made things a little sharper. This morning though, it was like they hadn't had enough rest to function – especially when I banged into the wall.

I opened the door just as two delivery guys, followed by Greg, the concierge, walked out of the elevator.

I understood why he didn't want it sitting in the lobby.

A wooden crate, the size of a large chair – maybe an extra-large chair – was being wheeled on one of those push carts, and for a second I panicked it wouldn't fit through the door – but I was wrong.

"Where do you want this, lady?"

I hadn't made any chair sized purchases recently. "I don't know what it is. Think you can help me out?"

"Sorry, we just deliver."

I looked at Greg, who shrugged.

I rolled my eyes. "Put in the living room then I guess, please."

The shorter of the two delivery guys handed me a clipboard and a pen with what looked like a Band-Aid wrapped round the top. "Sign here, and here."

I read the forms – twice. I couldn't find a single clue which could shed some light, so I scrawled my name and handed them back.

"Oh, this is for you too." He held out a thick cream envelope. *Marnie* was scribbled across the front, and I then knew exactly who was responsible for my annoying wake up call.

Greg coughed. "Ah, Doctor Matthews, if that's everything, we'll leave you to it."

"Yes, thank you," I replied, though I was still staring at the envelope as they said goodbye.

I saw the problem as soon as I heard the door click on their way out… "Wait, how am I supposed to open this?" I called after them, but it was too late. "Ugh!"

I knocked on the crate; it was nailed shut pretty good. Running my fingers along the edges didn't find any obvious way of opening it either. I was pondering what to do when I realized I was still holding the envelope, and ripped it open.

For stargazing.

And as you're not inviting me over, here are the coordinates for my roof terrace the next time you want to see me and my body… all that.

40.7336° N, 74.0027° W

I groaned again as my cheeks pinked, even though there was no one around to witness it. He was never going to let that go. I shouldn't have said anything, but he'd been standing in front of me after he'd broken into my room, naked save for a pair of thin pajama pants and his muscles were right there – still there whenever I closed my eyes. My mouth had pooled with saliva and my vocabulary had failed me. Plus, he knew full well what he'd been doing, and the effect he had on me.

The effect he continued to have on me.

Had always had on me.

Jupiter Reeves and innocent were not two words which fitted together.

My eyes flicked back to the box, then the card.

No way.

Excitement flurried around my belly, and I ran as fast as I could to the kitchen – the only place I could think of with implements remotely capable of opening the crate. I returned with a rolling pin and an impressive thick bladed chef's knife; not sure when Lowe and Beulah thought I'd have time to do all this baking and chefing, but it was good to have a fully stocked kitchen if only to help me break into things.

Easing the knife through one of the joints, I banged hard on the end; it loosened with a loud creak. Five minutes later, I'd repeated it at every corner, and one side of the heavy wooden crate fell to the floor, followed by an avalanche of packing peanuts.

Another ten minutes and it had been fully dismantled. I was standing in a sea of Styrofoam and protective cardboard casing, staring down with an open mouth at one of the most beautiful telescopes I'd ever seen.

The Celestial PlanetMaster G20 T edition X.

It made the telescope I'd had as a teenager look like a pair of Fisher-Price plastic binoculars.

It was like gazing at a piece of priceless art, or the stillest lake under a full moon.

I wanted to touch it, but I couldn't bring myself to get closer than the foot away I was currently standing. I wanted to run my fingers along the steel axis and peer through the finder, but something was stopping me.

The butterflies had ceased with their fluttering, replaced by the gnawing of the unknown; of what this meant… because it wasn't just a telescope.

I knew Jupiter too well for that.

It was one thing to buy several years' supply of candy Life-

Savers, or a coffee made exactly how I liked it. But it was quite another to spend seventy-five thousand dollars on a telescope that only the most hard-core stargazers would consider purchasing. Most hard-core couldn't afford.

I also knew this one wasn't readily available – yet. It had a limited-edition release, so how he'd managed to get hold of it was anyone's guess.

All of a sudden it felt like something was sitting on my chest, squeezing hard, trapping me, and I stared at it until a yawn broke through. It was time to go back to bed.

The Lions had a game later this afternoon, but as it was Saturday I didn't have to be at the stadium until it began. I'd planned to go in early and work on the One Percent program, as it was now called, but now I was sorely tempted to creep back under the covers and sleep for the rest of the day.

I lay there. And lay there.

The more I tried to sleep, the harder I squeezed my eyes shut, the less I was able.

Jupiter.

Even when he wasn't around, Jupiter was my tormentor; his presence was everywhere. Naked, clothed – it didn't matter. He was just *there* wherever I turned, whether I wanted him to be or not, with his broad shoulders and sculpted chest, his blue eyes sparkling bright, his smile wider every time… and it always made my heart skip a beat in the way I wished it wouldn't.

In a way my body made sure I couldn't ignore.

But it was there, the low *throb, throb, throb* like a distant helicopter somewhere in the skies above.

In the week since we'd been working together, we'd fallen in a routine bordering on familiar, *possibly* even comfortable, possibly enjoyable – even if he refused to let up on his incessant teasing.

Perhaps this is what happened when exes were forced to spend time together. Perhaps this is how exes became friends. I hadn't expected to ever see Jupiter Reeves again, let alone be in a room with him and having a civil conversation; an achievement I was surprisingly proud of myself for.

Friends.

Friends was something I could handle; something my heart could handle.

Friends didn't have the power to shatter your world into a trillion pieces.

But friends did not send you presents with a price tag that equaled an annual salary.

I was pulling the covers back over my head when my cell buzzed. I was about to ignore it when I noticed Beulah's name flashing across the screen.

"Hey!"

"Hey! How are you? I didn't wake you, did I?"

"No, I wish," I groaned. "I've been awake for a while. What's up?"

"Me, too! It doesn't matter how late I go to bed, I seem to be hardwired to wake up at dawn."

I didn't have the energy to tell her about my delivery, so instead replied with, "tell me about it," at the same time she said, "Do you wanna come boxing with me?"

I shuffled about on my pillow, making sure the cell's microphones weren't covered. "What did you say?"

"There's a boxing gym I pass on the way to the stadium, and I always wanted to try it. There's a class this morning. You in?"

I rubbed the sleep from my eyes. "Have you asked Lowe?"

Beulah chuckled. "She had plans which didn't include boxing."

I stretched long into my bed, arms over my head with a groan as bones cracked and muscles engaged. I wasn't going to do myself any good staying here and stressing myself out trying to solve my Jupiter problem. And a couple of rounds with a boxing bag might even help.

"Sure, but can we get coffee on the way? Otherwise the boxing bag will be doing the rounds with me," I laughed.

"You got it. Meet at the Coffee Grind near the University on Amsterdam in an hour?"

Yes! I knew where that was. I hadn't been in the city long, but I had remembered where the best coffee spots were.

"See you there." I hung up and jumped out of bed, impressing myself with the level of energy I'd managed to summon.

I got to the Coffee Grind in under the hour, beating Beulah, though I was only waiting a minute before I saw her jogging around the corner to me, dark curls bouncing on her shoulders. There hadn't even been time to text and ask for her order.

"Hey," she greeted, squeezing me in a hug. "Thanks for coming to this with me. I've wanted to go for ages, but I'm too chicken to go alone."

I grinned at her. "Any time. I need to get some frustration out anyway."

She raised an eyebrow. "Oh, yeah?"

I nodded; she knew exactly what I was talking about. "Yeah."

"Okay, let's get coffee then we can discuss it on the way. You'll feel so much better once you've beaten the shit out of a giant leather bag."

"I hope so," I laughed. "Okay, what's your order?"

"Ice black drip, please."

"You got it, I'll be right back."

The coffee shop was much busier than it looked from the outside. Much, much busier, and pretty loud. I joined the line behind a couple of guys wearing Lions caps, pulled out my cell and brought up Jupiter's contact details.

My fingers hovered over the letters. I needed to say thank you.

Thank you seemed too basic for the immovable object now sitting in my living room; for the trouble he'd gone to. And thank you wasn't right. I had a lot of feelings about Jupiter Reeves swirling around my brain, but I wasn't sure if thankfulness was one of them.

I hadn't figured it out before my name was called, so I slipped my cell back into my pocket, put my order through, and stood aside to wait with everyone else.

"Marnie," the barista called my name, quicker than I'd expected. "Marnie."

"Me!" I pushed through the rest of the customers waiting for their drinks and grabbed the two cups, then made my way back to where Beulah was standing under a row of blossom trees. "Come on, let's go."

She dodged a guy not looking where he was going. "It's so busy!"

I glanced around; fifty percent of the people were wearing some form of Lions logo.

"The game today," I gulped my coffee, gagging at the bitterness. "Ugh, this is disgusting."

I looked at the cup. Unless my name had changed to Barney in the last fifteen minutes, this was not mine.

"What's wrong?"

"I got someone else's coffee," I grumbled. I really wanted coffee, but this was undrinkable. However, that would require me going back through that crowd. But… coffee… "Do you mind waiting? I'll see if they have mine. I can catch you up if you want to start walking."

"No, we're good for time," Beulah replied, and then her smile turned flat while her eyes moved to over my left shoulder.

I spun around to find a preppy-ish looking college guy holding a large coffee cup. "Marnie?"

"Yes?"

He thrust the cup at me and pointed to the one I was holding. "I think we got each other's."

My eyes widened with relief at the trip I'd been saved, "Oh! Thank you! I really didn't want to go back in there."

"Yeah, me either," he grinned. "Here you go."

I took it from him and sipped. Much better. "Ah, awesome. Enjoy your day." I smiled at the guy, expecting him to walk off as I turned to Beulah, gesturing with my head for her to lead the way.

Coffee guy didn't move. Instead, deep dimples formed as he grinned. "Your coffee order is disgusting by the way."

I scoffed; eyes widening at Beulah, then at coffee guy. "No, you're mistaken. *Your* coffee is disgusting. I nearly spat it out."

"You're wrong."

I wasn't about to stand and argue with this guy, no matter how cute he thought he was being, especially as I was becoming aware of Beulah's head switching between the two of us like this was playing out on Center Court at Flushing Meadows, wearing a wide smile of her own that I didn't understand, but it looked like trouble.

"Okay, well, enjoy your coffee." I pulled a laughing Beulah away in an attempt to shut this down.

"Oh, I will, Marnie," he grinned. "See you around."

The way he said my name… all arrogant and self-assured, but not in the way it tripped off Jupiter's tongue, because when Jupiter said my name, it felt like there was no one else around.

Beulah nudged me and lowered her voice. "That guy was flirting with you."

"What?" I blew out. "No, he wasn't."

She pulled her sunglasses down her nose. "Um, yeah, he was definitely flirting with you."

"Beulah…"

"What?" She lifted her palms defensively. "I'm just saying. He was flirting with you, and he was cute."

"He was a college kid. He couldn't have been older than twenty-two." I took a big gulp of coffee, coughing at the temperature scalding my throat.

She smacked me on the back until I stopped then put her arm around my shoulders. "Let's go boxing and you can tell me about this frustration you need to get out. I'm assuming it's big and covered in tattoos?"

I nodded with a sigh.

"What's happened?"

"He sent me a telescope."

"Ohh… kay…" she drew out the word as she dropped her arm so we could let a couple pass between us. "And that's bad?"

"No. But in this case, a car would have been cheaper. And you don't just send someone a car, do you?"

"A car? What kind of telescope is this?"

I shrugged. "One to remind me we're connected, that we have a past, that we once meant something to each other. It's another way for him to manipulate me, like he did for me to come here. But all I remember is him leaving me on the doorstep with a broken heart that took years to mend."

She put her arm round me again and squeezed. "But you've been spending time together. Has that helped?"

I sighed even deeper. "Yeah, it's been good, it's helped. But we're spending time together because he somehow convinced Jesus Rodriguez – who thinks I'm a waste of time, by the way – that he alone should be helping me."

Beulah chuckled quietly. "The boy's tenacious, I'll give him that."

"Right! And I can't think around him or have time to think about what I want, because he's always there telling me what I want! Telling me we're supposed to be together. Telling me I belong to him. In reality I don't know him well enough, not anymore."

We both sipped our coffees and walked in silence for a dozen paces before Beulah broke it. "That's hard. I met Rafe, my fiancé, at college, and we hated each other. It took me a long time to realize that I didn't really hate him, and that we were supposed to be together. Perhaps it took longer than it needed to because of our past."

"I've made peace with the fact I'm in New York because of him, and if I really want to admit it, I'm enjoying myself. Penn's been taking me seriously; he's so enthusiastic that it's hard not to love it. It might be too early to tell whether I'm making a difference, but the team has won the last five away games."

I met Beulah's raised palm for a high-five.

"You're doing an awesome job."

I smiled, thinking that perhaps I might succeed in this made-up role after all. "Thanks, but it doesn't change the fact that I thought I was going to work on my newly resurfaced broken heart by myself, and the guy that broke it in the first place is here. It's hard and confusing. And overwhelming," I added, after a beat.

"Yeah, and I can't imagine Jupiter's helping with that."

I threw my hands in the air too enthusiastically and my coffee sloshed out, thankfully missing my clothes. "Exactly! He thinks he can click his fingers and everything is forgotten and forgiven. That he can send me boxes of LifeSavers, or bring me coffee, or have a seventy-five thousand dollar telescope delivered to me, and it's all okay."

I turned as she gasped. "Seventy-five grand?"

I nodded deep. "Yep. But you know what the real kicker is? He won't apologize. He says he's not sorry for bringing me here."

"Oh, Marnie." She stopped walking suddenly, and I turned to see her standing a step behind me. "You know what?! We need a girls' night. You need a little fun. You just got divorced. Forget about Jupiter for the moment, and do what you want to do."

Yes! Do what I want to do… which should be so simple. It sounds so simple, but when your head's a mess and you've been consumed by one person since the day you met him, it's hard to separate it out.

To know exactly what you want. I didn't have time to think about it then either.

"We're here! Let's sweat it out."

I peered up at the non-descript brick building. In fact, on closer inspection, it wasn't nondescript, and discounting the neon flashing four leaf clover which read O'Malley's Boxing Gym, it looked like a building site.

"Here?"

"Yep." She held the door open and I peered in. It was filled with heaving, sweaty bodies. I counted eight boxing rings, each with two people sparring. Along the brick wall on the far side stretched twenty punching bags, evenly spaced and hanging from the ceiling. "This place is supposed to be the best. Classic, old-school boxing."

It really didn't look like the sort of polished, elite gym I'd have expected Beulah to frequent. I could already smell the sweat, and… was that blood?

"I understand why you didn't want to come by yourself."

"Ladies, you gonna stand there or you gonna wrap up?"

I startled and my eyes shot up to find an older man who could only be described as a retired boxer with a partially toothless smile, and a nose that looked like it was missing all its cartilage, waiting expectantly for an answer behind a counter.

"This is awesome," Beulah whispered, then walked over and handed him forty dollars. "Two for the eleven a.m. class please."

He looked slightly amused. "Have you boxed before?"

I shook my head, as Beulah said, "Not for a long time."

"Okay." He placed two sets of gloves and four bandage rolls on the desk. "Drop your bags in the lockers. Barney will show you how to wrap, and then go warm up on the wall."

He pointed to a tall guy facing a small group of people. He was wearing a tank top and a pair of long shorts, showing off a well sculpted body. My brow furrowed; it was clear he was in good shape, impressive even. But that's where the appreciation stopped. My heart rate didn't rise, butterflies didn't flap their wings. His perfectly chiseled body did nothing for me, nor his clean shaven jaw and smooth cheeks.

It was beyond irritating. I should be feeling all of those things, all the throbbing and heart racing and… I was so zoned into trying to get my pulse to rise at the guy's very tight ass – the way it did with Jupiter's – that I didn't notice him turn around.

"If it isn't Ms. I-don't-know-how-to-order-coffee."

I tried to cover my embarrassment with a shock of loud laughter. "I can order it just fine."

"That's still up for debate," he grinned, while Beulah nudged me. "You need help with those?"

I held up the bandages. "Yes please, we both do."

"I'm good," Beulah the traitor, replied. "I can remember how to do them."

Barney took mine, unraveling one until it pooled on the floor, then took hold of my hand. Slowly, he wrapped my wrist and fingers; he was so close I didn't know where to look, especially as I knew he was staring at me.

"You work here?" I spluttered as he began on my other hand. "How did you get here before us?"

I tried not to frown as he winked.

"I know a shortcut. And yes, though only on Saturdays. I'm third year at Columbia, but I've been coming since I was a freshman. John lets me train for free in exchange," he nodded toward the guy at the desk.

"Oh, cool." I stepped closer to Beulah, who seemed to be trying to leave me alone.

Barney picked my gloves off the floor and eased them over my wrapped hands. "There you go."

"Thank you." I smiled as the trainer in the closest ring hollered. "Buddy up!"

Barney leaned in closer, a smirk on his face. "I'd say let's be buddies, but I need someone tough enough to handle a proper drink."

"You're assuming you'd have had the option," I shot back. The way he was looking at me had me squirming with unease. "I've already got a buddy, thanks."

Beulah was grinning as she lifted up the rope and we stepped into the ring to join everyone else.

"Shut up," I hissed, which made the grinning worse.

"Okay, class! Let's get warm."

A sweaty hour later and every single muscle I had, plus many I didn't realize I had, were screaming in pain as I guzzled down a bottle of water. It felt incredible.

I felt alive and invincible, like I could do anything.

An equally sweaty Beulah threw her empty bottle in the trash. "Now I need to pee. Give me five minutes."

"You looked good out there, a natural right hook. I'll remember that."

I spun round to find Barney standing behind me.

"Thank you," I chuckled. It was hard not to smile at this guy. There was a certain charm in spending an hour with someone and sweating until you're borderline dehydrated.

"So I was thinking I should probably teach you what proper coffee is like. What do you say? Maybe next Saturday?"

Not that much charm though… nervous knots began tightening in my belly. "Oh… Um…"

"What's going on?" Beulah asked, returning to my side.

He turned to Beulah. "I'm just asking Marnie here, if she'd like to meet me for coffee next week. You know, on a date."

"Oh, really? That's interesting." She looked between us, at my face, and the fresh sweat droplets rolling down my cheek. "Marn, can I talk to you a second?"

I didn't get the chance to object before she pulled me to one side. "This is the fun you should be having."

"What?"

"Fun." She stared, daring me to argue. "Go on the date and have some. He's cute."

"He's too young," was the first argument I could think of.

"So?"

"What about Jupiter?" was my second.

"What about him? You don't owe him an explanation," she shot back, and I knew she'd have an argument for every point I raised.

I looked to the floor, shuffling a piece of dirt with the tip of my sneaker, while I tried to think of some more reasons to say no, beyond me not wanting to go out with him, because Beulah did have a point, kind of. I owed Jupiter nothing. Yet why did the thought of going out with this guy cause little balls – balls that felt a lot like guilt – bounce between my ribs like it was a pinball machine.

"Look, you're not going to marry him, his name is Barney. So I say give him your number and have some fun."

My eyes flicked up, confusion plain on my face. "What's that got to do with anything?"

"You can't be Marnie and Barney." She threw her head back and laughed loudly. I cracked a smile.

"I guess it was nice to be asked politely, and not ordered with the assumption I'll follow through," I conceded, looking over to where Barney was in conversation with one of the other trainers. "I guess he's kind of cute."

"Exactly. You never know, it might help you realize what you actually want – or who you want," she added, pulling me back to where Barney was now unpeeling his wraps.

He glanced at me eagerly. "So, whaddaya say? Might I have the honor of taking you on a date?"

"He's asked nicely," Beulah whispered with a nudge.

It was like I was on top of the highest rollercoaster, right at the pause – the exact moment when you desperately wanted to get off but couldn't because the car was going to plummet any second.

And I did what I would have done if I had been on the rollercoaster. I ignored the brewing of unease in my belly, and instead focused on Beulah's words. I did need fun. I did need to get my head out of the Jupiter fog, "Sure, sounds good."

The smile he gave me – genuine, warm, happy – alleviated a little of the guilt. I punched my number into his cell.

"It was a pleasure to meet you, Marnie coffee drinker." He threw his water bottle into the trash to join the rest. "Count on me calling you soon. Bye, Marnie's friend."

Beulah rolled her lips, waving as he walked away.

"Nice work, Marn." She pushed me gently with her shoulder. "He is seriously cute. Look at his butt."

My head dropped in my hands; I didn't want to look at his butt. I wanted to take my number back. "Shit. What have I done? I shouldn't have done that. Jupiter is going to be so mad."

"You don't have to tell him!" She frowned before her eyes flared. "Though I bet he's hot all riled up anyway."

"Oh, God…" I couldn't stop the onslaught of throbbing; I'd never seen him properly mad, and wasn't sure I wanted to. Not now he was all mean and tattooed. "You're not helping."

She laughed. "Not trying to. Come on, let's get to the club. We can shower in the gym then go for lunch."

We waved goodbye to the instructor, and walked out past Columbia, cutting through to Riverside Park and along the Hudson. A couple of boats were already anchored up, ready to catch any balls which flew over the stadium boundaries, and the closer we got to the stadium, the thicker the crowds. I'd gotten used to seeing thousands of REEVES shirts, though Ace Watson was a close second.

I hadn't spent much time with The Lions' pitcher, only seen him in passing on occasion. But the fact he annoyed Jupiter so much did make me smile every time I thought of him… which then reminded me of what I'd done.

"When Barney texts me, I'm going to tell him I made a mistake. It was dumb. I shouldn't be dating anyone until I've sorted my head out. Jupiter and I should be friends," I blurted. "That's the best idea for now."

Beulah looked at me, offering me an "Okay," in response. "Whatever you want to do, we'll be here to support you. Just make sure you're happy."

We flashed our badges at security as we passed through the stadium doors.

"I just need to grab some clean clothes from my office, I forgot to pack them. I'll meet you in the locker room."

"Okay, see you in a second."

I took off in the opposite direction, running down the stairs and along the corridor.

"Star! Wait up!"

I spun around just as I reached my office; Jupiter was jogging toward me. It wouldn't be possible for him to get more stunning every time I saw him, and yet he did. Or maybe I just forgot how utterly beautiful he really was, because for a split second, he stole my breath.

Every time.

"Hey," I smiled as he reached me.

As always, the scent of him engulfed me; overpowered me like the rest of him.

"Hey, how are you?"

"I'm good, you?"

"Sleep well? Dream of me?" he winked.

I held in the sigh, just hitched my backpack further onto my shoulder. "I was going to message you this morning, but then thought I'd see you anyway. The telescope… thank you, it's incredible. I'm so grateful. But… Jupiter, it's too much. I can't keep it."

He blinked, confused. "Don't be ridiculous. Of course, you can."

I ignored the dismissive shoot down. "I don't even know how you managed to get hold of it."

"I have my ways," he grinned.

"Jupiter…"

"Marn, the telescope is yours. I'm not arguing." He leaned against the wall, his biceps rippling from the movement, making it seem like the stars really were twinkling across the planes of his muscles. I wanted to touch them; I itched to touch them. Every time I saw him and he was dressed like he was heading to the gym I had to keep my fists clenched to stop me from reaching out, especially when he crossed his arms over his chest. "Tell me what you've been doing this morning. Worked hard by the looks of it."

Flames licked along my skin as his gaze thoroughly traveled the length of my body. Not an inch of me was left overlooked by him.

"Actually, I went boxing," I relented.

"Yeah?" he reached over and squeezed my bicep. "Check out those guns."

I glanced down at where he was still stroking my arm, his thumb slowly moving back and forth hypnotically. "Yeah. I just had to picture your face." I teased.

His thumb stopped moving and his lips rolled as he tried to hold back a smile. "Touché."

I twisted slightly, relieving myself from his hands. I couldn't concentrate when he was touching me.

His playful tone dropped. "Come on, Marn, when are you going to forgive me?"

"It's not about forgiving you; too much has happened between us, I need time, but…" I looked up hesitantly, "I think we could be friends… if that's okay."

From the way his eyes darkened, I hastened a guess that it wasn't. "Friends?"

I plastered on my best smile and nodded.

"We were best friends, Marn. We were more than best friends."

"*Were,* Jupiter." I sighed, not wanting this conversation when I was stinking of boxing, and desperate for a shower. "We *were.* We've lived half a lifetime since then. So much has happened. I got married…" I added, quietly.

His eyes bulged wider than I'd ever seen them, hot with a rage that had me stepping back, "What? You're fucking married?"

"No, I'm divorced. I got divorced when I realized…"

I stopped talking.

Jupiter stopped moving, his brow furrowing deep. "Realized what?"

I took a beat. This wasn't the time or place to tell him. I didn't want him to know in the midst of a somewhat heated conversation. "It doesn't matter."

His face dropped closer, nearer to my height. He wanted to see the look in my eyes, because he knew exactly why I'd divorced my ex-husband.

Exactly what I'd realized in the D.C. elevator.

I'd always been a shit liar, and he could read me better than any book.

"Is that why it took you six months to get here after Shepherd offered you the job?" He searched my face, but I wouldn't look up from the J.R. initials embroidered above The Lions logo on his t-shirt. But he'd always been able to read me, and that was his answer. His tongue clicked in confirmation. "And you still won't admit we're meant to be together? That it's always been that way?"

I took another step back, needing air again, because my brain was on the verge of frying. "It doesn't matter what I think. Friends is all I can offer you right now."

He said nothing, just stood there shaking his head with a piercing glare as his jaw worked back and forth.

Suddenly all his rage transferred to me and flooded my blood. "You haven't even apologized! You said you weren't going to. You expect me to forgive you for something you're not even sorry for!"

"I said I'm not going to apologize for bringing us back together."

I stepped back, throwing my hands in the air. "Of course. How dumb of me to forget. You just snap your fingers and everyone trips over themselves to do your bidding. You've just assumed that because I'm in New York that we're going to be together. It doesn't work like that."

"Marnie…"

But I was on a roll, and had no room for interruptions. "You know, I was asked out today. He asked me if I would do him the honor of letting him taking me on a date."

Jupiter face screwed up, then he scoffed hard, which set my teeth on edge. He was laughing until he saw the look on my face. "Seriously?"

"Yes, seriously. And I'm not quite clear on why you're finding it so funny," I spat.

"Because…" his jaw tensed while he searched for a reason.

"Yes?"

He pointed at himself. "Me, for a start."

I crossed my arms over my chest, and narrowed my eyes. "You?"

"Yes, me. And you. You and me."

"Jupiter, there is no you and me. There's you, who brought me to New York, and me who is trying to figure my life out. And this," I flicked my hand back and forth, "this isn't helping. You aren't helping. You can't just say that we're together because you decreed it."

He blinked slowly, then stared as he realized what I was saying, "Hang on, have you said yes to this chump?"

"He's not a chump!"

When Beulah said Jupiter would get riled up, she had no idea. The vein on his neck bulged, his eyes narrowed, then his voice dropped to an eerie calm. "Have you?"

I couldn't move back any further, I was already pressed hard against the wall. "No, but even if I had, you have no say in the matter. I'm free to date whomever I want."

One big hand pressed to the wall above me. "And what's this guy got that I haven't?"

I swallowed thickly, determined to hold my ground and prayed he didn't get any closer. "Manners. He asked me if I would like to go for coffee. He didn't manipulate me into moving two thousand miles, he didn't break into my hotel room wearing only pajama pants, he doesn't make jokes about me wanting his body." I dropped my head and whispered, "And he hasn't already broken my heart."

He moved away, his fingers running through his hair just like I used to do for him. I could see a hefty dose of hurt framing his eyes as they roamed my face, and I wanted to feel remorse – but I didn't. It was nothing compared to the hurt he'd caused me. I waited. I thought he might leave, but I was wrong.

He crossed his arms over his chest, just like me. Except when he did it, his tattoos stretched out as his muscles flexed, and he looked like he'd belonged in a biker gang. He looked like the menacing guy on the posters around the city, and I was doing an excellent job at not crumbling under his intimidation tactics.

He spoke, finally. "Okay, Star, I'll play along."

My eyes shot up to catch his glinting.

"You'll play along?" I spat.

"It's cute that you think you'll find someone better than me, but sure… you need to get something out of your system, go for it. Go on a date with this guy, try and prove me wrong." He failed to notice that the tick under my eye was going double time as my jaw clenched. "But tell me this… is there anyone else?

"Anyone else?" I breathed out, trying to stay as calm as possible, but inside I was burning red-hot. My throat was thickening with scalding tears I didn't want to give him the satisfaction of seeing. Tears he didn't deserve.

His head tilted. "Yes. Is it just this coffee douche? Or are there others?"

"No, there aren't others!"

What did he think I was doing? Lining people up around the city?

"Good." He nodded slowly, casually, though he was anything but, "Just checking if there are any more barriers in my way that I need to deal with. But make no mistake, I am getting you back."

"You are so fucking arrogant! You're an ass. An actual ass!"

His grin was only missing a cutlass and a gold tooth. "You always said you loved my ass."

"You know what? I take it back. And I take my offer of friendship back too," I choked, but it was too late to stop him from witnessing the tears. I pushed open the door to my office and slammed it behind me as they poured hot and angry down my cheeks.

I hit the lock, not wanting him to follow me.

Drawing the back of my hand across my sniveling nose, I snatched up my phone. If Jupiter Reeves wanted me to go on a date, then that's exactly what I was going to do. Just as I realized I didn't take Barney's number, my cell buzzed.

Barney: When are we taking you for your first lesson in proper coffee?

Marnie: As soon as possible.

I hit send, and sobbed harder.

Maybe I could sob some sense into myself… or at least until I figured out what I was doing.

11

Jupiter

Present Day

"FUCK!"

I hurled my glove so hard that it dented my locker. It was right next to the dent I'd made with a ball yesterday.

At this rate I'd be paying out for another door.

At this rate I should just hand my Amex over to the club.

I sat down and kicked off my sneakers. There was a clang as they hit the back of the locker.

I slumped back, raking my fingers through my hair.

What a fucking mess.

I was off. Everything was off.

I'd just finished running drills, and I could've done fifty

more. I hadn't missed one ball at base practice; I'd caught everything.

And I couldn't give less of a shit.

I didn't bother looking up from my hands when the locker room doors swung open. Noise levels went up from silent to fucking annoying. Lux Weston was complaining about his hamstring; Parker King was pissing himself laughing at something Ace was showing him on his cell, and Stone was… on his way over to where I was sitting.

With any luck he hadn't heard my tantrum, because I couldn't be fucked to have a conversation about it. But from the way I'd stormed off the field the second we were done, he knew something was up.

Luck wasn't on my side.

"Okay, Reeves, spill it. What's up your ass?"

I pulled my shirt over my head. "Nothing."

"No, that's a fucking lie. Three days ago you were a moody bastard, but now you look like you wanted to rip Coach's head off because he called time. It was like you were on a suicide mission with those drills."

"They're called suicides for a reason," I snapped.

"I didn't see anyone else taking it literally," Stone snapped back, sucking down a Gatorade between breaths. "So I'm asking again, what is up?"

"Fucking nothing!"

"Okay…" he pressed on, "then I'm asking this. That was a phenomenal practice. We've won eight games in a row. Everyone's talking about us. Jones and Simpson are still with reporters discussing the early season success. I'm telling you, you should be buzzing, and you aren't." He was quiet for a whole ten seconds, though even if Locker Room One didn't now resemble a tail gate party, my brain was too busy for any peace. "Reeves!"

"What?"

"I asked you a question."

My teeth ground together. "Actually, you didn't."

I kind of enjoyed the way his nostrils flared. I wondered how long it would take to snap his endless patience. The moodiest I'd ever seen him was when he told that story about his girlfriend shopping, or not shopping… whatever it was, but maybe if I riled him enough he'd join me under my black cloud.

Misery loves company after all.

"Okay, why aren't you buzzing?"

Ah, there it was; the million dollar question. Why wasn't I buzzing?

Probably because I hadn't slept.

Probably because the jealously raging through my blood was stopping me from being able to do anything else.

I didn't look at him as he sat on the bench opposite me. One thing I'd learned about Stone was that he'd wait and wait, and wait some goddamn more until I talked. It was fucking annoying.

Not as annoying as the next person who spoke, but still annoying.

"Is this to do with Science – I mean Doctor Matthews?"

My eyes shot up to where Ace was standing in front of his locker, which reminded me that I needed to talk to whoever was in charge of lockers to have his moved far away from mine. "What's that supposed to mean?"

He shrugged, pulled off his shoulder support, and stripped off. "She's got a date today, right?"

I was in front of him so quickly he didn't have time to

blink.

"What? What the fuck do you know about her dating?"

"Dude! Easy!" He took a dramatic step back. "You're practically touching my dick!"

My head snapped round to where Stone was watching in amusement, though he was the only one, and translated my expression like an expert.

"Watson, answer the question."

Ace grabbed a towel from the cubbies so slowly it was like he didn't realize my brain was about to short circuit. Or maybe he did and wanted to annoy the fuck out of me. In which case, mission accomplished. "I came in early. I was getting coffee, and she was in the dining room with Shepherd's fiancée and the hot chick from legal."

"Ace, man, you gotta stop calling them chicks. They're on the exec board, dude." Stone got up then parked himself in front of Ace and me, like a fucking umpire.

I snapped my fingers to get Ace's attention back on the topic in hand. "And?"

He focused on me, though he was still clearly confused about whatever Stone has chastised him for. "And they were talking about a date. I listened long enough to figure out it was your…" he looked to Stone then back at me, "lady friend?"

Stone rolled his eyes, but nodded.

"What else?"

"Um," his brow furrowed, "only that it's today at Riverside Park. She wanted a lunchtime date so that she could keep it on a time limit. Being honest with you, man, it didn't sound like she wanted to go, but you've clearly fucked up enough that you got your lady dating someone else. What did you do?"

He grinned like only a twenty-two year old who stuck exclusively to one night stands could. My fist clenched.

"Reeves, sit down there." Stone pointed to a spare bench. "Watson, you can get in the shower."

Another loud chatter erupted as a couple of other guys walked in. Stone nodded to them then came and sat by me.

And fucking waited.

I groaned. "I think I fucked up, man. I know I did. Big time."

"Okay, what did you do?"

I looked up at him, his eyes filled with concern.

"I think I've been pushing too hard."

He sat forward, his mouth set in a hard line, though the edges were twitching, like yeah, he could've told me that for free.

"We've been spending time together for her program, and it was starting to feel like when we were kids again..." I raked my fingers through my hair, pulling hard on the ends. "Fuck. I've waited so long for this, and now she's here and my chest feels as though it's going to cave in from wanting her. I didn't even realize how badly, and then she asks me if we can be friends."

Fucking friends.

"And that's not all." I rubbed my chest; I swear I could feel every single crack. "She got married."

"Oh shit! She's married? Sorry, dude, that's fucking rough."

"Yeah," I dropped my head. "I'm certain that's why it took six months for her to come here. She was getting divorced."

"Oh," Stone's shoulders dropped anti-climatically, and he let out a loud tut. "So she's single?"

I pulled on the ends of my hair, again. "I can't believe she got married."

"Um, dude, you've slept with hundreds of women."

"I didn't want to marry any of them. I didn't pledge my undying love to someone else."

"Sounds like it did die though. She got divorced." His eyebrows rose, daring me to disagree. "Do you know why?"

Out of the corner of my eye, I could see Boomer Jones making his way toward his locker which was next to mine, but he took one look at me and turned around.

"Why she got divorced?"

"Yes."

As I shook my head no, the look on her face flashed into my memory again as it had done a hundred times since; the look she'd had after I'd asked her why she'd divorced. I knew from the way she couldn't meet my eyes that it was something to do with me, and it was the only thing keeping me within the realm of sanity, keeping me from smashing all the lockers, and knocking down all the doors.

"Reeves, you're losing me. What's this got to do with her date? How'd that happen?"

"She told me she'd been hit on, and I laughed. She got mad. And now according to the club gossip, she's going on the fucking date."

Stone winced, and I felt it right in the chest.

"She hasn't spoken to me since, and she won't see me. Three days… she's been ignoring me for three days! I went to her office and she refused to let me in. She just sat on her stool and stuck her earbuds in so she couldn't hear me knocking." I dropped my head, because what really bothered me was this… "And she hasn't been sitting in her usual spot at the games. I didn't realize how much I needed her there, but our last three games she was somewhere else."

It wasn't just about how much I needed to see her; it was the way her eyes always met mine from under the peak of her ball cap, making me feel like I was the only man on the field. It was the way she was the last person I saw after running round the bases, and stepping into the dugout. It coated me like a protective salve.

But without her, I'd been open to the elements. Vulnerable to attack.

I'd missed an easy catch last night; it was only a matter of time before it started to affect my game.

Huh, started. Who was I kidding? She'd always affected my game.

Stone stayed silent, then turned toward the showers, yelling, "WATSON!"

Either Ace didn't hear or chose to ignore him. Either way, Stone, wasn't waiting for an answer and got up.

I huffed out a huge sigh. What a total fucking clusterfuck I'd made of everything. The girl I loved was on a date with another dude.

Because I'd told her to go.

I launched my shorts into the laundry just as Stone returned.

"Put your clothes back on," he said, before adding, "you've got two hours before we have stretching."

"Two hours for what?"

"To find her. She should be in the park. He said she's using her lunchbreak. Go and find her, break up the date, fix whatever you fucked up. It doesn't matter, just be back in two hours."

I stared at him, not quite understanding until Stone opened my locker, grabbed a clean pair of shorts and a shirt, and threw them at me.

"Reeves, go."

I yanked them on as quickly as I could before I had any time to think about whether this was even stupider, whether it would only make things worse. Fishing around for my earbuds, I stuck them in and pulled on my ball cap. My sprint to Riverside Park began the second I left the locker room.

It took me ten minutes of running along the river to reach one of the side entrances and a fork in the path, which is when it occurred to me that a) I was recognizable, and b) Riverside Park was fucking massive, and I had no idea where she was.

I stopped. Fuck. Fuck.

Left. When in doubt, go left.

Left it was.

I took off again. She can't have gone too far because Marnie was nothing if not a stickler for punctuality. She wasn't ever going to take longer than an hour if she was using her lunch break; my girl was a rule follower.

Maybe because it was mid-week, maybe because it had rained the day before and the ground was damp, or because the air was still a little cooler than usual, but the park wasn't as busy as I was expecting it to be.

If it had been a little busier, I might have missed her.

It was only when a kid screeched and bolted up the path followed by a frantic mother that I finally spotted her.

I stopped dead and ducked behind the nearest tree. The heavy pounding of my heart had nothing to do with the sprint I'd taken to get here.

I dropped down and fiddled with my shoelace, pulling my cap down lower as a large group of schoolgirls passed by. Thank fuck my shirt was long sleeved; I didn't need to be outed while spying on my ex-girlfriend.

In fact, if no one ever found out about what I was doing, the better.

I waited until the girls passed, and got back to my feet. It was now or never.

I peered around slowly and watched; her hair was up, her glasses were on – not even resting on her head. They were on her nose.

My heart leapt, actually fucking leapt, and it was possible you'd have seen my grin from space.

Marnie Matthews might have gone on this fucking date, but she definitely didn't want to be there. Ace had been right.

I couldn't see Coffee Douche. I could only see her face and her smile, or rather fake smile, which told me everything I needed, and I almost felt stupid for panicking about it.

Even the past few weeks on the brief occasions I'd made her laugh, her eyes had lit up like the Fourth of July, and for the briefest second she'd look at me like she used to look at me; until she went back to the ever-present scowl. Even the scowl was growing on me.

But this moron couldn't even make the little creases fan out from the corners.

Yeah, I knew when Marnie was interested, and it was definitely not the expression she was wearing right now.

Coffee Douche had his back to me, and from what I could tell, he was pretty average. Average size, average brown hair, average shirt. Average and nondescript, which was probably why she looked so bored.

If I needed further confirmation, it came when she began chewing on her cheek as she nodded wide-eyed. I learned a long time ago that was how she forced herself to concentrate when she was struggling. She was a second away from yawning.

I turned and leaned against the trunk with a broad smile while I wondered what he was trying to impress her with.

He'd learn soon enough; it took a lot to impress Marnie Matthews.

After a quick chuckle to myself, I remembered the reason I was here in the first place.

Fuck.

This was all my fault.

What was I doing?

She was on this date because I'd forced her on it. I thought back to what she'd said about us not being an us, how I hadn't apologized… how I'd broken her heart.

I thought I'd just needed to remind her of what we had been, but I'd underestimated her stubbornness.

I hadn't taken her seriously enough, and I'd been handling this all wrong.

She'd asked for space, and I hadn't listened. I needed to let her come to me, and as much as I didn't want to, I needed to leave her here.

If friendship was all she wanted right now, I was going to snatch that shit up and be the best friend she'd ever had. Again.

We were meant to be, I knew it as well as I knew myself, so I could wait for forever to begin until she was ready.

I checked the time; I had to get back to the club before I got called out for missing our stretching session.

I stole one last glance at her, just in time to see her jump out of his reach. I couldn't hold in the bark of laughter, and if I didn't want to break his fingers for trying to touch her, I'd have almost felt sorry for the guy. Almost, because he'd done the classic 'oh, you've got something in your hair' move. It was the sort of shit Ace would definitely attempt, right before the follow-up lean-in kiss.

Douche.

He could try if he wanted a broken face.

I peered back around the tree to find her staring directly at the trunk, and jerked back immediately.

Double fuck.

I'd been louder than I thought, and there was no way I could move until she looked away.

For no reason, other than it felt like I was now playing hide 'n' seek with my niece, I held my breath and tried to shrink into the tree. At least I only exercised in exclusively dark colors, so was currently camouflaged.

I didn't work.

When I peered round a second later, Marnie Matthews was standing right next to me, arms crossed over her chest, doing her best impression of snarling dog.

"Hey, Marn, what's up?" I tried to play it off as cool as possible, and not like I'd been caught creeping.

She bought none of it, and we both knew I was busted.

"Are you following me?" she hissed.

"No," I shook my head, because technically, *technically* I hadn't. She'd already been here and I'd found her. "I happened to be jogging and I saw you."

Both hands went to her hips. "Doesn't look like you're jogging. How long have you been standing behind this tree?"

"Um…" I looked at my watch again.

"How long?" she gritted out.

"Twenty minutes."

"Twenty… Jupiter! Jesus," she spat, her eyes narrowed. "You should be at practice."

I held my mouth into a straight line, trying really hard not to smile, but my insides were skipping. "Do you know my schedule, Marn?"

Her jaw popped. It looked less threatening when the soft breeze blew the hair off her face like she was in an eighties music video, but I knew she was pissed.

I wasn't about to make it worse. I'd done enough of that lately.

My shoulders sagged in defeat. No more jokes. No more trying to make her laugh. Just me.

"Marn, I'm so sorry. I didn't mean to disturb you. I wanted to leave before you saw me, I promise."

I peered around her to see Coffee Douche was staring at us, and from the way he was staring and craning his neck, he knew exactly who Marnie was talking to. Me.

That gave me less than a minute before he made his way over.

Always under a time constraint when I had something important to say; then again, I would never have enough time.

I wanted all the time with her.

I pulled her out of sight, hiding her behind the wide trunk. Except for the brief second when I'd found her on the floor of her hotel room, this was the closest I'd been to her. I held my breath, expecting her to push me away.

Instead, her pulse ratcheted up. Her eyes flashed as she searched my face; big, and wide, and pleading. Those eyes were all I'd seen for the past three days, and when she dropped them it felt like I was witnessing an eclipse.

I softly tipped up her chin so she could see me, see for real how sorry I was. How desperately I wanted to fix my fuck up.

"He asked me, Jupe. That's all," she whispered.

My heart thumped. I took a step in, stealing the rest of the air between us as I caged my body around hers. "You haven't called me Jupe since we were kids."

Careful not to scratch her with my callused fingers, I used my knuckle to stroke along her jaw. Her skin was still as soft as I remembered, and my dick showed no care for how inappropriate it was to have a boner in the middle of a park on a Wednesday afternoon.

Her breath was kicking in bursts when I brushed my thumb along her lower lip, tugging on it ever-so-slightly. Every cell in my body wanted to capture it between my own, especially when she glanced up at me, green eyes flashing like night flares.

Now, *now* she was looking at me like she used to look at me.

I swallowed hard, trying to ignore my dick twitching and focus on the task at hand. I was so close I was breathing the air she expelled.

"I'll ask you, Star. I'll ask you whatever you want. I'll give you whatever you want, but right now…" I moved my thumb and replaced it with my lips; the softest graze, the most gentle of presses – but only a taste; not even the briefest slip of my tongue against hers. She so was addictive, once I got started I'd never stop, especially when she began quivering. "I'm sorry. I'm so fucking sorry for hurting you. This week, when we were kids… every single time."

"Jupe... seeing you again…" Her eyes filled with tears, and my stomach plunged. "I'm trying my best."

Every one of my muscles tensed. What had I done to her?

And I didn't just mean this week.

I wiped away the spillage. "Don't cry, Marn, please. It fucking kills me. Don't cry. We can be friends. Whatever you want, we can be. I'm so fucking sorry I was such a dick. Now, then. In the future."

For some reason that made her cry harder, so I cupped both sides of her cheeks.

"It's okay. I promise, it's okay. Do what you need to do. I'll give you the space, and I'll be waiting when you're ready. However long it takes." Her trembling jaw punched me right in the gut. "Just don't ask me to stop believing in us. I can't do that."

She sniffed so I took the sleeve of my jersey and gently wiped her runny nose, just as a loud throat clearing told me my time was up.

"Everything okay here?" Coffee Douche asked.

I tore my eyes away from Marnie. Jesus, no wonder he was behaving like Ace. He looked about the same age, and way out of Marnie's league.

Fuck, even I was out of her league.

"Everything's fine."

He didn't fool me with the fake gasp. In fact, I'd have had more respect for him if he'd come straight out and admitted that was why he'd interrupted in the first place.

"Shit, you're Jupiter Reeves. Holy Shit!" He bounced around like his brain was about to explode. "Can I get a selfie?"

And this was where my reputation for being an asshole came in handy. I peered at Marnie, my eyebrow raised, but she looked at her feet to hide her tears. She had yet to experience the Jupiter known to the public, though she'd definitely seen me being an asshole.

"Nope."

"Dude, come on, it'll just take a second," he whined, holding his phone up. "I gotta show my friends. They'll never believe it..."

"Move that any closer to me and I'll break it," I snarled, my eyes still trained on Marnie.

He recoiled, muttering "dick" and something about The Dodgers under his breath, but he now had a story for his friends – he'd called the great Jupiter Reeves a dick.

Unfortunately, he didn't leave us in peace like I was hoping. I guessed that was my cue, and Marnie now had some explaining to do.

Ignoring him, I leaned over and kissed her damp cheek, low enough to also catch the corner of her mouth. "See you later, Star. You know where to find me when you're ready."

She blushed, slowly biting her lip as her fingers ran back and forth over them. Forcing myself to look away took every fiber of self-control I had.

"Make sure you keep your hands off my friend," I growled at Coffee Douche.

Throwing a wink to Marnie, I sprinted back to the club, newly energized and much happier than I'd been when I left.

Threatening people really put a pep in my step.

12

Marnie

Fourteen years ago - March

“You know, by the time you’re done at M.I.T., I’ll be in the starting nine for The Dodgers, on my way to being the best third baseman ever. Tell me about what you’re going to study again.”

Jupiter cast aside the book on the solar system and smirked at me in the lopsided way that made me feel like I was sitting on a firework; crackling hot, and ready to explode. “I already told you a million times.”

“I know,” he leaned up and kissed my nose, “but I like hearing you talk about it. It makes me feel smarter just by hearing you being smart. You never know, maybe I’ll get to N.A.S.A. too, if baseball doesn’t work out.”

His smile widened when I giggled; it wrapped around my heart and squeezed. I couldn't imagine a day I'd ever get enough of it. There'd been more than a handful of mornings over the past two months where I'd woken up and convinced myself I was still dreaming.

"Okay…" I put down my book on astrophysics, and propped myself back on my elbows.

We were on the plinth; we'd taken to coming every lunch-break or free period we could, and because it was a slightly dirty, cold wooden platform, I'd taken to packing blankets in my backpack to make it cozier.

Jupiter was lying by my side; I stretched out my legs next to his, and even though I was slightly higher up on the blanket, my feet still only reached halfway up his legs, especially when he scooped them up and shifted one of his big thighs underneath.

I hoped I'd I never get used to the sensation of his skin against mine, especially when his fingers stroked up and down my calves, setting off a delicious squirming in my belly. I'd thought they were magic fingers after I'd discovered what they could do, but then I learned what his tongue was capable of.

I didn't know it could get better… I was wrong.

Every touch supercharged my skin, slowly driving me crazy as my body bent to his will. I wasn't even sure my body belonged to me anymore from the way it reacted whenever it was within a hundred yards of him, because since the first time we came up here – every time we were up here – he showed me exactly how he owned me.

I wanted his hands everywhere.

I wanted to feel him everywhere.

Jupiter Reeves had taken residence in my head – which

turned to mush – and my heart – which flip-flopped – every time I saw him.

And it was only getting more pronounced.

Is this what falling in love feels like?

"Star, what are you staring at? Tell me what Boston will be like." His long boy lashes fluttered as he blinked at me, waiting. He was so beautiful, like a meteor shower bursting across the sky.

I opened my mouth to say something, but closed it instead.

"What's wrong?"

I sat up, reaching out to push my fingers through his thick hair. The spring sunshine had brought more of his freckles out, like the stars at an indigo twilight.

"Marnie, what? What's wrong?" His brow furrowed with concern, only relaxing slightly when I smiled.

"Nothing's wrong, Jupe. It's good, it's all good. I was just thinking how happy I am."

He inched up, his smile capturing mine while his hands scraped roughly through my hair, desperate to get to me. I tasted the Dr. Pepper he'd been drinking, or maybe it was the cherry LifeSavers he'd become addicted to; whatever it was, it tingled along my tongue as his tangled against mine.

I let out a soft moan and moved back; it was too hard to concentrate when he was touching me, and I needed to get this out properly.

I'd been thinking about it for weeks.

That look was back on his face, the one where he wasn't quite sure what I was thinking. I stroked down his cheek, biting down on my lip to distract me from the nervousness.

In the last two months he'd helped me study and I watched his games. We'd stolen kisses in the hallways as he rushed to practice and I ran to the library; he'd tried to teach me about baseball, and I'd tried to teach him about the solar system. We'd spent time with his friends, and on one rare occasion outside of the times we all rode to school together, Emerson, where she'd made me laugh with how much she made fun of him. He'd met Lena and Byron, though neither of them had known what to say to him.

And we were so similar; we were both working our asses off to live childhood dreams. Even if they weren't quite the same, our drive was. We understood what it was like.

A physics student and a baseball player.

Marnie the nerd, and Jupiter the most popular of jocks.

There was nothing about this situation that hadn't surprised me; especially how sweet and kind he was, how patient he'd been with me. Not once had he pressured me into doing anything I didn't want.

Now, I wanted everything.

"I saw my mom this morning. Her and my dad have gone away for the weekend."

He frowned. "Are you going too? I thought we were going to hang tonight."

I shook my head. "No, I'm home alone. Will has a party that I know he didn't tell my parents about; it's why my mom thought she could leave me. They think he'll be home."

He smiled again. "Okay, cool. We can watch a movie or something. Then I have my game tomorrow. You'll come, right?"

"Yes, of course I will." I softly touched my lips to his before taking a deep breath, "But there's something else I want to do instead of watch a movie…"

I held his gaze, waiting for him to catch exactly what I was saying without the embarrassment of having to say it. It took him twenty seconds of searching my face for the ball to drop, followed by his jaw.

"Marn, are you sure? Don't you want to wait until your birthday?" he blurted.

I shook my head slowly.

"You're sure? You're really sure? I'm happy waiting until you're ready. I'm good doing all the other stuff." The way he was tripping over his words made me swear he was almost nervous as me.

"I'm ready, Jupe."

He stared at me then stood up so quickly the plinth shook.

"Let's get back to school. I need to go to the drug store, and if I sprint to practice, there's still enough free period left." He dropped back down when he caught the surprise on my face. "If that's okay… we can stay here if you want."

I laughed. "No it's good. I need to get to the lab early anyway."

He pulled me to my feet, smacking a quick kiss to my lips, before gathering up my text books and the blanket. We took off at speed down the hill to the main campus, him nearly pulling my arm out of the socket while we ran.

"Ouch, Jupe!" I squealed with laughter, and a little pain, as we passed the hockey arena.

"Shit, sorry. Sorry." He roped me into a hug; his free arm wrapped around my waist, and kissed my hair with a chuckle. "I'll walk at a regular pace. Where's your next class?"

"We can go to the sports building; I need to collect a new timetable before I go to physics."

"Perfect. Lead the way, professor."

I rolled my eyes making him laugh, and that's how we walked across the campus. It was becoming the norm; and perhaps I'd gotten used to the staring, or maybe people weren't staring quite as much as they used to. That was only if I discounted the harem of identikit girls who followed him around like I didn't exist.

I'd also gotten used to the length of time it took to get places with Jupiter, because everyone had to say hello to him, high-five him, or comment on his latest game. But he kept my hand in his through all of it. He didn't seem to care, or notice, how long we were, as long as he was holding onto me.

I definitely didn't care.

We walked up the steps and flashed our badges at the entry way, Jupiter hauling me against the wall before I had a chance to head in the opposite direction.

"What are you doing?"

Jupiter curled my hair through his fingers. "Marn, if you change your mind between now and tonight, it's okay. We can always watch a movie."

I grazed the edge of his shirt; his breath catching as my fingertips brushed his solid abs. "I'm not going to change my mind."

"Fuck, you're killing me." His lips lingered on mine for as long as he dared before the hall monitor forced us to separate. "Then I'm going to make tonight as incredible as you are. I'll see you later, Stars and Stripes."

I didn't turn around after I took off down the hall; I needed to bury myself in work for the next five hours so there was no time for the nerves to set in.

I'd never thought about how I'd lose my virginity until

I met Jupiter. And since then, or since the time he asked me to be his girlfriend, I'd read twenty-four separate articles in Cosmo on their best sex tips, and binge watched three seasons of Gossip Girl on DVD, plus the compilations of Chuck and Blair sex scenes on YouTube.

I'd always been a good student, but neither Cosmo nor Gossip Girl had told me about the butterflies, about the desperate fluttering like they were to trying escape. They also didn't say anything about how you should spend your time waiting for your boyfriend to arrive.

I'd stood up, I'd sat down. I'd taken a bath, because apparently it would help me relax.

It didn't.

I was more nervous than when I'd sent in my M.I.T. application.

I hadn't been sure what to wear, so I stuck to my usual sleep shorts and tank top; but kept it plain. Tiny hearts and clouds wasn't exactly sexy and mature. I didn't need Cosmo to tell me that.

I was trying hard not to have a panic attack when a quiet rapping at the window had me spinning round to find the boy next door standing there with the cutest smile on his face.

My boy next door with the smile I loved.

And when I saw what he was wearing, I relaxed measurably. I even let out a little laughter – shorts and t-shirt; we'd both gotten the memo.

I eased up the window. He climbed in and stopped on the spot he landed. The air shifted immediately, becoming thicker, heavier, like a vacuum was being sealed around us.

"Hey, Star," he murmured, his dimple popping.

"Hey."

"You okay?"

I nodded, but my hands were twisting into knots.

"Marn..." Three large strides and I was in his arms. He smelled fresh from the shower; musky and sweet entwined together – just like him. He tipped my chin up so he could look at me. "We're not doing anything tonight that you're not comfortable with, okay? Say the word. I've got some movies in my bag..." he nodded over to where he'd dropped it on the floor.

"Oh yeah, what've you got?"

"The Hangover to start." He grinned sheepishly and pulled a face; because he was always trying to me laugh, make me comfortable, relaxed.

But I was. Entirely comfortable. I trusted him unconditionally.

And I wanted this more than anything.

"I'm fine; just... go easy on me. I don't have the same experience you do."

We'd never openly discussed it, but in the same way he knew I was a virgin, I knew he wasn't.

"Star..." with the way he slowly brushed his thumbs back and forth along my jaw, he may as well have been laced in Valium; I took a deep breath as his eyes searched my face. "Let's take it step by step, and then we don't have to think about it. Does it help if I tell you I'm just as nervous?"

There wasn't an ounce of a lie on his face, even if he was only saying it for my benefit, "You are?"

When his thumbs halted on my cheek, I could almost feel his hands shaking, "Yes, I want this to be perfect for you, and I've never had a night like this either. I showered three times because I couldn't stop sweating."

He stuck his tongue out to the side, pulling a silly face with the one goal of making me laugh. His head dipped, catching my giggle, and he kissed me long and slow. My body melted into him and I wondered if he could taste my toothpaste as he explored my mouth. It was warm and soft, like always, but he kept on, not letting me up for air because he knew exactly what he was doing; turning me into a puddle until I swear I could feel him seeping into my bones. It was the balm I needed for the last of my nerves.

He pulled back with a smile. "So you wanna show me the balcony?"

I tried to focus, but after that kiss it was like asking me to run a marathon. "You just walked through it."

"Yeah, but I think you should show it to me anyway." His lip curled up as he winked and walked to the window.

"Okay…" I followed his outstretched palm and held onto it to step up on the window bench, and through the window.

The balcony did not look like it had when I'd last seen it.

My earlier panic and the ringing in my ears was likely the answer to why I hadn't heard him out there setting it up, because there's no way he'd been able to do this in silence. Roped lights hung between the palm trees, crisscrossing the tiny space and fastened onto the wall. My blankets had been laid out, along with more, and a dozen cushions I didn't recognize. Electric tea lights flickered in the twilight, positioned in every corner and crevice he'd been able to find.

It was stunning. More than stunning. Perfect. And Jupiter had done it all for me, actually… I removed my hand from my mouth. "How did you do all this?"

He looked at his feet, and for the first time ever, I swear he blushed. "Emerson helped me."

"Emerson?"

"I didn't tell her anything, just that I wanted to surprise you to watch the stars. She passed me the cushions, and let me borrow all the lights."

"She won't tell your parents?"

He shook his head, with a grimace. "No, I paid for her silence by promising to take her and Mallory to surf camp every day during the holidays."

My hand went back to my mouth to hide a giggle. Emerson really must have worked him hard on that negotiation, and the fact he'd agreed meant more to me than the fact he'd done this in the first place.

His arms snaked around me from behind, his head on my shoulder. "It was worth it, I told you I wanted it to be special."

I circled in his hold, his face searching mine for approval, desperate to know he'd done the right thing, "It's perfect. So, so pretty, Jupe. I can't believe you did this for me."

"I'd do anything for you, Star." His fingers combed through the strands of my freshly washed hair, lifting the ends to his nose. "I love it when your hair is down. I love feeling it slide through my fingers."

My chest rose and fell; the longer he looked at me, the tighter it felt. I needed to breathe, and I needed to stop shaking. The balmy April night air was doing nothing for me.

"Are you cold?" He snatched up a blanket, and wrapped it around my shoulders.

"No, just adrenaline, I guess."

"You're so beautiful. Some days I have to pinch myself to believe you're really real." His head cocked to the side, "What's so funny?"

"Nothing. I was just thinking the exact same thing earlier."

"Oh, yeah? Does that make me as smart as you then?" he

bent and kissed my nose.

"You're way smarter."

"I am for finding you."

Time began moving in slow motion as his warm fingertips inched underneath my tank top. I looked down to see his palms enclosing my waist; his thumbs drifting over my skin like a whisper, so hypnotizing. My breath shallowed the higher his palms slid over my too hot skin, and soon he'd be able to feel my heart hammering if he couldn't already.

"Arms up." His voice was thick and gravelly, and dragged across every nerve ending. The goosebumps I had were nothing to do with the cooling air; the heat from his gaze was doing a good job of keeping the chill at bay.

He dropped my tank top on the floor, swallowing thickly. I'd had a month of feeling his hands on me, but this was nothing like those other times. Now he was almost transfixed as his thumb swiped across my nipple, puckered so tight it hurt. I couldn't stop the groan from barreling up my throat.

His eyes found mine; they were no longer piercing blue – they were navy – and the little flecks of gold round the edges glinted in the flickering lights around us. If that wasn't enough to show me how affected he was, I could also feel it nudging against my stomach.

"That noise, Marn. I need to hear it again."

He got his wish when his lips replaced his thumb. "Fuuuck," he mumbled with his mouth full. His tongue, his magic tongue, circled around my nipple then popped off with a loud, wet slurp, and I let out a groan, deep and animalistic, a sound I'd never imagined I would make.

He reached over his head; his shirt landed on mine, and he fell to his knees. His lips grazed along my stomach. "I want to see you, all of you. Properly."

His fingers gripped the elastic of my shorts, and his eyes found mine again; this time searching for permission. Sucking my lip between my teeth, I nodded.

I'd never been naked in front of him. Not totally naked. We'd never been naked together. Up to this very second, Jupiter had always made sure there was a strip of clothing between us in case we were caught.

But there was no catching us now.

We were all alone.

For the first time ever, the flush across my body wasn't from embarrassment or awkwardness. It was from him, from the flame of his gaze. Sexy wasn't a word I'd have ever used to describe myself, but that's exactly how he was making me feel right now, especially with his hands cupping my ass.

"You're perfect, Marn."

His lips found my belly, and he laid a path of soft, wet kisses across my hips, which had me squirming in seconds. It was a good job his grip was firm, because the second his tongue found a home between my legs, they gave way; the sensation a thousand times more intense than it had ever been.

"Oh, God," I panted as my hands clutched tightly on the deep, rich brown strands of his hair, as he licked me slowly, "Jupiter..."

He carefully removed himself from my vice grip and stood with a chuckle, wiping his mouth, "Careful, Star."

I couldn't take my eyes off his shorts, and the very obvious tenting.

The first time I'd touched his dick, I'd tried not to be intimidated. I'd wrapped my fist around most of it while he guided me on how to jerk him off. The second and third time, it had been better.

But now it was all coming back, especially as his shorts had found themselves on the growing pile of discarded clothes, my thighs almost clamped shut.

How was I going to fit him?

I'd seen him with his shirt off; I'd stroked over the definitions of his muscles, but I definitely hadn't been looking properly. I swear I'd seen lesser mortals in my books on Greek Gods. Though I guess Jupiter was a God, a Roman God. The Roman King of Gods, of sky and of thunder… and he looked every single inch of it.

I glanced up at his inhale; at his pink tongue running along his bottom lip.

"No one's ever looked at me the way you look at me," he grinned. "Do you think it's possible to be addicted to a person? Because I think I'm addicted to you."

Yes, I did, because I knew I was addicted to him.

He held his hand out for me. "Lay down, Marn."

I placed my head on one of the cushions, and he moved beside me, positioning himself like we had sat earlier with my legs over his. Except this time, I was totally exposed, totally open as he gently spread my thighs. He propped himself up on his elbow, and behind him I could see the stars appearing in the sky, like they'd come to watch.

"You're so fucking beautiful." He dipped down to kiss me, lingering and slow, just like before. "Promise you'll tell me if you want to stop at any time?"

I nodded, but there was a greater chance of Hell freezing than of me stopping this. I'd become a dripping, quaking mess, and we hadn't even started yet. Every time I felt his dick nudge me, leaving his pre-cum on my thigh, it set of another surge of violent shuddering.

His hands were everywhere, gently stroking my belly or slipping between my legs while his mouth was shifting between mine and a nipple, like he couldn't go too long without tasting me. I couldn't concentrate; I didn't know where to focus.

I *couldn't* focus.

Every sensation intensified the heat coiling inside me a thousand times over, until I was a desperate, panting mess.

My legs had fallen wide open; his thumb was slowly pushing in and out, playing with me, toying, teasing. I knew there was a puddle underneath me; there's no way there wasn't. By the time he reached behind himself to pull out a foil packet, I was wound so tight he'd barely have to move for me to explode.

His mouth found mine again like it had been missing his whole life, and he shifted, nestling against my scalding skin until I felt him, hard and throbbing against my entrance.

Maybe I was the one throbbing.

He hovered over me, his hands either side of my face. There was steam coming off the heat of our bodies; so close, so hot.

"Marn, look at me." There was so much emotion in his eyes it was impossible not to look away. "Marnie, look at me."

I found him again, and couldn't stop the moisture leaking from my eyes and down the sides of my face. His lips touched mine, so tenderly it nearly ripped my heart out. I held on, not blinking as he slowly, carefully, pushed inside me, and I thought I might lose my mind at the sensation of him stretching me out; the bite of pain, the tightness, the way he fitted perfectly… like we were made for each other.

"Shit, this is… you okay?" he gritted out.

I nodded, and reached up to wipe a trickle of sweat from his forehead; he caught my hand in his and brought it to his lips.

"I'm gonna move now, okay?"

His mouth captured mine again as my fingers found the base of his neck and pushed into his hair. He was being so careful. The pair of us were shaking. His tongue moved in unhurried strokes while his hips slowly thrust, matching the same pace, and completely overwhelmed me.

Soon, it wasn't enough.

I could feel him tremble, feel how hard he was trying to hold back. But I wanted more. My hips acted of their own accord, taking what I needed, meeting him stroke for stroke.

My spine had become a corkscrew.

A vein I'd never noticed before was pulsing in his neck. He was losing control, and it was the sexiest thing I'd ever seen.

"Do you think you can come like this?" he asked, scooping my ass into his hand and lifted me higher. That movement alone pushed the pressure to breaking point. He was pushing something; a switch had been flicked.

Every atom in my body was burning. My synapses were shooting haphazardly under the surface of my skin.

I'd had orgasms at Jupiter's hand before, but nothing prepared me for the tsunami which hit and crashed through me until I was convinced I'd died. But it wasn't over. Jupiter offered me a kiss of reprieve, and thrust into me one final time, muffling a loud cry against my lips. I breathed it in, breathed him in, as my chest threatened to give way.

And just like that, I'd lost my virginity to Jupiter Reeves.

His head was still nestled in the crook of my neck when I realized he was speaking, and I tipped my head to the side so I could hear him better.

"I learned something today."

"Oh?"

"Yeah, in one of your books. Jupiter is the protector planet, so I guess my job is to always protect you."

"Yeah? I need protecting, do I?" I teased, making him laugh, and his dick twitched inside me setting off a torrent of mini aftershocks.

"Nah, I think you're tough enough to handle yourself, but I just like the thought that I can."

Another heartbeat passed and he eased out of me, moving away for what felt like the longest second. I closed my eyes until I felt him next to me, pulling me tight against his chest.

I didn't think it was possible to relax further, but then his finger began circling my belly button. "I think I love you, Marnie Matthews. I've never felt like this about anyone before, like my heart could burst at any second. The only other time I feel this alive is when I've got a bat in my hand and I'm running bases."

It was the first time those words had passed his lips. I'd been waiting to hear him say it first, because I already knew that's how I felt; that I loved him. But to hear him finally say it…

I wasn't sure if I could even speak, but he heard my breath catch.

After a minute, he pointed up to the sky. "You know how people say stuff is written in the stars? Do you think we are?"

I watched them twinkling above us, one shooting across the sky. "Written in the stars?"

"Yeah," he whispered as he dropped a kiss on my head. "That we belong to each other. I'm yours, and you're mine."

I didn't reply, just nuzzled into his chest. Something had shifted in the last thirty minutes and my mind was elsewhere.

I was beginning to realize how close the draft was.

How far Boston was from California.

And what I was going to do about it.

13

Jupiter

Present Day

New York City in the rain is not a fun place to be driving.

And… there was the thunder.

At least it summed up my mood.

Fuck, I missed California.

"Fucking move, already!" I leaned on the horn. The douche in front of me inched forward.

Jesus.

I should have walked. I'd have gotten home quicker, and given how everyone was hurrying along with their heads down, no one would have noticed me anyway. If I had to stay in this traffic any longer, it would be worth the fine for abandoning my car.

Shuddering as a droplet of rain trickled down my neck, I grabbed the towel off the passenger seat and rubbed it over my head again.

Goddamn rain. Even in the ten seconds it had taken me to run from the stadium to my car I'd gotten completely soaked.

It had been going for a solid two hours now. The heavens had opened the second I'd stepped onto the field at the start of the seventh inning. We're not talking about a trickle of rain, a couple of drops; we're talking apocalyptical; a torrential, thunderous downpour. If I didn't know better – that I couldn't actually summon meteorological changes in the atmosphere – I'd say I was living up to my name as the root cause, because it matched my mood perfectly.

The tarps had come out before I'd gotten around the bases. The boys and I sat there, frustrated, waiting for something we all knew was going to happen.

Rain-out.

We lost the game, and the mood I'd been sporting all afternoon hit rock bottom.

Before anyone had time to suggest a post-game analysis, I'd grabbed my bag and stormed out. The only thing I needed to completely top off this total bullshit of a day was seeing Marnie with that douche coffee guy again.

I thought I'd been okay with leaving her there, but by the time I'd gotten back to the stadium, it was clear to me and anyone in my path that I wasn't. No. I was definitely not fucking okay with that.

I'd left her, and every time I blinked, all I could see was them together. I saw him drying the tears *I'd* caused.

My punishment? That I'd kissed her, and now I remembered exactly what her lips felt like; I had a 4D memory of them imprinted on my skin, on every part of my body, and I could do absolutely nothing about it.

I pulled the visor down to check I hadn't turned into The Hulk from the thick, ugly green jealousy raging through my veins, but no. The same asshole I'd always been stared back.

Actually, not always. And not exclusively.

Because I was also a man of my word, and I promised I'd give her space… to be her friend.

I just didn't realize how hard it would be, and I was only eight hours in.

Fucking *friends.*

I should have asked for a definition, because as of right now, I had no clue what it meant. I thought it might have meant she'd come to the game. Scratch that, she's supposed to come to the game as part of her job; but as a *friend,* she could have been back in her usual seat.

She wasn't.

As a *friend,* I thought she'd support me.

Perhaps send me good luck message.

Nothing.

Maybe we had a different definition of the word.

Maybe she'd been too busy with Coffee Douche.

I must have been out of my mind when I told her to go on a date. What the fuck had I been thinking?! I was an idiot for thinking I'd be able to handle it, handle knowing she was with another guy.

Worse than that; kissing him. Or more.

My stomach convulsed at the thought. My knuckles whitened as I gripped the steering wheel and shook it hard. It didn't move.

Fuck's sake.

I eased forward to the front of the lights. Fucking finally! I'd be home in ten minutes, which was probably all the time my wiper blades had left before they flew off.

Lightning flashed in the sky, and pedestrians hurried along the sidewalk quicker.

A loud ringing cleared my black cloud enough for me to glance over at the dash to see my youngest sister's name. I sighed heavily and my chest sagged; I really didn't want this conversation, but she'd only call again, and again.

"Hey, Em," I sighed resignedly as I inched forward another couple of yards.

"You okay? I caught the end of the game."

On the far side of the traffic I watched a woman get soaked by a wave of water, sprayed by a passing truck. She stood there, her mouth wide open, while coming to terms with the fact she'd have been drier if she'd gotten into a bath fully clothed.

Oh well, hopefully she didn't have late night plans. Hopefully she was going home with a lonely broken heart, just like me.

"Jupe?"

"Sorry, yeah I'm fine." If she only saw the end of the game, I could get away with this being a short conversation.

"Sure?"

"Yes, Emerson! I'm fine."

"Then what's this Drew is saying about you smashing a bat in the dugout the during fourth inning?"

Goddammit. My brother-in-law had a big mouth. I muted the speaker and shook the wheel hard again, letting out a loud, frustrated cry. It didn't work if I thought it was going help me feel better.

Only one thing was ever going to help me feel better.

I returned to the call. "I wasn't playing well. I didn't even get off home plate. It was a bad game, that's all. With one hundred and sixty two games a year, they can't all be good."

"And you took it out on your bat?"

Yes. Yes, I had. My bat was currently in the morgue undergoing autopsy. Cause of death: Jupiter Reeves and his inability to be chill about anything concerning Marnie Matthews.

"Emerson… why are you calling me?"

She didn't even pause, because I knew the real reason she was calling, which was why I'd been avoiding her the past few days. "How are things with Marnie?"

I scratched through my stubble and rubbed hard on my still-damp neck, then sighed deeply. "They suck."

"I thought they were getting better."

"So did I, but then I fucked up, and now they suck again." I didn't want to get into details, because honestly, I didn't want to hear Emerson agree I'd fucked up, and I also wasn't sure I could keep a grip on myself long enough not to cry.

Fucking cry, with actual tears… just like Marnie.

"Oh, Jupiter..."

"Yeah." I zoomed forward into the next block of traffic. One more block and I could turn off. "I made her cry."

I heard her suck in a breath. "How?"

"Emerson, I really don't want to talk about it. I want to go home, drink a bottle of whiskey, and wake up next year."

The home part would happen, but the rest would be followed with hot tea, and tomorrow, which made me even more depressed.

"Okay. You know where Drew is if you wanna talk about it guy to guy."

"Thanks. I don't."

"Let's hope Marnie is somewhere as miserable as you are then, you grouchy fuck!" a deep voice called out in the background. There's a thought. My chest flickered with… hope, maybe, but it died before I could figure it out. "And you'd better be smiling when you come here next week."

Confusion and poor calendar management pulled me from under my cloud again, though the lightning strike at that exact moment reminded me it would only be temporary. "What's next week?"

"The twins' birthday. You said you had a free day and you said you're coming over to help with balloons. You promised." Drew had gotten nearer the phone, so near I could picture exactly what I'd said and when I'd said it – right after Opening Day when we'd beaten the Yankees, and I'd seen Marnie for the first time in fourteen years.

That's what happened when you were on a high. You promised shit you'd then come to regret.

"Haven't you got nannies for that?" I grumbled.

"Reeves, this is your niece and nephews…"

I held in the groan. Still, I did kind of like Emerson's kids. They were pretty cute, and funny.

"Yeah, I'll be there." The car in front moved forward, giving me an out of this call. "I need to go, I'm nearly home."

"Bye, love you. Try to cheer up."

I hung up without saying goodbye. There was almost enough space in the traffic that I could inch through and take my left, even if it did mean I was hopping the corner of the sidewalk.

Fuck it, the sidewalk was empty. Everyone was out of the rain, where I would soon be.

It took less than five minutes for me to pull into my space in the underground parking garage, and get in the elevator to my apartment. Because I had zero self-discipline, I checked my cell as I got in.

My head fell back as I slumped against the stainless steel.

My new friend had not messaged me. I didn't think she'd come running after I'd left her by the tree, but I thought she might have sent me something, anything.

Fucking friends.

Fourteen years I'd trained myself to function without her.

Now less than a month in, and I could barely get through an afternoon. I was a notebook away from drawing hearts around her name while I listened to Adele on repeat and tried to be patient.

I laughed to myself. Jupiter Reeves and patient are not two words commonly found together, but the thought did help me feel a little better.

I was still laughing as the elevator dinged and the doors opened.

The smile might have frozen on my lips, but every other part of my body heated up, and my heart bounced around like an excited puppy. My black mood vanished instantly; and if it was daylight, I swear the sun would be shining if I looked out the window.

No more rain.

Because unless it was an apparition, Marnie Matthews was sitting on the floor outside my apartment, dripping wet.

"Marn?"

She looked up as she heard me, scrambling to her feet with

a soft smile. "Hey."

This was better than checking my cell every twenty seconds. Much better.

Five yards out, and I stopped. Not because I didn't want to invade her personal space, but because when I said she was dripping wet, I meant it. Every item of clothing was soaked through, including the white Lions t-shirt she had on.

The one which clung to her body, accentuating the curve of her perfect tits that I knew fit just as perfectly in my palm, and the very clear outline of her nipples. It wasn't just me that noticed either; my dick was paying very close attention.

And I now wanted to kill every single guy who'd seen her like this, including…

"Not that I'm not overcome with happiness to see you dripping on my doorstep, but how did you get up here?" I leaned against the wall as casually as I could.

She looked at her feet. "I showed your doorman my Lions pass."

Yeah, and I bet he got a good fucking look.

"Inventive," I gritted out, trying to keep the jealousy from my tone. "Marn, what are you doing here?"

"I wanted to talk."

"Where's Coffee Douche?"

She pursed her lips, the annoyance I knew so well flashing across her face. "You left me with a lot of questions to answer, you know."

I smirked, I could imagine. I could also imagine Marnie had been less than happy answering them. "I'd say I'm sorry, but you know me too well for that. I think I've used up all my sorries today."

She was quiet for a second and her hands began twisting

nervously. "Did you mean it?"

"Yes, Marn," my bag fell to the floor; two large quick strides and I'd eaten up the space between us. My hands cupped her face and I met her stare, "Of course I did. I meant every word."

"I'm sorry about the game," she whispered.

From the way she was looking at me, she was just talking about the rain-out. "You watched?"

"Yeah, I was up in the box." She hesitated, catching her bottom lip in her teeth. "It's where I've been watching this week."

"I've been playing like shit." I searched her face, her green eyes gazing up at me. "I thought you'd skipped them all because you were mad."

"I am mad!"

I dropped my hands and picked my bag up with a sigh. "Marn, what are you doing here?"

"I told you, I wanted to see you and I want to talk."

"Look, I know you're pissed at me, but I said I'd give you space and I meant it." I dug into my pocket for my front door key and stepped around her, hoping to avoid inhaling any more of her scent; that freshness of apples and a freshly mown field. It was making me lightheaded. "Even if it'd be easier to rip a limb off," I mumbled.

"What?"

"Nothing." I pushed the door open, holding it for her to walk through. "But if you've come here to yell at me, please save yourself the job. I had a shit game, and I'm not in the mood to hear it. You can do it tomorrow instead."

She stopped on the threshold. "I haven't come to yell. I came to talk."

I was suddenly overcome with exhaustion and finding it

very hard to look at her when she was standing there, arms crossed over her chest which pushed her tits up so all I could think about was sliding my dick between them. I stormed over to the couch, picked up one of the blankets Emerson had left me, and tossed it at her.

"Put it on. I can't talk to you when you're all… like that." I jerked my head at her, hoping she'd get my meaning without me having to say it.

She didn't and her eyes flashed, switching to angry Marnie once more. "Are you making fun of me again?"

"No."

"Then what is that supposed to mean? What is… 'like that'?" she jolted her chin as I had.

"Wet," I gritted, and stormed over to the fridge. I might not be sinking the whiskey, but I still needed something to take the edge off. "I can see through your shirt."

She picked up the blanket, and wrapped it around herself, muttering the obvious, "It's raining outside."

My mood clearly hadn't gone far, and I spun round to face her. "I don't give a fuck. You can't come here looking like that and expect me to be…"

"Be what?"

"Friends."

Her face dropped, and I wasn't sure if the trembling of her jaw was because she was suddenly cold, or because she was about to cry. Whatever it was still had my heart melting the armor I'd been wearing all day.

My shoulders dropped. "Marn, if you want to be friends then we can do it during office hours. I can deal with that. But you can't come to my apartment at nine p.m. dressed like that, and expect me to keep my hands to myself."

I blinked in rapid succession, making sure I'd heard correctly and not just wishful thinking, but I swear she said, "What if I don't want you to?"

She was still by the door, and I stepped slowly toward her until I was so close I could see my eyes flashing in hers. But on closer inspection, it was her eyes flashing.

"Is that a joke? Because it's not funny," I growled.

"No, Jupiter, it's not fucking funny! There's nothing funny about this. It's not funny and it's not fair. You don't get to just interrupt my date, my work, turn my entire life upside down… and expect me to fall into your lap."

My hopes, which had been up for a split second, were dashed to smithereens once again.

"We had this conversation already. I heard you loud and clear."

"I'm not done."

I rolled my eyes. Of course she wasn't. All I wanted to do was have a shower, jerk off to memories of her, and go to bed… then start again tomorrow.

"Do you remember the first time you kissed me?"

I couldn't believe she even had to ask; it was burned into my memory, branded onto my heart. It was still one of the top five nights of my life. But instead of telling her all that, I just nodded and said, "Yes."

"I thought I'd never felt anything better. You made me feel safe, secure, hot... I'd never felt anything like it. And every single other time you kissed me, I thought the same thing – that I'd never feel anything better."

I thought I knew every tell she had, but right now, I couldn't read the expression in her eyes. It didn't help that she was looking at her feet.

"I know, Marn. Me too."

"And today… it was the same."

Up until then, she maybe had seventy percent of my attention, because the other thirty percent had already heard what she was saying the first time, and therefore was concentrating on not getting a semi or thinking of her wet shirt underneath the blanket, and what was underneath that. I probably should have offered her a change of clothes, but then she'd be naked in my apartment, and I wasn't sure I wanted to push myself to test how I'd handle that.

Not well was my guess.

Now, however, she had one hundred percent of my attention fully invested in every word coming out of her mouth.

I spread my legs to drop down nearer to her height, and narrowed my eyes, "What happened with Coffee Douche?"

"He wanted to know how I knew you, and what you'd said to me."

"And what did you say?"

"I said you were apologizing for being an asshole as part of a rehabilitation program." Her laugh rang like a tiny bell in my chest. "And then he wanted to know how much further down the line his apology was."

"He's gonna be waiting a while," I gritted out. "You're not going on a date with him again."

It wasn't a question. Marnie looked like she was about to argue, but her face softened.

"I'd already told him that before you turned up. I hadn't wanted to go on the date in the first place. I shouldn't have gone, but I was so mad at you! You're in my head all the time, it's like I can't escape!"

"Now you know how I feel," I challenged her back.

She held onto my gaze, and sighed in defeat.

Now for the question that had been going around and around in my head since I'd discovered the news. "What happened with your husband?"

Just like earlier, her lip caught between her teeth, but this time I pulled it free.

"Tell me what you realized."

Her pupils flared, her chest rising and falling quicker with each breath. My fingers pushed through her wet hair until her head was against the wall, neck craned to look at me.

"Tell me."

"I realized that I had never gotten over you."

And there they were. The words I'd been waiting to hear my entire adult life from the girl who'd owned my heart for the duration.

My thumb ran roughly along her plump bottom lip. I was captivated by the way her soft, wet skin reddened under my touch as I pulled it down. But the second she moaned, I snapped.

"Starlight, star bright," I breathed into her mouth before capturing her lips with my own.

I sucked, tasting her like I'd wanted to earlier, like I'd been at sea for years and had finally reached dry land. Like she was the lifeline I never knew I needed.

No, that's bullshit. I'd always known she was my lifeline.

Surrounding her mouth with mine, I kissed her hard, desperately. There was no savoring, because I had no intention of giving this up ever again. I didn't need to make it last. It belonged to me, had always belonged to me, and I was finally taking it back.

My tongue tangled with hers, hot and wet, and everything

I missed. She reached up on her tip toes, her fingers combing through my hair, and the blanket fell to the floor. At the feel of her nipples grazing against me, my dick thickened instantly, and I pulled back.

She was breathless; her cheeks were turning that unique shade of pink I loved as she looked up at me through thick lashes, her green eyes hooded and glassy.

She could have been sixteen again, and she'd never been more beautiful.

My forehead rested against hers. "I've fucking missed you, Marn, and I'm not just talking about the past three days."

"I know," she whispered back, her breath hot on my skin, "now kiss me again."

My dick was screaming to get out of my pants. "I'm gonna do more than kiss you, Marn, and you have to forgive me in advance."

"What for?"

"Because I'm about to fuck you like I need to make up for the past fourteen years, and I have no plans to be gentle. Then I'm going to do it again."

My mouth latched back onto her. The air caught in her throat as I scooped her up and carried her through to my bedroom and put her down. The blinds were still open along the wall of windows, and I was tempted to close them but stopped myself.

Fuck it.

People could fucking watch. I wanted the whole world to know she was mine again.

I stood back and looked at her panting hard. There was the tiniest shard of hesitancy in her eyes, it was exactly the same as the night we'd first slept together; the night I'd taken her virginity. The apprehension had my dick swelling because I knew where it came from, and I was going to fuck it right out of her.

By the time we were done, she wouldn't have any doubt.

Her shirt was still clinging to her skin. It might have been wet, but it wasn't cold. Her body was feverish under my touch, under my palm running over her tits; she flinched as I squeezed a nipple.

"Clothes off," I ordered.

I knew she could have removed them quicker; anyone else and I'd accuse them of putting on a show. From Marnie, however, it was a message; she wasn't going to bend so willingly to my demand.

But it only spurred me on, especially when her shirt was the last thing to come off. It dropped to the floor, along with her bra.

Then I saw it, and my legs nearly gave way.

"Star..." I hissed, not quite believing what I was seeing. A shiver flew down her side as my thumb brushed over the tiny hand-drawn thundercloud and lightning bolt, sitting to the right under her left boob; over her heart.

I might be covered in her, but this was all me.

"You're not the only one with a tattoo," she whispered.

I dipped down, my cheek nestled against her tit and my tongue ran over the delicate lines, coating the tiny ridges with my saliva. My girl covered in me, painted in a permanent reminder *of me.*

Her hand brushed through my hair on the way to gripping the back of my neck. I felt the moan erupt from her diaphragm; deep, and rumbling, and desperate. Shivers flew across her skin like wildfire as my hands slipped into the elastic of her panties and tugged hard.

The scent of her need hit me, and I stood, my hands breezing over her curves, leaving a ripple of goosebumps in my wake.

With her head thrown back; my lips tracked up her neck before I pinched her jaw between my fingers and dragged her gaze up, forcing it to meet mine.

"You're going to be leaking my cum for days."

Shock didn't have the chance to cross her face before she was launched onto the bed, her tits bouncing when she landed. My dick needed out of my pants, now.

I took my time; reaching behind and yanking my shirt off, enjoying the heat of her eyes trailing over me, the way she glanced up with an almost pained expression as my pants came off, and my cock bounced against my stomach; thick and hard.

All for her.

Her lips parted, and the tiniest gasp flew out.

I dreamed about this so many times over the years, it was hard to believe she was really there in front of me; whether the throbbing deep in my balls was purely down to my vivid imagination.

Then I remembered my imagination had never been this good, and I'd just made her a promise I fully intended to keep.

"We're not teenagers anymore, Marn. Spread your legs. I want to see what I've been missing."

I waited, giving my balls a gentle tug to distract myself while my eyes locked on her; feasting. Even the claps of thunder and flashes of lightning couldn't break my connection.

Her knees dropped apart a fraction, but nothing like what I had in mind.

"Wider," I growled.

Another small parting; her chest flushed pink with shyness, but there was going to be none of that in our bed. She knew me better than that.

She was going to know how much I worshiped her; I planned to show her every fucking day.

"Star… when I say wider, this is what I mean." The mattress dipped under my knees, and I wrenched her legs apart. Her thighs glistened. Arousal seeped out, and a single drop ran down and hit the sheet beneath her. I caught a second on my thumb and sucked it into my mouth. Sweetness hit me harder than any sugar rush. "I think I've died and gone to heaven."

My tongue tingled, my mouth pooled with saliva. I bent down, running my nose either side of her lips until I was coated in her. She shot up the bed with a groan as I took my tongue and dragged it up the length of her slit.

"That noise, Marn. Fuck! I've only heard it in my dreams."

Another flash of lightning illuminated her, as I resumed my position.

"Ohhhhh… God," she cried.

I wanted to remind her of my name, but my mouth was full. Scooping her ass up, I lifted her high, my arms under her thighs. Opening my eyes, all I could see was a line straight down her body through the space between her soft tits, to eyes rolling back in her head.

The mewling turned to whimpering turned to heavy, thick rasping.

I ate her like she was my obsession. The harder I sucked on her clit, the firmer my fingers dug into her ass, because the more she squirmed. And then came those telltale signs I remembered so clearly… her thighs trembling, her stomach convulsing, her delicate hands fisting the sheets.

Call me selfish, but the first time she came was going to be on my dick, wringing every drop from me. We had all night, and I'd waited too long. Placing a soft kiss on her pussy, I rose up to find her chest heaving and covered with a sheen of sweat. Her skin was silky under my touch as I ran my hands over her curves, like I was upgrading my memory.

Then I was hovering over her, surrounding her with my body; her face turned and she nearly eviscerated me with the fire blazing in her eyes.

"Marn," I propped myself on one hand, wiping away the hair stuck to her forehead. "Are you ready?"

"Yes…"

As gently as I could, I placed a kiss against her lips, already slightly swollen from our kissing. Shifting her knees, I hitched a leg over my hip, and lined myself up with her.

I tried to go slow, I tried to ease in so I could feel her taking every last inch of me, but I failed miserably.

In less than a second, I'd bottomed out.

In less than a second, I was home.

Her body shuddered beneath me, her pussy fluttered and her eyelids flickered. I thought I was having an out of body experience with the tightness at which she was gripping me; a velvet vice squeezing the life from me.

But it was the way she said my name which broke me from her spell, not quite whispering it, not quite speaking, but dripping in desperation.

"Juuupiter…"

I needed to hear it again.

My tongue tangled with hers, dancing together as I unlocked her hands from around my neck and gathered them into my fist.

"Can you taste yourself on me? Can you taste how much you've missed me?"

She replied with another gravelly moan.

Circling my hips, getting as deep as I could possibly go, I ground against her clit, setting off more contractions which had both our groans colliding and bouncing off the walls.

"Move... please, I can't take this," she rasped.

I let out a dark chuckle and obeyed her command.

Soon, rocking inside her wasn't enough. From the way her back arched, I knew she needed more. Her nipples were impossibly tight, her chest flushed the deepest shade of pink, and the pair of us were sheened in sweat; our skin slicking together. We were both hurtling to the end faster than an eighteen-wheeler.

I didn't want it to end, but I didn't know how much longer I could go on for. Marnie Matthews had stripped me of staying power.

She was gasping for air, and I was the oxygen.

I shifted until I was caging her in with my arms, twisting her so she couldn't move. I pulled out slowly then drove back into her with such force, her cry could have been heard over the loudest clap of thunder.

"Did you ever scream my name when your husband was fucking you? Did you ever think about me?" Her eyes flared, and I stopped moving. "I'm not letting you come until you tell me. Did you wish it was my dick sliding inside you... just... like... this."

Her head fell back with a groan which shook my bones.

"Say it, Star," I gritted out.

"Yes. Yes, I did."

Once more I pulled out the full length of her, and drove

back in with an almighty force which nearly burst my balls. "Let me hear it. Make it worth it."

Another deep thrust.

"Jupiter! Fuck! FUCK… JUPITER!"

Fuck my balls, my heart was about to give way.

"Tell me who your pussy belongs to. Who it's always belonged to."

"You, Jupiter… always you."

"Mine is going to be the only name you ever scream again. Understand?"

She couldn't nod, she couldn't move. She was too gone to do anything except come.

One final thrust was all it took.

She almost gagged when her orgasm hit; sucking as much air as she could into her lungs, and choked on the speed.

And I was undone.

I burst inside her, my balls emptying and my bones liquefying until I swear my soul was being extracted by force. Black dots swam in my vision, like she was sucking me into her center of gravity, never to return. I collapsed to the side, pulling her next to me. I wanted to feel her heart beat in time with mine, settle next to mine.

Sync with mine.

I'd never felt anything like it. Every cell, every atom in my body was dancing.

"Oh my God, Jupiter." Every word punched out as she caught her breath, "I don't… I don't think I can move. I think you've killed me."

"Funny," I kissed along her shoulder, "I was going to say I've never felt more alive."

Later, much later, I fell asleep listening to Marnie nestled into my chest breathing in and out for the first time since I was eighteen years old.

And my world righted itself.

14

Marnie

Present Day

Turns out, sex is a lot like riding a bike. Once you know how to do it, it's hard to forget.

And lying right next to me, one huge bicep curled into his side while the other was flung over his face, was the most elite, top-of-the-range bike I'd ever ridden.

My fingertips had been tingling since I woke thirty minutes ago. Even though we'd only collapsed a couple of hours ago, I was surprisingly full of energy. It was almost as though I hadn't been fucked to within an inch of my life.

But I had, and I didn't need to see my reflection to know I was a knotty, crumpled mess, while he lay there as though he'd just stepped off a catwalk; peaceful, content, his pouty mouth soft and quiet.

Blissfully quiet.

I held mine together to stop a giggle from erupting.

I was desperate to touch him, skate my fingers over the convergence of planets running across his impressive chest, follow the shooting stars down the thick vein running the length of his bicep. I didn't need to look at the sky if I had him.

The set of eyes I could do without though. My eyes, tattooed on his triceps, made me feel like I was constantly being watched, like I was judging myself.

Maybe I was, but for now I was happy to soak in the bliss.

On those rare times we got to spend the whole night together, I'd wake up before him and trace the divots in his shoulders, the lines of his abs, and brush my fingers over the perfect dimple in his cheek.

I kind of missed that dimple, the one now covered in thick whiskers.

That boy I loved was now *all* man; possessive, controlling and unapologetic.

That toned body now rippled with muscle, thick from years of training. Harder, meaner, more refined, and capable of moves I'd never imagined in my wildest dreams.

My aching thighs were proof of that.

Whoever said confidence was sexy had never met Jupiter Reeves. His confidence wasn't sexy; his confidence oozed from him. It was in the air around him, and it possessed you like a demon the second you breathed it in.

His confidence was why no one ever said no.

How could they?

Goddamn, I hated it when Jupiter was right.

After weeks and weeks of resisting him, I couldn't ignore it. He owned me, body and soul.

"I know you're watching me..." came his sleep-roughened voice as one dazzlingly blue eye opened. Mine widened in surprise, accompanied by a giggle.

The arm covered in shooting stars and the date of our first kiss snaked around me and pulled me close so he could plant a big, wet kiss on my lips.

"That noise, Marn."

"My laugh?"

"Yeah, I could listen to it on repeat and I'd never get enough." He smiled back, but it wasn't playful; it was kind of bashful, vulnerable. "Did you sleep well?

"All three hours of it, yes." I yawned, stretching my arms above my head.

He grinned and threw back the covers. "Wait here. Promise you won't move?"

I wasn't sure I had the energy or the skeletal composition to move even if I wanted to, seeing as my bones hadn't totally regained their full strength after turning to Jell-O.

"I promise." I yawned again, taking full advantage of the sight before me.

He leapt out of bed, giving me a perfect view of his ass; his tight, very smooth ass. He must do a thousand squats a day to maintain an ass that rivaled a peach for peachiness.

How was I ever thinking I missed his old body?

I was just beginning to doze off while dreaming of it when he returned, two coffees in hand. Or one coffee and one cup of green froth.

"What's that?"

"Matcha," he laughed as I pulled a face then waited until I

scooched up the mattress so he could slide back in next to me.

I propped myself against a pillow then took my coffee from him. "Thank you."

"You're welcome." He watched as I blew away the steam on mine. "I've been waiting to do that forever."

"What?"

"Bring you coffee in bed again," he grinned.

My heart softly thudded and I looked at him curiously. This wasn't the Jupiter who'd commanded me with his dick last night, who'd taken control of my body and mind until they bent at his whim.

This was the Jupiter who'd made me hot chocolate to watch the night sky when I was sixteen years old, and set a thousand flickering lights out so we could make love on blankets under the stars; the one who'd pulled me against the tree and begged forgiveness, finally giving me the words I didn't realize I'd desperately been waiting to hear.

I'm sorry.

No arrogance; just him.

I was beginning to realize two Jupiters existed, and I never knew which one I was going to get.

"Jupe..." I began as I set my coffee mug on the nightstand. "How are you like this, and also such a dick to people? You know everyone thinks you're an asshole, right?"

"It's special for you, babe," he winked and sipped his green froth, but he wasn't getting away with it that easily.

"Come on, be serious."

He puffed out a long breath of air. "I just don't really like people."

I pursed my lips and tried to catch his eye, but he wasn't looking at me. "That's total bullshit. You used to."

That got him, and his eyes sparkled with amusement. "One night of wild sex and you've become quite the swear machine, Missy."

One of his long, thick fingers poked me right in the ribs, and I was incapable of holding in the bark of laughter. Herein lies the problem when someone knows you so well – they know your weak spots, including the space between your upper ribs where you can't do anything but howl with laughter when they squeeze against it.

"Jupiter!" I could barely wheeze out his name, as he rolled on top of me, almost forcing me into the mattress with every wiggle of his fingers. "Stop! Ohmygod, I can't breathe. Stop… stop... Please. I'll do anything. I'll beg, please!"

After what seemed like a lifetime his hands finally stilled, though they didn't move, his thumbs ghosting over the exact weak spot, silently threatening, and reminding me what they were capable of just in case I fell out of line.

"You can beg me again if you'd like. I'll make it worth your while." His voice had turned distinctly gravelly; a direct contrast to the fat raspberry he blew on my neck, which set off another round of laughter until I was convinced my sides were actually splitting.

He stayed on top of me and wiped away the tears that clouded my vision. This time I stayed silent until he gave me the answer I was waiting for.

"I think it started when we broke up. I didn't want anyone but you, and all the attention I was suddenly getting was too much. It was a hundred times worse than it had ever been at school. I didn't ever want them to think they had a chance, and being a moody asshole made that easy."

I took as deep a breath as I could, seeing as how he was still lying on my chest.

"I know I broke your heart, Marn, but I broke mine, too. Believe me I did."

And there was the in to ask the question which had kept me awake for months and months.

Years almost.

"Then why did you do it, Jupiter? Why did you break us up?"

He looked down, resting his head on my chest. "We were kids, Marn. It doesn't matter anymore. What matters is that you are here in my bed, and I've just brought you coffee exactly how you like it..." he looked over to where our cups were placed side by side, "and we have a couple of hours before I have to be at the club. But most importantly, tonight will be my first pro game where my girlfriend is watching."

This time, the breath I tried to take caught hard. "What? Girlfriend?"

He heard the shock in my voice, the tone that said I wasn't expecting *that* word to come out of his mouth. "Give me a chance, Marn. Please. Just see how we are together."

"But how are we going to do this? We work together."

"We're going to do it the way we have been doing it, with me coming to see you every chance I get, but with more sex." He rose over me, licking his lips. "I can't wait to spread you over your desk and eat your pussy."

The deep throbbing told me my pussy was fully aligned with that idea.

"In fact..." his lips touched mine for a nanosecond, "no time like the present."

His head was between my legs before I could blink, and any anxiety trying to make itself known at the fact he hadn't answered my question was extinguished the moment his tongue got to work.

"Shit! I really need to pee. I'm not going to make it to the box."

An almighty roar rent through the air. We were running through the lower tiers of The Lions stadium on the way to Penn Shepherd's box. We were all late, but only Beulah was hopping up and down.

"There," I pointed to the restroom sign a little ways up, and the three of us ducked inside, only to be greeted by a long line.

"Ugh, this needs to move quick."

"Why didn't you go before we left?" asked Lowe.

"I was finishing up some new contracts, and then you were outside. Plus, I didn't need to go when we left, but now I do."

"Stop hopping. It'll make it worse."

Beulah stood still, though she was clearly struggling. "Can we message the girls and let them know we'll be five more minutes?"

That'll be five to add onto the fifteen we were already late. We'd missed the warm ups, the National Anthem, and from the sounds of the crowds, the first pitch. I'd have run ahead, but Lowe and Beulah had invited some friends of theirs whom I hadn't met yet, and I wasn't that great at turning up unannounced.

"Who's coming again?"

"A couple of girlfriends – Kit and Peyton. You'll like them a lot, they're super fun. Kit is a professor at Columbia, and Peyton is a book editor."

One thing I loved about Lowe and Beulah was how unapologetically accomplished they were. One reason I'd always struggled with new people was the small talk and opening questions, because when it came to my turn, eyes tended to glaze over. But with these two, they were more genuinely interested in me, more so than anyone else I'd met outside of the field of science and space. I liked it, and for the first time ever, I was enjoying having real girlfriends.

"Sounds fun. The more the merrier."

"Yeah, it should be."

We shuffled forward a few feet. The line was so long that by the time we got to the front, I'd need to pee too. Another muffled cheer echoed through the walls. At this rate we'd probably miss half the game and I really didn't want to. It was a big game tonight, Lions versus Mets. The stadium was fuller much earlier than usual as this was the first time The Lions had met the number two New York team.

Girlfriend comment or not, I was desperate to see Jupiter play.

I glanced up to find Beulah and Lowe staring at me.

"What?"

Lowe tapped a polished finger to her lip. "Why do you look all glowy?"

"Glowy?"

"Yeah. It's like you've been dipped in an Instagram filter, but this is definitely natural." Her finger moved from her lip to circle my face, and I tried not to shrink under her scrutiny. "Why do you look like that?"

I didn't have a chance to reply before her face lit up. "Oh! I got it! The date! Did it turn out okay in the end?"

"Um, you could say that." I tried to hold in the smile tugging at my lips.

Neither of them bought it. "Something is going on."

I was just about to put them out of their misery when Beulah shushed us and nodded to the girls in front. They were talking so loudly I was surprised we hadn't been forced to pay attention to them when we'd walked in. From the empty Lions cups in their hands – the ones you paid ten dollars for, and entered into a drawing to meet the players – they weren't exactly sober.

"Did you see Ace Watson stretching? Jesus, his ass is obscene. It should be illegal."

"OMG Watson is so cuuute. I heard he likes older women though."

"Ew. How old?"

"I dunno, like thirty maybe."

"Gross."

Lowe and Beulah's eyes shot wide open, and Lowe mouthed 'thirty' at us. But the girls were only just getting started. I should have known from the shirts they were wearing.

"Thirty isn't that bad, Jupiter Reeves is thirty-two."

"Yeah, but he's a guy. And fucking hot. So hot. Those tattoos… mmmm."

I'd overheard so many of these conversations over the past month, and they were only slightly more explicit than the conversations I used to overhear at school. In fact, I'd heard so many that I could now block them out. But maybe it was because of what happened last night, or because it was exactly like the conversation I'd overheard by the team posters on my first day at work, that this was grating a little bit harder.

Jesus, had that really only been a month ago?

"He'd definitely set fire to your bed."

"Think of all that experience."

"If he was teaching, I'd never miss class. And I'd let him bite my apples."

"Do you think he's as good at sex as he is at baseball?"

"God, where's a good pair of ear plugs when you need them?" hissed Lowe. "They're not even original."

But I wasn't listening to Lowe.

What I was doing, however, was interrupting the girls before I could stop myself.

"He's better…"

All four of them stopped gossiping, turned around, and glared at me. I met every ounce of their annoyance with my own, and a healthy dose of snark for good measure. Especially when the blonde one raised a brow as she slowly glowered, starting at my feet and gave me a thorough once over. "Yeah, right. As if you'd know."

"Oh, I'm sorry. I thought anyone could join in."

If she pursed her lips any tighter, the filler would pop. "This is a private conversation."

I plastered on my best fake smile and gave her a non-committal shrug. "If you wanted a private conversation then you shouldn't be standing in the restroom of a baseball stadium talking at the top of your voice."

They each shot me a death stare worthy of a hormonal teenage girl, but turned back to their conversation.

"Nice," grinned Beulah.

"Oh my God, that's why you're all glowy!" whispered Lowe just as a stall finally opened up.

Beulah snuck through before any of the girls noticed, because they were now too busy using their inside voices.

"Hey!" the blonde one shrieked, but it was too late.

"You snooze, you lose," Beulah winked, slamming the door in her face. Lowe muffled a snort behind me.

"I really should talk to Penn about who he lets in here."

"Yeah, guess I'll have to get used to it all over again," I rolled my eyes.

"What does that mean? Did something really happen?" she whispered.

I nodded but kept my mouth schooled in a straight line. "Yeah, you could say that."

"Oh shit." She stopped me from continuing with a wave of her hand. "Wait until Beulah is here, then you won't have to repeat it. Plus, not sure we need any ears."

I looked over to the girls, a slightly smaller group now two had managed to get into a stall together.

"Beulah, hurry up!" Lowe called.

"Coming, sorry." She emerged still doing up her jeans, but didn't have time to get out of the stall completely before the other two girls pushed her out of the way. "Watch it."

"Shouldn't have jumped line."

"God," Beulah muttered, rubbing her elbow after she'd washed her hands. "Girls are the worst."

"Some girls," Lowe countered as she linked arms and we walked back out into the corridor, into a sea of black and gold. The crowds had doubled in the five minutes we'd been in the restroom. "We're not so bad. Come on, we've already missed the first inning."

"At least Penn is in his seats so he's not going to be wondering where we are."

We hurried through the crowds as quickly as possible, dodging the beer and pretzel lines, plus a couple of Lions' staff selling foam fingers. The line for the merch stand we passed was nearly as long as the line for the restroom.

I grabbed my stomach as it rumbled loudly, though not enough to be heard. A sex marathon really worked up an appetite, and I'd already eaten a double bagel and a chocolate muffin, plus a bowl of granola the size of my head for breakfast. It was like I was carb loading for an actual marathon.

I was in luck. We arrived just as the food was being brought out.

"Hey, there you are! Where've you been?" a brown haired woman asked as she rushed forward, her face filled with excitement, and pulled Beulah and Lowe into a big hug. "You're missing a good game. We already scored."

Shit. I hoped that didn't mean I'd missed Jupiter.

"Do you know who it was?"

"Yes, Lux Weston, who is quite the hottie. You must be Marnie." I was roped into the same hug the other two had been, and all I could feel was relief I hadn't missed Jupiter hitting big. "I'm Kit. I've really been looking forward to meeting you."

From the way she was looking at me, like Lowe and Beulah had done the first time I'd met them, I hazarded a guess that she knew about Jupiter bringing me to The Lions.

"Oh… um, thank you," I blushed hard.

"Put her down, Kit," Beulah ordered. "Marnie, this is Kit, a good friend of ours."

Kit blushed almost as much as I had. "Sorry, I just got excited for a second."

"Where's Payton?" asked Lowe.

"In the restroom. She said she's only going to pee when The Lions are at bat. That way she doesn't miss Ace Watson's ass."

My hands didn't shoot to cover my mouth in time for me to catch my shocked bark of laughter.

"I think that's a fair and logical point to make!"

I spun to find a very beautiful woman walking toward us, wearing a pair of skinny jeans and a Lions shirt; one of the ones Lowe made which said 'I caught a Lion' on it, though I couldn't imagine her out on a boat in the middle of the Hudson. A mass of thick black hair was tied up with a Lions bandana, and her face was completely bare of makeup, save for a slick of lip gloss. For the second time in as many minutes, I was squeezed in a hug.

"Oh, Marnie, I've been so excited to meet you."

"So I guess you all know about Jupiter then," I asked when Payton released me.

At least Kit had the sense to look bashful, Payton just looked overjoyed.

Lowe held two drink options out to me; a glass of champagne or a bottle of beer. I took the beer. "Sorry, we should have warned you that you'd been the topic of conversation for a while before you arrived. We've been so excited to have you in our group."

I laughed. "It's okay… what else have you said though?"

She shook her head. "Nothing. There's been nothing to tell, right? Nothing before now, anyway."

"What? What's this?" Beulah looked between us, and then pointed at me. "Oh! Is that the glow?"

I glanced around the room to see four sets of eyes desperate for information. I'd become comfortable sharing with Beulah and Lowe, but two more… this was turning into twenty-four hours of new experiences.

"Um…" I looked longingly as one of the executive wait staff brought out a plate of burgers. Lowe followed my gaze.

"Hey, let's eat first, have a few drinks, and we can talk while the game is on."

"Awesome idea."

Another roar bounced around the stadium. Our boys were in the field, which meant either we'd caught out one of The Mets, or The Mets had scored. Either way, something had just happened. "Come on, let's hurry. We're missing this and I'm gonna get quizzed if I'm not careful."

"Penn and his quizzes," Beulah griped, head slowly shaking as we all rushed out to the balcony overlooking the field. It wasn't the closest we could get; the owner's seats where I'd been for most of Jupiter's games were practically in the dugout, but I preferred these. We had a full view of the field while still being close enough to get the atmosphere. "Have we all got drinks?"

"I do." I put my hand up while I made a beeline to the where the food was being laid out, heading straight for the fattest and juiciest burger.

Stools were lined up along the balcony overlooking the field, and I sat at the one on the end. The Mets were at bat; the next batter was walking out to home plate. I could see Jupiter stretching and rolling out his shoulder, his left hand gloved. I wanted to take some time to watch him, watch his movements, the way he grinned over at Stone Philips like the two of them were sharing a secret no one else knew. But as he always did, he sensed me the second I'd walked out. He knew I was here and he'd found me. I couldn't see his eyes behind the sunglasses he was wearing, but from the way his head tilted, I knew he was looking straight at me, just like I knew that his eyes were licking flames across my body.

I knew because I could feel them, like I could still feel him between my legs.

I shifted on the stool, in an attempt to ease the tension

building, only to remind myself of another ache – the one in my glutes. I should probably join Jupiter on his next gym session and get some squats in myself.

"Shall I take a stab in the dark and say we're Team Jupiter now?"

I turned to Lowe, a mouth full of burger. "What?"

"Well," Lowe nodded toward the girls and back at me, "we want to stick together. As long as you don't like him, we don't like him. It's girl code. But if you're looking at him like that…"

It must have been the lack of sleep that caused the overwhelming tidal wave of emotion to hit, one that had me tearing up before I'd had a chance to swallow.

"Yeah, I think we can be Team Jupiter."

"What happened on the date then? Was it a bust?" Beulah jumped on the stool between Kit and Lowe, followed by Payton; all five of us sitting in a little semi-circle so we could talk, eat, and most importantly, watch.

"Ooh, here we go girls," Payton said, rubbing her hands together. "Ace Watson is quite the pitcher, isn't he?"

She turned to look at the big screen on the wall, the one showing Lions TV, and a close up of Ace's face.

"He's a real cutie."

"He's popular too. We bumped into some fans of his in the restroom earlier."

"Yeah, they were a real treat," I agreed, the sarcasm loud and clear in my voice, then picked up my beer and took a long sip.

"Anyway, come on, tell us what happened."

Kit was loading ketchup onto her burger. "Can you give us a quick recap first?"

"Jupiter turned into Marnie's shadow, Marnie said they could be friends, Jupiter went postal, Marnie met a cute guy at boxing and went on a date with him."

I glanced over to Lowe, my eyebrows raised. "I'm impressed. Yeah, that pretty much sums it up."

"I work in P.R., what can I say? I excel at summarizing succinctly. Why use five words when you can use two?"

"So then what happened? God, I can't imagine Jupiter having to work at getting a girl to like him."

And therein lay some of the problem.

"Jupiter turned up on my date."

Eight eyes widened; a rainbow of shades; blue, honey colored, palest brown, and two so dark they were almost black. Two mouths fell open, and Kit choked on her beer.

"Shut up. He didn't!" Payton spluttered, and slammed her hand down on the ledge. Luckily, nothing fell off.

I nodded.

"Oh, I can totally imagine him doing something like that."

"What happened?"

I crunched down on a pickle with a grin. "He claimed he was going for a jog and just happened to see me."

We all burst out laughing, because just like I'd known the second I'd spied him behind the tree, we all knew it was bullshit. I saw him way before he thought I had too.

"It was so pathetic. I'd tried to ignore him but he kept peering round the tree, so I stormed over, and he…"

"He what?"

My shoulders dropped, and I let out a groan. "He kind of looked like a lost puppy. It was so hard to be mad, and then he apologized. Really, really apologized. And…" I bit my lip to halt the barrage of memories, "then he kissed me."

"Holy shit."

Another huge cheer rent the air and we all looked out, remembering why we were here. The Mets had a new batter; the ball flew out of Ace's hand, and made contact with the bat

It didn't get very far – to third base in fact, and straight into Jupiter's outstretched glove. He caught it so casually he looked almost disappointed on the Jumbotron as the camera zoomed in on his face.

Then he smiled, a proper wide, honest-to-God smile.

Even though it probably wasn't the correct response, we all sighed deeply. In fact, I suspected that the entire collective of female fans in the crowds followed suit, even though everyone else was cheering.

None of us spoke for a good two minutes; we just absorbed the atmosphere. Finally, a voice asked, "Then what happened?"

I swallowed the final bite of my burger before answering. "Barney, the guy from boxing, walked over to us behind the tree, but he was more interested in getting a selfie than in what we were actually doing. In fact, even after Jupiter left, all he wanted to do was talk about him, and not because of anything to do with me. He went to call his friends."

"Didn't he want another date?" asked Payton, and for some reason right then, I couldn't imagine her without a fistful of numbers, guys lining up for a second date with her.

I shook my head. "No, I'd already told him it wasn't happening. I would have got there quicker, but Jupiter was distracting me."

We all turned to the field again; The Lions were switching out.

"What happened between then and now?"

"Well…" I picked at the label on my empty bottle, only for it to be switched out for a new one by a guy behind us I hadn't noticed. I waited until he left, then admitted, "I went over to his place last night, and..."

"You left this morning. The glow," Beulah interrupted, pointing at me accusingly.

I blushed, but I couldn't stop the smile they'd be able to see from the far side of the stadium.

"I'm so glad we picked you out a comfortable bed!"

I knew I was squinting quizzically. "What?"

"In your place. That bed is super comfortable is all I'm saying," she winked.

"It is; thank you."

"So... what now?" asked Kit.

"Now we see, I guess. He's already calling me his girlfriend, but I'm not ready for that yet. I know I want to give it a go and I know I want him. I just need a little time to get used to the Jupiter those girls want. That Jupiter..." I pointed as he ran off the field, turning in enough time to see him take his sunglasses off and wink up at me.

"There is not a dry pair of panties for anyone who saw that," laughed Payton, and I couldn't do anything but agree. "God, baseball players are hot. And now Ace has disappeared, it's time to pee again."

She jumped off her stool and ran off, leaving me to my thoughts. My gaze was firmly trained on the screen showing Jupiter in the dugout, downing a bottle of water in a way that made me need to quench my own thirst.

And from that moment and for the rest of the game, whenever he was on base, or at bat, or on the screen, my eyes were glued to him.

Because I was once more being pulled into Jupiter's gravitational field, something I knew from past experience was near impossible to get out of.

The Lions beat The Mets six to four. After Lux Weston had scored, Jupiter had hit two home runs, which had brought a couple of other guys home. Saint Velasquez hit the final home run of the game, and was named Player of the Game, down to the three balls he'd caught.

And now I was walking out to the parking lot; Jupiter's arm slung over my shoulder with no care in the world, even though I kept looking around to check no one could see us.

"Marn, my place or yours?" We reached his car and he was grinning at me like I was in on the joke, though I was certain I wasn't.

"What's so funny?"

He shook his head, but the smile didn't drop. "Nothing, just how happy it makes me that I get to ask you that. So…"

I thought of my super comfy mattress. "Mine. We can stay at my place."

"Yeah." He kissed me quickly as he opened the passenger door for me. "A sleepover at my girlfriend's."

There was that word again.

It had me hesitating before I got in the car. "Jupe, do you remember when we were kids before you asked me to be your girlfriend… we basically made out for a month?"

"Yeah, it was amazing."

I tried not to grip onto the doorframe; I didn't want this to go the way of the friends suggestion. "Do you think we could do that again? Try it on for size?"

"What?" His grin turned into a frown as he balked. "You wanna make out for a month? *Just* make out? After last night? No sex? I mean..." He stopped talking and I could see him trying so hard to be calm. I had to hold back my smile just to see where he went with it, especially as he now looked like a little boy who'd dropped his ice cream cone in a muddy puddle. "Um... yeah, I guess."

I cupped his face. "No, I mean, can we just see how things go?"

He blinked slowly. "I don't know what that means. Things are... we're back together, right? We are, aren't we?"

"Jupiter, it's been a long time. I want to take it slow, get to know each other. Is that okay?"

"Okay," he kissed me again, as though needing to check. "We can do that, but you're okay, right? We're okay?"

"Yes, I'm good." I gave him my biggest smile, and he finally closed the door to get in on his side. "We're good."

It was true, I was. We were.

But it was a leap from sex to girlfriend, and I didn't add that if my heart was broken again, I wouldn't recover this time.

15

Jupiter

Present Day

"So what's Emerson been up to since school? Will Piper be there, too? What about Jenson? Do you still talk to him?"

I took my eyes off the road for a second to glance at Marnie, again. For the past five minutes, instead of holding my hand she'd been smoothing down her jeans.

"Star, you okay?" I leaned over to give her cheek a quick kiss, and squeezed her thigh – where my hand was still unheld. "There's no need to be nervous."

We've been doing *our thing* for over a week now, and were on our way to the twins' birthday party. She'd been quiet most of the morning. I was certain it had everything to do with seeing my family again, and overthinking the situation as she had always been prone to do. Though I wasn't quite sure which particular element of it she was overthinking; though it was likely all of it, or more probably the questions which were bound to come flying thick and fast. I'd already warned Emerson and my mother, who was visiting for the weekend, that they needed to go easy, but I couldn't imagine they'd pay any attention to what I wanted.

I was still trying to do my 'listening and give her space' thing, which I was no doubt excelling at. It didn't matter that as far as I was concerned, she was my girlfriend, even if I wasn't quite sure what she was calling me, and even if she had dropped my hand twice this week when we'd been walking down the hallway to her office.

"I'm not, just, you know, I'm interested."

"Okay… is that why you're firing questions at me?" I stared at her hands, which were still moving. She looked up and stopped with a grin. "Yes, Jenson and I are still close. He's a sports' lawyer; he's mine actually. He gave Beulah hell on the negotiations of my contract."

"Wow, really? That's cool, good for him."

I nodded. "Yeah, he did okay for himself. I would have still loved to play with him though. As for the rest of your questions… no, Piper isn't coming. One of her kids has chicken pox, so they luckily got to bail. Emerson moved over here a couple of years ago. Her husband, Drew, used to play for the Rangers – it's the hockey team in New York."

"I know that!"

I shot her a side-eye and raised my eyebrow.

"Okay, I didn't," she smirked.

"They have three kids; the twins, who are three today, and an eight-month-old boy."

"Do they have names?"

I shifted gears, moving out from behind the Sunday driver and put my foot down. "Yeah. Gabriella and Grey are the twins, and the baby is…"

Shit. My mind blanked, and it didn't go unnoticed by my passenger.

"Oh my God, Jupe! Don't you know?"

Xander. That was it.

"Of course I do, it's Alexander, but everyone calls him Xander. Drew already has Grey in ice skates, so I'm going to be working on Xander for baseball."

She gave a quiet chuckle, mumbling, "Wow, three kids. She's my age..." under her breath, then went back to smoothing her jeans. Any longer and she'd smooth a hole in them. "Is it going to be busy?"

I groaned. "God I hope not, or we're doing a gift dump and leaving."

"You don't like kids? Or is this The Grouch talking?"

I laughed. The Grouch, as she'd taken to calling me whenever I got, well… grouchy, but coming from her I only found it amusing, and it almost counteracted any mood I might have been in. I even managed to have a conversation with Ace yesterday without wanting to throttle him, because I kept picturing her.

It wasn't just that either… it was like all the sex we'd been having had given me superpowers with Go-Go-Gadget arms. I hadn't missed a ball all week when I definitely should have been falling asleep on the field. But I'd caught them all; not a single one dropped.

And we were in a new winning streak; six games in a row, putting us firmly third from the top of the National League East table.

Several times over the past week I'd given thanks that we worked for the same team, because if we hadn't, I'm not sure I'd have seen her during daylight hours. As it was, I still didn't get to see her as much as I wanted, though I did make sure I kept up our daily brainstorming sessions, even if a total of zero brainstorming had been done this week.

I zoomed across four lanes and pulled off the interstate. "I like kids. What I don't like is screaming kids and lots of them hopped up on sugar, which is what today will be, but as long as I have you to protect me, I'll be fine."

I brought her hand to my lips, even though I distinctly heard a tut-tut from her.

"Do you want kids?"

"Marn, are you asking me to get you pregnant? Because if so, I'll pull over right now and do it."

"Jupiter!"

"I'm serious." I stopped at the light and turned to face her. "I want babies with you. I want you to have my kids, lots of them, so say the word..."

Unfortunately, she didn't say any word so I carried on driving, and five minutes later, pulled off down the street leading to my sister's place. Before they had Xander, they split their time between their loft in the city where I was currently crashing, and their house upstate, but once he came along, they moved out here permanently. Emerson owned a successful gym in the city, which had grown into three locations, the newest of which was in nearby Scarsdale for all the bored housewives to keep themselves occupied when they weren't shopping.

Five minutes later we pulled up to the gate, and even Marnie groaned as they opened. Emerson and Drew's house wasn't small. The same went for the long-ass driveway, except you wouldn't know from its current state. The entire space was full, and the party was apparently being sponsored by Range Rover. There were so many black ones parked that it would be impossible to tell the difference when guests eventually left. I was adding to the mix, though at least mine was navy.

The upside of this was that Drew clearly had plenty of people to help with balloons, and I was officially taking myself off the hook.

"Jupe, there are so many people!" Marnie cried. "I thought you said this was going to be small."

I cut the engine behind the car I knew was Emerson's. "I hear you, but let's just go in and see. If you need to get drunk to get through the day, I'm fully supportive of that."

She pursed her lips, giving me an opportunity to kiss them. "I don't need to get drunk."

At that point, an adult I didn't recognize passed by with a child under his arm, the kid's back legs flailing. "Sure? Because if that's the case, you can drive home and I will," I winked.

She dropped her head, only for me to slip my finger under her chin and tilt it back up.

"Marn, you don't have to say anything about us. The only people who will really care are my parents, and you can tell them the truth – that we reconnected and we're spending time together." I tried to ignore the slow twisting in my gut that I had to explain this to her. "It's no one's fucking business anyway."

Her light laughter put a halt on any further gnawing.

"See? It helps to be a grouch sometimes." My fingers caught the ends of her hair, and I pulled her toward me for a quick kiss. "Come on, we've got gifts to dispense."

I'd just opened the trunk when I heard a screech and peered round the car in time to find Emerson hugging Marnie. I'd known that screech hadn't been for me, seeing as it had only been weeks, not years, since I'd seen Emerson, plus I'd spoken to her last night – not that she'd ever greeted me like that.

"Nice of you to finally join us, you lazy bastard," drawled my brother-in-law, Drew, before pulling me into a one-armed hug so he didn't crush his baby son cradled in his other arm.

I snorted, which turned into loud laughter. "Dude, you've forgotten what it's like to work for a living. You're lucky I was up before lunchtime on my first day off in weeks. Serves you right for listening to me in the first place." I swept my arm around before continuing, "It doesn't look like you were short of help anyway."

"Oh, I know! Everything was done yesterday. I just wanted to see how early I could get you here."

I saved the eye roll but called him a dick anyway, then nodded at the trunk full of gifts. "Here, you carry these in, and I'll take Xander."

"Did you clear out FAO Schwartz?"

"I might have gotten carried away, but I haven't been to a birthday party since they were born, so figured I needed to make up for being an absentee uncle. In hindsight, I probably should have gotten them delivered here instead of my place."

He handed Xander over to me. Even though his hair was dark, like Drew, he had Emerson's eyes, which were almost exactly the same color as mine, and they were now staring at me, "Hey, Bud, how's it going?"

He responded with a spit bubble, as his little hand reached up for my beard. "It's better than your dad's huh? His is going grey, but not Uncle Jupiter. He still has lots of life left in him. Stick with me, I'll teach you what it's like to work hard."

Drew ignored the jab, shaking his head instead as I followed him inside. Marnie was long gone, swept up by my sister who I noticed hadn't bothered to say hello to me, and I walked into the kitchen just in time to see her being taken into the backyard by my mom.

I could go after her, check she was okay, but Marnie Matthews had reminded me plenty of times she didn't need protecting, and what was I to do but listen.

"Fucking finally, wondered when you'd roll out of bed!"

I spun around to find a group of degenerate dads, at least two of whom were holding a baby, standing in a corner. Though they weren't really standing, more like strategically placed to avoid getting called for Kid Duty by their significant others. All of the guys were friends of Drew's from his days playing hockey, and before the kids had come along, I'd often spent time with them during my off-seasons when I visited Emerson.

Plus, as fellow members of the elite sportsperson world, I used to cross paths with them occasionally.

"Dude, are you supposed to swear when kids are around? Isn't that rule 101 of parenting or something? Even I know that." I smirked at Felix, Drew's best friend and business partner, who was casually throwing popcorn into his mouth.

The pair of them retired from hockey a few years ago to set up a foundation for kids with disabilities to help them get into sports. It was cool, and I'd donated a truck load of signed bats, balls, sneakers, and shirts for their bi-annual foundation galas that always raised a ton of cash. Then I sent it all again when I started at The Lions.

"Yeah, moves to New York and stays on Pacific Time."

I grinned wide and walked to the corner where they were all standing.

"Clearly, as I told Drew, you lot have forgotten what hard work means." I moved around the group, hugging them. "I see you're already hiding."

"This is not hiding," Drew said as he returned with a couple of beers, and handed them around, saving the non-alcoholic one for me. "We're in the way out there."

We all peered into the enormous yard. The entire space looked like a fairground without the rides; face painters, a ball pit, a barbecue… and there were the balloons in a giant arch – yeah, I wasn't going to be helping with that. Down at the bottom was the pool, and even from this distance I could see how many kids were in it. A giant unicorn slide was roped into the middle, and currently had six bigger kids on the top from what I could see.

It looked intense.

I swigged my beer. "How long have you all been here?"

"Couple of hours."

A round of chuckles sounded as they got a look at my face. I know I said I wanted to have kids with Marnie, and I did, but the early mornings… I'll pass on that, thank you very much.

"I dunno," Jasper, an old teammate of Drew's, nodded at me. "You look pretty at home with a kid in your arms."

I looked down at Xander, still content being held by me and slapping my cheek every couple of minutes. If I could have a kid like this, I'd be happy. But with my luck I'd get the one who was outside and currently smashing up the flower beds with a full-size hockey stick.

"Fuck's sake," one of the guys growled as he took off and removed said hockey stick, then marched his kid back down to where the moms were.

"Anyway…" Jasper said as he swigged his beer, "the new season started well, and you've been playing well. Did Shepherd change the whole team?"

I narrowed my eyes at him. "Are you trying to say you haven't been avidly following the New York Lions?"

"Dude, between the Rangers, my wife, and kids, I have my hands full, so how 'bout you catch me up?"

I chuckled. Jasper Jacobs was also having a good season, and was well on his way to his first Stanley Cup win as part of the Rangers coaching team, so I guess I could cut him some slack. I showed support with a quick punch to his shoulder.

"Yeah, he changed the whole team, save for Lux Weston, Boomer Jones, and Parker King. You need to come to a game, man. The Stadium is top notch. He's pumped nearly a billion in, if you include the players too."

"Didn't most of that go on your salary?" snorted Drew. "Why are you not paying me rent again?"

I smirked and sipped my beer, willing myself not to rise to his bait, because this was our relationship. It started when he first started dating Emerson and I hadn't been too happy about it, but truth be told, he was a decent guy, and she couldn't have gotten anyone better. I still liked to give him shit though.

"I'm going to teach your son to play baseball for free, remember?"

He leaned over and snatched Xander from my arms. "This is a hockey kid."

"We'll see." I gently patted Drew's face. "We will see."

Xander looked like the only thing he actually cared about was where his next meal came from; and the conversation moved between baseball and hockey as quickly as a puck across fresh ice, or a home run.

"Well, something's working. I can't believe you beat the Mets! That was a fucking awesome game, dude."

Yeah, what a fucking game. That was the day after I'd

found Marnie at my door, and knowing she was watching had started my superpower. But more than that, it had been a couple of weeks since we'd started trying out the One Percent program of hers, and it was working.

I wasn't being biased either.

I'd overhead some of the guys talking about it.

"Yeah, that's all Marnie. She's been working her butt off, and it's starting to happen."

Jasper's brows knotted. "What does that mean?"

"She's got this theory that if we improve the tiny things that annoy us, we'll improve exponentially overall as team."

She'd already got me my little bat baggies, so I was happy. I was still working on the tape to keep Ace's trap shut though.

"Huh, sounds interesting," was all he said, but I could see the cogs turning. I wouldn't put it past Jasper to have the Rangers signed up to it next year.

"Wait, hold up." We all turned to Felix, who actually had his hand up. "Marnie? We're not talking about Marnie Matthews? *The* Marnie Matthews?"

I cringed and was about to accuse Drew of blabbing, because I'd momentarily forgotten about a night during the off season a few years ago when I'd gotten drunk with him and Felix, and we'd spent the night lamenting our love lives. Or they did; I just doled out sage advice while they'd been crying.

But I had let it slip about Marnie.

"I said nothing." Drew held his free hand up in defense, before an expression you could only describe as devilish crossed his face. "I haven't even told them you brought her here today."

That was enough for Felix to choke on whatever snack he'd been shoveling into his mouth, because the dude did not stop eating.

"The girl that came in with Emerson?" His eyes widened when Drew nodded. "Are you telling me the famous Marnie Matthews is here, and we get to meet her?"

The eye roll I saved from earlier came out in full force, but then I nodded slowly, at the same speed the grin spread across my face.

"One and the same."

"So you actually got her? Like, you're dating?"

I could safely agree to the dating question, because we were definitely fucking dating.

"Yes. And yes."

It took a while for him to close his mouth, then… "How?"

Drew hitched Xander up on his hip with a smirk. "Yeah, Jupe, how? How did you get Marnie? Why did you come to The Lions again?"

Felix and Jasper looked between us, back and forth, and back again – with identical confused expressions.

"Shepherd paid me a visit when he took control of The Lions. I said I'd only join the team if he found Marnie. It was a gamble that paid off." I shrugged, casually. "It's taken me a month to convince her we belong together, though."

"Have you met her yet?" Felix asked as he turned to Drew, who shook his head.

"Nope, but it's literally all Emerson has talked about for a month. Then your parents turned up…"

I glanced outside just in time to see Emerson go running to the side of the pool as one of the kids fell in, or was pushed. There seemed to be a lot of crying, but Marnie and my mom were still off to the side, deep in conversation.

"Actually, where's my dad? I should probably go and find

them."

"They don't care about anything except Marnie, believe me. And your dad is in the pool, where he's been all morning," replied Drew, sounding more amused than annoyed.

I looked again. Unless he was under the unicorn, I couldn't see him. "Okay, well, I should probably head down there. Wish me luck."

I wasn't about to add that I'd spent long enough away from Marnie for my liking, and I was beginning to fidget. Me, Jupiter Reeves, fidgety because he'd been separated from his girlfriend…

"I'll come with you, just in case Emerson needs rescuing," said the guy who was equally twitchy at being separated from his wife, and I followed him out of the kitchen. "Come on then, spill it."

"Spill what?"

"You know what."

I stopped walking and waited for a creepy-as-fuck clown to pass us. "I thought it would take longer to happen because she was so mad and wanted nothing to do with me. I wasn't entirely convinced I'd even manage to get her back."

"How did you manage then?"

"My winning personality, how else d'ya think?" I slapped his cheek again, just because I knew it irritated the living shit out of him.

He crossed his arms, both brows raised, and waited for the real explanation.

"I threatened anyone else with a beat-down if they so much as looked in her direction," I grinned. "Oh, and I forced her to work with me."

"There it is…"

My voice dropped. "It's only been a week, but… shit, I dunno. I thought I was in love with her before, but getting her back… I feel like I'm falling so hard I didn't even realize this kind of love existed. Like the whole world stops when we're together."

Drew's eyes got all watery; because while he might have been one of the meanest wingers in the NHL, he was also a massive cry baby.

"Jeez, pull it together. There are kids here, man. It's embarrassing that you're the only one crying."

He wiped his eyes. "I'm good, just happy for you, Jupe. You deserve it, really. Maybe you'll smile a bit more now."

I grinned. "Maybe I will."

"So are you officially a couple? Do we need to get Ella sized up for a bridesmaid's dress? Or is it going to be a housewarming present situation?"

I ran my hands through my hair, feeling a little less confident than I had a couple of minutes ago. "Not exactly. She wants to take it slow…"

"Sounds normal."

"Does it?"

Drew looked at me like Marnie did the time she was trying to explain black hole theory to me. "Yes, it's normal. Girls are..." He paused. There wasn't a good way to end that sentence. "Why are you rushing anyway?"

"I'm not!" I grumbled, because it sounded like the sort of thing Marnie had said to me. "I just… I never thought I'd find her again, and she's all I thought about for so long. I'm not good at being patient."

"Dude, I totally get it, but if you can keep your shit together, it'll pay off." He put his arm around my shoulders. "Now come on, I want to meet this girl who's finally untwisted your panties."

"Oh, fuck off," I grinned, narrowly avoiding two older kids charging past with Super Soakers. "You're the worst brother-in-law."

"Nah, I'm the best and we both know it. But keep swearing in front of my son, and I'll staple your mouth shut."

I looked at Xander who let out an ear piercing shriek, and nearly tipped out of Drew's arm because he'd spied the group of ladies we were heading toward, which included both his mom, and mine.

"There he is! Where've you been hiding?"

"Me?" I leaned down and kissed my mom's cheek, peering over to where Marnie momentarily looked up from a conversation she was deeply involved in; her smile was like a rainbow to my chest. Then she went straight back to it, and I wasn't sure what I was so worried about. "You disappeared with Marnie the second we arrived! You didn't even bother to say hi."

"I'm saying hello now," she said, like my suggestion she should have greeted her only son any sooner was preposterous. It wasn't like she hadn't been calling every single day either – I spoke to her less when I'd lived a mile away, though now it became clear why she'd been so clingy.

"Uh huh," I muttered and released myself from her grasp. "Enjoying the party?"

She clasped her hands together with the same kind of look that Drew had been sporting. "Oh, Jupiter, it's so wonderful seeing Marnie again. She hasn't changed a bit. I'm so happy that you've been able to work things out."

I tried not to roll my eyes. It was no secret my mom wasn't exactly a fan of me being single, and while she tried to avoid any of *that* type of press, the tabloids still loved to couple me up with anyone I was photographed with, even ones I hadn't been spied with – someone new every week. Then after Emerson settled down and the kids came along, she really made her feelings about my social life known.

The fact Marnie was even here would probably be enough to sustain her for all future Christmas and birthday presents.

"Okay, well, I hope you had fun catching up with her. You guys are all sitting together tomorrow night at the game." I twisted around as a cry let out from the unicorn to see my dad jumping off the top in a cannonball, then turned back to my mom. "What is he doing?"

"He's been teaching them how to make the biggest splash." She sighed the way you only could when you'd been married nearly forty years, then went back to find Marnie, clearly done with me.

I walked over and stood on the edge of the pool, just in time to see my dad emerging. "Hey, Pop."

"Jupe, buddy! You coming in?" he asked, swimming over to me.

"Not today, no. I didn't bring a change of clothes."

"Shame, you should have. You were always the best at cannonballs."

I grinned. "True, but I learned everything from you. You planning on staying in there much longer, or are you gonna come and have a beer with your only son?"

He laughed loudly. "Yeah, I'm coming. Let me get dressed and I'll meet you by the barbecue."

He hopped out and shook off the water. I was fit; a professional athlete in his prime, but I sincerely hoped that when I finally reached my dad's age, I was still in as good a shape as he was now. That's what a daily surf and living on the beach did for you.

"Deal."

"Uncle Jupiter!"

I glanced down at the tugging on my shorts to find Gabriella standing wide-eyed and looking like butter wouldn't melt in her mouth, something she got from her mom. I scooped her up in my arms, planting a kiss on her cheek. "Hi, birthday girl. How're you doing, cutie pie? Where's your brother?"

"He's digging for slugs with Samson." She pulled a face, and I pulled one right back.

"Slugs? Gross."

"I know." She shuddered dramatically and pointed across the yard. "Who's that lady?"

"Which one?

"The pretty one with the long hair talking to Mommy."

I grinned. Marnie did look beautiful today. She'd been wearing her hair down all week, big fat waves tumbling down her back. When we were kids, I used to try and separate out the little gold strands bleached from the Californian sunshine. It was darker now, but I couldn't wait for more to lighten during the summer. Her nose was crinkling up with laughter at whatever Emerson was telling her, and the apple of her cheeks had pinked.

I stopped staring when Gabriella prodded me. "Uncle Jupiter?"

"If I tell you, can you keep it a secret?"

She nodded with utmost seriousness.

"That's my girlfriend. Her name is Marnie."

Her eyes widened even further, like only a newly three-year old's could. "Grey has a girlfriend."

It wasn't the response I expected. "Does he now?"

She nodded solemnly. "I saw him give her his Animal

Crackers." She chewed on her bottom lip and asked, "Do you love your girlfriend like daddy loves mommy?"

I brushed her hair back from her face, and straightened her unicorn headband. "I do."

"What's going on here?"

"Mommy!" she squealed, making my ears ring. I wouldn't be surprised if my eardrums had actually burst. "Uncle Jupiter is telling me about his girlfriend, but I'm not allowed to tell you."

Emerson threw her head back and laughed while I muttered 'traitor' under my breath. "You should know better than to confide in a three-year-old, especially this one. She's the blabbermouth of the family."

"Now you tell me." I rolled my eyes and put Gabriella down so she could go and destroy someone else's hearing. "Have fun reconnecting?"

Emerson pulled me into a hug. "Oh, Jupe, I did. I really did. It's so good to see her. You too; you seem calmer."

I frowned. "What does that mean?"

But she just shrugged.

"I'm glad you've finally found her again, it's been long enough. Though," she pinned me with a look, "you haven't told her why you broke up in the first place."

I glanced over to where Marnie was now talking to Drew, which meant I likely needed to rescue her. "Emerson, it doesn't matter. It's the past, and we're together now."

"Just as long as it doesn't come back to bite you on the ass…"

"Why would it?" I snapped, not wanting to continue this conversation, especially when she gave me another pointless shrug.

I went in search for Marnie and found her heading down toward the restroom, so I jogged after her.

"Hey," I whispered, snaking my arms round her waist and pulled her against the wall. "Are you ready to go? I think I'm partied out, and I want to show you something before we get home," I kissed her head, "and then we're spending the rest of the afternoon naked."

In a less than a flash her pupils widened, and her pulse ratcheted up.

"I'll take that as a yes," I chuckled.

"You do that." She thumbed to the restroom, "Can I pee first though?"

"Yes. I'll go and find my parents. Meet you in five?"

"Make it four," she grinned.

After all the goodbyes and calendar schedules my mom made to meet Marnie before tomorrow's game, it actually took fifteen minutes to get out of there. I was expecting her to have some kind of freak-out the second we drove out of the gates, but she was perfectly calm, quietly smiling to herself.

I peered over at her. "You okay there?"

She nodded slowly. "Yes. I was just thinking how good it was to see Emerson. She seems really happy, and the kids are adorable."

I wasn't quite ready to divulge exactly how pleased it made me to hear her say that, but I leaned over and kissed her quickly. Marnie changed the music, and then went back to her thoughts as I took a left out of Emerson's place and headed down the road, driving through the town and out the other side in contented silence. I hadn't spent much time actually *in* the town, because whenever I was visiting, I tended to camp out at Emerson and Drew's house. Plus it was usually too much hassle going out in public, but I think it was a place I could get used to. It reminded me a little of Malibu, just without the beach, Pacific Ocean, and year-round sunshine.

Finally we came to a turning down a dirt path that I'd missed the last time I'd visited. I slowed almost to a stop which had Marnie paying more attention to our surroundings and the large red PRIVATE PROPERTY: KEEP OUT signs to either side.

"Jupe, where are we?"

I laced my fingers between hers, bringing them to my lips. "You'll see."

She sat up straighter and peered out the window, though all she could see was giant hedgerows. Her frown turned confused as the path opened up to us, and a ramshackle farmhouse in the middle of a field appeared.

"Whose house is this?" Her eyes kept flicking between me and the No Entry signs. My girl was not a rule breaker. "I don't think we're supposed to be here."

"It's okay." I pulled up and stopped the engine, then removed my sunglasses and turned to her so she could search my face for an explanation. "This house is mine… well, ours."

"Jupiter…" she gasped, her eyes widening. "Wha… what? You bought us a house?"

Fuck. I could feel my insides flip-flopping. It was still a sensation I was getting used to whenever Marnie was concerned.

"I bought it when you agreed to come to New York. I haven't touched it. In fact, I've only been here the one time because I didn't want to jinx anything. I was hoping… well, waiting, I guess… until we got to the point where we could build a home together. I'm not saying that's today; I know we're still getting used to things, but I wanted to bring you anyway."

Her mouth dropped, then she started chewing on her lip, but it wasn't in the way I liked. I ignored it and jumped out of the car, running to her side before she could object. "Come on, I want to show you something."

She took my hand quietly and followed me. "I haven't been around the house because I wanted you to be here with me, but there is something I do have plans for. It's the reason I bought it."

I wasn't sure whether it was a good sign she hadn't said anything yet as I led her through to the huge field behind the house, which stretched all the way down to a little stream at the bottom. The structure in front of us was what had sealed the deal; an old stone outbuilding, just like the farmhouse, also falling down in equal parts.

"It feels like we're in the middle of nowhere."

I laughed, because that was exactly the point. "I know, even though Drew and Emerson are ten minutes away."

"Was this what you had plans for?" She pointed to the outbuilding, her face saying everything else.

It was a dump.

Still, the birds chirping in the surrounding trees did add a little something.

"It is. Wanna hear them?"

She nodded. I pulled her into the building, which was almost pitch black, so pulled her back outside because I wanted to see her face when I told her. Plus, it didn't look that safe, and we could do without the concussion from a stray falling brick.

"You can totally veto it, but hear me out..." I took hold of her hand and laced our fingers together for a tour around the outside. "I thought that we could replace the top half of this stone with glass – you know, for walls of glass. We can put in heated flooring and turn it into a cozy space, add a bed... then above us would be a retractable glass roof so we can watch the stars all year round. Even when it's freezing cold we can sleep under the stars, and it'll feel like we're camping back at your place. And the best bit," I grinned, "as we're in the middle of nowhere, we won't get so much light pollution. It's not Joshua Tree, but it'll be closer than New York's skies."

She let out a little gasp, slowly turning around. I stood still as she let go of my hand and walked off, her fingers trailing along the stone until she vanished around the corner. I was about to go searching for her, but another minute and she was back, glancing up at me. "You're building me an observatory?"

I nodded. "It's not round, but... yes"

Her eyes filled with tears that soon streamed down her face. "Jupiter... I... I don't know what to say."

I wiped her cheeks dry and dipped down, brushing my lips to hers in the most gentle kiss I could muster. "You don't have to say anything."

She sniffed hard, rising up on her tiptoes to kiss me again. Her arms wound softly around my neck. "It's the kindest, most incredible thing anyone's ever done for me. I can't believe it."

I shrugged, suddenly feeling all kinds of self-conscious which was freaking me the fuck out.

"You deserve it. You deserve everything, and I want to be the one giving it to you."

"Thank you." Her hand cupped my cheek, while her eyes

roamed around my face. The tears were making it hard to read the expression behind them, because the harder I looked, the more I wasn't altogether convinced I'd done something good.

"Whaddya say? Think it's too early to christen this place?"

She looked down to the semi-dried mud we were standing in and then back up at me with a tiny grimace. "Isn't it too muddy?"

"Maybe, my little Star, maybe," I said, an idea forming. "But I think we could make it work, somehow."

She squealed as I scooped her up and carried her over to the car. Everything else was forgotten the second her lips joined with mine – where they stayed until long past sundown.

16

Marnie

Fourteen years ago - April

"Ahhh… gahd, Jupe, please… Jupiter." My head fell back on his pillow with a throaty moan.

Every muscle in my body was coiled tight, ready to explode; *desperate* to explode. But I wasn't allowed to, as for the past thirty minutes I'd been kept on a slow and steady simmer. I was struggling to breathe, struggling to do anything except concentrate on what his tongue was doing to me – or not doing.

I definitely wasn't concentrating on the question he'd asked me.

"What's the answer, Marn? Two more answers, then I'll let you come." Another long drag of his tongue reminded me of exactly what he was doing.

It was the worst kind of torture.

"He-proposed-that-comets-with-very-long-periods-originate-from-a-cloud-of-small-bodies-orbiting-the-sun-at-a-distance-of-one-light-year," I blurted as quickly as I could. Anything to stop this sexual torture.

I could hear him checking if I was right.

"Good girl. You're gonna ace this, Marn! Okay… last one… shit, I don't even understand half these words, let alone the entire sentence. What is the MHD approximation?"

His fingers slowly pumped inside me. They hadn't once picked up the pace, no matter how much I'd begged for it. I scoured the recesses of my brain for the answer; I know I'd been reading about it earlier in the week.

"A reduction of the equations of fluid mechanics coupled with Maxwell's equations."

"Correct. Now you earned your prize." He said no more, but his tongue got to work.

Long, thick strokes, each one applying more pressure, the pressure I'd been craving, that I needed. His fingers were still pumping inside me, each pass rubbing against *that* spot; the one that made me see stars.

My thighs were heavy, my breathing labored, and every sensation was magnified a thousand times by my hyper-sensitive skin. He'd been building a dam, and all I wanted to do was crash through it until there was nothing but rubble.

I was vaguely aware of his head lifting, his tongue switching out for his thumb, but I didn't get time to register properly as my orgasm was finally, *finally* wrenched from me as viciously as if I'd been ripped apart.

If I thought I'd have a second of reprieve, some time to suck fresh oxygen into my lungs, I was mistaken.

"Fuck, you're stunning when you come." Jupiter scooped me up like a rag doll. "Straddle me in case you're too sensitive. I want your tits bouncing in my face."

I was so wet that I took him easily, but the sensation of his thick cock stretching me out when I'd barely arrived back on earth was almost too much. Even a month of having sex as often as we could was still not enough to get me used to that initial sting of him inside me. I was still fluttering as he began pumping into me, gripping my hips so tightly that if I looked down, I knew there'd be little white patches under his fingertips where he'd stopped my blood flowing.

His hand smoothed along my chest until his whole palm cupped my breast and his lips found their way to my nipple. When his eyes finally held mine, his pupils were so blown I could barely see the blue iris surrounding them.

"I can't get enough of this. I can't get enough of you," he gritted out, his voice like gravel over my skin. "Marn, fuck, I'm gonna come, watching you… look at you taking my cock. It's too much for me to last long."

My fingers scratched through the sweat-dampened tendrils of hair at the base of his neck, and I began rocking in his lap in the exact way he loved me to do. "I want it, Jupe. Let me feel it."

His mouth hit mine with precision accuracy, hard and bruising, just as his hips thrust wild and frenzied into me. A deep, animalistic rumble charged up his throat, becoming trapped against my lips as he erupted inside me.

We collapsed together; the softy downy comforter cushioning us as we fell back.

"Holy shit, Marn, that was another level. If I knew studying was this hot, I'd have been getting straight As years ago." He gently kissed me when I frowned. "You know what I mean."

I wasn't actually sure I did, but I let it go because he was right about the study sessions. They were hot, and I couldn't keep my hands off him. I'd aced every test I had since we'd begun studying like this, and even Jupiter was averaging a B now instead of a C. He even got an A on an English paper.

That had been the best study session, and after his grade, his mom had handed us a hundred dollars to go for burgers and a movie, but we went down to the boardwalk instead and made out on the Ferris Wheel.

He adjusted us so I was underneath him, hovering above me with his perfect smile as he brushed away the mass of hair stuck to my forehead.

"I'm serious. This past few months with you… it's been incredible. My grades are amazing and I'm playing better than I ever have before. I heard some Dodgers scouts are coming to the game tonight, and it's all because of you."

"I don't know any Dodgers scouts," I said with a grin.

"You know what I mean," he repeated, running his nose along my neck before nipping me. When he looked up his eyes had changed; they'd become softer, bluer. "I love you, Marnie Matthews."

Out of nowhere, my throat thickened, and I couldn't swallow down the tears stuck in my throat quickly enough to let out more than a rasped, "I love you, too."

"Hey, don't cry. It's a good thing."

"I'm not, I'm just… they're happy tears. I just…"

"What?"

I tried to move on the pillow, but I was trapped between his elbows resting either side of my head. I didn't want him to see the anguish that had started creeping in. "It's nearly the end of the year. You'll get drafted, and I'm going to Boston."

He smiled softly. "I know, but we'll figure it out. I'm not

letting geography get in the way."

"Actually, I've been thinking about it."

A lot. I'd been thinking about it a lot, so much so that I had the beginnings of a plan.

At least he looked intrigued. "Oh?"

"I've come up with a couple of options. One, I don't have to go to M.I.T. early. I can stay in school here for another two years; or two, I stay in school and apply to CalTech." I smiled, ready to deliver my wild card. "You can practically see the campus from Dodger Stadium. I'd get in there, easily, and once you're in the majors, it would be so easy to come to all your games."

He shifted his body until he slipped out of me. I immediately missed the warmth of him, especially as it felt like the air was cooling around us from more than just the A/C. "Marn, all you talk about is M.I.T. Even I know how perfect the program is there, because you told me about it a hundred times when we first got together. You've wanted to attend since you were a kid, when you found out Buzz Aldrin went there. You've always wanted to go to M.I.T., just like I've always wanted to play for The Dodgers."

I tried to ignore the way my heart rate spiked; not in the good way, in the way that it did before panic set in.

"I know, but there are still fine programs for me at CalTech. It's an excellent school. I'll still get to do what I want."

"Where's this coming from?" He searched my face but I didn't want to voice it, because it was dumb. Because I knew I'd miss him so much it would feel like my heart had stopped, but he could see it from the way my eyes filled with tears before I could stop them. "Marn, don't worry about us, we're strong enough to survive a little distance for a while. I'm not letting you give up your dream." He dipped down, trying to calm my worries with a kiss. “We’ll make a pact; we won’t go more than three weeks without seeing each other. If you can come in term time, then I can travel during the holidays and breaks I get. Deal?”

I nodded.

“Good,” he kissed me again, a light smack of his lips. “I need to get in the shower before my parents get back from taking Emerson to the mall, and then head to warm ups. You’re still meeting Emerson to come to the game later, right?”

I nodded, and tried mustering up a smile. “Yeah, wouldn’t miss it. I’ll see if I can find the scouts and talk you up.”

“That’s my girl.”

My smile still hadn’t reached my eyes as he ran into the bathroom.

“I didn’t expect it to be so busy.”

Emerson and I were walking through campus to the stands. I wished we could hurry a bit quicker, but the way she kept turning around was slowing us down. At this rate we’d be standing in the wings instead of getting a seat near home plate.

“Yeah, it’s a big game today. Jupe said he thinks there’ll be Dodgers scouts there, too.” I frowned as she spun again and nearly walked into a couple of guys from the football team who jogged past us. “What are you looking for?”

“Mallory said she’d meet us here with the McAvoy twins, but I can’t see her anywhere.”

“Have you called her?”

She held up her phone. "No cell reception. It's always so shitty when the crowds are big. Seems kind of pointless as that's when you need to find people the most."

I was just about to suggest we went and found seats to save, because Mallory would figure out eventually that we'd gone to sit down, and then at least she'd have a spot once she arrived. But then I heard a loud cry, and the problem was solved.

"God, I've been looking for you everywhere!" she huffed, as she tried to catch her breath from wherever she'd sprinted, which seemed to be somewhere with water given the drips still flying off her short blonde hair. "Hey, Marn, how's it going?"

"Hey, I'm good. Why are you wet?" I pulled the two of them off the path, as another crowd of people surged past us, all heading to the stadium.

"I came from the beach. I didn't realize the time. I just had enough to rinse the sand off and wash my hair."

Emerson's nose wrinkled up, her freckles spreading almost the exact same way as Jupiter's. "Where are the others?'

"They not here?"

Emerson and I both shook our heads.

"Oh, they said to meet them here…" She looked around like Emerson had done. "But if they're not, I say let's go and get seats. They can find us there. My legs are already like Jell-O, I don't want to be standing all night."

Finally, a plan I could get behind.

"Great, let's go."

We got back on the path and joined the swarm, a bright shock of orange as everyone headed in the same direction wearing team shirts or school sweaters. I was wearing one of Jupiter's baseball sweaters, his initials sewn into the breast, along with his name across the back. Emerson had one on too, while Mallory was wearing her own school sweater.

The crowds in front of us had begun to bottle neck as everyone tried to get into the stadium. Mallory and I found ourselves being swiftly yanked to the side by Emerson. "This way, it's quicker."

We snuck behind a row of billboards and found ourselves going through a darkened tunnel underneath the stadium, made darker by the early evening twilight. Turning a corner, we were blasted by the bright floodlights and finally came out the other end… and onto the side of the field.

"Ohmygod, Emerson, how did you know about this?" Mallory hissed.

"Crew showed me." The only Crew I knew was Crew Hollander, wide receiver, which would make sense seeing as this stadium housed the football team in the winter. "Come on, we don't want to get caught here."

We ran along the far outside wall of the field until there was an opening we could sneak into. I spied an empty bench halfway up, and pointed. "We can sit up there."

All three of us sprinted up the steps to get there before anyone else could, and then collapsed.

"I need to do more cardio," Emerson wheezed, looking at her phone as it pinged. "Ooh cell reception. Spread out, we're going to have to save some seats between us. I'll let the twins know where we are."

Where we were was in really amazing seats halfway up behind home plate. We couldn't have gotten better ones if we'd been lining up outside since lunchtime. I had just enough view that I could make out our team in their tunnel by the dugout. I pushed my glasses up to get a clearer picture, and my heart thumped hard. Jupiter was in the shadows with Jenson. I could make him out by his shirt, though I'd probably have recognized his ass too.

I stared until I couldn't see any longer, given the speed at which the stadium was filling up, and the amount of people passing through my eye line, as well as trying to squash me closer to Emerson.

"How'd your parents get down at the front?" cried Mallory when she spotted Emerson's mom and dad, sitting behind the dugout.

"They always sit there. The parents get preferential seating."

"Huh, that's cool." Mallory rolled her lips, then spun around to a guy trying to sit next to her, "Sorry, saved."

He trundled off.

"The twins had better get here soon," she grumbled. "We can't save seats all night."

I shifted up a little as someone wedged themselves into the space next to me, and he was too big to argue with. "Have you never been to a game before?"

She shook her head. "Not this year. I've been struggling with time because if I'm not surfing, I'm studying. I've been to a few, but it's a bit boring."

"Yeah, I understand the studying part." Jupiter naked flashed into my head, and I squeezed my thighs shut.

"When are your exams? I'm so done with it all. School blows sometimes."

I shrugged looking a little sheepish. "I don't have any. I've done all the work I need to for M.I.T. when I applied early, but I'm trying to get ahead of first year so I don't fall behind."

She nudged me. "Shit, Marn, that's some big brain you have. No wonder we never see you in class. Ours are like elementary school compared to yours. At least chill out a bit, come down to the beach and surf with me," she grinned. "You can even bring Jupe if you want. I'd love to see that lump on a surfboard."

My laugh was drowned out by an announcement over the loudspeakers cutting through the music playing, asking us all to sing the National Anthem. We all stood, more out of habit than anything else, until it was time – made known by the vocal expertise of the crowd hollering and whooping.

Then the boys arrived. My belly flipped as Jupiter appeared and took position on third base. His eyes traveled through the crowd, past his parents, and the second I thought there was no way he'd spot me, his gaze hit me brighter than a spotlight, followed by a grin I felt deep in my core.

I was brought back to my present with a hefty nudge from Emerson. "Don't make me need to hurl, please."

I snorted hard. "Sorry, Em. I'll try my best."

She grinned back before she shot up and began waving enthusiastically, adding to the chaos of the stadium. "Twins!"

I hadn't met Emerson's friends before; identical twins called LJ and Ainsley. As they got closer to us, it dawned on me I'd seen them around school but never together, so I hadn't realized they were two different people.

Mallory and Emerson gave them both a hug before Emerson pulled me up. "Hey guys, this is Marnie, my brother's girlfriend."

I waved shyly. "Hey, nice to meet you."

"Marn, this is LJ," Emerson gestured to the twin in black, then to the one in a Jupiter sweater, just like most people here were wearing, "and this is Ainsley."

LJ hugged me hello, while Ainsley just stared at me. I was beginning to think I had something on my face but then she smiled, weakly, and sat next to Emerson. The entire interaction was incredibly weird, but maybe she was one of those people who warmed up a little slower than others.

I could definitely relate to that.

"Glad you found us. We were going to have to give up these seats soon."

LJ removed her jacket at sat down. "Sorry, it took us ages to get in. It's a busy game tonight."

I almost fell into her as I was shoved forward by a guy moving onto the bench in the row behind me, who in turn had been shoved by the group behind him. I bent to pick up his wallet which had fallen on the floor, along with a couple of credit cards and his – HOLY SHIT! LA DODGERS I.D. CARD!

This was HUGE.

"Thank you," Dodgers guy said. "It's busy tonight."

I nodded, forcing myself to blink. "Oh, it's always like this. It's a great team."

I spun back around as the stadium erupted in cheers; the first runner was thrown out at first base. I wanted to go back to The Dodgers guy, watch him while he watched, but instead I crossed everything I could in the hope Jupiter had a good game.

If he played well, there was no way they wouldn't want him. Everyone would want him.

By the end of the third, Santa Monica High was up three to one. The baseball gods were shining on Jupiter because he'd been having an awesome game, the best I'd seen him play.

He'd caught four balls straight off the bat, and his aim had hit the bullseye every time, wherever he'd been throwing it.

S.M.H. was next at bat, and Jupiter was fifth in the batting order. The diet coke I'd been drinking had gone straight through me.

"I'm going to the restroom before Jupiter is up."

I ran up the steps to find the nearest, praying there wasn't a line. Thankfully I found one.

"Oh, look who it is." A hard shoulder barged into me, pushing me forward, and I had to brace myself against the wall before I hit the hand dryer. "Little Miss Perfect."

"What?" I looked in the mirror to find an ice-cold stare belonging to one of the many hordes of girls I'd seen following Jupiter around.

I was a nerd. I wasn't oblivious to the comments which shot my way on occasion or a little light bullying. But for the most part I avoided it, which was due to me either being locked in the lab with my head down, or tutoring a jock. And I was smart enough to know the jocks bought me some protection.

But Jupiter had propelled me to the front of the crowds. Being seen with him, holding hands, being kissed; I knew we'd been at the top of school gossip since our first lunch together had created a touch of drama, I just hadn't realized quite how much. Except now, the queen of it was standing right behind me. I wasn't entirely certain, but I think she belonged in the Laurens group.

"You think you're so special because you're the one who finally snagged Jupiter Reeves," she spat.

I spun slowly, making no sudden movements, like you would if any vicious animal was hissing over your shoulder. This would be easier face to face instead of viewing her in the mirror. "Do I?"

"I can tell you, you're not. You're just warming him up for the rest of us," she snarled.

Ew. I wasn't even sure what that meant, but it sounded gross. It also sounded like…

"Are you jealous? You're jealous of me?" I laughed.

She startled, as if the notion was really absurd. "As if! I'm telling you it how it is. The second he gets drafted, you're getting dumped for someone more his level."

I stepped to the side and slowly inched toward the door. My fists clenched to hide the shaking as I tried to summon my best Blair Waldorf. At least the hours and hours of watching Gossip Girl wouldn't go to waste.

"I have to say, green really doesn't suit your skin tone. It makes you look sallow."

I flicked my hair to the side as I stormed past her and walked out, but before the door swung closed, I could hear her mutter, "what the fuck is she talking about? I'm wearing pink."

Blair Waldorf vanished into thin air.

I ran down the hallway, ducking into a side door just before I dissolved into a fit of wrenching sobs I muffled with the neck of my sweater. Hot tears fell down my cheeks while my chest juddered as I silently gasped for air so no one would notice me. It wasn't even what she said – okay it was a little about what she said – but mostly it was all my fears being voiced aloud by someone wearing Pepto-Bismol pink, which was ironic seeing as she'd made me feel like I needed to run to the nearest drug store to guzzle a bottle as though it were milkshake.

The worst bit? I was crying in a doorway when I should be out watching my boyfriend. Maybe if I dried my eyes and ran fast enough, I'd make it back in time.

I made it back, though I kind of wish I hadn't. I also wish the girls had seen me coming, but as I snuck along the row behind because it had less people on, they didn't.

"Oh God, Ainsley, give it up will you?" Emerson huffed, and from her tone it sounded like this conversation had been going on a while.

"Sorry, I just really love him, and Marnie's our age, the same age as me. Do you think it'll last?"

"I dunno. Probably not, knowing Jupiter, but it doesn't mean he's going to date you either, and he's happy right now. Can we please stop talking about him?"

My body was slowly going numb, one limb at a time. If Emerson didn't see us lasting, then what hope did I really have?

"Just one more," whined Ainsley.

"No, you're grating on my last nerve, Ains. Watch the game, will you?" snapped Mallory, just as she caught my eye. It was too late though, she knew I'd heard everything. "Hey, Marn, thank God you're back. Jupiter is at bat next, and he'll want you watching."

I knew the last point she added wasn't for my benefit.

I almost felt sorry for Ainsley as I silently stepped onto our row. I knew full well how intoxicating Jupiter was, and I couldn't imagine it was easy getting out of his pull once you were in it.

But he was mine, and I wasn't about to let him go.

"Sorry you heard that, but don't worry about Ains," whispered Mallory as I took my seat again. "She's harmless. Jupiter doesn't even know who she is."

I know she was trying to make me feel better, but it didn't.

Ainsley might have been harmless, but there'd be a hundred girls after her.

I wish I could say I paid attention to the rest of the game, but every time Jupiter was on the field, all I could think about was losing him once school finished. And every time he was off the field, all I could think about was what I was going to do to stop it to make sure I didn't.

Back and forth, back and forth, until a cheer erupted throughout the stadium.

Music echoed off the billboards once more. We'd won. The game was over. Jupiter had hit the home run which secured it, all in front of The Dodgers scout sitting behind us.

He was still running the bases as students poured onto the field. That was my cue. I pushed past Mallory and ran down the steps as fast as my legs would carry me.

Faster.

Jupiter passed home plate, picked up his bat, then turned. I could see his eyes searching for me where I'd been sitting, and when he finally spotted me, he took off into a jog heading straight in my direction. I launched myself onto him, wrapping my legs round his waist; one hand scooped under my ass, the other still held onto his bat.

"You did it, Jupe. I'm so proud of you! What a game." His eyes sparkled like the evening's first stars, and I couldn't wait to tell him the news. "The Dodgers scout, he was here. He was sitting behind me."

His eyes flared wide. "Shit, really? Fuck! They were really here?"

I nodded, a grin splitting my face.

He spun his hat round so he could get as close as possible, burying his head in my neck. "I fucking love you, Marn. What a fucking day."

"I love you, too. I'm so proud of you."

I held onto him, breathing in his sweat, licking the salt off my lips from when he'd kissed me. I thought my chest might cave in.

This. This was mine. Jupiter was mine. And I was going to do everything in my power to make sure it stayed that way.

17

Marnie

Present Day

I pressed down hard on my legs, trying my best to halt the *tap, tap, tap,* but I could still feel them jittering underneath. It was possible I'd had too much caffeine already.

It wasn't like I'd been mainlining it, but that was only because I hadn't found a suitable I.V.

Yawning, again, I peered over to the glowing red clock above The Lions' field.

"He's on his way up. I just had a notice he walked in downstairs."

I smiled over at Penn Shepherd's P.A., Melony. I'd been waiting outside for the last thirty minutes, no doubt getting on her nerves.

It didn't occur to me that he wouldn't be here, because he was *always* here. Always somewhere in the stadium; usually hovering over me, checking on what I was up to next, sometimes lurking in the hallways, straightening one of the framed team shirts which hung along the walls of the executive entrance.

One time I found him arranging the sweat towels in the gym.

Penn Shepherd was *hands* on.

Even Lowe had started complaining that he never seemed to sleep, and we weren't yet half-way through the season.

I jumped up as he walked out of the elevator. Finally!

Taking the wad of messages that Melony was holding out for him, he flicked through them, only then noticing that I was standing right next to his office with a large box under my arm.

"Oh, Marnie! Did we have a meeting?" he startled, "or are you trying to make me look bad by being at work before me?"

"No, to both," I scoffed.

What a ridiculous thing to say.

A wry smile flashed on his lips as he passed by, walking straight into his office. "So to what do I owe the pleasure then?"

I took a second to blink my sight back after being momentarily blinded by the sun hitting his windows. It really was a beautiful day outside. My old office had been underground, in the depths of the Johnson Space Center, and I'd almost forgotten how much better a sunny day made things seem.

"I wanted to show you something." I lifted the box up as much as I could. "But I can come back if you don't have the time."

"I always have time for you Doctor Matthews. You are turning my team into winners. Want some coffee?"

I kind of did… but instead replied, "No thanks, I've had some already."

He shouted his coffee order to Melony, then perched on the edge of his desk and nodded to the box. "What's that then?"

That was something I'd been waiting nearly a month for, after I'd had the green light on the One Percent program. *That* was Phase Two.

It's not so much that time flies when you're having fun, but more like when you're working so many hours you forget what day it is. It was hard to believe it had been six weeks since I'd sat in this same chair and presented my One Percent idea to him, because even as I'd spoken the words, I hadn't been entirely sure it would amount to anything.

We'd started gradually; a system of phases and tiny tweaks that wouldn't create attention – the tape, the sleep schedule, Jupiter's bat baggies – which had proved to be surprisingly popular, were all Phase One.

Overall, it had gone relatively seamlessly. Even Jesus Rodriguez seemed to have come around, especially after I'd shown him the data I'd been studying – the results of which said, without doubt, The Lions were leaps and bounds ahead of where they'd been in the standings at this point in the season compared to any of the previous five.

And he should know, because he'd been with the team for the entirety.

On the unofficial grapevine – loosely translated as the pillow next to Jupiter – I'd heard that the boys were holding up better than expected against the grueling travel schedule imposed on them. We were currently thirty-one wins to twenty-three. And following the weekend, Lux Weston was now leading home runs for the league after a grand slam hit bottom of the eighth that saw us eventually beat the Mariners by two runs.

Beyond Jupiter and his cherry LifeSavers, I'd learned that baseball is full of the most superstitious people in the world, and as soon as they'd realized the changes they were making could be helping them win, they'd been begging for what would come next. I was getting visits from some of the guys, adding things to my list of what frustrated them most. More than once I'd arrived at my office to see two or three of them hanging around outside. Ace Watson and Parker King were there daily.

Ace's non-stop talking was exclusive to Jupiter, however.

I dropped the box onto one of his chairs and ripped it open. "You remember I told you about that material? The one that can detect sweat levels?"

He nodded, taking the shirt I was holding out to him and rubbed the fabric between his fingertips. "This it? Feels just like a normal shirt to me."

"It's supposed to, that's what makes it so revolutionary."

I waited while he held it up to the windows, letting the light shine through to he could examine every stitch, every seam. He stretched it taut, then turned it inside out, and repeated it all. I watched a pigeon land on the railings outside, but he didn't care so much and flew off.

"Where do the sensors go?"

I nodded at the shirt crumpled in his hand. "They're there."

"Where?"

"In the shirt. They're microfibers sewn into the material; they're part of the cloth. The whole thing is made of sensors. It can detect anything."

Even in the brief time I'd known Penn Shepherd, I'd learned it took a lot to impress him. And right now, if I wasn't mistaken, I'd just achieved that badge of honor.

"Anything?" His eyebrows shot so far into his floppy blonde hairline they almost disappeared.

I nodded with a grin.

"Anything?" he asked again, but slower this time.

"Yes." I looked at him, interrupting before he asked a third time. "Yes, anything."

"Steroids?"

I'd always understood that Penn Shepherd had genius level intellect, but maybe I'd heard wrong if he didn't realize what anything meant.

"Yes. If it can be found in blood or urine, it can be detected through those sensors." I waited for him to say something, but he was still inspecting the shirt. "For today's purposes though, it's just the sweat we're looking at."

I grabbed my laptop from the box and spun it round so he could see.

"What's this?"

"This is the dashboard." I tapped the screen which showed a series of graphs and dials. "Each player has his own; and then they're all compiled on the main screen here." I flicked onto another page.

"How does it know what to monitor? You must need to find a base rate first, right?"

I nodded. "Right. When we first set them up, we record everything we want the sensors to detect; base heart rate, hydration levels, metabolism – that kind of thing. During each game we observe the changes, and can make adjustments as they happen." I watched a frown form on his face. "It seems complicated, but it's easy to set up. Maybe an hour for each player to be tested, then the program does the rest. But eventually we can use the information to design specific training programs for each player."

He took the laptop, swiping across the screens. My eyes began wandering around his office, to the framed pictures of him and Lowe; one of him with a couple of guys and a dog; another of him and someone I knew to be Lucian Shepherd, his grandfather. I'd seen him once; he'd been with the N.A.S.A. Administrator in Houston. It wasn't hard to understand where Penn got his drive from.

I glanced back at him just as his mouth straightened into a line. "If I put the shirt on, will it come up here?"

"No, not that one, it's just a demo, but I can get one for you this week if you want to try it.

"Yeah, I do." He tapped against a graph of wavy lines. "What's this right here?"

I peered round the screen to see what he was pointing at. "Muscle fatigue."

His eyes bulged in excitement. Personally, I thought sweat rate was more exciting, but each to their own. "Marnie, what the… are you serious?"

"Yeah," I grinned again.

"And they use it in Space?"

I nodded. "Something similar, yes."

He stood up and rounded his desk before sitting again. "How did you get ahold of it?"

"An old colleague of mine has been developing it. I've been talking to him, and he's said we can have it."

"Have it?" One thick brow shot up skeptically.

"Well… buy it. He's interested in getting into sports because he thinks it'll be more lucrative than the government, so we'll likely get it cheap."

"I have two questions." He held up one finger, followed by another. "How many zeros are we talking, and how soon can we get it?"

"I'll follow up with him this morning and ask. We're not talking less than six zeros, and I don't know. Soon, I hope, but it'll take a little time to set up."

He leaned back in his chair, arms linking behind his head. "Give him another zero if we can get it finalized in the next two weeks, and we have exclusivity on the material for a minimum of one season, preferably two. And," his eyes widened as another stipulation came to him, "The Yankees or the Mets aren't ever allowed to access it. Talk to Beulah; she'll help draw up the contract, but don't do anything without her present. I don't care if you are friends with this guy. I want this, and I don't want anyone else to have it."

There was that famous, not-taking-no-for-an-answer Shepherd I'd met last year. He was the same as the Shepherd with the seemingly bottomless pockets.

I nodded. "Sure, I'll see what I can do."

"Great," he looked at his watch, "MELONY!"

I nearly fell off my chair as he yelled, then again when Melony peered around the door less than a second later. Christ! This caffeine was driving me crazy!

"You have an intercom you know."

"I know," he replied, though I wasn't sure that was entirely true. "Can you get me the Commissioner's office?"

And just like every other time, the meeting was over without him ever really saying it was over. Penn's day just seemed to flow from one appointment to the next.

"I'll see myself out." I thumbed behind me, then gathered

up my things as he waved me goodbye.

I left his office feeling much less jittery than I had while I'd been waiting for him.

Or a little bit less.

However, the jitters started up again as soon I got back to my office; or they fluttered up from my belly until they were banging a rhythm against my heart.

Or maybe it was just my heart.

Jupiter jumped up from my desk as soon as I walked through the door. If I'd been a little quieter on entry, I knew I'd have caught him with his feet up.

"Hey!"

In descending order, my eyes lit up from seeing him, then the bagel he was holding out for me; not so much the coffee. I snatched the bagel, and took a huge bite.

"Thank you!" I moaned.

He wiped the smear of cream cheese from my lips, and then leaned it to get the spot he'd missed with a delicate swipe of his tongue that had my toes curling. However, it was hard to sink into a kiss with a mouthful of dough, no matter how much I wanted to.

Jupiter moved back, but only enough so I could take another bite of bagel. His arms were still wrapped firmly around my waist, which was fine with me.

"Where've you just come from? What's this?" he asked, taking the box from under my arm.

"The shirts," I mumbled through my mouthful.

"The German space ones?" He pulled one out and looked over it in almost as much detail as Penn had.

I nodded. "Yep, the German space shirts. I showed Penn a sample."

He stood there staring as I finished my bagel. "Well, what did he say?"

"He said yes!" I grinned, and received another smack of his lips on mine. "But it wasn't like he was going to say anything else. He wants the edge, and he doesn't want the Yankees or the Mets to have it."

"Oh, babe," he squeezed me tighter, "that's amazing. I'm so proud of you. You're doing an awesome job."

I grinned up at him. Two months ago I had no clue what I was going to do, or how I was going to do it. I planned to stay a year and then leave. But now, I could honestly say I was enjoying myself, in no small part due to the enormous man wrapped around me.

I watched his smile soften, and he pulled me in another fraction, enough so the flats of his palms could run up and down my back. "Where were you? I missed you this morning."

I tried not to stare but his eyes were so blue, so hypnotizing, and when he smiled, the little golden flecks sparkled like sunbeams hitting the ocean.

"I'm sorry; I thought you deserved to sleep." I curled my fingers around the strands of hair at the base of his neck. The sun had been lightening it so much they were turning the color of melted toffee. "We got in late last night."

"We both got in late," he countered as he rubbed his nose against mine, "and you look tired. You should have stayed in bed. You've been working so hard."

"And we'd have got so much sleep?" I pinned him with a look.

"I am capable of cuddling you know!" he protested, but as if to prove himself wrong, his hands inched downward and under the band of elastic on my yoga pants. Then under my panties, and we both felt my body melt; I had no control.

I'd lost that badge weeks ago.

Somehow his lips found my neck, something I was making easier for him with the way my head automatically lolled to the side. "I missed this when I woke up."

"Next time I'll make sure that I wake you up." My voice had turned raspy, and my legs were struggling to hold themselves up against the strength of the deep, primal throbbing between them.

Because this is what happened; Jupiter only had to touch me and my body lit up like the Empire State building. My vagina, though, she could detect him the second he was within a hundred yards, like a silent alarm. I know we'd been kids back then, but the sex was better than I remembered; explosive, mind-blowing, and I couldn't get enough of him, just like he couldn't get enough of me.

Just like I hadn't got enough last night, and we'd finally collapsed, exhausted, before falling into the deepest sleep.

Or he had.

His comment about me being tired was right on the money. I'd caught sight of myself this morning and I couldn't image that I looked any better right now, so I wasn't going to bother checking.

I was tired. Drained, almost. But it was more than sex, more than the fact we couldn't keep our hands off each other. It was a lack of sleep due to not sleeping.

Or to be factually correct, not being able to sleep.

Jupiter Reeves, my first love. The man I knew for certain was my only real love; my true love.

My love, who knew me better than I knew myself; knew what I needed, what I liked. How to make my body respond in a way it never had in anyone else's hands. Or mine.

There was no question I'd never find anyone or anything better than him.

Which was the problem.

For every single night since our first night, over the past few weeks, I'd stay awake after he'd fallen asleep. I'd stay awake and watch him sleep, watch him dream; sometimes listen to his soft snoring, and other nights listen to the conversations he'd have with himself.

But I would *be awake.*

I would sync our breaths to rise and fall.

I would trace the constellations over his shoulders, and watch the stars shoot across his chest.

I would run my lips across his biceps, link our fingers together, and relish in his thick arms slung across my belly.

But as the night darkened and shadows appeared, I would need to push away the terror slowly taking hold of my insides at how much I wanted him. Then I would ignore the unease creeping through my bones like a dense fog at the start of a horror movie.

I would have to remember my breathing exercises; and if I was lucky, once the hours had past and the sun was getting ready to rise, I would finally fall asleep.

"Well, you can give me a special wake up tomorrow morning," he winked, setting off a fresh flurry of ripples in my core.

"I'll remember that when you're snoring away," I teased, and his eyes widened in the way that I knew I was about to get it. I held my palm up, a futile attempt to stop him. "No, Jupiter. Don't even think about it. Do not!"

I couldn't step back because I was already pressed hard against the door. I was trapped, and a fight was useless, but I'd try and put one up none-the-less.

"I mean it. Do…nnnaarrghh!" His thick finger found my ribcage, and tickled hard.

I was gone.

That feeling of his fingers rubbing against the delicate bones always had me wheezing with laughter like I was an eighty-year-old woman smoking sixty a day which set him off too, without fail, because our laughter was contagious, and there was nothing funnier than the two of us laughing together.

It took a minute, but I finally managed to escape his clutches when he bent over double, laughing so hard he nearly lost balance; especially when I shoved him to one side.

"Fuck, you're so funny when you're laughing." He was still wheezing as he wiped away the tears streaming down his face, and stepped toward me.

"Don't come near me!" I shouted louder than I needed to from where I was now standing, using the metal desks as protection. "You've lost your touching privileges."

His bottom lips protruded like a naughty boy, but I wasn't going to be swayed. "No, I have to get these shirts organized. If you're going to stay in here then you need to be a minimum of six feet away, and you have to be working."

"Oh, Doctor Matthews, you drive a hard bargain," he grinned, but stayed where he was. "Want to bring your lab coat home and play naughty patient and doctor? I could pretend to pull my hamstring during the game tonight, and you could make it better by sucking my dick."

I couldn't hold back the snort of laughter, especially as it was clear he was being deadly serious. "Oh, dear God."

He winked then held his hands up in surrender and resumed the position I'd found him in. I knew his feet had been on my desk. "Hey, something to think about."

I nodded to the white wall, where the list was now extensive thanks to my daily visitors. "I created a spreadsheet to log all the phases, and where we can monitor the results. You could input the new ones; that would be helpful."

I waited for him to answer, but when I looked up it was clear he either hadn't heard me, or he'd chosen to ignore me. Probably the latter. "Jupiter?"

He put down his phone and whatever he'd been reading on it. "Oh, you're serious? You want me to work on a spreadsheet?"

"Yes! Aren't you supposed to be helping?"

"Noooo…" he drew out. "I mean, yes, but we're back together now, and you're doing a great job, so you don't need my help any more. My visits to your office are purely recreational. That's why I brought you a bagel and coffee."

I frowned. "So you're not going to input my data into the spreadsheet for me?"

"Nope, I draw the line at spreadsheets. I only tolerated them for our study sessions, but if that's what you're talking about, hop up on the desk right now." He patted the space in front of him, right between his legs. His eyes darkened instantaneously.

Visceral. Absolutely visceral. The memory of our study sessions slapped me hard in my drooling vagina.

"I can't, I have to work." I tried to keep the whine out of my voice, but I knew it was there somewhere.

"Okay…" he went back to his phone.

I looked at the clock; I'd give him sixty seconds before he started talking again. I reached for my laptop, opening my email to find the one from my old colleague, Jorg. I shot off a reply to set up a conference call with him and Beulah, then dropped a note to Beulah updating her on who Jorg was. All that took five minutes, and Jupiter still hadn't said a word.

He was still staring at his phone.

"What are you looking at?"

From his expression I could see he was either up to no good or up to something he didn't want to share, so obviously I wanted to know about it, immediately.

I moved over to where he was sitting, only for him to pull me into his lap. I held my hand out, and he placed his phone in my palm.

"Pinterest?" My face screwed up at the screen, and then up at him. "How do you know about Pinterest?"

"Hey! I know about stuff!" He held my hand and swiped his phone screen, bringing up a board filled with houses, textiles, and interior design inspirations. "When I built my house in Malibu, my architect showed me Pinterest. It helped me find exactly what I wanted by taking bits from lots of different places. It turned out perfectly." He looked up and smiled. "I can't wait to take you there. It's right on the cliff above the beach."

"What were you looking at just now?"

He tapped the screen and moved to a new board, one that looked more countryside than beachy. "I've been making one for our new place."

I scrolled through the images; there were hundreds. *Hundreds.* Farmhouses, English gardens, wooden beams, roll-top bathtubs, tiling, theater rooms, and… planetariums.

That middle of the night feeling began scratching at my gut. I handed the phone back to him.

"I'll share this with you, and then you can look through and delete anything you don't like, and add anything you do. We'll build our dream house, Marn." He leaned up and kissed me, his tongue swiping across my lips before I could stop it.

Lifting me off his lap, he stood me back on the floor, pocketing a roll of LifeSavers I'd already opened and started for the door. "Okay, I have to go for a meeting with my third base coach. I'll call you when I'm done. Love you."

He stopped. I stopped. Time might have also stopped. His hand was hovering halfway to the door handle. I'm not sure I blinked.

His eyes widened, and a broad grin broke through his shock as he walked straight back to me. Warm hands cupped my face, and I could feel the calluses on his thumb as it brushed over my cheeks. "I should have been a bit cooler with that, but hey, you already knew. I love you, Marn. I love you so fucking much, and getting you back..."

His tongue did the rest of the talking with more than a swipe across my lips. It sunk deep into my mouth, caressing mine, twisting together, hot and soft. Every swipe filled with emotion, and I returned it a hundred fold, especially when I could feel him smiling against my lips.

This man, this fucking man.

He was going to be the death of me.

Again.

I pushed him gently. "Go, you're going to get in trouble if you're late."

"Okay," he winked. "I'll see you later." He stole one last kiss and ran out of the door.

I walked to close it, peering down the hallway until I knew he was really gone, only then did I shut it and slump onto my desk. My head fell forward, cushioned by my arms.

The sex, the hand-holding, the winks, the laughter, the present…

I could do those. I could manage that.

The girlfriend-thing, the house, the Pinterest board planning, the future…

My heart was pumping so hard that it felt like I'd taken a weightlifter's pre-workout shake. An Olympic weightlifter sized one. I sat up and rubbed my chest. It made things hard to concentrate when it felt like your heart was about to give way any second.

Either that or crack a rib.

I didn't think this had anything to do with my caffeine consumption either. Before I gave myself any time to ponder it, I snatched up my phone and earbuds, and walked out.

I needed air.

Fifteen minutes later, I found myself along the boardwalk; on one side of me were the canoes setting up for the game tonight, and on the other, Jupiter was staring at me. Or rather his poster was. The one I'd seen on my first day.

Who knew six weeks could feel like a lifetime?

I uncrossed my legs, then crossed them again, settling back into the bench opposite.

Fans, tourists, passers-by; they were all out in full force; every other person wearing a black and gold shirt. It was busier than usual. Since the boys had settled into the season and were playing well, Penn had opened up practice times. Tickets were on a first-come, first-serve basis, so for the last week, there'd been lines forming from eight a.m.

There were a few guys in front of Jupiter's poster today, but they were soon pushed out of the way by another posse of girls.

It was never going to change.

Everywhere Jupiter was the girls would follow, desperate for any breadcrumbs he left them. And while in school it might have been his winning smile they dropped their panties for, even I could attest to the tattoos as a verified vagina magnet.

I chuckled to myself. He might have become an asshole to build a blockade, but all he'd done was create a challenge.

He looked so dangerous, and every single female wanted to be the first to tame him.

I almost felt sorry for them, because they'd be waiting a while.

And I knew all about waiting for Jupiter Reeves.

Waiting brought me here; to New York; to this bench.

And I still hadn't been ready.

I should have known it was inevitable the second I'd discovered he was at The Lions. I should have protected myself better, but it hit me before I'd had a chance. It took hold of me, just like he had.

I was in love with Jupiter Reeves, again, for real. And he loved me back.

But it didn't take a rocket scientist to figure out why I didn't feel good about it – or why I hadn't been sleeping.

Because when I'd broached the subject of our breakup again, he brushed it off just like he'd done before.

Because what if I opened my eyes and he wasn't there? Just like last time.

Because when I closed my eyes I was sixteen again, my heart bleeding and beaten.

And blindsided.

I didn't see it coming the first time, but the second… that I needed to prepare for.

18

Jupiter

Fourteen years ago – June

If Emerson was trying to win the Biggest Pain in My Ass award, she was running a good campaign. It was becoming harder to concentrate on Marnie's pillowy lips wrapped round my cock when Emerson's shrill voice was shouting up at me from the yard.

Not ideal at all…

Even when Marnie did that thing with her tongue – the one I swear sent a memo straight to my balls telling them to get ready for explosion – I could only picture Emerson, which made it all too fucking weird.

The message wasn't getting through; connection lost.

"JUPE!! JUUUUP…IIII…TER…"

My jaw clenched.

Opening my eyes, I looked down at Marnie's perfect face, her long lashes fluttering against her cheekbones as she took me deeper. I was so fucking proud of her; it had taken a few tries, but she could now almost get the full length of my dick in her mouth. Sex with Marnie – discovering what she liked, learning what it meant when she made that noise, or when her head lolled to the left instead of the right, and how the gentlest brush of my thumb under her boob really got her wet – had become my favorite lesson.

My favorite ones to study for.

My balls were tightening again, and I brushed my hand over her cheek. "Fuck, Marn, you're so good at this. Don't stop."

"JUPE. JUPE. JUPE. I KNOW YOU'RE THERE!"

My dick shriveled again.

I'm going to kill her.

Marnie pulled off me with a wet pop, and a bead of saliva strung out from the tip of my dick. I ran my thumb over her lip, and wiped it off.

"Babe, let's pick this up later," she sighed, leaning back on her haunches and staring at my rapidly deflating dick.

"JUPITER!"

I ran to the window, to find Emerson looking up. "Fucking what?"

"Come down."

I glanced over to Marnie who was gloriously naked, and holding out my shorts and shirt. I took them with a sigh, yanking them on then grabbed my sneakers. I reckoned I had just enough time to wrap my arms round my girlfriend and kiss her before my sister started up again.

"You're perfect, Marn. I love you. I'm so sorry about this. I'll make it up to you later. We'll watch the stars," I winked at her, "and then I'll make you see them."

She smiled, forgiving and soft, when any other girl would be bitching for days. But that was Marnie. "Can't wait. I love you."

I was still pulling my sneakers on when I jumped onto the balcony, and over the railings.

"You're a pain in my ass, Reeves," I grumbled, climbing down the palm. "This had better be good. I was busy."

"Dad's been looking for you," she shrugged. "He's got his serious face on, so I thought I'd better come find you. Didn't have to look far though, did I?"

I swiped the back of my hand over my mouth, making Emerson gag.

"You're gross. You're such a slut boy."

"I have a girlfriend," I shot back, and pushed her hard enough that she almost fell into the nearby bush. "Tell me what's going on."

"I dunno," she shrugged again.

I mentally flicked through the list of things I kept on standby, but nothing came to immediate mind for what I could have possibly done wrong. I'd finished the year with a B average, I hadn't missed practice, and the draft was in a few days. When I'd seen him this morning he'd high-fived me, or maybe that was yesterday morning.

He didn't look in the high-five giving mood as I walked into the kitchen, however.

Emerson had been right. He had his serious face on. It didn't come out often, but when it did, he meant business. In fact, the last time I'd seen it was when Piper had gone off to college in September and he gave her 'the talk', or a talk. I hadn't stuck around to listen.

"Um, hey, Pop. What's going on?"

He looked up from his coffee. "Take a seat, Jupe."

I frowned, but did as I was told. "What's going on?"

He took off his reading glasses and sat forward. "I wanted to talk to you about Marnie; you and Marnie."

Me and Marnie had not been one of the subjects on my list. In fact, of all the things in my life, Marnie seemed to be one they approved of, almost more so than baseball.

"Okay…" I began as it dawned on me that maybe they knew what we did during 'study' time. "We're being careful if that's what this is about. We haven't been having sex long, but we're being careful."

He waved his hand, a grimace flashing across his face. "No, no that's not what this is about, but I'm glad you're being careful."

I sighed in relief, especially as my mom chose that moment to walk in.

"Hey, sweetie." She kissed my cheek then sat next to my dad, and I realized they were both here to talk.

This wasn't good.

"You're in on this too? What's going on?" I snapped. My agitation was beginning to fester. I might have been a little more relaxed if Emerson had waited another five fucking minutes, but on top of having to deal with this, I still had a latent tingling in my balls.

"There's nothing going on, there's nothing to be in on. We just want to make sure you're okay, that's all. We have some concerns."

I looked at my dad. "If this isn't about sex, what is it about?"

My mom leaned across the table like my dad had, her fingers steepling together. "Jupiter, sweetheart, we like Marnie, she's a nice girl, she's been great for you."

"Yeah, I know..."

They glanced at each other, and I knew I was about to be hit with nothing I wanted to be hit with. "Noah Matthews came over to see us last night. He said Marnie's requested to stay in school. She asked him to sign her note rescinding her acceptance to M.I.T. She's decided she wants to go to CalTech instead."

My brows dropped down so low, a headache almost instantly appeared. "What? No way, that's not possible."

My dad cleared his throat. "You didn't know about this? Noah seemed to think this could be coming from you, which is why we wanted to have a talk."

"What? No! Marnie wouldn't do this without telling me, and she wouldn't do it, period, he's lying. Marnie and I made a pact for when she goes to college and I'm drafted."

Mom rolled her lips together, and I could tell she wasn't convinced. "He seemed pretty sure. He said she'd told him the courses were better at CalTech. He wasn't happy; she's his little girl and he thinks she's throwing her future away."

"Guys, I'm telling you, Marnie wouldn't do this." My jaw ground hard. "I wouldn't let her either, that's why we made a pact. She's going to Boston, and we'll see each other as often as we can."

But they carried on as though I hadn't spoken. "The draft is in a few days, Jupiter, and it's going to be full-on. You'll barely have time to come home, let alone travel to Boston. We'll support you either way, but it's not just your life we're talking about. Marnie's not seventeen yet."

"Mom, she's seventeen in a few weeks," I snapped. "We'll figure it out. But I'm telling you, Noah Matthews is full of shit. Marnie is going to M.I.T."

"Okay, we just wanted to check," she conceded, and then she smiled. "Let's grill tonight, ask Marnie over."

I stood up, needing to move; needing to think. Needing to get away from this conversation, I thumbed behind me. "You guys done? I'm going to my room."

I took off before they could reply, sprinting up the stairs two at a time, and slammed my door behind me.

What the fuck?

We'd talked about a pact.

I walked over to the window, then fell onto the bed.

Where had this come from?

When we first got together she would talk about M.I.T. all the time; her courses, what the campus was like, the library… but if I really thought about it, she hadn't mentioned it for a few weeks. Not since that brief conversation we'd had about CalTech.

And the last time I'd talked about visiting Boston, she'd changed the subject.

A dull gnawing started up in my belly. Ten minutes ago, I'd been so certain Noah Matthews was lying, but it was possible there was a shred of truth.

I jumped up from my bed; lying down wasn't doing it. Thinking would be easier if I was standing.

"EMERSON!"

My bedroom door flew open; it wasn't a lucky guess she'd been walking past, I'd heard the floorboard creek outside my room. She was either listening or passing by weirdly close to the wall.

"You bellowed?"

I gestured to the bed. "Sit."

She was too nosy not to be a little inquisitive about what I wanted from her. I linked my arms behind my head as I tried to figure out what to do, and how I could do it.

If I asked Marnie straight out, she'd want to know where the information came from. She'd blow up at her dad, who in turn would hate me even more than he already did.

Alternatively, she'd blow up at me, and I didn't want that either.

If I could figure a way to find out whether it was the lie I hoped it was without Marnie knowing, then I wouldn't cause any unnecessary distress. Then we could all go about our lives as planned.

Dodgers and M.I.T.

"Jupe, can you stop pacing and tell me what you called me in for? I'm meeting Mallory at the mall and I don't have all day!"

I stopped, my eyes narrowed at my sister. "I need you to do me a favor, can you take Marnie? I need to do something, and don't want her around."

She looked at her nails. "I think you're all out of favors."

"I've taken you to school or the beach every single day."

She simply raised a single eyebrow at me.

"Fine, what do you want?" I snapped.

I'm not sure why she bothered with the prolonged pause, drumming her fingers against her lips; it was clear from her answer that it wasn't an off-the-cuff negotiation.

"Your truck."

"Fuck off."

She stood up from the bed, and walked slowly toward the door.

"Fine, you can have it for one afternoon."

"A whole weekend," she shot back.

"An afternoon and an evening."

Her smile was more simpering than any of the girls at school. I glowered back.

"I'll call her now and tell her Mal and I will collect her on the way. I'm assuming you need me to tell you when the coast is clear?"

I nodded, ignoring the guilt and anxiety twisting into a cyclone in my gut. "Yep."

"It'll be in the next hour."

"Thanks. And Emerson," I called after her. She put her head back around the doorframe. "Make up something about why you wanted me earlier."

True to her word, Emerson's message came through an hour later, and I made my way over to Marnie's, the way I usually did. I knew her brother was out, and her parents had left first thing to collect some shit or other from Santa Barbara, which was going to take all day.

The house was clear.

I stepped softly through her window.

I'd never been in her room without her.

It was so still; whispers of her perfume floated in the air, and I breathed them all in, filling my lungs as deeply as I could; filling them with her.

I stayed in the middle, circling slowly, seeing it differently to every other time I'd been here. A voyeur.

I could see the pin board in the corner above her desk; a photo of us she'd taken a few months ago – our first day at the beach – nestled among drawings of stars, her class schedule, my games schedule, and her favorite quote – *The Stars Don't Look Bigger, But They Sure Look Brighter.*

Her snuggly teddy had been relegated to the bookshelf 'so we didn't corrupt him too much', she'd said. The sweater she'd been wearing this morning was slung on the back of her chair, and there was a pile of laundry yet to be put away, on top of which were five rolls of cherry LifeSavers, making me smile wide.

Her laptop was on the bed, resting innocently on the pink comforter as though it was lazing in a field of wildflowers. My heart thudded heavily, giving me an unnecessary reminder that I shouldn't be here, and I shouldn't be opening it up. And I definitely shouldn't be typing my name in as the password.

The screen lit up and my stomach bottomed out.

Noah Matthews had been telling the truth.

The letters were still open. Two side by side; one to M.I.T. Admissions, the other to Santa Monica High School.

Her plans laid out in black and white, as clear as the promise she'd broken, along with our pact.

I don't think I'd ever loved her more. I don't think I'd ever been angrier at her.

She was blowing her life up for me; the brilliant life she had planned, for *me.*

I didn't know what she thought our future was going to look like, but I could tell her right now it didn't involve giving up on her dreams for me.

Her drive to get to M.I.T. was one of the things I loved most about her.

I sat back, reaching for the baseball I'd left on her nightstand, and tossed it into the air.

The stitching flickered as it spun as quickly as my mind was spinning.

I wasn't sure what was making me angrier – that she'd lied to me, that she'd done this behind my back, or that she thought I'd be okay with it when I found out.

Or, as my throat became scratchy with the threat of tears, that I wouldn't do the same for her.

If it came down to it right this second, would I give up the chance to play for The Dodgers?

No.

But I'd never doubted we wouldn't last long distance.

And that meant there was only one thing I could do.

I didn't let her know my parents invited her for dinner. I didn't want to see the lie in her eyes if the subject of graduation came up. I ignored Emerson when she told me she'd returned from the mall. I replied to Marnie's text with a simple, "I'll see you later", because while I knew what I needed to do, that didn't mean I wasn't going to hold her in my arms one last time.

Kiss her one last time.

Sneak out of her window one last time.

The full moon lit my way to her place, and I crept under her comforter when she held it open for me.

"Hey," she breathed sleepily, wrapping her arms around my neck.

I twisted her into the little spoon, and kissed along her shoulder. "Hey, sorry I took so long. Did you have a fun time with Emerson?"

"Mmmmhmm," her head softened on the pillow. "I'll show you everything tomorrow. How was your day?"

"Just getting a few things ready for next week, and trying to plan out my calendar for when you're in Boston." My arms wrapped tighter around her body and I placed my palm over her heart. “I was thinking we could take a trip there before spring training begins. We can go and see your dorm, what do you think?”

Her chest caught, and her pulse quickened. I knew she’d heard.

“Star?”

She spun around to face me. “Jupe, stop talking and kiss me.”

My heart cracked.

I didn’t say a word as I pulled her underneath me, crushing my lips to hers, surrounding her, bruising us.

One last time.

MARNIE

“I’m getting really worried about her. It’s been a week. I think she needs to go to the doctor.”

“I’m going to murder that kid.”

I raised my head just enough to hear the muffled voices outside my room. But it wasn’t Jupiter, so I laid it back on the pillow and pulled the comforter over my head to block out the light creeping through the blinds.

Maybe if I was quiet enough, the voices would vanish.

Maybe if I was quiet enough, I would vanish.

Then the pain would stop.

I would hit the bottom of the black hole I seemed to be tumbling down.

If I hit the bottom, perhaps the sensation would come back to my limbs; the emptiness I felt deep in my marrow would refill; the numbness would disappear; my body wouldn't feel like it was being ripped in half.

I would no longer be shrouded in the darkness I'd lived in for seven whole days.

The never-ending tears would stop falling.

My last thought as exhaustion took me; death must be easier than this.

19

Jupiter

Present Day

"But my birthday isn't for two weeks…"

I kissed her nose on my way to the kitchen. "I know, but we'll be traveling, and I don't have another free day until after it. And then it's the All Star Game, and we'll be back in L.A."

She popped her hip, her elbow crooked. "Are you at least going to tell me where we're going?"

"The Polo Bar."

That got her attention. She pushed her glasses up onto her head. "How did you know?"

Pulling her toward me, I rested my arms on her shoulders. "I asked Lowe and Beulah if there's anywhere you'd been talking about. I wish I'd known sooner; I can always get a table there. I did seven years of campaigns for Ralph Lauren."

There was that look again. It always took me a second to remember that she knew nothing of my life between when we were kids and up to a few months ago. Years and years of my face being plastered on billboards; stuck between the pages of magazines; spread over the sports pages; not to mention the award ceremonies, exclusive interviews and television appearances, along with dozens of social media accounts dedicated to me – she'd missed it all.

Marnie had taken herself to the only place where it was possible to escape me, or as close as…

Space.

"Alright, big head. I just… I'm still getting used to that side of your life. You know, the one who can buy telescopes that cost the same as a car, and old farmhouses…" She paused and pursed her lips. "But… also… I never realized how full-on the season was going to be. Days off should be spent relaxing, and I like spending them in with you, eating popcorn, watching movies. I like us hanging out and getting to know each other again."

I brushed my fingers through the ends of her ponytail. "I love those nights too, but today is special, it's your fake birthday," I smirked. "Plus, you're my girlfriend, and I want to show you off."

I swear I felt her tense under my arm, but she kissed me too quickly for it to register properly. It wasn't the first time it had happened either.

"Thank you, I'm a lucky girl."

"You're welcome. You've got an hour, but then we need to leave to meet Drew and Emerson." I flicked on the television to catch the start of the Braves game. They were playing the Giants, who we had next week. "Go get your ass in the shower."

"An hour? How long do you think it's going to take me to get ready?" she tutted.

I chuckled. Not one woman I'd ever met had complained I'd given them too much time, and most of that was spent applying a shovel-full of makeup that took nearly as long to remove. With Marnie, however, she could have five minutes and still look perfect, but I'd allowed for some extras just in case.

"Hey, I know what it's like if you stand between a woman and time. I've made that mistake before."

Marnie was halfway to the bedroom, but turned and stared at me with narrowed eyes.

"Emerson! I meant Emerson."

"Hmmm."

I'd never given her a reason to be jealous, but I wasn't going to lie and say I didn't enjoy it a little. We hadn't talked much about our previous relationships, mostly because I'd never had one and wasn't overly enthusiastic about discussing my one-night stands. The only thing I cared about hers was that they were done. My body still swarmed with jealousy at the idea of her being married, so I'd decided to pretend it never happened.

She was mine now, and anyone else was irrelevant.

And while tonight might have been a fake birthday, there was a present in there for me too. We hadn't been out as a couple before, never been photographed together. In fact, I'd never been out on a date, not a proper one. Dates were for girlfriends, for women you planned to see again.

And I couldn't fucking wait to date the shit out of Marnie.

I focused back on the game; nothing was happening, so I jumped up at the commercial break and went to shower. Twenty-two minutes later, I'd left Marnie with a towel wrapped around her, head upside down as she dried her hair, and returned to the game where there still wasn't much going on.

The Braves had scored, now leading one-nothing, and that was the most interesting thing I could say. I must have been watching longer than I thought, because when I got up to grab a drink, Marnie appeared in the bedroom doorway, and I forgot everything that had ever happened up to this very second in my life.

My dick throbbed so hard I needed to keep myself from toppling over at the blood rush.

Fuck me. I'd never seen her look like this.

I'd gotten used to seeing her at the club in tight yoga pants, or jeans and a tee, or walking around my apartment in a bra and panties, sometimes naked.

But I'd never seen this. *Ever.*

If I had, we wouldn't have surfaced for air.

"What's wrong? Why are you looking at me like that?" She was fixing her earrings and hadn't noticed me walking toward her.

No, *stalking* would be more apt.

I was the hunter and she was my prey, and I wasn't just going to eat her. Fuck dinner, I was about to devour her.

Her dress was a thousand shades of blue silk, all flowing over her body like a moonlit waterfall, the clearest waters cascading into the deepest, darkest pool. The pool which stopped mid-thigh, showing off the longest, leanest, curviest legs. I'd never seen them look like this, and all I could think about was having them wrapped around my head while I went to town on her; dragging my tongue over her clit, and spearing it into her tight, wet pussy.

I dropped my cufflinks on the side table, and slowly rolled up my sleeves one at a time.

"Jupiter..." she frowned.

"Marnie."

She took a step back and blinked rapidly. Nerves. She should be nervous.

"Answer me one question, has anyone else seen you in this before?"

"No." Her head hastily shook from side to side.

I gently brushed a thick curl off one of her soft, apple-rounded tits, pushed up high and ripe for my teeth to sink into. "I'm glad I got to see you in it, but you will not be wearing it out of this apartment."

Her neck jerked back so she could look at me. "What?"

Ignoring her, my fingers hovered over the tiny shoulder straps – the ones barely holding up this scrap of material, the ones which tore from the seam with the slightest tug from me. The flap of silk floated down until her boobs were scarcely contained.

"Jupiter! What are you doing?"

"I'm illustrating how flimsy this dress is."

She opened her mouth to protest, but it was as my thumb brushed over a nipple as hard as my dick, so instead, it simply dropped open with a soft moan.

My hand crept up her thigh, pushing under the hem. "See, Marn? It's better if I do a full inspection of it before we leave. Don't you agree?"

She was wearing heels which brought her a little closer to my height, but I still needed to spread my legs slightly to meet her eye line. Big green eyes widened more with every inch my finger edged closer to her ass.

I leaned in, brushing the shell of her ear with my lips. "I asked you a question. Don't you agree it's better?"

Her head fell back as I pushed under the elastic of her underwear.

"You're soaked, Marnie. Fucking drenched. And that won't do at all… it's not just your dress you'll need to change; you'll need fresh panties too."

The groan she let out as I brushed her clit sounded almost painful; raw and animalistic, hitting deep in my balls; an arrow spiked with pure lust.

This was going to be quick.

One finger buried itself in her pussy. I added a second, then a third, curling them up as I pumped inside her until we were both vibrating with desperation.

Desperate for release.

Desperate for each other.

"You need this so badly, don't you? Your pussy is dripping on the floor."

I spun her round until she hit the wall, her hands bracing her from falling forward. Her back was against my chest as I unzipped my pants, my cock jumping free like a prisoner making a break for it. "We don't have much time."

Bracketing her in with my thighs, I yanked her dress up and pulled her panties to the side, then drove upwards with one long stroke. Tight. Hot. Wet. So, so wet.

She cried out, and I wanted to feel those cries in my chest, I wanted to breathe them in.

Wrapping my fist into her thick mane of curls, I jerked her head around until I could fuck her mouth with my tongue while my dick thrust hard, frenzied, and wild.

I was so affected by her it was more than an addiction, and

it came with no cure.

I needed to touch her wherever I could, whenever I could, because I'd go crazy if I didn't.

Claim her. Own her. Make her mine.

"Get ready, Star. I'm about to explode so hard you're going to be wearing my cum to dinner."

A throaty moan almost pushed me to breaking point. My hand slid around her body, bringing her even closer to me as my arm held her hips in place while my fingers ground forcefully on her clit. With every long, rough stroke, I swallowed her cursing until I could do nothing to stop my orgasm barreling through me, except take her along for the ride.

I gripped tighter as her knees buckled, and waited until we could both stand upright without support. I might be a professional athlete, but she knocked the wind from my lungs every single time.

I eased out, gently sliding her soaked panties back into place; she definitely needed clean ones. I could probably do with changing too. There was no way I wasn't covered in her.

I found the delicate stretch of skin just above her collar bone and kissed it, whispering, "Marn, please don't wear that dress. I won't be held responsible for my actions if you do. And that includes murdering any guy who so much as glances your way."

She took a deep breath and silently went to change, but not before I caught the smirk crowning her lips.

"That dress is so cute," Emerson said as she forked a

mouthful of birthday cake into her mouth.

We'd continued with the fake birthday throughout dinner, including presents from Emerson and Drew, and were now sitting in front of an enormous chocolate cake with candles, though we'd been strictly forbidden from singing Happy Birthday.

After two hours of eating and drinking, that suited me fine.

"Thank you. I thought so, too," Marnie took a long sip of her wine. Thankfully, for my sanity, she'd changed into something slightly less revealing before we'd left, though she could be wearing a garbage bag and I'd still want to jump her. "I bought it a few weeks ago. I went shopping with the girls at work. It actually came with a really pretty slip underneath, the lace layered together at the neck." She brushed her fingers across her chest, then her gaze slowly moved my way. "But when I tried it on earlier, it ripped. Guess it was too flimsy."

I didn't know what the fuck a slip was, but from the way she was looking at me, I should probably learn.

I coughed into my iced water and put my glass down. "That wasn't your dress?"

She shook her head slowly as a couple of wait staff cleared our table of plates, removing all the chocolate crumbs Drew had dropped, and left with the cake and the promise of boxing it up.

"Oh." My brows dropped in confusion. "Why were you showing it to me then?"

"I wasn't. I was coming to ask you to fix my necklace, but I didn't get the chance."

"Oh, man, what did you do?" Drew chuckled, while Emerson's hands flew up to her ears.

"Ugh, God, don't answer that. It's like we're back at school again. You two were at it more than the bunnies Piper and I had as kids!"

There was a memory to laugh at. "I seem to remember you guys splitting a hundred bucks after Mom and Dad made you sell all the baby bunnies that arrived."

The smirk was knocked clean off Marnie's face. "We weren't that bad,"

"Yeah, you were. All that 'studying'…" Emerson air-quoted aggressively, "you thought you were so sneaky, except Jupiter's bed always squeaked on the floor, and that wooden platform overlooking the sports fields…!"

Now it was my turn to look shocked. "What? No one knew about that!"

"Everyone knew about it."

Marnie's bright red face dropped into her palms. "Ohmygod!"

Drew's head fell back with a loud guffaw. "This is amazing. You should see your faces."

I grinned wide, putting my arm round Marnie so I could pull her into me and drop a kiss on her head.

"It's all good, we got a happy ending."

"Sounds like Jupiter's the one with the happy ending. OUCH!" Drew rubbed his ribs after Emerson elbowed him. "What? He did."

"Can we not talk about my brother having sex please?" she whispered aggressively as a waiter came out to refill our glasses. I stopped him from pouring anything into mine; I'd allowed myself one glass only.

"You want to talk about us having sex instead?" Drew asked with a wicked grin.

"No!" I interrupted before my sister could answer. "Subject

change!"

The smile Emerson shot my way came straight from her sixteen-year-old self.

"Hey, I'm making the most of having a night away with my wife. We're gonna get buzzed later, and spend the whole day in bed tomorrow."

I shot a little side glance to Marnie who was now quietly in conversation with Emerson. When the season finished, we'd be spending weeks in bed.

I focused back on Drew. "Where are you staying?"

"The Mark. I swear the mattresses are made from actual clouds."

"Yeah, I like it there. Marn, you want to take a little city break with me?" I waggled my eyebrows at her, making Drew laugh.

"Okay, I'm going to the restroom, see if I can't cool my cheeks," Marnie announced, standing up.

"I'll come too." Emerson pointed at Drew and me. "Try and come up with some suitable conversation topics please? School, dirty diapers, vacations… all better than talking about sex all night."

"Yes, boss," I saluted and she walked off, heads together with Marnie.

As always, I took whatever opportunity I could to watch my girlfriend's ass; the dress she'd changed into really shouldn't be legal for what it was doing to her. I stared until Drew snapped his fingers in my face.

I glanced back at him, and saw the wry smile twisting his mouth.

"You guys seem good, a bit more relaxed than you were a few weeks ago."

"Hey! I'm always relaxed."

Drew scoffed. "All I'm saying is at the birthday party you were watching her like a hawk."

"That's because Emerson and mom got their claws in before I had a chance to get out of the car."

I thought back to that weekend. It was true, we were better. I hadn't realized how nervous I'd been about her seeing my family again, but she'd loved it as much as they had. She'd seen my mom a couple of times while my parents had been in town, and met up with Emerson and the kids. We were connecting on every level; laughing until we cried, and reminiscing about high school while she massaged my shoulders after a long game. And the sex? It was better than I'd ever imagined; the best I'd ever had.

It was almost as though we'd never been apart.

Almost.

Because she still hadn't called me her boyfriend, and occasionally I'd catch her hesitating, tensing, faltering; like she was about to say something and then decide against it.

And not that I was counting, but she still hadn't told me she loved me, no matter how many times I told her.

Okay, I was counting.

"But it's good?" he pressed on.

I nodded slowly. "Yeah, it is. I think it's taking Marnie a little longer to get used to it." I thought back to her comment earlier. "Maybe getting used to me being me as well."

"That's understandable though. You're a much bigger dick now than you were in high school, I'd imagine," he grinned.

"You're lucky it would be frowned upon to reach across and slap you," I rolled my eyes, "but seriously, it's good between us. I just feel she's holding back sometimes." I shrugged. "I dunno. I love her, and I want everyone to know it."

Drew rolled the stem of his wine glass, spinning the dark red liquid. "I'm sure it'll feel like that for a while. When Emerson and I found each other again, it took us a few months to really figure shit out."

"Yeah, I hope that's all it is." I glanced over to the waiter as he appeared with the check but handed my credit card over before he could place it down, along with my valet ticket. "Thanks, man. Can you get my car brought around the back?"

"Certainly, sir."

Drew peered around me. "The girls are coming. You want to come back with us for a nightcap?"

"Raincheck?" I shook my head. "I want to get Marnie home. We're flying out tomorrow night. Thanks for coming out tonight though, dude. We can do this more now I'm not third wheel."

He nodded enthusiastically. "Anytime. It's good to get away from the kids too, if only to sleep past six a.m. I will never get used to being awake at that time."

"Tell me about it," I shuddered. I was looking forward to a long sleep in tomorrow.

We both stood as the girls returned. "Can we call the driver?"

"Already done." I looked at Emerson, who was now wrapped around Drew. "Want us to give you a ride?"

She shook her head. "No thanks, we're going to walk a little."

It took five minutes of hugging and organizing when we'd see them next for the car to pull up, then another fifteen to get back to Marnie's apartment, where I pulled her onto the couch and planned to spend the next hour snuggling while the highlights played. According to the sleep schedule she had everyone on, I also had another hour after that to get lucky before it was lights out.

I caught her hand as she pushed it through my hair, and pulled her down into my arms.

"Thank you for dinner tonight, it was perfect." She kissed my cheek, moving her legs to rest on mine, and I was only slightly disappointed she'd changed out of her dress.

Maybe if I asked nicely I could convince her to put the first one on again, even if it was ruined.

"You're welcome." I ran my palms up and down her legs while I flipped through the games played tonight. "I'm sorry about your other dress; I'll buy you a new one. But you still looked so beautiful tonight, Marn. So fucking beautiful. I couldn't keep my eyes off you."

"It was totally worth it." Her fingers were twisting the ends of my hair, which was almost long enough for her to wrap around her index finger now.

My eyes flicked from the Mariners game to her. "Happy fake early Birthday, my little Star. I love you."

"Thank you. It was the best fake birthday I could have asked for," she grinned, and slightly drunkenly scooched onto my lap. Her arms slid around my neck; her lips trailed a path along my jaw until they found home on my own. My dick got hard the second she'd flung her legs on mine, but now her hot little body was pressed against me it was throbbing. "Now, please stop talking and kiss me."

My lips were a hairs breadth away from brushing hers when a flicker went off in the far, *far* recesses of my brain.

When I think back, I don't know what possessed me to do it, but I didn't kiss her. Instead, perhaps stupidly, I pulled away. I wanted to hear it. "Marnie, I love you."

"I know," she smiled, leaning in again.

I squeezed the tops of her arms, lifting her off my lap and stared her down.

"I love you."

Her arms crossed defensively. "I heard you."

"Why won't you say you love me?" My jaw was clenched too tight for it to come out as a whine, though I was surprised it didn't.

Her eyes flared, her mouth parted, and the way she looked at the floor had my belly twisting in on itself.

"Marnie, answer me. Do you love me?"

She sucked in her bottom lip; she needed to stop it quivering.

"What the fuck, Marn?"

She held out a shaky hand to me. "Jupiter, let's go to bed, please. We don't need to talk about this now."

"Oh, yes we do!"

"Jupiter…"

I sat back. My world was in danger of shifting. As if I could stop it, my fists clenched and rammed hard into my armpits.

"No! Tell me! I want to know."

She started to push her toes back and forth along the floorboards, focusing on her feet instead of my face like I wanted. It felt like I was waiting an eternity for her to speak, longer still when her eyes filled with emotion and her hands began balling into fists.

My heart stopped.

"Do you… do you not love me?"

"It's not that simple, Jupiter." Green eyes swimming in fear shot up to meet mine.

"Why isn't it?" I snapped, harder than I meant to.

Our first date had changed on a dime. Back and forth her feet went again; my eyes never left her face, and I was about to speak when she cut through the tense silence with a whisper.

"I'm worried…" A single fat tear fell down her cheek and splashed on the floor. "I'm worried that if I say I love you… if I say it, then everything will backfire and I'll lose you again; that you'll leave me again," a loud sob caught in her throat. "The last few weeks have been amazing, and I didn't want them to end."

She looked away, and another tear fell.

My heart cracked imperceptibly. I almost brought her into my lap again, but then something stopped me. Whatever it was I wish it would also stop the past which was now hurtling back at light speed to haunt me, right alongside Emerson's words.

Yep. Pretty sure my ass was about to be bitten. I fucking hated it when Emerson was right.

I took a deep breath and reached out for Marnie's hand, but she snatched it away before I could touch her.

"You left me on the porch."

"We were kids, Marn." I tried to use my best calm voice, the one I used with Grey and Gabriella, because if I stayed calm then I hoped she would too. Or at least lessen the snarl that was now present in her tone.

Suffice to say, from the way she was glaring, it didn't work.

"We didn't break up because we were kids!"

I sighed, but it was pointless hoping she'd let this drop. "The reason doesn't matter. What matters is I love you, and I hope you love me."

"You loved me the day before you stood on my doorstep

and said I was too clingy, that I wasn't girlfriend material. You loved me the day before you said you didn't. I never understood it…" she stopped to suck in a breath as her sobbing started up again. "You loved me, and the next day you were drafted and broke my heart, out of the blue… poof. We were broken. You broke us."

I shouldn't have avoided this conversation. I should have been honest with her from the beginning that I might have ended it, but she was the one who broke us first.

I was trying to stay calm, but each of her last points was made with an angry prod to my chest, and every one cracked my façade a little bit more, until…

"I broke us up because you lied!" I snapped hard, pushing up from the couch.

She stared up at me, mouth wide open. "Wh... what?"

I stormed over to the kitchen, and took a bottle of water from the fridge. "I knew about CalTech, Marn."

She blinked several times, and then her arms crossed her chest again. I couldn't tell if she knew she'd been busted, or genuinely didn't realize what I was talking about; not that either one made this situation better.

"What does that mean?"

"I found the letter you wrote to M.I.T. that said you no longer wanted your place, and the other one to S.M.H., and the CalTech application. Your dad went to my parents and asked if I was behind it." Like it was yesterday I remembered how pissed I'd been, how hurt I'd been. But mostly I was pissed because I was getting blamed for something I was adamantly against.

"So you broke up with me?!" she shot back.

"Yes," I replied simply, because back then it had been that simple. Back then it was the only decision I thought was right.

Since she'd been in New York, I'd gotten used to Marnie's angry face. I knew when she was pissed because her eye twitched a little, and the tops of her ears reddened. But right now, she surpassed any levels of anger I'd seen before. A tiny vein was pulsing in her temple, and any second there'd be fire shooting out of her nostrils with the way they flared.

And it only served to flick the switch on my own temper.

"Don't you look at me like that! I wasn't about to let you give up on your dream, because I wasn't going to give up on The Dodgers. You would never have let me do that! And look," I threw my hands in the air, "you went to M.I.T. and you went to N.A.S.A.! FUCKING N.A.S.A., MARN! Just like you always wanted."

To give her credit, she didn't even flinch. She just stared at me, her chest heaving and her eyes narrowing.

"Do you know how long it took for me to feel myself, to feel right, to feel whole again? I cried for six months! I cried until I couldn't cry anymore." It didn't come out as a hiss; it was more angry than that. She'd surpassed anger to reach a level where every word was quiet and damaged, dripping with pain.

I was desperate to make it stop, but even more desperate to make her understand.

"Marnie, I'm sorry. I'm so fucking sorry. I know I broke your heart, and I'm begging your forgiveness to mend it. I'm not going to apologize for why I did it."

Thankfully her eyes flared again. The anger was back. It was easier to deal with her when she was angry.

"OF COURSE YOU WON'T! BACK TO THE SAME GODDAMN ARGUMENT!"

"NO! IT'S NOT! You broke our pact! You lied! You owe me as much of an apology!"

"I didn't know where you'd end up. You wanted The Dodgers, but they didn't have first pick. You could have gone anywhere, and I wasn't going to risk it!"

I wished my dick would ignore the way her boobs bounced when she threw her hands in the air.

"You were giving up your career!"

"No, I wasn't! I was giving myself options!" she spat out, like I should have realized all along. "It was the same course at CalTech. It was the same course just on the other side of the country, so wherever you went, I would pick the closest."

My jaw popped so hard I could feel my back teeth ripping from the root. "No, Marnie, it wasn't the same course. I checked."

"What?"

I swigged my water, willing some calm to return. I didn't have the fight in me if she was going to keep lying, or maybe she'd convinced herself of an alternate truth. "It wasn't the same course. You were postponing a year, and then downgrading."

"I was sixteen! I was completely in love with you, and I wasn't ready to be three thousand miles apart. Sixteen, Jupiter!"

From the corner of my eye, I could see The Dodgers game playing out. Almost fourteen years I'd spent there. I could tell you how the field smelled after a rare Californian rainstorm; I could tell you about Vince, the head grounds-man, and how he used to spend an hour every morning cleaning the bases, because it had been his first job at The Dodgers' and he believed in it with the same fervor people believed in God. I could tell you what the dugout looked like after every game, but while I'd spent all that time with a hole in my chest, I couldn't tell you I regretted it, because if I did, I might not be standing here now, the love of my life in front of me, looking like she wanted to murder me. And if those years were the price to pay for the rest of my life, then drain my fucking bank account and make a run for it.

"Yeah, and I was eighteen and completely in love with you. Was it the best decision I've ever made? Fuck, no! And could I have handled it differently? Yes! But I was just as pissed and heartbroken as you were. You can't hold it against me now, Marnie. It's not fair."

She was biting down so hard on her lip I was afraid she'd bite though it. Tears fell thick and fast down her gorgeous face. "You don't get it, do you? I got married to a man I didn't have to spend time with, and then divorced him. But you… ours was the relationship I mourned. You are the one I mourned. You died. We died. I can't survive that again!"

There was no anger in my voice, but her tears were piercing my heart like they usually did because she wasn't listening to me. "Not good enough. I'm not dead, Marn. I'm alive and kicking, and I live for loving you. Maybe I could have made a better choice back then, but so could you. I can't change the past, but I can make sure our future has us living it together." She dropped her head, but I lifted it. She needed to see me when I spoke my next words, needed to see it in my eyes; see the love that coursed through them, that always had. That she was the fluid that ignited me, she was the fuel that burned through my veins and scorched my blood. "Fourteen years, three months, and thirteen days, Marnie. That's how many days I've loved you, and you've been my first and last thought for every single fucking one. So I guess the question is whether you're going to let me."

Her arms dropped to her sides, and her shoulders fell. "What do you want me to do, Jupiter?"

I put the bottle of water down. "I want you to admit I'm

your boyfriend. I want you to admit that we're meant to be together. That you love me."

"Where are you going?" she asked as she followed me to the door, almost at a full sprint, panic building in her voice.

I couldn't stop myself from brushing my knuckles against her cheek. "I'm going home. You need to figure out what you want your future to look like, and I don't want to be here if you decide it doesn't include me."

I kissed the top of her head as she broke into heavy, rasping sobs; every single one a bullet to my chest.

When I reached the elevator and glanced up, her face had dropped into her hands, her chest heaving like she couldn't breathe. I watched until the doors closed, and for the second time in my life, I left Marnie Matthews on her doorstep, holding my heart while I walked away.

20

Marnie

Present Day

"Oh. What are you doing here?"

Emerson held up the Fed-Ex package I'd been expecting when I opened the door, the one the concierge said was on its way up.

He failed to mention it wasn't being brought by the Fed-Ex guy.

"Nice to see you too, Marn," Emerson said somewhat sarcastically as she kissed my cheek when she walked in.

I took the box she pushed at me and closed the door behind her.

"In my defense, I wasn't exactly expecting you." I followed her through to the living room, and dropped the box on the table. "You wanna tell me why you're here?"

I walked over to the kitchen and flicked on the coffee machine, expecting her to answer but she didn't. I peered around the kitchen wall to find her sitting at the telescope, which Jupiter had graciously moved nearer to the window. And that was only because he said he couldn't 'adequately fuck you in every inch of your apartment if this is in the middle of the floor'.

A full body shudder erupted at the memory.

Pulling the hair tie off my wrist, I scraped everything up into a messy bun. "Emerson?"

"You know there's a guy over there jerking off?"

"What?"

She moved away from the telescope, stood up, and squinted out of the window before returning to the telescope. "Yes, there," I followed her finger to the huge glass and copper building thirty blocks away, the one that bounced the sunlight off its beams every morning, blinding me for fifteen minutes before the earth shifted a little further along its day.

I nudged her to the side and looked through the scope; there was indeed a guy jerking off. I briefly wondered if it would be hotter if he were hotter.

"Gross." I turned to my guest who still hadn't answered my question. "Em…"

Emerson moved away from the live porn show. "I just wanted to check on you, see if you were okay. But actually…" She tilted her head, and gave me a very thorough once over, "you look like you are, so now I want to know why."

I peered down at my pajamas; the one covered in eggs and bacon, toast and coffee. Beyond me wondering what gave her the impression I looked okay, they were making me hungry. And Emerson looked like she'd come straight from the gym.

"Are you hungry? I mean for proper food. If you're expecting green juice you've come to the wrong place. I can make you some of Jupiter's matcha though."

Her head shook vigorously. "No thanks, I've been in New York long enough to drink coffee. Drew would never have matcha in the house."

"Sensible," I grinned. Jupiter and I had had many discussions over the virtue of coffee versus matcha.

"You make the coffee, I'll make the eggs." She started crashing around the kitchen before I had the chance to agree. Instead, I followed in silence and scooped the remainder of beans into the grinder. "Tell me then, why do you look good?"

I glanced into the stainless steel of the coffee machine. I definitely hadn't miraculously unwrinkled in the last fifteen minutes. There was no fairy godmother situation. "Emerson, I'm in my pajamas and haven't brushed my hair – or teeth for that matter. The delivery woke me up."

Her eyes bulged. "It's ten a.m.!"

I turned on the grinder before she could say any more, and yelled over it, "I was asleep. Not everyone gets up before the sun."

She started cracking eggs into a bowl. "I wasn't expecting you to be asleep. I was expecting you to be blotchy and tear stained, and rocking slowly in a corner."

I stopped, ground beans in one hand, coffee filter in the other. "What? Why?"

"Because I spoke to Jupiter, and he told me about your conversation…"

"Oh." I watched the first drip hit the bottom of the pot.

I knew her being here had everything to do with Jupiter, but I hadn't expected her to say that, or be surprised at how I looked. I did feel good though; better than I had in a long time. More accurately, better than I had since I'd arrived in New York.

In the last three days I'd grounded myself. My world was finally spinning in the right direction again.

"Marn…"

I reached onto the shelf and removed two coffee mugs. "You know, I heard you once. You were talking to that friend of yours, the one who had a crush on Jupiter. The twin."

A little crease appeared on her forehead. "Ainsley?"

I nodded. "Yeah, her. We were at Jupiter's game, the one where The Dodgers' scout was sitting behind us, remember?" Emerson took a second, and then she nodded. "I'd gone to the restroom. One of his fan club members accosted me, telling me there was no way Jupiter was going to stay with me once he got drafted, that he'd find a new girlfriend as soon as we were separated. I cried all the way back to my seat, only to hear you telling Ainsley you didn't think Jupiter and I would last."

Emerson had been watching me the whole time. Her hand stopped whisking the eggs and flew to her mouth. "Oh, Marnie, I wouldn't have meant it…"

"I know," I muttered, my mouth turned downward, "but I loved him so much, I couldn't bear the thought of leaving him – or him leaving me. I did what I thought was the best thing for us; it wasn't a big deal for me to stay in school another year, and it definitely wasn't as big a deal as he seemed to think, so I requested to stay. I was seventeen, Emerson. I was trying to keep us together but he left anyway, and I always wondered why. Wondered what happened. I drove myself crazy for years. I blocked him out of my life so I'd stop thinking about it."

She reached out and touched her hand to mine, but I

wasn't done.

"It was easier than I thought it would be. The M.I.T. School of Engineering is where you want to go if a baseball player breaks your heart. Science nerds do not compare," I laughed dryly. "The past month, I've been falling back in love with him. There was no way I could stop it, but he's been buying houses, and telescopes, and a boxes of LifeSavers, and planning our future, while I've been lying awake too scared to sleep in case he decided the next morning that he was done with me again. I've been trying to protect myself..." I laughed through my words, because I was done with beating myself up. "Turns out, I was the cause in the first place."

Emerson looked at me like I was a little crazy. Maybe I was, because over the last three days I'd realized something that I probably should have realized a long time ago... especially as a scientist.

I couldn't control the future; I could only control my choices.

And I choose Jupiter.

"It wasn't easy on him either you know." The eggs sizzled as Emerson poured them into the hot pan. "The weeks after the draft, he was a mess. It's the first time I remember him really crying... like not from a ball smashing into his face or something, really hard sobbing. I heard him one night and didn't know what to do. He was my big brother, but for two weeks, he only left his room to eat or train."

I blinked. My heart skipped a beat. He'd told me over and over that our breakup had been hard on him too, but to hear it from someone else really helped it sink in. "Really?"

"Yes. And this time I didn't realize anything was wrong until I watched the game last night. The only time he plays that badly is when it's to do with you." She frowned at me. "Why are you smiling?"

"Because I watched the game, too. He did play badly, didn't he?"

She narrowed her eyes as she scraped the eggs onto the plates I'd laid out. I poured out two cups of coffee, pushing one over to her.

"So tell me why you're okay, and you look like you've slept for a week. The other day you looked tired… hot, but tired," she added with a grin.

"Because I have. I've almost slept solidly, but I also had sleep to make up for."

She stared, waiting for the real answer.

"Jupiter stormed out the other night and told me to figure out what I wanted my future to look like, but I already knew. I wanted my future to be our future; I've never not wanted that. I was just scared of it all blowing up; scared of him leaving me on the doorstep again… Except when he did, I expected it to be a thousand times worse than it was." I took a massive bite of my toast and eggs. Sleeping had almost given me a bigger appetite than sex. "Understanding that I was partly responsible for our breakup lifted a huge weight off my shoulders, and when I finally stopped crying, I slept. And sleeping really helps you think clearly."

She pursed her lips as I winked at her.

But it was true; I'd made an excuse to Penn about not traveling because of the shirts, but instead of working, I'd slept. I'd slept for three days, and healed my heart.

And I felt fucking fantastic, like I could take on the world.

Or at the very least, Jupiter's army of female fans.

Emerson picked up her coffee and sipped. "Have you spoken to him?"

I shook my head. "No, not yet. I wanted to see him in person, and he's been away. But I'm going to the game today."

"What are you going to do?"

I chewed on my lip. It was probably best to have at least one person's opinion. I put my dirty plate in the sink and ran to get the Fed-Ex box.

I placed it in front of Emerson with a nod. "Open it."

Her brows dropped a little as she ripped the tape off, then pulled out the contents and held it up.

"Oh my God."

I cringed. "I know. It's lame."

She stared at me, her eyes wide again. Eyes so similar to Jupiter's my chest suddenly ached from how much I'd missed him, how badly I wanted to see him, and I had to concentrate hard on not crying,

"Are you kidding? It's perfect! He's going to lose his shit!"

"You think?" I asked as I rolled my lips. "Lowe's putting it on the Jumbotron, so you'll see if you watch."

"Oh, I'm definitely watching. I'm coming tonight."

I grimaced, though I guess one more in the crowds wasn't going to make a difference. "Really?"

"Hell, yes. And I'm bringing everyone I know."

She laughed at whatever expression my face held, which was mostly wondering if it was too early to start drinking.

Lowe and Beulah grinned down at my chest, so I crossed my arms over it.

"Stop staring will you?"

"No way, this is going to be fucking awesome." Beulah laughed so hard she nearly fell off her stool. "I can't believe you're doing it!"

I groaned. "Please stop saying things like that. I need encouragement before I change my mind."

I wasn't going to though. No matter how much I hated being the center of attention, Jupiter was worth more than mortifying levels of embarrassment. I was also only doing this because more than I knew he'd love it, he *needed* it.

"Sorry, I'm just so excited!" She clapped her hands together and then outwardly composed herself. "Sorry, I'll be calm."

"Thanks," I turned to Lowe. "Is it all set?"

"Yes, first inning. Penn's requested it be early so that Jupiter starts playing better again."

"You told Penn?!" I glanced around; I was still here and the ground hadn't swallowed me up like I'd wished. This was so unprofessional.

"Well, he was going to see it… plus he loves love, and he loves Jupiter almost more than he loves me. He just wants him to be happy. This is seriously cute."

I scowled at her and looked out to the field. The stadium was full. The KissCam had already been around twice.

From the shadows I'd watched the team warm up and do their stretches. I hadn't wanted Jupiter to see me and I knew he'd be looking – except he didn't turn up for stretches.

I could see ten thousand gold foam fingers, signs with player's names on, and message banners I'd be adding to.

The teams took the field.

The first bars of the National Anthem played out.

It was time.

I grabbed my belly. It was possible I was about to puke, but

I couldn't tell whether it was from nerves or excitement.

Both probably.

"Okay, I need to use the restroom, and then I guess we're going to have to go out there and sit."

Lowe picked up the giant piece of cardstock. "Let's go. It'll be over soon, and then you can get on with your lives."

Yes. Her words enabled me to take the first deep breath I had all afternoon.

Our lives. Mine and Jupiter's. *Together.*

I started for the door but another arrow of doubt hit me, and my heartbeat skyrocketed with the threat of a panic attack. I spun around to face them. "What if he says no?"

The giant card slapped me on the ass as Lowe hugged me. "Marn, are you kidding? I bet he runs off the field in the middle of a play and whisks you away."

"You think?"

"Absolutely, now come on," Beulah said as she linked her arm through mine.

I couldn't tell whether I was walking or if she was dragging me, but we almost passed the restroom.

"Stop! I still need to pee." I turned just before I ran in, and pointed at the cardstock Lowe was carrying. "Will you wait here with that?"

She nodded, but I didn't miss the smirk. I should have thought to cover it with a cloth or something while we were walking through the stands. I should also have put on a sweater given the amount of people staring, or perhaps I was imagining it.

No. On second thoughts, they were staring. I'd left my hair down, curled it into the big waves Jupiter loved to run his fingers through, but now used it to pull over my shoulders in an attempt to hide my chest.

It didn't work.

"Cool shirt. Where did you get it?"

"Oh," I crossed my arms, trying to cover what I could, "I made it."

"That's hilarious. Imagine if he sees it." The blonde girl in front of me nudged her equally blonde friend while I stayed as still as I could and prayed the stalls would open quickly. "Stace, look at her shirt. How cool! We have to get these!"

Stace twirled around to see. "OMG! I love Jupiter Reeves! I'm from California, and I cried so hard when he left The Dodgers."

I blinked in surprise. "Are you serious?"

"Yes, but I'm at school here, so I'm lucky. I'm his number one fan." Her little nose wrinkled as she screwed it up.

I didn't want to break it to her that according to my shirt, I was officially Jupiter's number one fan. Nor did I want to share I wasn't talking about the California part of her sentence, though I probably shouldn't have made fun of her crying. Sure, she seemed cute; friendly and perky, but her nails said she could scratch my eyes out in under a second.

"We have to make these!" she cried to her friend. "We come to all the home games. We haven't been able to figure out where he parties after though. Do you know?"

"Oh," I tittered back, nervously, "I don't think they go out; the scheduled is pretty tight."

"No, they definitely party!" she shot back with all the confidence of someone who spent hours on social media tracking the team's whereabouts. It was something I hadn't believed people did until Lowe showed me, though I was still unclear how anyone found the time. "We were out with Ace Watson, Parker King, Lux Weston, and Tanner Simpson last weekend.

They got us into the V.I.P. section of Vitamin D. Ace said Jupiter always goes with them, but he had to bail. We're meeting them later though, and fingers crossed he'll be there." She held her crossed fingers up.

My head fell back with a loud laugh. Last weekend Jupiter and I had gone straight home after The Lions had beaten the Red Sox and gotten into the bath where he'd spent thirty minutes grumbling about how much Ace didn't stop talking in the dugout. In the end, I'd soaped up his cock until he was forced to concentrate on something other than Ace, then had to hold onto the sides of the bath so he could fuck three orgasms out of me.

There was something to be said for post-game sex.

"What's so funny?" Stace frowned.

"Nothing." I shook my head, still picturing Jupiter's face for when I told him Ace was using his name to pick up girls. "Stall's free."

She scowled, and then marched into it. I peed as quickly as I could, then ran out to find the girls.

"Quick, let's get out of here. Jupiter's number one fan is in the bathroom." I was still laughing as I filled them in on the story of Ace, and the three of us snickered the rest of the way to our seats where the smile was wiped off my face.

Emerson was in the row behind us, and true to her word, had brought everyone she knew. Half the people from the twins' birthday party were here. My mouth dropped open as my eyes ran down the row, taking everyone in.

"Hi, Marnie!" Drew's hand shot up in the air and waved, both enthusiastically and unnecessarily, considering he was barely a yard away which meant everyone turned to look at me.

"What did you do?" I hissed at Emerson. "I thought you

were kidding!"

"I would never kid about watching Jupiter on the Jumbotron," she winked. "Turn around, you're going to miss them coming out."

My stomach gurgled and dropped as hard as I did into my seat. Harder, even.

I shrunk down, pulling my cap on as the boys took the field. My heart didn't even give a little flutter as Jupiter ran out, not one flap at the sight of his ass running to third base.

I was too nervous. My entire body was no longer made of atoms; it was built solely on nerves. I'd become human Jell-O; shaky and trembling.

I wished these seats came with puke bags, especially as I'd left my purse in my office.

I was trying hard to stare into the distance when Beulah nudged me, then nodded to the Jumbotron – or one of them. My face was going to be on all three around the stadium.

Oh, God.

I took the card from Lowe, stood up, and waited.

The first Brewers' batter walked out of the dugout, and got into the batters' box.

Then I remembered Ace had been told to delay the first throw, but I hadn't given any thought to how he'd do it.

Jumping Jacks.

Jumping Jacks was how Ace was delaying the first throw. He wasn't hard to miss because the mound was right in front of me, but I barely glanced at him before my gaze finally landed back on Jupiter, who still hadn't noticed me on the screen.

He hadn't noticed me period.

His head was down, his foot marking the dirt near third base. He hadn't even noticed the game had yet to start because Ace was fucking around.

Everyone else except Jupiter had noticed, especially as the crowds were very obviously laughing.

Ten seconds of Jumping Jacks, and Ace was done.

"Reeves, you fuckhead! Look!"

Jupiter's head snapped up to Ace, and then turned slowly to the left, to where Ace was pointing – to me on the Jumbotron, holding my sign. In a flash he whirled back around to the crowd, then back to the Jumbotron, and once again to me.

He'd found me. From the way his body turned and his massive biceps crossed over his chest, I knew he'd found me. I couldn't see his face, but I was willing to bet all the stars in the sky he was glaring at me, eyes narrowed and piercing, his jaw clenched tight.

Just like his poster.

He didn't look away, didn't look over to the Jumbotron, just stayed trained on me, my sign, and the huge black letters which read:

JUPITER, I HAVE A QUESTION.

I waited, staring straight at him, and not over to the Jumbotron where I could see myself in perfect color; big and bold.

"Turn it around," Lowe hissed.

"Oh, right."

WILL YOU BE MY BOYFRIEND?

If I thought the crowd was laughing loud at Ace, it was nothing compared to the roar going through them now.

Behind me I could hear whispers, light laughter, and then a snort to my right – or a chorus of them. There was too much ringing in my ears for me to hear properly.

I was suddenly thankful there was a whole row of Emerson's friends between me and the strangers who thought I was certifiable.

Thank God we were in the front row so no one could turn around to look at me. It was bad enough the entire stadium could see me on the screen, and it didn't take long for the crowd to realize they were possibly witnessing more than a joke, evident from all the cell phone camera raised in the air.

"You're gonna be on the news later," sing-songed Beulah quietly from her seat.

I groaned just as quietly. I could picture the headlines, especially as Jupiter had yet to answer.

He was still staring at me when another snort of laughter echoed behind me, and it was enough to have me stamping my foot like a petulant child.

"JUPITER!"

The Jumbotron screen split in two, one half on me, the other half on Jupiter.

A grin spread slowly on his face, stretching out his full lips until it was a smile reaching from ear to ear; bigger than I'd ever seen it.

The stadium was so silent you could hear the birds singing outside, and the jets flying overhead.

You could have heard a pin drop.

Then, he nodded. Slowly, teasingly, but he nodded. Nothing could stop the smile taking over my face as I slowly dropped the sign so he could read my shirt. He glanced at the Jumbotron then bent back, throwing a laugh out high enough and loud enough to startle the birds.

JUPITER REEVES IS MY BOYFRIEND

I'd never heard the crowd cheer bigger. It was deafening; booming; resounding; thunderous.

I snatched away the tear before it fell. I wasn't going to cry on the Jumbotron as well as make a total idiot of myself. Not that I cared, but thankfully the umpire decided he'd had enough of the Jupiter and Marnie show, and the game got underway.

The final batter walked up to the batters' box for the end of the Brewers' first inning. Ace did his thing. The bat cracked. The ball flew through the air, and straight into Jupiter's glove.

I swear he hadn't even been looking, because I swear he'd been staring at me since the first pitch.

He sprinted toward the dugout, ball still in his hand. I didn't know he was capable of scaling walls more deftly than a cat, but in a blink, he was on the roof of the dugout, standing in front of me with the ball in his hand.

I barely noticed the movement around us, of cellphone cameras coming out as he bent down and leaned forward.

"Hello, Marnie Matthews."

I blinked away the emotion in my eyes. "Hey."

He held his hand out. "I caught you a ball."

I took it, soaking in the soft smile as he looked down at me. I wanted to bathe in this feeling forever; warm and glowy, and perfect. "Thank you."

"Nice shirt." He reached out, his fingers slipping under the neck and pulled me to him. His hand fisted the material, and I didn't have a second to think before his lips crashed onto mine, not that I would have changed the outcome under any circumstance.

I wasn't sure what was louder; my groan or the cheer from the crowds watching us around the stadium. But I didn't get a chance to enjoy more than the briefest taste of him, the quickest swipe of his tongue before our perfect moment was ruined.

"Okay, show's over. Get down, right now Reeves!" yelled Coach Chase. "You're acting like a goddamn teenager!"

Jupiter smirked but did as he was told and disappeared into the dugout.

"I told you he'd run off the field," whispered Lowe.

When Jupiter came out for his first time at bat, I finally got to enjoy the butterflies fluttering round as they dissipated all the nerves. And I really got to enjoy the way he turned and winked at me, just before he took position.

Then I got to see the wavy line he drew in the dirt, the way he always did. But for the first time, I realized that it was more than a wavy line… much more than a wavy line.

I saw it for what it really was.

An M – for Marnie.

How had I never recognized it? Though I knew a small voice, Jupiter's inside voice, was telling me it was because I'd never truly acknowledged his truth, that he'd never stopped loving me, and his future was our future.

That he loved me as much as I loved him, and this time he wasn't going anywhere.

I could finally allow myself to believe it.

For the rest of the game I sat in a beam of his sunshine, warmed through to my bones with the knowledge that Jupiter Reeves once again belonged to me.

Jupiter Reeves was *my* boyfriend.

The Lions won, seven to two. Jupiter would be forgiven for delaying the start of the game because four of those runs were his, along with the handful of Brewers players he'd caught out.

The crowds were still cheering as they dispersed, clearing out of their seats when he pulled me down the steps by the dugout and yanked me onto the field. His callused palm wrapped around mine and stayed there until he found the quietest spot he could, because he was too desperate to see me to wait until we got home.

His blue eyes bored through me as he stopped us on the other side of the tunnel, the side away from fans leaning over the railings for autographs. He stared, really stared, as though seeing me for the first time.

It was the way he'd stared at me that first day in Penn Shepherd's office.

The way he stared as he helped me pick up my text books in the hallway after Josh Ridley knocked me over.

His fingers flattened out a crease on my t-shirt, tugging on the hem to straighten it, but it was like he was buying time, trying to believe I was really standing in front of him.

"I didn't notice you. I thought Ace was being the dickhead he usually is, so I didn't notice. I hadn't wanted to look up and not see you there."

I brushed my hand over his soft whiskers and cupped his cheek. "I know, but I'm here now, and I won't miss another one."

He took my palm, placing it to his lips. His breath was hot against them as he said, "I want to read what's on your shirt."

I stepped back, so he could. He read it over and over, until his eyes misted. "I fucking love you, Marn."

"I know," I pushed up on my tiptoes for a kiss, then reached into my back pocket and passed him a thick cream envelope, nodding for him to open it. "I want to show you something,"

He ripped the seal and unfolded the paper, pulling out four more behind it. His brow creased deeper the longer he continued to study it. "What is this?"

"Well..." I peered over the first page and pointed to a crudely drawn little box. "This here is the kitchen. See? There's the kitchen table, and that's the stove top you had fifty different pictures of." I glanced up at him, but he still looked confused. "I'm not great at drawing, but I took inspiration from your Pinterest board."

"But, Marn... what is it?"

My eyes flicked to his, and back to the paper. "It's our house."

It took a couple of seconds for him to blink. "You drew out our house?"

I searched his face like he was searching mine. It had taken half our lifetimes, but we'd finally found each other again. For good.

The knowledge of that, the weight of it in my chest was so overwhelming, it caught in my throat and spilled from the corner of my eyes.

"I love you, Jupiter. I love you so much. I've never stopped loving you, ever. In all these years, you're the only one who's ever truly owned my heart. I'm sorry I didn't say it to you the other day, I was just scared; terrified, really," I sniffed, "but you asked me what I wanted my future to look like, so I'm showing you. My future is our future. I see you and me, in this house, a home that we build together."

He rolled his lips, chewing lightly on the bottom one. "What else does the house have?"

I smiled softly, wiping the back of my hand under my nose, and went back to it. "Okay, well, I like the way the kitchen wall at Emerson's opened up into the back yard, so I added that here," my finger passed over the pages, "but I made the pool closer to the house, because I thought it would be good to see the water from the window, and it would remind us of California."

"What else?" he asked again, just like that day in my office, the day we started working together, which was the first day I knew for certain I'd fall in love with him again.

"Here's where the playroom would be."

His eyes shot up. "Playroom?"

"For our kids. I was thinking three, maybe four."

His arms snuck around my waist, and rested just above my ass. "What about the observatory?"

"No changes. It's perfect exactly how you described it." I glanced up at him, my heart filled to the brim, which carried on and overflowed. If I looked down I'd be standing in a puddle of it; a puddle of my love, for Jupiter. "For real, Jupe, will you be my boyfriend?"

He smiled that smile again; the once-in-a-lifetime one which threatened to split his face. The one witnessed by millions today.

He didn't sink into the kiss like I wanted him to, but I had the impression he'd rather not stick around by this wall on the other side of the tunnel.

"Yes, you bet your ass I will. Now let's get the fuck out of here so I can start being your boyfriend the second we get home." He took my hand and led me off. "Maybe in the car if you're lucky."

And that's how we left the field, my hand in his as I was dragged off as quickly as he could drag me without dislocating my shoulder.

But I didn't care because my hand was in my boyfriend's hand, where it belonged.

Jupiter Reeves, my boyfriend.

Jupiter Reeves who belonged to me.

Again.

Finally.

Epilogue

Jupiter

Four months later

"Marnie! Will you move your ass?!"

"Calm down, Grouch," Marnie said as she walked calmly out of the house, putting on sunglasses like I hadn't been waiting outside for fifteen minutes. In fact, 'excels at waiting outside for women' should be put down on my résumé for whenever the time came for me to retire. "What's the rush?"

"I'll show you Grouch." She squealed as I slapped her ass. "Get in the car before I put you over my knee, and you make us even later."

She slowly pulled the sunglasses down her nose, her eyes glinting mischievously, and I nearly, *nearly,* made good on my promise… but I had more important things to do.

We had more important things to do.

I slammed her car door shut then ran around to mine and hopped in. If there'd been dust on my driveway, it would be swirling through the air with the speed at which I'd hit the gas. Marnie was too busy fiddling with the music to notice I was having a mini panic attack while running through a mental checklist to make sure I hadn't forgotten anything. But as long as Marnie was sitting next to me, and the small velvet covered box was burning a hole in my pocket, then I figured everything else could be bought.

"You wanna listen to pre-game commentary?"

I shook my head, picking up her hand and kissing it. "Nope, I'm good. You're in charge of music, and I'll be in charge of the volume."

"If you change your mind..."

Saluting the security guard at the gates as we passed, I turned right onto P.C.H., and away from the private estate where I lived.

Or *we* lived.

Because when we weren't in New York, Malibu would be our residence. We were now officially bi-coastal. The season had ended two weeks ago; Marnie and I had spent a week packing our things and then hopped on a jet to the warmth of California.

More specifically, the season for The Lions had ended two weeks ago, in the first round of the playoffs. We'd lost against the Cubs.

We'd lost, but you'd never know it from the celebration, which lasted three days – five if you counted the amount of time Ace went missing for, only to resurface at the Hard Rock Hotel in Atlantic City. Penn Shepherd certainly knew how to throw a party.

And boy had we partied.

The last time the New York Lions had made the postseason was fifty years ago, and we made sure everyone knew it.

It had never happened in my lifetime.

Never in the lifetime of any of the current team members, or the executive board.

What we'd achieved, not only as a new team, but a team made up of guys who'd never played together before, was immense. Virtually implausible.

The formerly almost washed-up, almost forgotten about Lions, were once more walking proudly with their heads held high.

New fans cheered loudly, old fans cheered even louder. The flags flying along Lions Boulevard flapped hard in the breeze.

The team New York had long considered a joke was now a serious contender for next year's World Series. We'd had a taste of victory, and there was no way we wouldn't do everything in our power to beat ourselves in the standings.

Especially as we had The Edge.

The Edge, who was now softly snoring away in the passenger seat, catching up on all the sleep she didn't get last night. The Edge I was totally taking credit for.

Penn Shepherd might have spent a billion on improvements, but we'd have never managed it without Marnie and her One Percent.

And Marnie would still be sending rockets into space if it hadn't been for me.

Therefore, credit.

The bat baggies, the bat tape, and the sleep schedule had all been improved on. I still didn't have the velvet pouches, but the starting nine now traveled with their own mattresses which were carefully wrapped and set up in the hotels on each away game by a team which rivaled a Formula One pit crew for speed and precision. I didn't think it would make that much of a difference, but The Lions had the longest winning streak of all the teams this season.

We went fourteen games in a row without a loss.

There were now two guys on The Lions' staff whose sole job was to make the dugouts we visited exactly like our dugout at Lions stadium; down to the cubby where our helmets were kept, and the positioning of the water cooler. We kept to the same snacks, same meals, same everything.

The technology in our shirts had proved inordinately successful. After the first trial, Penn Shepherd had bought it, and Jorg had moved over from Germany; because once Shepherd wanted something, he usually got it – which was another reason why The Science and Analytics Department now existed.

Jorg and Marnie had grown into a team of ten, which was great for Marnie, less so for me and the afternoon delights I could no longer partake in due to all of the people being around *all of the time.*

Sex with Marnie had been relegated to mornings and evenings. Occasionally I persuaded her to stay in bed longer, but unfortunately, the team winning had awakened a monster in her. She was almost more desperate to reach the World Series next season than I was.

And I fucking loved her for it.

The nightstand on her side was piled high with books on sports data and analytics. I'd get into bed every night and have to answer twenty questions on what I thought may or may not work, based on that evening's game. Sometimes she wouldn't stop talking unless I made her stop talking, usually with my dick.

Because whenever my dick was involved, I always had one hundred percent of her attention.

The nightstand on my side was piled high with books on design and architecture; because now the off-season had begun, we had the time to dedicate to our New York house. It was our project. And if she peppered me with twenty questions about the different types of tape, or the best ways to break in new cleats, then I was asking about styles of flooring she wanted, or the size of the bed, or whether she had time for a conference call with our architects. And to get my attention, she just needed to stand in front of me.

Naked.

Just the thought of it now had my dick twitching.

Marnie didn't wake up until we were about to pass the turning on I-10 for Palm Springs. She stretched sleepily and looked around at the scenery, which wasn't in any way what she was expecting. It took her a second to figure it out, and then her head shot up. "Where are we? How long have I been asleep? Jupiter, why are we going to Palm Springs?"

Her entire body spun around, and a deep crease formed on her brow.

"We're not," I grinned.

"We're supposed to be at my parent's! They're expecting us."

Marnie's parents; Noah and Bryony Matthews. I no longer sighed internally at the mention of their name, which was progress on my part.

If I thought I'd been nervous about seeing Marnie again, it was nothing compared to how I felt about seeing her parents after fourteen years. When Marnie and I officially got back together, I thought I'd have a bit of time to see them, to figure out how exactly I was going to persuade them that I was for real this time. Because after she'd found out how I'd known about CalTech, her dad became her new enemy number one. It took a whole night in bed and the whole of the following morning to convince her not to say anything.

But then she announced they were coming to New York for the weekend, so I needed to call in the big guns.

The big guns being Drew and Emerson.

In return for them spending the weekend with Marnie's parents while I was at the stadium – talking me up at each and every opportunity, bringing them to both games, even wheeling out Grey and Gabriella to squeal about how much they loved their Uncle Jupiter – I had to promise Drew that he could auction off an entire week of training with me for his foundation.

That's right, an entire goddamn week of someone following me around.

But… I'd let someone follow me around for a year if it meant getting Noah on my side, because Marnie was worth that, and more.

She was worth everything.

I still wasn't entirely convinced Noah thought I was genuine, though the conversation I'd had with him this morning – the conversation I'd snuck out of the house to have, while Marnie thought I was on a run – had certainly helped sway the arrow in my direction.

I laced my fingers with hers and squeezed. "Plans changed, my little Star."

"What?" she barked out, because my girl liked changes of plans about as much as she liked surprises. "Why? When did this happen?"

I shrugged but offered no verbal response, because in about thirty seconds, her focus would be taken.

Twenty.

Ten.

She let out a loud gasp.

Bingo.

"Oh… Jupiter," she breathed out in a way I definitely wanted to hear again later, maybe even as soon as we checked into our hotel. Her eyes widened. "We're really going here? You're taking me to Joshua Tree?"

I leaned over and kissed her, slowing down as we passed the 'Welcome to Joshua Tree' sign.

"Yep. I thought it would be good to get away for the night."

Her mouth opened then closed, then she said "but-I-didn't-bring-my-telescope!" so quickly, it took me a second to figure it out.

"Don't worry, there's something in the trunk just for you," I winked.

She whipped around in her seat, forgetting momentarily she couldn't see through leather, and then let out a little giggle. "Joshua Tree! I can't believe it. I haven't been since my seventeenth birthday. Thank you! This is definitely better than a barbecue with my parents."

I wasn't about to argue with that.

"Oh God, Jupe, look at it! It's so beautiful." Marnie's neck craned back so far she slipped down the tub with a splash.

I made a mental note to add a bath to the observatory at the New York house.

After we'd checked in and I'd spent the afternoon showing Marnie exactly how much I loved her, we'd taken a walk while the veranda of our suite had been transformed into a sparkling, flickering, stargazing wonderland by the hotel. We'd returned at twilight to find the outdoor bathtub steaming full and overflowing with bubbles, all catching the light of a thousand candles, and a trillion emerging stars.

We'd now been in the bath close to an hour watching the sky.

An empty bottle of champagne was resting in a slowly melting ice bucket off to the side.

We'd blown out all but five candles, though even those which had lit the space couldn't have distracted from the incredible night glittering a thousand shades of blue and lilac.

"It is." I brushed a damp tendril off her forehead, my gaze never leaving her face as I kissed her softly, quickly. Her expression was so filled with wonder, delight, and happiness I could watch her forever. My heart was fit to bursting. "Do you remember the first time you introduced me to the Milky Way? The first time we watched it together and I saw a shooting star?"

She tore her eyes away from the sky and met mine, with a nod and a broad smile.

"I wished for you."

"What?" Her head tipped back, and the bubbles rose up as she moved closer. "What d'you mean?"

"I'd never been in love before, but that night… laying there, drinking hot chocolate and eating popcorn… I never wanted it to end, so I wished for you forever. I knew that night I would fall in love with you, that we'd always be together. Even when we broke up, somehow I always knew I'd find you again, that we'd find each other. It wasn't easy. I'd wake up some nights and miss you so much I could feel my heart cracking again, but all I had to do was look up to the sky, and I knew you'd be somewhere else doing the same."

I swallowed down the emotion threatening to break in my voice and reached under the bath for the little box I'd placed there while she'd been setting up her telescope.

"I love you so much, Marn. So, *so* much. I can't imagine ever being without you, and I don't have any intention of it happening again." I swallowed once more, this time to buy me a second to calm my racing heart. "Therefore, my perfect Star, I need to tell you that I no longer want to be your boyfriend." She didn't blink as I opened the box, and the only way I knew she was breathing was from the movement of air over the bubbles by her chest. She stared down at the ten-carat blue diamond set in a gold band twisted with diamond dust; a hazy, glowy Milky Way of her very own. The Milky Way was where it all began. "If you'll have me, I'd like to be your husband."

Her brows creased so much they nearly touched, and her nose crinkled in confusion. "You're asking me to marry you?"

"Yes," I nodded.

She brushed her fingers over the stone, and delicately removed it from the velvet casing holding it in place. Just as delicately, I took it from her.

"What do you say, Marn. Will you marry me?"

There were ten seconds of shocked silence before she replied, "Yes! Yes, of course I'll marry you."

I slipped the ring onto the fourth finger of her left hand. She was still looking at it, twisting her hand and watching as the diamond caught the light, when I reached down through the water and grabbed her ass to pull her as close as I could possibly get her.

This time when I kissed her, I didn't stop.

Water sloshed over the side, and the candles extinguished.

The rest of the night was spent with only stars guiding our way.

It was all we needed.

THE END

ACKNOWLEDGMENTS

Wow, you guys. I can't believe we're here.

Jupiter was never supposed to be more than a side character in Drew; never more than Emerson's brother. But you loved him so much that I changed everything up. That was almost two years ago.

Jupiter and Marnie's story has been two years in the planning and I've loved every second of bringing them to life, I really hope you've loved them too. I would never have been able to do it without all your support for the world I've been building, and I will be eternally in your debt.

The past few years has been a wild ride, and I've made some incredible friends along the way, many of whom I send daily voice notes of total rubbish to - Steph and Jen I'm looking at you. Gemma, thank you so much for beta reading, and your total honesty I can always count on. Amanda for the ease at which you run The Jupiter Reeves Fan Club - because it literally wouldn't exist without you!

To Valentine, Nina, Amy, Kim, Sarah and everyone at Valentine PR. I'm so grateful to be working with you, I think I would have lost my mind without you the last five months. You've been utterly incredible.

Emily Wittig. OMG. I was so lucky to find you, please don't think I'm not fully aware of this on a daily basis. Your cover is so perfect and beautiful and and and… it brought the book to life. I can't wait for every other one we make together.

And Ryan, again, for being so patient with all my questions especially when I made you read all the girl bits.

If you've made it to the bottom of this I also want to say that I am fully aware how lucky I am, that I not only get to write these stories every day but that YOU read them. My readers are THE BEST. I wouldn't be here without you, and so many of you have been with me since Jasper; but I want to give a special shout out to my Insta Buddy reader group. I have so much love for you all, SO SO MUCH. You give me life and fill me with so much joy, every single day. I can't thank you enough for being part of this crazy road with me.

To everyone on this journey, thank you from the bottom of my heart.

Lulu xo

ABOUT THE AUTHOR

Lulu started writing by accident, and somehow found herself stuck in a fictional world of ice hockey, baseball and billionaires. A world she has no plans to leave.

She's a big fan of strong heroines, because those fierce alphas need someone to keep them in check. You'll find her navigating her way through Romance Land one HEA at a time, and trying to figure out the latest social media platform she needs to post to.

She'd love to hear from you, loves hearing your opinions and thoughts, so please message her on any of the below @lulumoorebooks. Or check her website - lulumoorebooks.com

And lastly, she'd love you to come and join her reader group on Facebook - aptly named The Jupiter Reeves Fan Club.

ALSO BY LULU MOORE

The New York Players

Jasper

Cooper

Drew: The Vegas Edition (extended prologue)

Drew

Felix

Huck will return early summer 2023

The Tuesday Club

The Secret

The Suit

The Show

The New York Lions

The Third Baseman

The Shake Off is coming late summer 2023

READ ON FOR MORE…

Want to know more about the origins of The New York Lions, and how Penn met Lowe? Read on for an excerpt from The Show…

THE TUESDAY CLUB
BOOK THREE

PENN

Do you know what it's like to have your world implode? Where everything you thought you knew was ripped away from you in the blink of an eye, and nothing makes sense anymore?

It's happened to me twice.

First, the day my dad died.

I was eleven, and he was on his way from a meeting to watch me play Little League when he had a massive heart attack. I'd hit three home runs before I noticed my nanny waiting in the stands next to our coach, her eyes glistening.

Growing up in a household with four older sisters, my father had been my best friend. My buddy. We'd sneak away from the squabbling girls and head somewhere quieter, just the two of us boys. We spent our time together watching baseball, or he'd take me out to the backyard and play catch - it didn't matter as long as baseball was involved.

It was *our* thing.

He instilled in me a passion for the game, and most importantly, a love for his favorite team – the mighty New York Yankees. During the season, we'd go to watch them every chance we'd get. Sometimes if I'd finished my homework in time, we'd go to the stadium during the week, and he'd sit me on his knee and romance about the magic we were going to witness; which players to watch, the teams we needed to fight hardest against. And then he'd tell me how one day he was going to buy it.

That one day we would own The Yankees.

Even now, for the first minute I enter Yankee Stadium – inhale that musky scent of the ballpark clashing with the freshly cut grass, or hear that first crack of the ball – I'm transported back to our seats, to my dad's knee, and my chest tightens until my breath catches… and I miss my dad so fucking much it's tangible.

Which leads me to my second implosion. Prepare to be outraged.

Let me set the scene…

When my dad died, I took his place as the next male heir to my grandfather's conglomerate. My dad was his only son from his four kids, and out of his eleven grandchildren, I am the only grandson.

Yep, surrounded by women.

My grandfather, Lucian Shepherd, is one of the most formidable businessmen in the world.

He started out helping his father - my great grandfather - in the small publishing company he owned, moving paper from the printers to the binding machines. He spent two hours there every day after school, and three hours each weekend for an entire year while he was finishing his studies, before going to work full time as a manager.

It took him twelve years to turn it into the number one publishing house, globally.

While he was doing that, he started investing. He invested in anything he could get his hands on – failing businesses, start-ups, property, tech, healthcare, food and beverage companies, textiles, aerospace and automotive – you name it, and my grandfather will likely own it.

And any company he doesn't wholly own, he probably owns part of.

By the time my father died, Shepherd Holdings Inc. was number one on the Fortune 500 list, and my grandfather was one of the richest businessmen in the world, worth circa one hundred and fifty billion dollars.

Neither has lost their spot since.

It had always been the plan that my father would take over the company when my grandfather turned sixty-five, except him dying unexpectedly put a wrench in the works. As a result, my grandfather postponed his decision to step down, and instead declared that he would hand over the reins when he turned eighty.

Hand them over to me.

Overnight, I went from being a kid who dreamed of playing ball to a kid whose destiny was laid out. A kid who would become the head of his family business - whether he wanted to or not.

But I did it, because it's what my dad was going to do.

Because it took me one step closer to buying The Yankees – my father's dream.

This sounds amazing, I hear you cry.

It's not.

Owning a conglomerate… Is. So. Fucking. Boring.

Like I'd rather be anywhere else boring.

Like I'd rather stick rusty nails in my eyes boring.

I was not built to sit in board meetings and discuss quarterly report fluctuations.

Board meetings lived up to their name, and were always timed with a much-needed nap. I'd rock up when I had to, sign what I had to sign, then be on my merry way – usually to meet Murray and Rafe for a drink and see what mischief we could get into, because my freedom was finite. The less I stuck around the office the better, because I knew that one day I wouldn't be able to leave. That one day the company would be the Albatross around my neck, with all eyes on me to lead it into the next generation.

But I behaved, sort of.

I towed the line, within reason.

I went to Harvard and studied for my MBA, even when I'd rather have had my fingernails pulled out. My only saving grace at school were my two best friends – Murray Williams and Rafe Latham. It wasn't that I couldn't do the work, or that the course was hard; quite the opposite. I have been cursed with a genius level IQ, and graduated top of my class with very little effort and a relatively poor attendance record. It didn't matter, because I can pretty much do anything.

(Except cook, but I have a chef so it's irrelevant.)

Given my future had been mapped out for the last twenty years, imagine my surprise when I get wind of a coup a few months ago. Well, not exactly a coup when I wasn't yet in power, but suffice it to say my eldest sister, Nancy – the family brown-nose – was doing everything she could to stop me from taking Gramps' leadership.

A pre-coup if you will.

I should have known it would happen, seeing as Nancy has had her eyes on it since she started working there. She had planned to go to law school, but instead, when dad died, she went straight into the company and learned from the ground up. And she's been doing awesome work.

She's become my grandfather's right-hand woman.

If you ask me, I don't know why she couldn't have been given the role in the first place.

But point is she wasn't, and I was.

You might wonder why I care about not having a job I didn't want anyway. The answer is, I don't. I don't care that I don't have the job. I *care* that I've wasted my entire adult life preparing for it when I could have been doing literally anything else.

I *care* that I'm now behind on my dad's goal to buy The Yankees, especially when Steinbrenner won't sell them.

I *care* that now I have no fucking idea what to do with myself.

So I'm sure you can imagine how angry I was. Like Randle McMurphy angry.

In a very drunken moment with Rafe where we pledged to never trust women again, and *fuck everyone,* I fired off an email I probably shouldn't have.

Which was how I found myself summoned to the Lexington Avenue headquarters of Shepherd Holdings Inc, by the great Lucian Shepherd himself.

That was two days ago.

Yes, I've made my grandfather wait for two days; probably the only person in the history of time, but that's how pissed I still am.

Printed in Dunstable, United Kingdom

65186207R00234